# IDYLL HANDS

## ALSO BY STEPHANIE GAYLE

*Idyll Threats*

*Idyll Fears*

# IDYLL HANDS

A THOMAS LYNCH NOVEL

# STEPHANIE GAYLE

**SEVENTH STREET BOOKS®**

AN IMPRINT OF PROMETHEUS BOOKS

59 JOHN GLENN DRIVE • AMHERST, NY 14228
www.seventhstreetbooks.com

Published 2018 by Seventh Street Books®, an imprint of Prometheus Books

Cover design by Jacqueline Nasso Cooke
Cover image © Dave Ellison / Alamy Stock Photo
Cover design © Prometheus Books

This is a work of fiction. Characters, organizations, products, locales, and events portrayed in this novel are either products of the author's imagination or used fictitiously.

Inquiries should be addressed to
Seventh Street Books
59 John Glenn Drive
Amherst, New York 14228
VOICE: 716–691–0133
FAX: 716–691–0137
WWW.SEVENTHSTREETBOOKS.COM

22 21 20 19 18     5 4 3 2 1

Library of Congress Cataloging-in-Publication Data

Names: Gayle, Stephanie, 1975- author.
Title: Idyll hands: a Thomas Lynch novel / by Stephanie Gayle.
Description: Amherst, NY: Seventh Street Books, an imprint of Prometheus Books, 2018.
Identifiers: LCCN 2018016761 (print) | LCCN 2018021138 (ebook) | ISBN 9781633884830 (ebook) | ISBN 9781633884823 (paperback)
Subjects: | BISAC: FICTION / Mystery & Detective / Police Procedural. | GSAFD: Mystery fiction.
Classification: LCC PS3607.A98576 (ebook) | LCC PS3607.A98576 I382 2018 (print) | DDC 813/.6—dc23
LC record available at https://lccn.loc.gov/2018016761

Printed in the United States of America

*For Todd*

# FRIDAY, SEPTEMBER 22, 1972
## CHARLESTOWN, MASSACHUSETTS

She watches the clock, checking the second hand to see if it's time to go yet. Her freckled hand trembles as it brings a forkful of mashed potatoes to her mouth. She sets it down. The fork clanks against the dinner plate's blue rim, and her mother's eyes are on her.

"Not hungry?"

Her mother assesses the plate. Peas untouched, potatoes furrowed by fork tines, meatloaf covered in ketchup to conceal only a small piece has been consumed.

She tries to smile, but her cheeks feel tight. "Guess I ate too many chips." She will accept this small sin if she may be forgiven the larger one coming. She touches the chipped crystal salt and pepper shakers. Years ago, she and her siblings had held the crystal shakers up to sunbeams, to create rainbows. "Rainbow makers," they'd called them. "Can you pass me the rainbow maker?" they'd say at dinner, and their parents would exchange confused glances. And they'd laugh, giddy in the power of their shared secret. Secrets are not so nice now. They are dark and make her sick.

Her father, at the head of the table, says, "Drink your milk." He doesn't look up, but she knows the remark is aimed at her. You'd think her parents worked a dairy farm, the way they push milk. She lifts the sweating glass and swallows a mouthful. It is cold and wet and tastes of soap. Someone didn't rinse the dishes well. It wasn't her, not this time.

She pokes at the meatloaf and watches her brother, Bobby, eat. He is the only one left at home with her. Her other brothers and sister have

7

grown up and moved to their own places. He will leave too, in a year or so. Bobby shovels potatoes and peas into his mouth. Then he chews and chews, twenty times at least, before he swallows. Has he always done this? He is the brother who scared her with stories of the boogie man when she was little. Who told her there were monsters under her bed. But he is the same brother who saved her from choking. Who stuck his grubby index finger down her throat and fished out the butterscotch candy blocking her airway. Tears come to her eyes and she blinks them away. They cannot see her cry. They'll know something is up. She pinches the web of skin between her left index finger and thumb.

Her mother asks Bobby about his job, and he talks about a customer who didn't know the difference between a spark plug and . . . she drifts off. Her father's fingers are stained brown at the tips, and his hair is going gray. Even his mustache is streaked with silver. He would die if he knew what she was about to do. It would kill him. She bites down until her front teeth indent her lower lip, and then she asks, "May I be excused?"

Both parents eye her plate. Both frown. Her mother is about to tell her to eat more.

"I told Lucy I'd meet her at 6:30." When they don't respond immediately, she adds, "I'm sleeping over, remember?"

"Whatcha doing?" Bobby asks.

"We're going to a double feature." She twists the napkin in her lap, strangling the fabric. Thank God she checked the paper for this weekend's listings. "*The Last House on the Left* and then *Bluebeard*."

"Double feature?" her father says. "Is Mr. MacManus picking you up?"

"Yes." She pictures Mr. MacManus, reading the paper in his recliner, balancing a cigarette on his lower lip. He won't be picking her up from the movies. Not tonight.

She prays her father won't argue, that she won't have to explain again that she is sixteen years old, old enough to go to the movies with her best friend. She doesn't want to argue that she can be trusted. She's not sure the lie would make it out of her mouth.

He sighs, but she recognizes the hollow sound in it that means he will give in. Her mother looks at her father. He sets the rules. He nods. Her mother says, "Be careful."

She rises from her chair. The smell of her mother's perfume, Wind Song, makes her wince. She used to love the smell, but now it makes her queasy.

"Clean your plate," her mother says.

She takes the plate into the kitchen and scrapes her food into the trash, the potatoes sticking, refusing to budge, until she pushes them with her knife. They land atop empty cans and cigarette packets and discarded circulars. She sets the plates and utensils in the sink, where her mother will wash them using Palmolive. Her mother wears bright yellow gloves to prevent "dishpan hands." She hums songs as she washes, Simon and Garfunkel or "She Loves You" by the Beatles.

The girl's eyes water and she blinks, fast. On the yellow fridge is a picture of her and her siblings two Christmases ago. They are arranged before the Christmas tree. Bobby has his arm wrapped around her neck and Dave is making rabbit's ears behind Mikey's head. Carol ignored them all, posing. Her pregnant belly upstaged her smile. The girl will not allow herself to think of her nephew, Jimmy. Not now.

She grabs her knapsack from outside her bedroom. She will be gone two days, she tells herself. Only two days. And then she'll be back, and it will be okay, things will be okay. She calls, "See you later!" and hustles downstairs, her feet thumping heavy on each step. Then she's outside, and the sun is sinking and the air smells like hot dogs and lighter fluid. The neighbors are grilling though the air is nippy and it's past grill season.

She sets her eyes to the road ahead and counts every car that passes. It keeps her from looking backward, to thinking of what lies ahead. It keeps her centered and present in the moment. That's what she must be. She pushes her long hair behind her and leans forward as she walks, away from home and her life before. When she returns, on Monday, it will be fixed, and everything can go back to the way it was.

# FRIDAY, MAY 14, 1999
## 0945 HOURS

**M**y sneeze erupted in wet spray. Droplets landed on an accident report. "Bless you!" Billy called from across the station. "Allergies bothering you, Chief?" Forty-six years I'd been on this planet and until last year I'd never had allergies. Had never had my eyes itch for weeks, had never woken each morning with a phlegm-coated throat, had never blown my nose through a tissue box in three days.

"My mother has hay fever something awful," Billy said as he approached.

"I never had allergies in New York." As if I could lay the blame at Idyll, Connecticut's feet. Idyll had too many trees, shrubs, and flowers. You couldn't walk four feet without stepping in a puddle of acid-green pollen. The crap coated cars and houses.

"My doctor says you can get allergies any time, even when you're old . . . older."

Old? I was in the prime of life. I sneezed again and grabbed a tissue. It tore in half. I fished the other half from the cardboard box. Blew my nose. God, when would this end?

"You take anything? Mom says she wouldn't survive spring without Allegra."

"I'll check it out." A paper airplane sailed past, coming to land atop a phone. "Is spring always this quiet?" It was my third here, but it seemed slow, even by Idyll standards. Idyll = idle. That joke never got old.

"Slow?" Billy said. "We got that problem up on Piper Street." Right. Someone was tossing clamshells along Piper Street. The shells had meat inside and were creating a rotting, stinking mess. It was the season's greatest crime.

"Saw your fitness plan," Billy said.

"How's that?" It was supposed to be under wraps for a week.

He got red. "Mrs. Dunsmore was upset, so I asked what was wrong."

"She's upset about the requirements? They're for policemen." Mrs. Dunsmore was the station's secretary and had been here as long as the building. Okay, maybe not quite that long.

"I figured," he said. "Is it because of Dix?"

Two weeks ago, Dix lost a footrace to a kid who'd defaced school property. The kid was nine years old. The guys had been teasing Dix, calling him Carl Lewis, ever since.

"No." One look around our station revealed that many would benefit from a regular exercise regimen.

"I think it's great." Not surprising. Billy was young. He could do all the activities listed and barely break a sweat. Hopkins hauled himself out of a chair and waddled toward the newly hired dispatcher. Not everyone was so lucky. "It'll get us in shape in time for the softball game, yeah?" He referred to the annual Idyll Cops and Firefighters match, which raised money for St. Jude's Hospital. Historically, the victories had been largely one-sided. Not on our side.

"Hope so," I said. "Would be nice to win." I'd never played on the team. My first year, I didn't know about it and so failed to volunteer, and last year the game was scheduled during my vacation break. I'd promised my nephews a trip to Six Flags and decided being the World's Best Uncle trumped propping up the sad collection of Idyll Police soft-ballers. This year, though. This year would be different.

The front door opened, and Mayor Mike Mitchell breezed inside. I walked swiftly toward the building's rear. The mayor was Billy's uncle. Those two could chat about Idyll's softball games for hours. Me and the mayor? We had a more complicated relationship. He'd once been a fan. But then I'd come out as gay, and he'd tried to interfere with an arson investigation. Now he delighted in taking jabs at me during town meetings.

I walked inside the Evidence room and locked the door behind me. I hadn't been inside in a year or more. No need. The room was the size of my guest bedroom, but it contained more stuff. Because this was Idyll, a lot of it was random. Sure, there were drugs and a couple of guns, but most stuff represented petty shenanigans: spray-paint cans, baseball bats, two bicycles, and a shelf full of fireworks. Leaning against the back wall were the twenty-two plastic flamingoes we'd recovered from the middle school principal's lawn. They'd been arranged to spell "DICK." There were also the rolls of toilet paper we grabbed every Homecoming. Apparently, it's a high school rite of passage to toilet paper the trees of the football players' houses. Startled kids, caught in the act, often dropped half a case rather than be caught. We used the toilet paper at the station, over time. It being May, we had only four rolls left. On the shelf nearest me were the cardboard boxes containing evidence from the North murder that took place in summer 1997, seven months after I started as police chief. On the highest shelf were three moldering boxes that looked as though they'd been placed there when Mrs. Dunsmore was hired as a fresh-faced secretary wearing a short skirt and tall hair.

The leftmost box looked soggy. It was labeled "COLLEEN." The one beside it was marked "Vacations, 1978–82." Why would they keep vacation records that long? The one closest to me wasn't marked at all. It was a blue-and-white banker's box. When I pulled it down and opened it up, it smelled musty, like old books. The box was filled with calendars of past police chiefs, detailing the exciting series of local town events they'd chaperoned. Memorial Day Parades, July Fourth Blast Offs!, and of course, the town's biggest event, Idyll Days. Dear God, this was my future. No more murders or kidnappings, only a long string of town events and charity pancake breakfasts. I didn't even like pancakes.

Another sneeze erupted from my nose. Too much dust back here. I moved to the door and set my hand on the knob. I heard the mayor say, "Where has the chief gone?" I dropped my hand and stepped back. A few minutes here wouldn't kill me. I returned to the boxes and pulled down the one marked "COLLEEN." I set it on the floor and unfolded the top flaps.

I'd been a homicide detective for twelve years before I came to Idyll. The foot-long bone lying in the box, its yellowed knobby end jutting above a plastic bag, didn't startle me. It was a humerus bone, the one that linked the elbow to the shoulder. Under it, a plastic bag held a plaid fabric swatch. A smaller bag contained a watch with a cracked glass face and a pale pink wristband. At the bottom was a folder labeled "JANE DOE." At last, something interesting.

A sharp squeak brought my head up. The door opened, and in stepped Michael Finnegan, our part-time detective, with a book in his hand. Originally from Boston, he had the accent to prove it. He whistled a tune, his eyes on the key he'd used to get in. He placed his keychain in the pocket of his mustard sports jacket and looked up. He saw me, a bone in one hand, and then looked down at the box by my feet. A line bisected his forehead, and his mouth turned down. "Oh. I see you've met Colleen."

His frown was unusual. Finnegan was my sunny detective. He left the bad moods to Wright. I wondered if the frown had to do with the bone.

"Who's Colleen?" I asked.

# FRIDAY, MAY 14, 1999
## 1010 HOURS

"Hiya, Mike!" Hugh called from his dispatcher's seat. "Or do you prefer Finny?" Hugh was hired two weeks ago. He still had that new hire shine. I gave it another three weeks before it dimmed.

"Either is fine." Most guys called me Finny, a few called me Mike.

"How goes it?" he asked.

"It feels like Friday the 13th." I'd had a call from ex-wife number two about her broken hot water heater, and my car was falling apart. It was shaping up to be a humdinger.

"The mayor is here," he said, voice low. He was new, but he wasn't stupid.

Sure enough, Mayor Mike Mitchell held court by the water cooler, pontificating about policing. I'd been a cop since 1971, so I figured I could skip his lecture. "You never saw me," I said. Hugh nodded, and I walked toward Mrs. Dunsmore's office. She'd offer me sanctuary. Besides, I'd finished *The Girl Who Loved Tom Gordon*, and wanted to discuss the book with her. Try to convince her to read it. She thought all Stephen King could do was scare people with monsters. This would change her mind.

She wasn't in her office, and her door was locked, so I headed for the Evidence room. I'd gotten a hammer, a flashlight, and many rolls of toilet paper from Evidence over the years. Maybe I'd grab the duct tape we'd impounded. A group of teen girls had used it to affix signs to utility poles declaring that Stacy MacMoore was a SLUT (the key word in pink glitter). The duct tape was heavy-duty, and my bumper was in need of repair.

Inside the Evidence room, Chief Lynch fondled a bone like a modern-day Neanderthal. I said, "Oh. I see you've met Colleen," before I thought it through. He asked, "Who's Colleen?" as he turned the bone in his large hands. Chief's a big guy, well over six feet, and handsome if you like Rock Hudson–types. He squinted at it, and I wondered if he needed glasses. Not that I'd suggest such a thing. I'd leave it to my pal Lewis to make that mistake. He would, someday soon. I'd put money on it.

"Mayor's outside." I looked over my shoulder. "Guess you knew that, huh?"

"Finnegan," he said. "Who's Colleen?"

So much for distracting him. "Colleen. Well, that's a hard question to answer."

"Why?"

"Because no one knows," I said. "But I found her."

"When?"

How much had he seen? He'd opened the box, but the folder wasn't in sight. He hadn't read it, or he'd be asking different questions.

"Wouldn't you rather sit down while I spin you the story?" There were no chairs back here, and it was cramped quarters for a guy his size.

"Mayor's still out there, right?" he asked.

"When will he be back?" the mayor shouted. We could see his outline behind the frosted glass pane of the door. The chief winced. No way he was stepping out there, into the line of fire.

"Okay." I set my book on a shelf, crossed my arms, and leaned against the metal shelving unit. "It was summer 1983. July. And I was reciting poetry in the woods. Robert Frost's "Stopping by Woods on a Snowy Evening." Only the woods weren't lovely. The woods were hotter than Hades and full of mosquitos looking to suck my blood."

"Why were you out there?" He set the bone back in the box, carefully. Some guys would've tossed it.

"Mr. Graham had called to complain, *again*, that bonfire parties were being held in the woods behind his house."

"Mr. Graham?"

"Dead now. He used to live on Oak Road. The house with the wrap-around porch, though that's new. Belongs to the Crawfords, those folks from California. Back when it was Graham's, it didn't have the porch or the blacktop driveway. Just a gravel drive sprouted with weeds."

He nodded, and I continued. "That day, Chief Stoughton was in a mood to assign his 'lead detective' to check out Mr. Graham's property. As if tramping through the woods at two o'clock on a Tuesday afternoon was going to solve the problem. I told Stoughton it was kids looking to drink during vacation, and there was no way they'd be outside in ninety-two-degree weather, hosting a bonfire." But reason had held no sway with Chief Stoughton. He'd been nursing a hangover that hot day, and he'd been eager to dish out punishment. "I went and beat back tree limbs as best I could. After twenty minutes, I hadn't seen a thing. I thought maybe Mr. Graham was losing it. He was eighty-six and fuzzy at the edges."

Chief Lynch waited. Other cops would've asked, "When did you find Colleen?" or begged me to skip the boring bits. But Lynch enjoyed a good yarn.

"I headed back to my car, waving my arms to keep the mosquitos at bay. My foot kicked a log. Something bright winked on the ground. It was a watch. Its glass face was broken."

"The one in the box," he said.

"I thought it was evidence of Mr. Graham's nighttime trespassers, so I looked around. The pine needles and leaf cover looked disturbed, but that could've been from me lumbering through. After a minute or two, I saw something else under the leaves. It was a dirty piece of fabric. When I got it up, I saw it was a skirt, a plaid skirt. Could've been the bonfire kids had gotten frisky, but it bothered me. I was thinking, *Why someone would leave a skirt in the woods?* when I spotted the bone. My first thought was it was a rotted tennis ball."

I'd knelt to examine it and the ache in my gut sharpened. It felt like I'd caught the soft skin of my belly in a zipper.

"There were divots and pockmarks, where scavengers had chewed on it. I tugged it out of the ground, turned it over, and saw it was the upper arm bone, the humerus."

"Then what did you do?" His face was alive with interest, and I realized I'd played this all wrong. I should've stressed that it was a dead-end case with no good angles. Now he'd want to know more. He'd definitely go through the box and read the folder, cover to cover. Damn it.

"I marked the site with my handkerchief. Then I got back to the car and called it in."

But not before I'd stood where the woods met Mr. Graham's yard. I'd stared at an old charcoal grill that hadn't cooked a hot dog in a decade. Tilted to one side, its cover so rusty I couldn't make out its original black paint. And I wondered why there was a bone in the woods, and how much trouble it was likely to cause.

"I got on the radio and told dispatch what I'd found. Jonathan said, 'A bone? You mean, like a deer, right?' As if I'd call in about finding a fucking deer bone. When I told him it was human, he asked, 'How can you tell? You take one of them adult ed classes?'"

"Jonathan sounds like a delight," Chief said. These comments made me like him. Some of the other cops thought he "talked funny." They weren't as fluent in sarcasm.

"What did you think about the bone?" he asked.

"It had been outside for years. I wondered why there was only one and how it got there."

He glanced at the box. "I'm guessing they didn't recover much else?"

I leaned away from the shelving unit's metal frame. "They found signs of a bonfire, burnt logs twenty feet from where I found the bone. There were beer cans and cigarettes. Some food wrappers and a discarded condom."

"July 1983," he said. "A cold case."

"The coldest."

He cocked his head. Looked toward the door. "Mayor's gone."

"You sure?"

He grunted. "He's not capable of staying silent for so long." He bent and picked up the box. I hoped he'd put it back on the shelf, but he carried it, in his arms, toward the door.

*Damn it.* "Chief, how 'bout I grab that for you?"

"I've got it," he said, and walked out.

"I don't mind."

"You been talking to Billy? I'm not old. I can carry plenty heavier things than this."

"I wasn't implying—" I stopped. And let him go. I needed to get my hands on that box before he read the folder, but there was no need to make a scene now. That would tip him off.

If you live your life like an open book, if you keep 90 percent of your info out there for anyone to see, they assume you've got no secrets.

That was the Chief's mistake. He was 100 percent secrets when he arrived in Idyll, so we assumed he was hiding stuff, important stuff. He should've flooded us with information, most of it nothing we'd want to know. It would have silenced us, made us wish he'd stop talking. That's how you go undetected for years—decades. How everyone thinks they know you so well. Trust me. I've been doing it for so long, I've forgotten I'm doing it most days.

# FRIDAY, MAY 14, 1999

Billy walked into my office. "My application for the drug squad program we discussed." He thrust the papers at me. Professional development. We had a small budget for it. Billy was one of three men who'd approached me about using those funds to get more on-the-job training. I promised to look the sheets over. "They're due Friday of next week," he said.

"Got it."

He stared at the bone on my desk. "That a human bone?" Got closer to it. "The humerus, right? Back in Boy Scouts we learned the differences between human bones and animal bones. People were always reporting they'd found body parts, and usually they were deer legs or bear bones. Our scoutmaster, Mr. Mulaney, he worked as an EMT, and he taught us to spot differences."

"I thought Boy Scouts went camping."

"We did that too." He peered at the bone. "Where did this come from?" Billy didn't know. Interesting. Then again, Billy was young, and Finny said he'd found it back in 1983.

"Woods back of Mr. Graham's place," I said.

"Whoa." Billy's eyes widened. "Is this Colleen?"

"What do you know about Colleen?" Finny had made it sound like nothing was known about her.

"She was our local ghost. As kids, we'd dare each other to spend the night in the woods behind the Graham place. Story was that a young woman had been murdered there. Her ghost was seen amongst the trees, screaming. People heard her. They wouldn't always see her, but they'd hear her. That was the bit that freaked me out, the screaming."

"Anyone ever do it?" I asked. "Stay overnight in the woods?"

"Kids claimed to, but without witnesses, who's to say if they did? I wouldn't sleep out there. Tons of mosquitos, and, back in the day, Old Man Graham kept a shotgun he threatened to fire at trespassers. I figured Colleen was made up by him to keep kids out of the woods. But this bone . . . Are you saying there *was* a body in the woods?"

"Just this bone," I said. "Sounds as though they never identified it."

"Shouldn't that be at Farmington?" Even a young patrolman like Billy knew the rules.

"Let's keep it between us, okay?"

"Sure thing." He looked at the bone. "Huh. Never thought she was real. I mean, not now, not as an adult. Weird to think the story was based on truth." He frowned. "I guess some legends turn out to be real, huh?"

"Guess so," I said.

He left me to dab at my eyes with a fresh tissue. My direct line rang. Outside call. 212 area code. New York City.

"Tom?" my brother, John, said when I answered. "How are you?"

"Fine. Everything okay?" He didn't call me midday, at work. We communicated through his wife, Marie, or our parents.

"Yeah, everything is fine. We're having a get-together, and I wanted to invite you."

"Get-together?" Had I forgotten someone's birthday? Anniversary? My mental calendar came up blank.

"I won a teaching award, and they're having a ceremony. Mom wanted to do dinner afterward." John had followed in our parents' academic footsteps.

"Congrats," I said. "Do you get money? A statue?"

"My name goes on a plaque, and I get a tiny, one-time bonus."

"When's the ceremony?"

"Next month on a Tuesday night. You're probably working."

"Probably," I said. "But let me look into it. What time does it start?"

"Well, the award thing is at 5:30 p.m. Mom wants to go out afterward."

"Kids coming?" I hadn't seen my nephews since Christmas. It seemed like they grew an inch between my visits.

"Yup."

"Where's it at?" I'd been to NYU just often enough to realize I'd be lost without explicit directions. John gave them to me.

"It'd be great to see you there." His voice was resigned. He didn't expect I'd come. I had a history of missed holidays, birthdays, and family outings. As a homicide detective, my excuses were solid. As chief of police in a sleepy small town? Not so much.

"Is it okay if I call you later and let you know?" Hedging my bets was my standard MO.

"Sure," he said. "Talk to you later."

No sooner had I hung up, when in came Mrs. Dunsmore. She wore her hair in a bun, and her trademark scowl was absent. Today she wore a lavender scarf. The ends floated behind her as she walked. She stopped abruptly and asked, "Why is that bone on your desk?" The scowl appeared.

"I found it in the Evidence room."

"And you decided it belonged on your desk?"

I sneezed and grabbed a tissue.

"Bless you," she said. "Your allergies are getting worse."

I honked like a goose into the tissue.

"Don't worry—they'll probably subside next month."

"Next month?" I'd been hoping for a few days more, a week at the outset.

She neared my desk. "Ah, *that* bone." As if we had a bunch of them lying around and she'd only recognized it now that she'd gotten a closer look. "There's a ghost story because of it." She went to my windowsill and began fussing with the plant she'd given me as a welcome-to-the-station gift. She'd repotted it because it had grown too big. At least one of us was thriving.

I waited, but she didn't say anything more except, "Looks like it might rain," and then, "That'll help with your allergies. Wash the pollen away. . . . And that physical-fitness memo you had me type up." Her lips flat-lined. "If you're looking to make yourself unpopular, you created a surefire way to do it."

"What? They're baseline fitness standards I've adapted from several state departments. Exercise is good. It'll make those guys better able to do their jobs—"

"Is this because Dix lost the race to that nine-year-old?" she asked.

"No. Take a good look at our officers. They can barely lift road works signs. They're out of shape, and it's not good for them. Fit officers take fewer sick days, you know."

"This wouldn't have anything to do with your new health kick, would it?"

"What health kick?" I asked.

"The one that has you eating salads and working out in the interview room during lunch."

"I think the men are going to respond more positively to this program than you think. It's got built-in incentives."

"You think you can convince the selectman and mayor to approve cash bonuses for meeting fitness goals?"

"The firemen basically get paid to work out all day. We'll be looking to fund an hour."

She tsked twice. "Sometimes you act like you haven't learned the rules of small-town politics at all."

I pointed to the bone atop my desk. "Speaking of rules, shouldn't this be in Farmington?" Bodies and their parts went to the Office of the Chief Medical Examiner.

"Yes, but I wouldn't send it there if I were you."

"Why not?" She was a stickler. Why advocate for keeping the bone?

"Detective Finnegan wouldn't like it." She and Finny had a funny relationship. She scolded him, and in the next breath recommended books he should read. He smiled, took the scolding, and read the books. Every now and again he'd offer to make her his fourth wife. She'd laugh and say he couldn't keep up with her.

"You ever try to put your hand between a dog and its food bowl?" she asked.

I said, "Thought that was a surefire way to get bit."

"Exactly. ME isn't missing that bone. No need to bring it to his attention." Was Finnegan the dog in that story? I swore she spoke in riddles to confuse me. "Put the bone in the box and give it here," she said.

"What? Why?"

"Because you are the chief of police, not a detective. It's not your job to investigate crimes. You already took on two of the biggest cases we've ever had. You think Detective Wright's going to join your fan club if you do it again?"

Lewis Wright was my full-time detective, and, it was true, he got peeved when I elbowed my way into his cases.

"Finny says it's an ice-cold case," I protested.

"Then it surely doesn't need your attention while I'm waiting for your crime statistics for the next town meeting."

"Fine." I took the bone from my desk and set it atop the bagged skirt swatch. Then I refolded the cardboard flaps and handed her the box.

"Was that so hard?" she asked before she left.

"No," I said, louder than necessary. The door closed and I grinned. Then I opened the manila folder on my desk. What she didn't know was that I'd made a quick copy of the papers within the Colleen box while Hallihan talked my ear off about John Elway, as if I cared about anyone who played for the Denver Broncos. I was a Giants fan. I'd thought I'd look at the papers later—maybe this evening, since a cold case wasn't part of my job duties.

But since she'd tried to make sure I'd leave well enough alone, well, there was no time like the present, was there?

I scanned the papers and stopped. What was this? A DNA test. Wait, who?

# FRIDAY, MAY 14, 1999
## 1115 HOURS

Across from me, at his desk, Lewis aligned his stapler, labeled with his name. His office-supply possessiveness was silly. It meant his stuff routinely went missing. When the fellas got bored, they'd make off with his scissors. Lewis would bluster and storm about. A little afternoon diversion for those who enjoyed it.

He said, "I haven't eaten. Wanna grab a sub from Papano's?"

"My turn?" It was, and I knew it. But giving in too easy took half of his joy away.

"Definitely your turn." He handed me two fives. "Ham and cheese."

"Lettuce, tomato, mayo, and sweet peppers," I said. We knew each other's lunch orders by heart. I tucked his money into my back pocket. I should've paid. It was my turn, and Wright had a wife and two kids, but I had three exes and three kids and two jobs that barely paid for all of them, so Wright picked up the tab more often. I didn't like it, but I appreciated it.

"Hey, detectives, you want in on the action?" Dix called. He was at the coffee machine, examining the stale baked goods on offer.

We wandered over, and I picked up a bagel, tapped it against the table. The thing nearly dented the wood. "Jesus. How long has this been here?"

"Three days," Lewis said.

"Hopkins will eat it," Dix said. He scratched his beard. I'd never known him to wear facial hair. His mustache was redder than his beard. The look screamed porn actor. Not star, mind you, just actor.

"What action are you promising?" Lewis asked. Surprising. He wasn't a betting man. His father had been a bookkeeper who'd taught him never to bet. House always wins.

"We're taking bets on whether the new dispatcher will ask Donna on a date before the end of the week," Dix said. Donna Daniels was the well-endowed bartender at Suds, who'd been nicknamed 'DD' by the brain trust of Idyll drinkers.

I filled my coffee mug. "He's been here two weeks. Maybe call him by his name."

"What's that again?" Dix asked.

"Hugh Bascomb. He likes fast cars, the Atlanta Braves, and the TV show *Friends*." In response to Dix's raised brows I said, "I'm a detective and he talks, a lot, in case you haven't noticed. Also, what are the odds that he'll ask her out?"

Dix rubbed his mustache. "Two to one on."

"Not worth it," Wright said.

"True," I agreed. "Besides, he'll do it."

"Why so confident?" Dix asked.

"I know people, Dix. It's one of my many skills. He'll ask her, before the week is out."

"Ah, yes, but will she accept?" he asked.

"That, Dix, is up to the lady."

Lewis said, "And the lady, by all accounts, doesn't take on fixer-uppers."

Dix whistled. "Harsh, Detective."

I said, "If you'll excuse us, Dix, we have important work to do." Lunch was important. Second most important meal of the day.

Dix called, "Oh yeah? What? Another house party thrown by sophomores, or did you finally catch whoever has been tossing clamshells along Piper Street?"

"Who *does* that?" Lewis asked, not for the first time. "Those things stink, and they're covered in maggots." I'd only driven past the carnage. Lewis was head of the investigation. Lucky guy.

"Someone on that street pissed off somebody. And the pissed-off person has access to a lot of clamshells," I said, for the sixth time, or was it the seventh?

"I've talked to everyone who lives on that street," Lewis said. He held up his hand. "Eighty-year-old widower who makes World War II dioramas." He curled his index finger to his palm. "Young married couple with a set of twins." He curled down his middle finger. "The couple who run the dry cleaners, the Silvanos."

"Maybe they ruined someone's shirt," Dix said.

"I looked into customer complaints," he said. "None of 'em were that angry. And none of the complainers owned a clam farm or a boat. Next up we have the Jax family." He curled in his ring finger, which told me he'd discounted them as targets.

"Hey, the Jax kid is the QB of the Idyll Marauders. Maybe someone doesn't like his record?" Dix asked.

"They were 10–1 last year," Lewis said. "Besides, the clams appeared the last week of April. Not during football season."

"Maybe the QB broke some hearts?" Dix suggested.

"That's possible," I said. "Teen girls can be aggressive in their displays of anger."

Dix said, "You still on about those posters? We got them down quick."

"Quickly," I corrected, out of habit. "Stacy MacMoore might have a different view." Her parents did. They wanted the girls who'd hung the posters branding their daughter a slut arrested.

"You think it's a rampaging band of teen girls?" Lewis asked.

"On the face of it, sure," I said. "Why not?" I had a daughter, and I remembered her teen years. They were not filed with sugar, spice, and everything nice. They were filled with sulky looks, hormonal exchanges, and heartbreaking episodes of self-doubt inspired by peer pressure.

My phone rang. I had to shift stacks of reports and empty chip bags to reach it.

"Michael, I have the box. Come get it." Her voice was breathy, annoyed.

I stood and tucked in my shirt. Checked myself for obvious stains. "I'm off to see Lady Du. I'll pick up lunch after that."

Lewis shook his head. "Barking up the wrong tree. She's known you too long. I still can't believe she lets you get away with calling her that."

"Lady Du? It's a title of respect."

"So you say. If I called her that, she'd ruler my knuckles."

Behind her office door, a typewriter was being abused. I opened the door and said, "Hello." She looked up. Her eyeglasses slid down her nose. Her pinned-up hair had gotten loose. That hair was grayer than when we'd first met, eighteen years ago, but I still saw her in there, the younger Grace Dunsmore. I was the only one who could. Even Hopkins, who'd known her as long, never saw the lighter, funny side of her. His loss.

"Detective Finnegan." She continued typing at the same rate an AK-47 discharges bullets.

"You have the box?" I prompted. It wasn't in sight.

She stopped and tilted her head to the side. "What've you gotten yourself into now?"

"Nothing. When the mayor came by earlier, Chief skedaddled into the Evidence room."

"And found the Colleen box," she finished. "What's in there he shouldn't see?"

There was no point lying. She'd ferret out the truth. I'd always said she was the best detective in the station. It annoyed Chief Lynch, but that didn't make it untrue. "The DNA report I had run, a few years back. It's in the folder."

"Ah," she said. "I see."

"How'd you get it back from him?"

She pointed to the small closet. "In there." She wasn't going to reveal her tricks. Okay. She'd gotten it away from him, and that was all that mattered.

Her gray raincoat hung above the box. I opened the box and pulled the Jane Doe folder out. There was my typed report from sixteen years ago. My name at the top: Detective Michael Finnegan. The report was short. One page and a half. Too many questions, and very few answers. I leafed to the back and pulled out a sheet. "DNA Test Results." The form was a tangle of scientific abbreviations and numbers. The top was easy to read, though. Under MOTHER was "Patricia Finnegan." Under FATHER was "James Finnegan." Under SAMPLE was "UNKNOWN." The DNA lab didn't use the term Jane Doe. They called them "unknowns." This was the sheet I couldn't have Chief Lynch getting his hands on. I tucked it inside my breast pocket and put the folder back inside, below the bone and the skirt and the watch. "Back in the closet?"

"Why not?" she said. "It'll keep the Chief honest. He can't investigate if he can't find it."

"You think he wouldn't look in here?" We exchanged a look, and then laughed. He'd sooner search the mayor's office.

And, like that, he appeared. In the doorway, holding up a paper. I peered. It couldn't be. I had that paper in my jacket.

He closed the door behind him and said, "What the hell is this?"

Grace looked my way and swallowed. She opened her mouth. I shook my head at her. She'd tried, but this wasn't her secret, wasn't her story.

"You had Colleen's bone tested against your parents' DNA?" he asked, incredulous.

"Yes."

"Why?"

I'd managed to keep it a secret from everyone here but Grace for over twenty years. I should've known it couldn't stay secret forever. The house always wins.

"I thought it belonged to my sister, Susan," I said.

"Susan? I thought your sister's name was Carol." He glanced at Grace and then me, sure he was being hoodwinked.

"My older sister's name is Carol. My younger sister's name is Susan. She went missing in 1972. She's still missing."

# MONDAY, SEPTEMBER 25, 1972
## CHARLESTOWN, MASSACHUSETTS

T he man held a dishtowel to his head. He sat on the stoop, his feet splayed. The towel was soaked with blood. "Fucking Walter," he said, only it sounded like "Walt-ah." You knew a local by how they said, "car," "bubbler," and "idea." Idea had an *r* at the end of it.

"Walter?" I asked, pen at the ready.

"I owed him dough for some broken filly couldn't race her way out of a paper bag. Name of Flash Lightning. Ha!" His laugh sounded like a rock tumbler in action. "He came 'round to collect. Told him I didn't get paid 'til Friday, just like everybody else. He broke a Miller bottle and cut me with it!" He pointed to a wet section of brick.

"Where's Walter now?" I asked.

"Upstairs." He pointed to the door behind him.

"He lives here? What's his last name?"

"McDonough, and no, he's up in my place." He pulled the towel from his head. The cut above his eyebrow was long and jagged. The bleeding had slowed, and the cut didn't look deep. Nothing time and ice and staying away from the racetrack couldn't heal.

"Might want to ice it," I said. "What's he doing upstairs, in your place?"

"Fucking my girlfriend, Sheila." He sighed. "He said that ought to cover half my debt."

I stopped writing. "You pimped out your girlfriend for half of your debt to Walter?"

"Well, I don't get paid 'til Friday, do I?"

When I signed up to be a cop, I pictured myself arresting drug dealers and low-level Mob flunkies, the scum that operated on street corners and outside movie theaters. I didn't see myself talking with idiot gamblers who couldn't pick a winning nag, and who paid their debts with whatever sad Betty was willing to shack up with them.

"I'm going up there," I said.

"Why?" he asked. "They ain't done yet."

"Because I'd like to hear that Sheila is okay with this arrangement." I stepped past him and jogged up the creaking stairs to the second floor, hand atop my club, just in case it got messy. From behind the door, Tom Jones sang, "She's a Lady." I pounded the cracked, blue door.

"Hold your horses!" a woman yelled. A half minute later the door swung inward. She wore a thin pink robe cut to mid-thigh, and her hair was half-done in curlers.

"You must be Sheila," I said.

"What do you want?"

"I'm Officer Michael Finnegan, and I wanted to make sure you're safe."

She cackled. "Safe as houses, boyo."

"Connor downstairs indicated he might have bartered you for some bad horse-race debt."

"Sure did." She gave me a smile that revealed a missing eyetooth. "Joke's on him. I'm gonna move in with Walter. He's got a steady job and a bigger place that isn't above his mother's." She shouted the last two words at the floor. A moment later, a thumping started up from below. Connor's mother with a broom, no doubt.

"Terrific. I hope you'll be very happy."

She grinned and slammed the door. I checked my watch. Only twenty more minutes. God willing, no more calls would come in and I could be inside the Dugout, drinking a cold one within the hour.

Outside, Connor was on his feet, holding a beer can. The dish-towel lay, discarded, on the steps. I wished him a good day and walked toward the police station. I arrived three minutes before end of shift.

That cold beer was almost in hand. "Hey!" my super called. "Come here." He snapped his fingers.

"What do you need?" My super was an okay guy, but a bear when it came to complaints.

"Call your mother," he said. "She's called here twice. Sounds worried. I asked what the trouble was, but," he shrugged. "Let me know if you need something."

"Thanks." I'd return my radio, keys, and activity log after I made the call.

"Ma?" I said when she answered. "What's going on? Is Dad okay?" My father had a bum ticker. He'd had a heart attack a year ago.

"He's fine. It's Susan. She's missing."

"Missing?"

"She hasn't come home since Friday. She said she was sleeping over at Lucy's house after they went to the movies. Then she called Saturday and asked if she could spend the night again."

"And Sunday?"

"She begged to stay over one more night. When I said it was a school night, she complained we didn't trust her, and I asked to speak to Millie. I wanted to be sure it wasn't a bother, but she said dinner was ready and hung up. This afternoon, the school called to say she'd been marked absent, and this was her third offense this term without a note."

"You haven't seen her since Friday dinnertime?" I asked. "What did Lucy say?"

"She hasn't seen her since school on Friday. Susan never stayed at her house."

"Where do you think she is?" I asked.

"I want to file a Missing Person report."

"But, Ma, what about last time?"

When Susan was fourteen, she'd run away. She was gone four days. An older woman who'd seen her hitchhiking in New Hampshire brought her home. My parents had grounded her for five months. She couldn't go to a friend's house or attend after-school games. When I'd stop by for dinner, Susan would glare at me from behind her too-long bangs. As if I'd done anything to land her in that jam.

"It's not like last time," she said.

"Are you sure?"

She hesitated. "Come over, when you get off shift, will you?"

"On my way."

I turned in my items and clocked out. On the way out the door, I ran into my super. "Everything okay?" he asked.

He and I had first met when Susan ran away two years ago. I'd come to the station to deliver a AAA map we'd found in her room. The destination was Atlanta. He'd taken the map, patted my shoulder, and promised to contact the police in Atlanta. So, when my super asked if everything was okay, I could've said, "She's missing again, my sister, Susan." And labeled myself as the guy with the runaway sister who wasted police time and resources. I looked at my newly polished shoes and said, "Nothing that won't solve itself. Thanks."

"That's good," he said. "Have a good night."

"You too." I hurried outside, where the wind tossed cellophane cigarette wrappers in the air. The Bunker Hill Monument loomed ahead, a reminder of Susan. She'd asked a million questions about it as a kid. *Who built it? Who cleaned it? Why were there only windows at the top?* Dave told her the monument was built by elves and was a secret portal to another world. That made her ask, *What kind of elves? What was the other world like? Could anyone go there? Had he been to the other world?* Bobby laughed himself breathless and said, "I can't believe you fell for that." I'd punched Bobby in the bicep, but I'd pulled the punch because he was younger.

Past the monument, I cut over and walked past the Sullivans' and O'Reillys' and McDonalds' houses. Too soon, I stood in front of 12 Wood Street, staring at the tan, aluminum siding. "Mikey!" my mother yelled from the second-story parlor window. "Come in!"

I wiped my feet. Ma hurried down the stairs. "Thank God." She clutched me like I was a life preserver. "Dave's out. Seeing if anyone saw her. Bobby is calling her girlfriends." My brothers were on the case. I'd been informed last. I tried not to let it bother me, and failed.

"What about Carol?" Carol, our oldest sibling, was a second mother to most of us.

"She had to go to the doctor's again." Carol was pregnant, and this second child had given her trouble from day one.

"I'll find Dave and help him."

Last time she'd gone, Susan had taken a suitcase she'd stashed behind the bushes in the Murphys' backyard. Maybe this time a neighbor had seen her with the suitcase. Damn. I should've asked Ma if it was missing.

Dave was talking to Charlie Houghman. Charlie had coached our Little League teams. "Hiya, Charlie." It felt odd to call him that. He'd been "Mr. Houghman" until recently, when he told me if I could vote, I could call him Charlie. It was meant to be a gift, but it felt like a burden.

He stood, pruning shears in hand. Charlie's wife had been a great gardener, until she got breast cancer. She was getting chemo now, and we rarely saw her.

"I haven't seen your sister since Wednesday. I was just telling Dave, she was playing on a skateboard one of the Ryan boys has. A skinny yellow board. She was with Lucy. Your parents must be out of their skulls, huh?" He shook his head. "I'll call you if I spot her."

"Thanks," we said. He nodded and picked up his shears.

Dave told me some neighbors he'd talked to had seen Susan on Friday, but none had seen her since. After dinner, she'd walked up Wood Street, toward High Street, dressed in jeans and a fringed top, her hair down, carrying a knapsack.

"A knapsack?" I asked.

"Not a suitcase."

"But not a regular purse."

We were both thinking it. She'd run, again.

Dave said, "Mickey Wentz said he spotted Susan walking toward the monument. Mickey said hi, but Susan didn't say hello." Mickey was an alkie who could be very nice and charming or not, depending on his intake levels. Susan might've chosen to avoid him for safety's sake.

"Why don't I go down High Street, to the monument? You check Cordid," I said.

"Already did, Officer." Dave's response was bone dry. Now was not the time to get into who was in charge. Dave was older by two years, but he wasn't a trained policeman. He'd argue I was barely a policeman, in uniform less than a year. I said, "Then search somewhere else."

"I'll check Elm," he said.

I stopped at every house and talked to folks. Neighbors were happy to chat. *Susan missing, again? How long had she been gone? Was a boy involved?* I answered more questions than I asked. "You look good in the uniform, Mikey!" said Mr. Sullivan. His comment emphasized how wrong it was that the family with the cop had a girl they couldn't find, again. It was like we were careless and had misplaced her.

At Bunker Hill, I flashed the photo of Susan at a ranger. He squinted. "I've seen her around. Cute kid." I got ready to tell him she was just that, a kid, and he better watch his step, when he said, "Sorry, haven't seen her recently."

"You sure?"

"Well, it's been busy since school started back up. Field trips. You know. But I don't think so."

"How about Kevin?" I asked. Kevin was a ranger who'd played in our neighborhood when we were kids. He was cousins with Jack McGee. Jack, who my dad warned me to "stay away from" when I was in third grade. Because Jack's family did "bad things."

"Kevin hasn't been on shift since Thursday," he said. "He's back tomorrow. She in trouble?" He looked at the picture again.

"No." I wasn't as sure as I sounded. "Thanks for your help."

I canvassed a few more blocks, but no one had seen her. They fired questions at me. *Why had she left? Was the fight they heard through their open windows Thursday night between her and my parents? She wasn't hanging out with Trisha Darling was she? Trisha was bad news.*

The sun was gone when I trudged back to the house. Inside, it was twenty degrees warmer. Ever since his heart attack, Dad set the thermostat to broil. Everyone was gathered at the dining-room table. It smelled of starch spray. Ma must've ironed in here, earlier. Dave drank a beer, a lit cigarette in his other hand. Bobby ate a cookie. When he finished, Ma handed him another.

"She's not at any hospital," Ma said. "I called all over. Brigham and Women's had a girl named Susan, but her last name's Lucas and she has appendicitis."

"Bobby?" I asked my younger brother.

"None of Susan's friends have seen her since Friday."

"What about Lucy?" I asked. "Do we think Susan really didn't tell her anything?" Best friends covered for each other. Lucy had been Susan's best friend since second grade.

"Are you asking if Lucy MacManus is a liar?" My father's dark eyes tried to bore a hole through my forehead.

"She might lie for Susan."

"I believe her," Bobby said. "She sounded worried. None of her friends had any idea where she'd gone."

"Boyfriend?" Dave asked.

"She doesn't have a boyfriend," Ma said.

"She's not allowed to have a boyfriend," Dad said, as if that settled that.

"Not one you knew about," I said, low.

"What was that?" Dad shouted.

"Enough!" Ma said. "Bobby, did any of the girls mention a boyfriend?"

"No," he said. "They said Susan has a crush on Andy Moretti, but he doesn't know she's alive."

"Moretti?" Dad said. "That oily piece of shit? He better not look at Susan. I'll put his damn eyes out."

"Dad," Bobby said. "Moretti's got a girlfriend, Sophia. He's never looked at Susan."

Was that true? Or was Bobby keeping peace? I'd ask him later, out of Dad's hearing.

"So, no boyfriend, she's not in the hospital, and none of her friends know where she is." Dave summarized it neatly.

"Has anyone searched her room?" I asked. If she'd run away, stuff would be missing.

"I looked this afternoon," Ma said. "And I didn't see much missing."

"Let's take another look," I said.

Dad and Dave stayed at the table.

Susan's room had twin beds, from when she and Carol had shared the space. Carol had left four years ago, when she married, but her bed remained, shoved against the right wall. Susan used it as a desk. There were books, papers, and school folders spread across it. Susan's closet had louvered doors that pulled off the tracks if you tugged too hard. The closet was shallow, so the hangers had to be angled so the doors could close. Inside were pants, skirts, blouses, dresses, and shoes. "There's an empty hanger," Bobby said.

"Just one?" Ma asked. "That's nothing."

Atop her dresser, an array of colorful lip glosses lay next to her perfume. Headbands with their small plastic teeth, ribbons, stickers, a keychain she'd won, and two copies of *Glamour*.

"Where's Mr. Growls?" Bobby asked, staring at the bed.

Mom frowned. "I don't know."

Mr. Growls had been with Susan since her fourth birthday. She'd taken the bear everywhere. Its fur was worn in patches, its head permanently atilt from years of hugs.

"She took it," Bobby said.

"And her lucky rabbit's foot," Ma said.

"Where does she keep it?" I hadn't been in this room since Carol lived here.

"Over there." She pointed to the satin-trimmed vanity table Susan had gotten five Christmases ago. It was comically small, built for a child, not a teenager.

"You know what this means?" I said. "She packed. She left. She ran away, *again*."

"Can you ask your department—?"

"Ma, she's a runaway. She hasn't been abducted." A low throb started at the base of my skull. I looked around the room again, hoping it would offer me some clue as to where she'd gone this time.

"We're going to have to find her ourselves."

# FRIDAY, MAY 14, 1999
## 2015 HOURS

**S**uds was packed with Friday-night drinkers, some of them UConn undergrads celebrating final exams. My polo shirt would smell like booze, fried food, and cigarette smoke when I got home, and I'd have to bring it back, another day, to the Laundromat side of Suds, for washing. Suds: half bar/half Laundromat, was the liveliest place in town. "Hi, Chief," Nate, the owner, said when I reached the bar. "What can I get you?"

"You have Brooklyn?"

He reached below the bar, grabbed a bottle, and popped off the cap. He didn't pour it, because I preferred to drink it from the bottle. "How's things?" he asked.

"Grand." Not true. My head was still buzzing from Finny's story about his missing sister. Missing twenty-seven years and no idea where she'd gone. I sneezed. Fished a handkerchief from my pocket. I blew into the cleanest spot I could find.

"Allergies," Nate said. "Nature's way of taking the White Man down."

"Don't Indians get allergies?" Nate was Nipmuc. How much, I didn't know. He said he didn't know either.

"Kidding," he said. "Most of my cousins are lactose intolerant."

Two college kids moseyed up to the bar. Donna took their orders. The boys tried not to hurt themselves ogling her. I scanned the room. Impossible to suppress the instinct to assess the crowd, check for trouble, make sure nothing looked amiss. Nothing seemed to, so I turned my attention to the little TV bolted over the bar. My mind wasn't on the game onscreen, though. It was still on Finny's missing sister. He'd thought the Colleen bone might belong to her. Jesus, what were the chances? Seven million to one? And still he'd had it tested. Completely against protocol. I'd told him so, but my heart wasn't in it because I could see, even now, how he'd wanted it to match. Twenty-seven years without any answers. That was longer than the dopey college boys at the bar had been alive.

"Hey, Chief," a man to my right said. I turned. Mr. Cullen. I recognized him from town events. He was a civic-minded businessman who dedicated time and money to the town's various projects. He held a foaming glass in one hand and a chicken wing in the other. "I drive down Piper Street every day. Any word on when those clamshells will be removed?"

"That's on DPW, Mr. Cullen." The stinking clamshells were supposed to be removed two days ago. "Have they not come by?"

"They say we need to bag 'em, but they're really gross."

*Grosser than a two-day floater out of the Hudson River?* No, I couldn't say that. "I hear you. Drove past a few days ago, and the smell was out of this world."

"My girls' best friend lives on that street. We can't let them play on the swing set if there's any wind," he complained.

"Tell you what. I'll call DPW and see what the holdup is." I knew what the holdup was. DPW didn't want to pick up maggoty, stinky clamshells, and not on a day when Piper Street wasn't on the trash route.

"You talking about the clamshells?" Another guy, one I didn't know, joined in. "Who dumped them there?"

"We're looking into it," I said.

"I spoke to a detective the other day. Guess this kind of crime doesn't happen in the big city, huh?"

"Not exactly." I'd come from New York City. The locals never forgot, or let me forget. What I didn't tell them was that petty crime was the same in intent, if not in execution, the world over.

"Remember in 1990, was it, when they kept finding those broken bottles on people's steps?" Mr. Cullen asked. "Glass bottles, and it was summer, so if you stepped out barefoot—"

"You cut your foot," the other guy finished. "Yup. They finally caught the guy, right?"

"Yeah. He was caught dumping glass shards onto someone's steps."

"Why'd he do it?" I asked, intrigued despite myself.

"I don't recall," Mr. Cullen said. "Do you?"

"Nah," second guy said. "I remember one kid had to have stitches. Sliced up his heel something awful."

I sipped at my beer, just another guy talking about the past crimes of Idyll, almost a local. A hand grabbed my shoulder, hard. I slapped my palm over the hand and turned fast, nearly head-butting Matt. "Whoa!" he said, pulling his hand free.

"You startled me," I said. Mr. Cullen and friend eyed us like we might start shooting. "Sorry," I said. "Old friend. He has a weird way of greeting people. Excuse us." I steered Matt Cisco toward the end of the bar's counter.

He grinned. He wore jeans and a gray t-shirt. How I ever convinced him to sleep with me was a mystery for the ages. "How are you, *papi*?" He whispered the last word. His Puerto Rican terms of endearment were always delivered as half-joke.

"Before a federal agent assaulted me, I was great." Matt was at the New Haven branch of the FBI. We'd worked a case together, fifteen months ago. We'd been keeping each other company roughly the same amount of time.

"Hey, Matty, what'll you have?" Donna asked. She liked him, more than me. Maybe because he'd never misled her by pretending to be straight.

"Rolling Rock," Matt said. When he took his foaming glass from her, he said, "Cheers."

"Cheers." I drank and stared at him from the corner of my eye. I hadn't expected to see him until Sunday, at the earliest. I smiled. He was good to see, no matter when. "How's things?"

"Just wrapped up a human-trafficking case. Now here I am, in the sleepiest town I know."

"Sleepy? I haven't told you about the clamshell mystery on Piper Street then."

"Oh, Idyll," Matt said, amused.

"Hey, those clamshells are nasty and no one knows who's dumping them."

He patted my shoulder. "I don't know how you keep up with this place."

I wanted to tell him about today's big news, about Susan Finnegan and the bone I'd found in Evidence, but we couldn't talk here.

Nate came over to check on us. "You guys good?"

My beer was nearly gone, but I didn't want another now that Matt was here. "Hey, Nate, what do you know about Idyll's ghost?" Nate knew everything there was worth knowing. Benefit of his profession. "Out in the woods by the Old Graham place?"

"Oh, you mean Colleen?"

"That's the one."

"Not much. Kind of recent, as ghosts go. Dates back to the 1980s. Story has it a teen girl was murdered there and now she roams the woods. They call her Colleen, but they don't know who she is. Mr. Graham, who owned the place, died a few years after they discovered the bones." I didn't correct him, tell him that there had been only one bone. "There was gossip he was involved, but that's nonsense. He was a nice old coot."

"New Haven got ghosts?" I asked Matt. He snickered.

"Kids used to dare each other to sleep in the woods," Nate said. "Try to see the ghost."

"I bet every kid who did it saw her too." Matt set his empty glass on the bar. "I'll have another."

"Sure thing." Nate grabbed the glass and went to the tap.

"So, what are your plans this evening?" Matt slung his arm over my shoulder. It was heavy with muscle. It felt good, but I couldn't have him do that here. I tried to shrug it off. "What?" he said.

"Nothing. I'd just prefer it if you kept your hands to yourself, mister." The "mister" was an afterthought, added when I saw the storm clouds on his face.

"Sure thing." He jammed his hands into his pockets. "Why don't I keep them all to myself? Sorry to disturb you." Before I could protest, he stomped off and out the door. I felt the weight of curious eyes on me. I kept my gaze on the TV until I felt them drop off.

"Where's Matt?" Nate asked as he plunked the glass down before me.

"Something came up." I tossed some bills onto the bar. Nate complained it was too much, but I wasn't going to turn around. Better to exit quickly.

The chill air smelled like rain. Matt was gone. Probably peeled out and driving hell for leather back home. Damn it. He didn't care what people thought if he touched me, if we looked like two gay men, because that's what we were. I had a harder time. I was chief of police, surrounded by the people I worked for. Plenty of them didn't like that I was gay.

I got in my car and picked up my mobile phone. Dialed Matt, but he didn't answer, so I drove home. Settled in my living room recliner, I called someone I knew would pick up, if he was home.

After two rings, he did. "Hello?" Damien Saunders said.

"Hi."

"Thomas. To what do I owe the pleasure?" Damien's phone voice was very good. He could've run a sex line, if he wasn't a Medical Examiner.

"Hey, Damien. How are you?"

"Fine. Today was quiet. Please tell me you're not calling to change that."

"No, no. Hey, you ever play softball?"

"Poorly. Why?"

"Annual charity match is coming up. Us versus the firefighters. My guys always get their asses kicked. Wonder if I'm allowed to recruit outside talent?"

"Think your team roster had to be submitted by April 30th," he said.

"What?"

"Yeah, I was talking to your Captain Hirsch about a fire case he consulted on. Anyway, he mentioned the game. He's team captain. I thought your captain was some guy named Walter Dix."

"Dix." The same guy who couldn't outrun a child. "Yeah, that's right." Was it? Shouldn't I be team captain as chief of police? Was it an elected position? If so, why hadn't I voted? Maybe it was an oversight. But I'd told them that I was looking forward to defeating the Red Menace (my nickname for the firefighters). I'd told them last week. No one had said anything.

Time to change the topic. "I have a question for you."

"Case-related?"

"No. Relationship-related." Damien was the only gay man in the area I was friends with, which said more about me than it did about him.

He inhaled, a soft little *oh*. "This involves Matthew Cisco?" Damien had met Cisco through work, but not socially, as far as I knew.

"Yes."

"Well? Out with it," he demanded.

"Matt met me at Suds tonight, and he put his arm on my shoulder and . . . I kind of pushed it off. Then he said he'd keep his hands to himself and stormed out. He won't answer my calls."

"You know why he's upset?" Damien said.

"Yeah, I do. It's just . . . he's way more comfortable being together in public."

"And you're not."

"Suds is full of townies. It's not exactly discreet."

"Quick question. How many couples did you see at the bar?" Damien asked.

My mind reviewed the bar. "Five. Why?" I could feel I was being set up.

"How many of them were holding hands or touching?"

"Three, no four."

"Did it bother you?"

"It's not the same." Those couples had been men and women, paired like the animals on Noah's Ark.

"Isn't it? Do you think those people worried about discretion?"

"You think I was wrong." I rubbed my toes against the carpet, making a grid pattern.

"I think you think you were wrong."

"Yeah." I cradled my brow in my cupped right palm. "What do I do now?"

"Apologize."

"I thought you'd say that."

"Make a gesture. Something romantic and a bit public."

"How public? Do I have to tag a bridge with our initials inside a heart?"

His laugh was terrific, low and rumbly. "Not that public. How about flowers?"

"Flowers? Isn't that, I don't know, kind of girly?"

"You ever get flowers?"

"No." I associated them with hospital stays, funerals, and my mother, who liked to grab bouquets from the bodegas as "pick-me-ups."

"It's a nice treat," he said.

"Where would I order them?" On those rare instances when I'd needed them, I'd asked my mother for advice, and she'd done it for me. Damien didn't need to know that.

He named a shop. "Tell them it's for your boyfriend when you order."

"Wait. Why? They don't need to know that."

"A bit public, remember? You need to start getting over your anxiety. You realize everyone in this state knows you're gay, right?" There had been news coverage, though I denied interviews, both on and off camera. Gay chief of police? I still got calls from hungry reporters.

"Yeah. It just feels like there is a difference between that and . . . everyone seeing it."

"Do you really care that much about whether the citizens of Idyll like you?" He sipped a drink. I could hear the clink of ice cubes against glass.

"Yes?"

"God, Thomas, for a big bear of a man, you've got a squishy marsh-mallow center."

"There is no marshmallow in these abs." I patted them, as if he could see.

"Right. I'm sure there isn't." He cleared his throat. "Well, good luck, Thomas."

"Thanks, Damien. I'll let you know how it goes."

"Mmm-hmmm. Good night." He hung up.

It was too late to call the florist shop, and I wasn't ready to do it anyway.

"Hi, I'm calling to order flowers for my boyfriend. He's mad at me." I said it aloud, a practice run.

The florist didn't need to know why I was sending them.

"Hi, I need some flowers for my boyfriend, a bouquet, like on the commercials for Valentine's Day, but not roses. Do I have to get roses?"

Jesus, I sounded crazy.

"Hi, I need to order a bouquet of flowers, for my boyfriend."

I could do this. Of course I could.

# MONDAY, MAY 17,1999
## 1400 HOURS

The physical-fitness memo sat on my desk, marked up with red-ink comments. Next to my suggested 1.5 mile run times, Mrs. Dunsmore had written "faster than the Cooper Standards." Beside push-ups, she'd written, "They're men, not superheroes." I picked up the memo and went to give *her* some feedback. Her office was empty. Damn.

"Chief!" someone yelled. "You got a call on line two. Some flower shop."

I picked up Mrs. Dunsmore's phone, hit line two, and said, "Thomas Lynch."

"I'm calling from the Blossom Shop. You placed an order earlier? We ran your credit card, and it seems to be having trouble. Is it possible there was a mistake, maybe with the zip code?"

I recited my Idyll zip code. He said, "Ah! That's the problem. You gave a different one."

"Which one?"

He read it off. It was my old New York zip code. "Wait. What street address did I give?" He told me. It was correct. "Sorry about that. Must've had my mind on other things."

The door swung inward. Mrs. Dunsmore stepped inside and said, "This is unexpected."

"No problem," the man said. "Have a good afternoon."

I hung up the phone and said, "Sorry. I got a call."

"And you were in my office . . ."

"Chief!" Hugh called. The new dispatcher had pipes on him.

"What?" she and I yelled at the same time.

"I think you need to hear this."

Mrs. Dunsmore accompanied me to the dispatch booth where Hugh Bascomb sat at the board. He said, "We just got a call from some folks who think they found human remains."

"Pardon?" Mrs. Dunsmore said.

"Two people passing through town. They say they found bones in the woods off of Route 30. They're probably animals. I could send Hopkins. He's closest."

"No," I said. Hopkins had as much experience identifying remains as I did wooing women. "Wait. I'll get you someone."

I stalked to Wright's desk. Mrs. Dunsmore didn't follow. Wright sat, reviewing statements. The clamshell case; it couldn't be anything else. "Hey, someone reported finding human remains in the woods off Route 30. Talk to Hugh for the exact location, and bring Billy."

"Billy?" Wright wrinkled his nose.

"His Boy Scout group got badges in learning the difference between animal bones and human bones."

He didn't ask questions; he grabbed his stuff and yelled, "Billy! Come with me." He didn't look behind to make sure Billy heard or complied. Billy hustled to catch up.

"Hey, Chief," Mrs. Dunsmore said. I turned. She had followed me. "You know where that road backs up onto, right?" she asked. I didn't. "It's the same woods where Detective Finnegan found Colleen's bone."

"In 1983," I said. "And they didn't find anything else."

She pursed her lips.

"It could be a deer carcass. We don't know that it's human."

"And if it is?" she asked.

"Then I'm sure Detective Wright can handle it."

She said, "I'm sure he can . . . but if these bones have *anything* to do with the Colleen case, wouldn't it make sense to involve Detective Finnegan?"

"He's off today, working his second job." Finnegan worked at a security firm, the kind that installed home alarms. He called it his "alimony job." He had three ex-wives. I'd once pointed out to him that heterosexuality seemed awfully expensive, and he'd laughed and said I might be onto something.

The mountain of crap on Finnegan's desk distracted me. Discarded bags of chips and dog-eared magazines and broken pencils. Wright's desk was pristine. Surprised they never came to blows over it. Cops had, over lesser things. Only it wasn't the small things they fought over. It was the bigger stuff at home, and the work stuff was just the valve that released the steam. I uncrossed my arms, clapped my hands together, and said, "Tell you what. If it has anything to do with that bone, I will apprise Detective Finnegan when he returns to work."

She crooked her finger at me, so I'd come nearer. I did, reluctantly. Her voice was low, pitched so no one but me could hear. "Michael hasn't been able to find his missing sister. He went so far as to have that bone tested for familial DNA. If he can help find whoever it belonged to, it would mean a lot to him. But he will never tell you that."

Damn it. How was I to argue that point? The Colleen case had bothered him for years. And it wasn't as though he was busy pursuing other investigations.

"Fine," I said. Why was it that when she and I tangled, I never won?

I stalked off to my office to lick my wounds and caught sight of a note. John, NYU Award. Shoot. I needed to tell him whether or not I was coming. Well, no time like the present. He answered the home line, surprised by the sound of my voice. Shocked when I said I'd come.

"That's great." I heard him shout to his wife, Marie, that I'd be coming. Her "Really?" made it to the phone too. Anyone placing bets on my attendance could've made a mint.

We chitchatted about the Yankees' season, and then I said, "See you soon. Oh, wait. Is it, um, okay, if I bring someone?"

"Bring someone? Like a date?"

I was spreading surprise all over the place today.

"Well, I mean, sort of, I guess."

"Of course you can. Sorry. I was just, surprised. You've never brought anyone to a family event."

"What about Helen Mayes? She came to dinner several times."

He groaned. "Poor Helen. I wonder if she's stopped dating gay men. Last I knew, she still lived in the city, so maybe not. Anyway, we'd be delighted to have you with or without a date."

John hadn't expected me to accept. He had had good reason. I always felt awkward at academic affairs where I stood out for not having multiple degrees, where scholarly names I didn't recognize were lobbed about, and I'd nod and hope not to embarrass myself or my family. If another attendee found out I was a cop, I became the target of an interview I hadn't signed on for. *What was it like? What did I think about decriminalizing drugs? Had I ever shot someone?* John told me once to ask how their tenure process was coming along. It worked well. Those who were on the cusp got scared, and those who had it were offended by the question and walked away within seconds.

Finnegan's missing sister had reminded me of the fragility of family. They're easy to take for granted or resent. But our time with them is limited. Susan's disappearance drove that home. She'd been sixteen when she went missing. No one, including Finny, had thought that the last time they saw her would be just that, the last time. Did I want to make small talk with uptight liberal academics who looked down on me? No. But I would, for John and for the rest of my family.

Would I ask Matthew to come?

Guess it depended on how the flowers went over.

# MONDAY, MAY 17, 1999

## 1505 HOURS

By pushing my shitty car to its limit, I arrived at the site just fifteen minutes after Dix called. He knew I'd be interested in more bones found not far from where I'd discovered Colleen's humerus all those years ago, so he called me when Wright and Billy left the station. I'd left my security job, claiming a sudden stomach bug. No one had questioned me. A stiff breeze smacked me when I exited the car. Billy said, "Hi, Detective. Why are you here?"

"You got bones?" I asked, skipping the pleasantries. My eyes went up, off the road, into the trees.

He nodded. "We haven't looked at 'em yet. Detective Wright is taking the couple's statement. He's in there with them now."

Ahead of the patrol car was a Land Rover with muddy tires. "Why were they in the woods?" I asked. There were no public hiking trails in the area. Nothing to attract tourists.

Billy ducked his head and said, "Lady needed a pee break. They'd been hiking the Mattatuck Trail and were headed home. She needed to stop, urgently."

"I see."

"She went back a ways to do her business, and she saw the bones. She ran back to the car. Her husband took a look and agreed they seemed human, so he called 911, and here we are."

"Up there?" I asked, pointing.

"Yes, but Detective Wright said not to let anyone through because—"

I climbed the shallow incline, ignoring his warning. I'm sure Lewis didn't want patrol mucking about, but he didn't mean to ban me from the scene. About twenty feet inside the woods, past the budded trees, to a spot where you could hardly see the road, stood three people. Lewis and the couple. They were in their midthirties. She wore her hair in a ponytail and had skin tanner than was typical of May. His Ray-Bans were tucked into the vee of his shirt. They leaned against each other.

Lewis stood at a point on the ground that was littered with twigs where a few dead daffodils stood guard. The soil was sunken lower than the surrounding ground, and protruding from it were small bones. She had good eyes. The bones weren't obvious. They could be mistaken, at first glance, for bare twigs and limbs.

Lewis looked up, saw me and said nothing, though his brows were raised. "Did you touch any of this?" he asked the woman.

She shook her head violently. "No, no, I couldn't. I went back to the car, right away."

"Detective Finnegan, would you fetch Officer Thompson? He has expertise in identifying bones."

Billy must've been a Boy Scout with Mr. Mulaney as his troop leader. I tromped down the hill and whistled to Billy. "Time to make Mr. Mulaney proud," I said.

"Too bad he's not here." Billy hitched his shoulders. Mr. Mulaney had died of a brain aneurysm at the too-young age of fifty-six.

We walked back toward the depressed soil. I held back, though it was clear this wasn't a fresh grave. Still, best not to muddy the soil with my prints. Especially since I wasn't on duty.

Billy approached the site carefully, gloves on. The wind scattered dried leaves. "Go ahead," Lewis told him. Billy squatted to look at the bones. "This big one looks like a femur. Can I pick it up?"

Lewis hesitated. If this was human, it'd be best not to disturb the scene. But, if not, he'd be the butt of jokes for years to come. Pride won out. He said, "Yeah. Get it out of there."

Billy had to dig with his hands and wrestle the bone to free it from the soil. He rotated it. "Long enough to be human, but let's see. Same thickness you'd expect for a person." He pulled it close to his face and squinted. "Single. Not double."

"Single what?" I asked.

"Linea something." He tapped the top of the bone. Not the rounded knob, but the sharper end. "In other mammals, it's double. Man, Mr. Mulaney would be disappointed if he knew I forgot this."

"You're doing fine. What about that?" Lewis pointed to two small, gray-white bones.

"Looks like finger bones," Billy said. "Bears look similar, but the grooves on the end of the phalanges don't look notched enough for a bear."

The couple shuddered. The woman turned and put her face in her husband's neck.

Lewis said, "Okay. Billy, you radio for the techs. I'll stay here."

A low rumble came from far off. We looked up. The sun had disappeared behind clouds.

The woman piped up. "Can we go now?" She hugged herself; her teeth chattered.

Lewis said, "Leave your contact information with Detective Finnegan." He jerked his chin my way. "And then, yes, you may leave."

I walked them to their car and took down their address and telephone numbers. "Thank you," I told her, touching her right arm.

"For what?" she asked, surprised.

"For calling it in. Whoever is buried back there, someone is missing them. This may end a long search."

She seemed caught off guard by the idea and said, "I suppose." Her husband took her hand and tucked her in the passenger seat. He pulled the car out the way people do when they're near a cop. Checking mirrors three times and barely using the gas.

Billy was on the radio. I looked down the road. Nothing but trees and flowers and birds. Good place to hide a corpse. It wasn't picturesque. No walking trails ran through here. It was a spot on the way to other places. I tromped back into the woods. Lewis scanned the ground. "I found something." He pointed. Four feet from the bones was a gallon-size plastic bag. It was filthy, covered with dirt and leaf matter.

"The techs should photograph it before we look inside," I said.

"I know that."

I said, "I wasn't talking to you; I was telling myself because I *really* want to look inside."

He gazed at me, his dark eyes full of questions. But the only one he asked was, "Where's the old Graham place?"

"That way." I nodded, away from the road. "If you walk straight through, you come up onto the backyard. Take you maybe ten minutes, tops." I looked through the trees, their buds unfurled to small leaves. Soon the leaves would grow, making it impossible to see a foot ahead.

"How far away did you find Colleen's bone?" he asked.

"From here? Probably three minutes. It was closer to this end of the woods than to Mr. Graham's land." The woods had grown dark. No more sun. The wind had picked up. Ominous.

"What do you think?" he asked.

I pulled out my cigarettes, shook one loose from the pack. I didn't light it. "I think we found the rest of her."

"Colleen?"

"I always thought it odd that we only found the one bone."

He pursed his lips. "Think the rain will hold off until the techs get here?"

A low rumble of thunder came. Ten seconds later, lightning lit up the sky. Everything appeared hyper bright for one instant, as if a strobe light had flashed. "No."

The techs came as the first drops hit the ground. They got to work snapping photos and erecting a tent to preserve the grave from the storm. I watched as the water fell harder, turning the ground to mud. My hair got damp, then wet, and then rivulets washed down my neck. Lewis stood under an umbrella, picking up his feet every so often and shifting to drier ground. "You can head back," he called to me. "Don't think we'll have anything concrete for a while."

"I don't mind," I said. The techs took more photos and shifted soil. They dug. Their feet made squelchy sounds in the mud. I didn't want to leave.

"Hey, Detective!" Billy called. He'd come from the road where

Lewis had parked him to keep any rubberneckers from approaching our scene.

"What?" Lewis shouted. He refused to budge from the mini-hill he'd found to keep his loafers out of the mud.

"Sorry, I meant Detective Finnegan," Billy said. "Chief wants you."

Hell. He knew I was here. Not good. I wasn't on duty, not even at work today. He was probably less than delighted with me right now.

"Yeah?" The techs were discussing the grave. I wasn't going to budge until I knew what they knew. Besides, I was in no hurry to be scolded.

Billy waited for more. Then he said, "He's waiting."

"I'll come back to the station soon," I called. Not true, but it would buy me time.

"No. He's waiting down there." Billy jerked his thumb toward the road behind him.

"Fuck." So much for staying to see what they found.

"Trouble in paradise?" Lewis asked. This was the first time he'd seen me mixing it up with the chief. Usually it was him and Chief Lynch barking at each other, the two so similar they couldn't see it.

I didn't answer. Just watched the techs for a few seconds more. Had they found her? Would we at last know who she was and how she got here? I wiped the water from my face and half-walked, half-slid my way to the road. The chief's car was pulled over to the side. He lowered the passenger window and said, "Get in."

I opened the passenger door and sat. Rainwater dripped from me onto his car mats, and seat, and I felt a child's pleasure in defiling his car. Payback for dragging me from the site.

"We're going to dinner. Mulrooney's. It won't be crowded, and we can talk there," he said.

Mulrooney's was far enough away to guarantee we wouldn't run into locals or fellow cops. The food was third-rate, and the service awful. Interesting choice. "I'm not hungry," I said, a last-ditch effort to convince him to let me stay.

"We're not going because you're hungry," he said. "We're going because you shouldn't be here."

# MONDAY, MAY 17, 1999
## 1650 HOURS

**W**e took a table near the back, where the classic rock couldn't assault us. Finnegan ordered a beer and a basket of wings. I ordered a soft drink, though I didn't plan on drinking it. I opened with, "What were you doing back there?"

"Where?"

I didn't answer his dumb-ass question. I was annoyed. Finny wasn't on shift, and then Billy calls in to tell me he's at the woods where the bones were found. That he just "showed up."

I'd stomped out of my office and gone right for Mrs. Dunsmore, but she'd been surprised, not defiant. No, she hadn't informed Detective Finnegan of the bone find. No, she didn't know how he had found out. Maybe I'd be better served yelling at one of the men in the station, as she was busy, and by the way the onions from my sub were a bit strong and did I want a breath mint?

Back into the fray I yelled until Dix confessed he'd tipped off Finny. No, he hadn't meant for him to show up at the site. He thought he'd want to know since he found that other bone so many years ago. Yes, he had work to do. Plenty of work. He'd get right back to it. Yes, sir.

Finny's dumb act wasn't bringing my blood pressure down, so I asked again, "What were you doing in the woods?"

"Observing."

"You're not on duty. You had no business being there. You could get suspended."

"Look, I'm sorry. I was curious. I didn't interfere in any way."

"You didn't touch anything?" He shook his head. "Didn't examine the scene?"

"Only from a distance."

"Didn't talk to the folks who called it in?"

He hesitated. "Lewis asked me to take down their contact information." Well, well. Looked like my other detective would come in for a talk too. "But I didn't do anything else."

"Again, you had no business being there. Weren't you at your security job?" I asked. He nodded. "I'm assuming you left early?" He nodded. "Right. You're suspended. Three days without pay."

"What?"

"You heard me. You can't leave your second job to show up to a crime scene on an investigation that you're not involved in. You spoke to the witnesses. Your name is now included in an active investigation you shouldn't be part of."

"Come on, Chief. Those bones are human. The person in that grave didn't bury herself. You're looking at a homicide investigation."

"You don't know it's a woman in that grave."

He flinched, annoyed by my questioning his assumption. He plowed on. "Lewis is busy. He's going to need help."

"Busy?"

"The clamshell case and . . ."

I said, "His wife's expecting their third child, so he might be distracted."

"Says who?" As if he hadn't been about to spill the beans that she was pregnant.

The waitress plopped our drinks on the table, hard. Liquid sloshed over the sides of the glasses. "Wings will be out in a minute."

"Can't hardly wait," I said.

I wiped up the spilled beer with several napkins. "Wright's been taking time off. Plus, I overheard him on the phone, talking about an appointment. Obstetrician. I know what that word means. You didn't know?"

Finny said, "I knew. He swore me to secrecy. It's early days for her."

"Then it's unfortunate that the only other detective in the station is suspended, isn't it?" He moved on his chair seat. His pants squished. He needed to change out of his wet clothes. But I'd let him soak until I got my answers. "You know the Colleen bone belonged at the OCME in Farmington. Why did you keep it? After you had it tested, you didn't need it."

He rubbed the corner of his eye. His jacket dripped fat drops onto the tabletop. He leaned toward me and said, "And I'm pretty sure *you* know you shouldn't lie in the midst of an active murder investigation. But that didn't stop you during the North case. You think I don't know who the cop at the cabin was? The one who saw the murder victim and who never came forward? And what about interrogating a minor without his parent or lawyer present? Pretty sure you broke that rule."

My spine tingled. Whoa. There was real menace on his face and in his voice. And he was right. I'd broken more than a dozen rules in my investigation of the North murder. I'd lied to him, to Wright, to everyone.

"Okay. I see how it is."

"Do you?" he asked.

"You want in on the case."

"Yes."

"And you're threatening to rat me out if I don't include you?"

"I didn't say that." He sipped his beer, winced, and set it down. Pushed it away from him.

The music got louder. Aerosmith's "Walk This Way." The patrons near the speakers would be hard of hearing soon.

"You want something. I want something," I said.

"What do you want?" He shivered. The restaurant was blasting cold air, and he was soaked through from the rainstorm.

"Let me look into your sister's case."

"I told you, I've looked under every rock. There's nothing."

"Then let me waste my time." He opened his mouth, but I spoke first. "I'm bored, okay? I'd like to do some investigating. Right now, my biggest problem to solve is how to get our roof repaired within our budget."

"Here's your wings." The waitress used both hands to set them on the table, as if they were made of tissue-thin china. The chicken wings were coated in bright orange sauce. They smelled like a locker room. Finny's nose scrunched. He pushed the basket toward me. "Anything else I can get you?" she asked, her eyes on another table.

"No, thanks," I said. She left without another word.

"Look," Finnegan said, "I get that you're bored. Most afternoons you've got this dazed expression, like you can't figure out how you got here. But my missing sister doesn't need your homicide-detective experience, okay?"

"You don't know that."

"You don't think I investigated it? I've spent years, *decades*, on it." There was aggression in his voice, and wounded pride.

"I'm sure you did, but sometimes a pair of fresh eyes is a good thing, yeah? We both know it's unlikely I'll find her after all this time, but, then again, who knows?"

"What if I say no?" he asked.

"No problem," I said. "You don't want my help? I understand."

He eyed me like I was a suspect. Trying to figure out my angle. Whether he believed it or not, I'd told him the truth. I was bored. I spent too much time at my desk, where my biggest danger was paper-cuts. I missed crime scenes and bad guys and all the things I'd taken for granted every day I was a detective. "We better get back." I tossed money on the table.

"Wait." His eyes had a speck of gold in them. They were wide now. "You're not gonna let me work the case if I don't let you meddle in my family history? You're going to suspend me?"

I replaced my wallet and stood. "Someone has to solve the Piper Street clamshell mystery."

He cursed me out. He had one hell of a vocabulary. Evidence of a Catholic upbringing. When we reached the car, he said, "Fine. I'll give you what I've got on my sister's case. You know, I could tell the mayor what you did on the North case. You'd be fired by Fourth of July."

I leaned against the driver's side door and stared up into the cloudless sky. My eyes teared up. Fucking allergies. "You could, but you won't. You're not that kind."

"What kind?" he asked, jerking the passenger door open with too much force.

"The kind that rats out another cop." I sat in the car.

He stared at me. Angry enough to steam his own clothes dry. "You better pray that I'm not."

I started the engine and said, "I'll mention it next time I talk to God."

# WEDNESDAY, MAY 19, 1999
## 2220 HOURS

The carpet chafed my bare shoulder, so I rolled onto my side. Matt lay on his back, eyes closed. He breathed in short puffs. I reached out and stroked the skin below his rib cage. He yelped and thrashed as if being assaulted by bees. "Ticklish," I said. He squinted, considering retaliation. He leaned in for a kiss.

"So, you liked the flowers?" I asked, when I'd gotten my breath back. He must've. He hadn't waited until we reached the bedroom.

"I had no idea you were such a romantic. I'll tell you who else was surprised. Agent Waters. I believe her words were, 'I didn't know he had it in him.'" Agent Waters worked with Matt and had been in charge of the Cody Forrand kidnapping case. I'd liked her. "What's with the boxes?" he asked. His fingers skimmed the side of one. It was a miracle we hadn't knocked them over during our earlier activity.

"Cold case I'm looking into." Finny had stopped by earlier. He'd made me carry all five boxes from his car's trunk to my living room. A bit of rebellion that I'd allowed.

"Murder?"

"Missing person," I said.

"Someone local?" He sat up.

"No, not exactly."

"What then?"

Finnegan had sworn me not to tell others. Matt reached for the cover to the topmost box. "Don't!" I yelled.

He dropped it. "What?"

"I'm not exactly sanctioned to work the case, and the fewer people who know . . ."

"Okay. I won't press it." He dusted his hands. "But you'll have to entertain me another way."

"Again?" We'd just finished.

"Not that. Poker lessons."

I groaned. He'd been on a poker kick ever since he saw that Matt Damon movie about the poker whiz who takes down a Russian gangster. There was a group at his office that played, Thursday nights. One of the better players, Vic Carson, was a jackass who made racist comments. Matt had decided the best revenge would be to take down Vic at the poker table.

"Put your clothes back on." I couldn't teach him poker in his current state. Couldn't concentrate. He complied. I got dressed and grabbed the deck, sat down, and said, "Let's get started. First lesson. Tells and how to spot them. Let's start with yours. Stop looking at your feet when you have a great hand."

"What?"

"You do it, every single time. Might as well wear a neon sign that says, 'Full House.' Vic must have a tell or two. Learn to spot them. I'm going to let you practice by faking a tell. Spot mine within five hands, and I'll teach you something new. Miss it, and we rewatch *Apollo 13*."

"Again? Some of us aren't in love with Ed Harris." He sat on the edge of his chair, eyes bright. I dealt. He watched each card as it hit the table and then scooped up his hand. My fake tell would be sniffing if my hand was good, and looking to the right if it wasn't. Matt was good; not great, but good, so he picked up on the tells quick enough that he got to the next lesson.

I considered whether beating Vic at poker would satisfy Matt. Sure, it would make him happy, but it's not like it would make Vic stop using racist slurs.

At half past midnight, I called an end to the game and said I was ready for bed. He grabbed his keys. He had an early day out of town tomorrow, and it made sense for him to go home and grab some shut-eye.

He paused at the door. "Those boxes in your living room," he said. "They won't get you into trouble, will they?"

"Trouble? No." I waited a moment and then blurted, "I'm sorry. About what happened at Suds."

He ran his knuckle along my cheekbone. "I know you are."

Despite Matt's assurances, I didn't sleep well. Noises kept waking me: a car alarm and then a raccoon or skunk attacking a trash can. Plus, there were the boxes in my living room, calling to me to open them, to see what was inside. At 4:45 a.m. I left the bed and grabbed a pair of sweats. I brewed coffee and took a big mug of it with me to the living room. I sat on the carpet, arranged the boxes chronologically (Finnegan had labeled the sides), and opened each one. The boxes contained interviews, notes, photos, tips, obituaries, and other stray items related to the search for his sister. In one box was a well-rubbed rabbit's foot, the fur dyed purple. No tag on it. No explanation. I checked the photos first.

Susan was a teenager with waist-long brown hair and a gap-toothed smile. In a picture with her older sister, Carol, I saw that Carol looked like Finny. The brothers, David and Bobby, looked like carbon copies separated by time. Susan looked like an outsider. Maybe she'd felt it. Maybe that's why she'd run away. It was clear from the reports that it's what everyone assumed. She'd done a runner two years prior. Gone four days. Returned home by some Good Samaritan who'd found her on a road in New Hampshire. This time, they'd waited a week before reporting it. Her brother was a cop, and he waited a week to file it?

The pages in the boxes were yellowed by time and smelled of must. I sorted them into piles and stacks. The missing person posters the Finnegans had made, in the days before copy shops were common, were sad. Worn mimeographed sheets with small blotches in the corners and the text sagging and warped.

The neighborhood interviews contained eyewitness reports of Susan's movements. People from Finny's neighborhood were talkers. Most of them, anyway. There were a few terse statements from neighbors that said they "hadn't seen nothing" or "weren't around." Finny had added notes to the bottom of these. "Neighborhood enforcer for Dugan. Wouldn't rat out Jack the Ripper if he was on his pay list." One statement, from a Jack McGee, read fine. He'd seen Susan the day before her disappearance, walking home from school. But he claimed he'd been working on his car in the driveway when she left home. Finny had scribbled "bullshit" on the back of the report. Under that he'd written "no oil stain on driveway" and "hands clean." There was something personal there. My nose was tickled by the dust in the box. I sneezed and grabbed a tissue. My foot, numb, was falling asleep. I banged the heel against the carpet, the pins and needles unpleasant, but not enough to make me stop reading.

Susan's parents and brother Bobby reported that she'd left the house on Friday, September 22, 1972, at 6:05 p.m. She'd told them she was headed to a double feature with her best friend, Lucy. After leaving the house, she was seen by Mrs. Douglas, walking on Wood Street toward High Street. Miss Rivers saw her head down High Street toward Monument Square, as did Mr. Hertz. And then there was the statement from the Bunker Hill ranger. Finny had written "Bunker Hill in opposite direction from Lucy's house." From there, they had three sightings: one on Concord Street and two on Bunker Hill Street. A storeowner, Mr. Burt Ferguson, spotted her at the corner of Bunker Hill and Elm. He'd assumed she was waiting to meet someone. Said she was checking her watch. A few minutes later, he looked up and she was gone. He was the last person who reported that he'd seen her that evening.

They'd looked into the storeowner, hard. Mr. Ferguson had run his corner store for twelve years. No kids. Single. That raised brows. They'd interviewed him four times. Between the lines, they'd thought maybe he liked young people too much. They asked about him giving free candy to kids after school and helping a neighbor boy with his math homework. He didn't have a history. No one had ever made a complaint against him. That didn't matter. They decided they liked him for it. The Boston cops turned his store upside down. Found nothing to show Susan had been there recently. Six months after the disappearance, he'd sold the store and left the neighborhood. Innocent or not, he'd been the focus of a police investigation. The neighbors had probably stopped sending their kids there to fetch things. Maybe stopped shopping there. He'd been tarred by the police and feathered by neighborhood gossip.

My throat itched. I should get a glass of water. But the kitchen seemed another world away, and there were more suspects to examine. Next up was Antonio Moretti, known as Andy. Susan had had a crush on him for years, despite her father's insistence that the Morettis were Italian scum. The crush was unrequited. Finny had noted that Andy was older and liked girls who were faster. There was a picture of him in the file. Nice teeth, good hair, and an outfit best left to the wide-lapel-loving 1970s. Andy had been at his grandmother's all weekend, gathered with his family for her final days. She'd died Monday night. He'd never been out of his family's sight long enough to meet Susan that weekend. It was clear the cops didn't favor him for it. Finny seemed to agree with that conclusion.

The last suspect was the weakest of all. A simple kid who lived across the street named Levi. He was twenty years old, but his interview responses read like they were spoken by someone half his age. Finny had written "poor Levi" on the back of a transcript. Levi lived with his parents. He worked odd jobs. He loved Susan. He thought she was "super pretty" and "nice." But Levi loved a lot of girls. Any woman who showed him kindness. He said he'd seen Susan the day she left home, but his mother said he'd been running errands with her. A grocery clerk backed her up. Levi had been acting up in the checkout aisle, asking for a pack of Juicy Fruit. The clerk remembered. Levi was in the clear.

Foolish to feel disappointed. If there had been a lead, they'd have found her by now. I went to the kitchen and drank a glass of water. The papers in that box showed careful, diligent police work with no result. That was the worst of it. You could do your best, interview every person, pursue every lead, and still come up short. Hard enough for a detective to swallow, even after years of practice. But a rookie patrol officer whose sister was the missing person? I was surprised Finnegan had stuck with it, had continued being a cop.

Back in the files, I found that Susan Finnegan had been "seen" by people all over the country after her disappearance. In the first two years after her disappearance, fifty-six sightings were phoned in. In the next two years, it fell to twenty-four. After that, it was a few each year for five years, and then none for several. The last reported sighting came in 1996, three years ago. A prank call was the opinion of the cop who answered. A teenager had phoned, saying he'd seen a woman who looked like Susan Finnegan. Where? Portland, Oregon, buying fish at a wharf. Tuna fish. He'd cackled and hung up. I was surprised the cop had logged it. But he had. He'd even notified the Boston cops, who notified Finnegan. Nothing came of it, of course. Nothing had come from any of the tips.

But Finny chased all the leads, even the one that came from an old biddy in Arizona clearly desperate for attention. She told him she'd seen Susan hiking. This was in 1981. He'd written HIKING? Circled the word. Drawn question marks all around it. Guess he didn't take his sister for a hiker. He flew out there and interviewed the woman four times before she confessed that she hadn't seen the woman clearly, and she'd looked close to forty years old. Susan would have been twenty-five at the time.

Boxes four and five revealed that there had been other sorts of searches. Crimes that Finny thought might include his sister as a victim. A man from Long Island kidnapped two girls in 1974. Maybe he'd taken Susan? No. How long had that taken to determine? Two and a half months. Finny's handwritten notes contained multiple exclamation points. He'd been excited, thinking he was onto her trail. Another case of missing teen girls in New England had briefly made him hope Susan was a victim, but it was clear she didn't fit the pattern. Too old. Not blond. And there was the small problem that she hadn't been walking on a deserted rural road, like all the others. There were pictures of the other missing girls, all of them similar, young and blond and enough alike to be cousins, if not sisters. Though the files were about Susan, tens of missing girls populated them, later dismissed as trails to nowhere.

Also included were the visits he'd made to morgues to identify Jane Does who were never Susan Finnegan. His notes were terse. "Not her" or "too tall" or "woman identified by spouse." The period after 1984 filled one fourth of a box. Very little had happened since then. I sighed.

Back to the beginning. What did we know? Susan had run away from home. She'd taken clothes, her favorite stuffed animal, and a lucky rabbit's foot. The rabbit's foot I'd found in Finny's box wasn't Susan's. It had been found in a car searched for drugs. Finny was sure it belonged to his sister, but the sad fur was dyed a bright purple. Later, he'd noted that Susan's had sported pink fur. He'd been mistaken. The token had never been returned to its owner.

Her bank account had been wiped out. She'd taken her money, all $160 of it. Hard to start a new life on $160, even back in 1972. She'd told her family she was staying at Lucy's, but her cover was blown by Monday morning when she didn't appear at school. Everyone assumed she'd run away for good. But what if she'd planned to be gone for only the weekend? What if she'd reappeared Monday at school? No one would have been the wiser.

Where would she have gone for a weekend? Away with a boyfriend? It was clear her father, James Finnegan, had possessed old-fashioned views on dating. But Susan wouldn't be the first teenager to figure out how to see someone behind her dad's back.

*She leaves home to spend a weekend with Mr. Right, only he turns out to be Mr. Wrong and he kills her?* It was a stretch. I leaned back and stared at my ceiling. It hadn't changed since yesterday. Go figure.

Outside, I heard kids playing tag. The clock read 8:25 a.m. Damn. Time to shower and dress. A car door slammed. A baby cried. Baby. I stopped in the hallway. What if Susan was pregnant? I looked behind me at the boxes on the floor. Pregnant in 1972. That was pre-*Roe v. Wade*, right? Her options would be limited. Have the baby, give it up for adoption, or . . . go somewhere where illegal operations were done. If Susan had been pregnant, who would she have told? No one in the family knew. Who would she have told? The baby's father? Her best friend?

I thought of Rick, my former Homicide partner in New York, now dead. We'd kept each other's secrets. He'd never told anyone I was gay, and I'd covered up his drug addiction. Maybe we shouldn't have kept each other's secrets. But we had. Now Rick was gone.

Lucy MacManus, Susan's best friend, had married and moved to Portland, Maine. She was now Lucy Rogers. Finnegan had stayed in touch. His last notes regarding her were from 1993. Six years ago. Her telephone number was on a paper inside one of the boxes. If she was still at the same number, if she hadn't moved in the past six years. If, if, if.

I found the paper in box number three and dialed it. It rang five times before a breathless woman said, "Hello?" I introduced myself. Asked if I was speaking to Lucy Rogers.

"Yes. Police chief, you said? Has something happened to Lyle?"

Was Lyle her husband? Or her son? "No. No. I'm calling about an old missing persons investigation. Susan Finnegan."

"Susan." Relief colored the name. She'd feared for her loved ones. They were still safe.

"I understand you were her best friend."

She hesitated. "Yes."

"Susan said she planned to stay over at your house the night she went missing."

"She didn't." The words came fast and sounded as if she'd said them a thousand times. She probably had.

"I assume your parents would've told the Finnegans if she'd stayed the night."

"My parents?"

"Yes, well, as we've established, they weren't best friends with Susan. You were. So if someone was going to cover for Susan, to say she had spent the night if questioned, that would be you."

"But she didn't."

"But you see my point."

"I suppose."

"Here's the thing that bothers me. She had a plan in place. She said she was staying with you. She planned to reappear later and have no one the wiser."

"But she didn't stay with me!" She was upset, but there was also anger there and . . . fear?

"Something didn't go right." I didn't know what. I didn't know a damn thing, but I couldn't tell her that. I waited, but she offered nothing, so I played my trump card. "When, specifically, did she tell you she was pregnant?"

She inhaled sharply and asked, "How? Who told you?"

She had, just now. It was an old trick. Present information as fact and see if it lands. I'd thought my odds were twenty-eighty at best.

"When?" I asked.

"She told me three weeks before she left. She made me promise not to tell anyone, ever. I wanted to, later. But I was afraid I'd get her in trouble. What if she'd had complications and needed time to heal from the . . . procedure. When it was clear she wasn't coming home, I got scared." She moaned, low. "Oh, God, they'll hate me when they find out. I almost sent them an anonymous letter, two years after she disappeared, telling them about the pregnancy. But I didn't know who the father was, and I was about to go to college and I worried, what if they traced the letter and I got locked up, as some sort of accessory?"

"Unlikely."

"I know that now. Back then, I was a scared girl about to leave home for the first time. And I couldn't wait to go. The neighborhood never felt right after she left. I hated passing her house, seeing her brothers, her sister, her parents. They'd fuss over me, and I'd feel like the world's biggest traitor."

"How pregnant was she, when she left home?"

"About two and a half months, or so she thought."

"Where was she headed?"

"A doctor in Boston, out of some place in the Combat Zone. That's all I know. She didn't tell me the doctor's name. I gave her money, to help. The operation cost $500."

"Lot of money."

"Yeah. She took out all her savings. Took some cash from her folks. Got the rest from the baby's father."

"Who?" I asked.

"She wouldn't tell. I asked and asked, but she'd only say she'd made a mistake and it was over."

"What else did she say?"

"She wanted me to pretend she was sleeping at my house. Said she'd be back Monday, in school. But she wasn't."

I imagined Lucy, at school, staring at the empty desk where her best friend should be sitting in class. Wondering where she was. "Anything else?" I asked.

"No. I wondered if perhaps the baby's father had gotten upset with her, but I had no idea who he was. She didn't want to talk about him. Said she wanted nothing to do with him ever again."

"And you've no idea who he was?"

"Until she told me she was pregnant, I assumed she was a virgin, like me. Susan was a good girl. Aside from running away, she hadn't ever gotten in trouble. But then, after that, her parents watched her like jail wardens. She wasn't allowed out to basketball games or parties. She had to come straight home after school."

"And you're sure she planned to have an abortion?" I asked.

"Positive. She couldn't care for a baby, and she thought her father would kill her if he found out. She said once it was over she could get her life back . . . but then she never came home."

"What do you think happened?"

"I hoped she'd changed her mind, decided to take off and have the baby, raise it somewhere where no one knew her."

"You think she's raising a child under an assumed name and never thought to call her family, let them know she was alive?"

Silence. And then a quiet sob. "No. I know she's dead. I think she had the operation, and it didn't go well, and she died." She hiccupped softly. "I have a daughter, Jeanette, in high school. She's sixteen, the same age Susan was when she left, and, if anything ever happened to her . . . I always felt awful, not telling the Finnegans what I knew. Back then, I was just a girl covering for her best friend. Now I'm a mother, and . . . please tell them I'm sorry. I'm so sorry."

She hung up the phone. I imagined having to tell Finny this news. That his missing sister had been pregnant. Maybe it would have been better if Lucy had sent that anonymous letter.

# THURSDAY, MAY 20, 1999

## 0915 HOURS

T he police station felt funny. There was a crackle to the air, like before a big thunderstorm. At my desk, I found Lewis had taken a passive-aggressive swipe, setting a long mailing tube between our desks. It kept my stuff from spilling onto his pristine desk. Another guy would've tossed my stuff in the garbage. Not Lew. Give it a few days and he'd trace, "Clean Me" in the dust atop my cabinet.

He appeared, a giant Dunkin' Donuts foam cup in hand. He caught me looking at it and said, "Our youngest was throwing up all night. She caught some bug at school. I'm half-asleep." If he thought that was bad, well, in another six months he'd have a brand-new baby and he could kiss sleeping through the night good-bye.

"Chugalug, buddy. We got faxes from the OCME," I told him. "Autopsy report."

"Yeah?" He drank deeply and removed his jacket, hanging it on his chair back. He sat and extended his hand over my pile of crap. I slapped the faxes into his open palm. "Where's the first sheet?" he asked.

"Damn machine probably ate it." We'd had trouble with the fax. Cover pages rarely came through, and sometimes we got a fax ten hours after it was sent.

He made a few "hmmm"s while he reviewed the sheets. Every new page made him swallow another gulp of coffee. "Young woman. Early to midtwenties. Five feet four or so. Caucasian." My sister, Susan, had stood five feet four. But it wasn't her. The DNA hadn't matched.

"Blunt-force trauma to the skull," he read. "Looks like the arm was cut from her torso *before* she was buried, but after she died. Evidence of knife wounds via her clothing and her rib bones."

"So he kills her, and then he stabs her."

"Looks like it."

"Somebody was angry." Most people stop attacking once their victim is dead.

"Yep." He rubbed his eye. "Surprised they didn't chew us out about holding onto that humerus bone." He didn't look at me, though he knew I was behind it.

"Maybe they have bigger fish to fry."

"Still waiting on the soil tests," he said. "Might tell us what season she was buried."

I closed my eyes and imagined the woods where we'd found her. The woods, in spring, or, scratch that, summer, when the ground could be dug easily. The trees abloom so you could hardly see two feet ahead of you. Birds singing. A young woman in the woods. Dead or alive? Dead. He killed her elsewhere and used the woods as a dumping ground. That was intuition talking. Sometimes the gut knows things.

A thump sound brought my eyes open. "Napping?" Lew asked.

"Thinking."

"Funny, they look the same," he said.

I tapped my brow. "I am using my leetle gray cells," I said in my best Hercule Poirot voice. He looked at me like I'd sprouted wings. Not a *Masterpiece Mystery!* fan.

"They got us dentals," he said. "You want to go to East Windsor?"

Not really, but I was second fiddle, so he could order me about. The fact he couched it as a question was decent of him. I stood. "Looks like I have a date with a dentist."

"Maybe ask about finally getting that crown fixed." He knew about my crappy dental work. Most of the station did. My bad teeth were a favorite subject of complaint.

I drove to East Windsor where a state forensic odontologist worked out of a rebuilt Victorian with pink trim. Dr. Finch had red hair tucked behind her ears. Her handshake was firm and dry. "Come into my office."

She put the x-rays I gave her on the light box. She smiled as she peered at them. One of her teeth was slightly crooked. "I've got good news." She tapped a molar that was bright in the x-ray. "Tooth number two. She had a gold crown."

"Gold. Really?"

"Gold is good dental material. Very durable, but expensive, and somewhat rare. If the body pre-dates, what did you say, 1985?"

"1983."

"Even better. I doubt you'll find many people back then with a gold crown. Also, you can see she had all of her wisdom teeth." She tapped the very last teeth. "Likely she was older than 16 and younger than 25. In fact, probably younger. Maybe 21 or 22 at the outset. See this gap in front?" She pointed to the front teeth. I nodded. Susan had also had a gap between her front teeth, more sizable. It had made her self-conscious. Ma had told her that Lauren Hutton had a sizable tooth gap, and it hadn't held her back from modeling or acting. Susan had shaken her head, aggrieved at our mother's lack of understanding.

"If she'd had the wisdom teeth long, they'd have pushed the front teeth together and shrunk that gap. That it's still intact tells me she didn't have them long, a year maybe."

I focused on the two front teeth, rounded at the bottoms. "You think she came from money?" Gold was expensive.

"She'd have been middle or upper-middle class, or had a dentist in the family."

"Thanks for your help."

"Happy to do it. Beats lecturing kids on brushing and flossing. Last kid I had in here? I overheard his mom say that as a reward for being so good they're going to the candy store. This, after I spent half an hour scraping plaque from his teeth."

Lewis was delighted by what I'd found. "That ought to help us winnow these down." He pointed to a teetering pile of folders on his desk. "Missing persons. New England–area white females aged 15 to

25 reported missing from 1975 to 1983. One hundred eleven results so far." He picked up the pile and dropped them onto my desk, flattening some old chip bags and scattering dust particles.

"What are you up to?" Shouldn't he be working the stack?

He rubbed his forehead. "While you were out, they caught the clamshell vandal, so I have fresh paperwork to attend to, thank you very much."

"What? When?"

"Just after you left, Dix and Johnson radioed in that a young woman was chucking clamshells out of her car on Piper Street. They followed her home to Holland Ave. They knocked on the front door, and her mother answered."

"Wait," I said. "Her *mother*? How old is she?"

"Fifteen."

"I told you!" I crowed, whooping for emphasis. "Teen girls!"

He clutched his head and groaned. "Stop gloating."

"Ex-girlfriend of the quarterback?" I asked. Maybe I was two for two.

"Best friend of the ex-girlfriend of the quarterback. Now, if you'll excuse me, I have to finish this damn report. You work on whittling the missing persons, yeah?"

I whistled as I worked my way through the photos and sketches of missing women. Some had freckles and braces, others had braids or ponytails. They were smiling, none of them aware their futures would lead them here, to a pile of missing persons reports two feet tall. I stopped whistling. Susan had surely never seen herself in their ranks. I shook my head.

"You okay?" Lew didn't look up from his report. Guess my movement hadn't been subtle.

"Aces." I separated from the pile several girls who were too tall or too short to be ours. Into the "no" pile they went: Veronica, Mary, Jessica, Sara, Ann, Louise, Kelly, Nicole, Caroline, Polly, Gertrude, May, Heidi, Candice, Helen, Lisa, Teresa, Victoria, Melissa, Betty, Sophie, Amanda. All those girls, somebody's daughter, all of them missing. Last seen outside a bus stop, after a basketball game, never seen again after leaving for an aunt's house. They'd been gone decades. Maybe some had aged, acquired wrinkles and gray hairs, and fattened up where they were all angles and elbows before. But some had not. Some of these girls had vanished, and not to a better life. They might be buried in a woods grave or damp basement, or dumped in a lake. These girls, with their wide smiles, they never saw it coming.

I cleared my throat and went to the coffee machine. I hardly needed more, but I wanted a break from those smiling faces. Dix came by as I watched the coffeepot burble. "Hey," I said. "Heard about your big bust."

He shook his head. "Don't know how we didn't catch her earlier. She was just tossing the clamshells out her driver's side window, for all the world to see."

"Did she say why she did it?"

"Said Dylan Jax had cheated on her best friend, Cassie, and spread a rumor that Cassie had an STD, so she decided to pay him back."

"But why the entire street? Why not just dump the shells on his lawn?"

"Because," Lew said, refilling his Dunkin' cup from the coffee-maker. "She figured if she did that everyone would know *he* was the target and would blame Cassie."

"What's going to happen to her?" I asked.

"Probably have to clean up her mess and apologize to everyone on the block."

"No community service?" Dix asked.

"I don't think so," Lew said.

"Wow," Dix said. "To be a teen girl. You can get away with anything."

My mind returned to the papers on my desk, to those girls, who had disappeared. How many of them had gotten away with anything? Few, probably. And how many of them had paid for sins not their own? Had been made to answer for voices in someone else's head? "Yeah," I said. "Teen girls have all the luck."

Dix laughed. I didn't.

"Hey," Chief Lynch said. "How's it going?"

Lewis tensed, ready to take insult. He and the chief, both so ready to be wronged. "Isn't today your day off?" he asked the chief. He was right. Weird that Lynch had come in. Or not so weird. He didn't seem to have hobbies or a large social circle.

"Just needed something from my office," the chief said, failing to take umbrage at Lew's remark. Interesting. His day off must've mellowed him.

"Lew is wrapping up the case of the clam vandal." I played peacekeeper.

"Great. Can I see you for a minute?" Chief asked me. "It's not about the woods case," he told Lewis.

"Whatever," Lewis said. We began to walk when I heard him add, "Better not be."

Lynch heard it but said nothing. In his office, he said, "Take a seat." He remained standing, his hands in motion. He was nervous. Why?

I sat and asked, "What's up?"

"I learned something about your sister." He sat in his chair, but his hands kept moving.

"What?" His shoulders were creeping toward his ears. Shit. Had he found her? Was she dead? How?

"Susan was pregnant."

"What?" No. No way. "She'd barely kissed a boy." I knew exactly who she'd kissed. Marcus Shannon and Greg LeRoy. It was my job, as her brother, to keep tabs on her.

"Lucy said she was a couple of months along. Susan planned to . . . take care of it, and come home once she'd recovered."

I felt hot. The station noises sounded softer, like when you're underwater and can't hear the sharp edges of the world. "No," I said. It's all I could think. No. Susan, pregnant? By whom? I pushed myself out of the chair and strode to the window. And then his words caught up to me. I turned. "Lucy told you? What? When?"

"This morning. I guessed that maybe Susan had been pregnant. I presented it as fact to Lucy, and she confirmed it."

For twenty-seven years, little Lucy MacManus had lied to my parents, to me. She'd told us she'd never seen Susan. Had no idea where she'd gone. Had no idea why she'd left.

"Are you okay?" he asked.

My mind, buzzing. "Susan was going to take care of it?" That was a euphemism for abortion. "We were Catholic. She'd never—"

"Lucy said Susan didn't want to be a mother, she wasn't ready."

"Of course she wasn't!" She'd been a child. No way was she ready to have a baby.

"Lucy said—"

"Lucy said?" I yelled. "How come Lucy never said a fucking word to us? She practically lived at our house. Ate dinner with us at least once a week. Had a crush on David back in the day—and now you say she just kept all this to herself while we lost our minds?"

"She felt badly. She apologized. Back then, she thought Susan would return in a day or two. Abortions weren't legal, so she thought she was protecting her."

"Protecting her?" My hollow laugh bounced off the walls. "That little bitch."

"Look, calm down."

"Calm down? You want me to *calm down*? I just found out my missing sister might've died on some butcher's table, and you want me to be calm about it?" It's what must've happened. She'd gone to a back-alley doctor, one who took money in exchange for silence. Something must've gone wrong. I saw Susan, her long hair hanging off the edge of a filthy table, steel instruments by her torso, her body covered by a bloody sheet.

"Look, I know this is upsetting, but—"

Lewis pushed the door in and said, "What's going on? You okay, Mike?" He looked at me, and then glared at the chief. "What the hell did you do?" he demanded.

"Me?" Chief Lynch put his hands up. "We were just talking."

"I don't think so. What did you do?"

The mood in the room was bright red. Lewis looked ready to take a swing. "Stop," I said. "I'm fine."

"The hell you are." Lew was right. I wasn't fine. Fine was a dead star whose light would never reach me. My sister had been pregnant twenty-seven years ago, and I hadn't known. None of us had known.

This would kill my mother. We'd not only lost Susan, we'd lost her baby. There were two to mourn now.

"I've got to go home." I stared at the floor and plowed ahead.

"But—" Lewis said.

"I'm sorry. I can't stay." I opened the door and charged through and out, nearly stepping on Jinx's tail. Jinx was the station's dog, a German Shepherd trained to sniff out drugs and take down bad guys if the situation warranted it.

"Hey!" Jim said, on behalf of his dog.

"Everything okay?" dispatch called, but I didn't answer, didn't stop. I pushed through the doors and went outside, my breathing labored.

Pregnant. I turned the fact around and around. Who had she had sex with? Did the father know she was expecting? Had she told anyone other than Lucy? How hadn't we noticed? I reviewed the few boys who'd expressed interest in Susan: the dweeb from her choir, Mark; the skinny kid on the track team, Joe; and Frank, who I'd suspected wasn't really interested in girls. None seemed a likely suspect, which meant that someone who wasn't on my radar, on anyone's radar, had impregnated my sister.

I got home and contemplated calling Lucy to yell at her for twenty-seven years of silence. But what good would it do? Maybe it would relieve the pressure in my brain for a minute or two. No longer than that. I thought about phoning a brother, but Dave was on vacation with his family, and I wasn't sure what Bobby would say. He was the only one still living at home when Susan went missing, and his life was affected in ways the rest of ours weren't. He had to listen to Mom cry and Dad vow to take the legs off the monster who'd taken Susan. He couldn't catch a break, except to escape to a friend's house. My parents monitored his movements closely. They weren't going to lose another child. No, sir. And phoning my sister, Carol? I felt uneasy. She'd wed and had children young. I wondered if she'd be sympathetic to Susan's decision to have an abortion. And, somehow, I couldn't bear to break the news to someone who'd judge her harshly for it.

I sat on the edge of my bed, staring at the stained carpet, trying to come up with answers to a question I'd never known to ask.

Who had knocked up my baby sister?

"**W**hat the fuck did you do?" Lewis demanded.

"Watch your tone, Detective."

"In the five years I've worked here, I've never seen him explode. He was fine when he came in to see you. Did you suspend him for showing up in the woods?" When I didn't answer, he asked, "Did you fire him?"

"Fire him? No!"

"What the dickens is going on in here?" Mrs. Dunsmore demanded before slamming the door closed. "Please tell me you two have joined the Idyll Players and are practicing a two-man scene called 'We Don't Know How to Behave in an Office.'"

Wright and I stared at her, confused. She pounced on our silence and said, "You've got every man out there, including citizens, listening to you two carry on. By all means, if you want an audience, I can open this door."

"No," I said. "I forgot it was open. Finny stormed out without closing it."

"And why was Detective Finnegan screaming?" she asked.

I cut a glance to Wright, then back to her, and moved my head, fractionally.

"Oh, come on!" he said. "Now you two are in cahoots to keep secrets?"

Mrs. Dunsmore said, "Hardly. Was it about Susan?"

"Yes."

Mrs. Dunsmore said, "It's about his missing sister, Susan."

"Oh," Wright said.

Not, "What missing sister?" or "Who's Susan?"

"You *knew*?" I asked him.

Wright said, "Yes, but he doesn't know I know. I had a buddy whose father joined the BPD back in 1978. He knew about the case. Girl goes missing, and she's the sister of a cop? It was news. Anyway, years later, I mentioned Mike's last name and my buddy asks if he could be *the* Michael Finnegan. Guess Mike got into it with a cop at the station over his sister's case once. Threw a punch. Got suspended. Decided to move here not long after." Well, go figure. I wasn't the only cop who'd made my way to Idyll after making poor decisions back home.

"He doesn't know you know?" I asked.

Wright's laugh was a short, sharp bark. "He really underestimates me at times."

"Did you know he thought Colleen—"

"Might've been his sister? Of course. Dummy left a DNA report in the box for anyone to find. Thank God he stuck it in the one police station where curiosity runs low. So, did you find her? Is that what wound his clock?"

"Did you?" Mrs. Dunsmore echoed.

"No. I discovered Susan was pregnant when she went missing. That got him hot under the collar."

"Oh," Mrs. Dunsmore said.

"Maybe she took off with the baby's father?" Wright suggested. He grimaced and shook his head. "No. That didn't happen."

"Don't think so," I said. "Her best friend says she was going to have an abortion."

Mrs. Dunsmore said, "Now I see."

"See what?" Wright asked.

"Why he was upset. He finds out his sister was pregnant and planning an abortion, and who finds it out?" She pointed at me. "This guy. Michael has been searching twenty-seven years, and he never knew.

Plus, he feels guilty. He told his family not to alert the police at first, when she went missing. She'd run away before and come home. He was a rookie and was worried it would reflect badly on him if he went running for help at the first sign of trouble, so he sat on it."

"That's why they waited a week to file the report," I muttered.

Wright said, "Poor Mike."

She cleared her throat. "Great. Now I've got to figure out what to tell the gossips out there." Damn. The entire station had heard Finnegan's blow up. There had to be some explanation. "I know," she said. "Chief, I'm distributing the physical-fitness memo."

"But I thought you said . . . oh. But the detectives aren't subject to that."

"The memo doesn't state that," she said.

"You think they'll buy it?" I asked.

She said, "I think they'll project their own rage onto the plan and see his reaction as reasonable."

"The plan is *not* bad." Since when did everyone become so damn opposed to fitness?

She said, "Excuse me, gentleman, while I go clear up this mess."

"And make me a target," I pointed out.

"You drafted the memo. Your idea. Your consequences." She left.

"She really loves to stick it to me." I rubbed my hair. Checked my watch. I could leave any time since I hadn't needed to come in. Maybe I should've waited another day to tell Finny. Maybe I shouldn't have done it here. Maybe, maybe, maybe.

Mrs. Dunsmore stayed true to her word. When I left my office, all eyes were on me.

"Chief, are you for real with this?" Hopkins asked. He held up the fitness memo.

"Absolutely," I said.

"Even the *detectives* have to participate?" Everyone paid attention. No one pretended to work.

"Yup."

"What about police chiefs?" Yankowitz asked. Jinx barked. Everyone laughed.

"I'm happy to meet the physical-fitness requirements." Was I? Most of the stuff I felt confident about, but how was my run time?

"Get your sneakers laced up, Dix," Hopkins called. The men chuckled. As if Hopkins should talk. No way he could've caught a running nine-year-old. He'd be hard-pressed to catch his shadow.

"Enough," I said. "This has nothing to do with Dix. I've had this plan in the works for months. Was just waiting for the weather to turn nice before I unveiled it."

"Great. We can suffer heart attacks outside in the sunshine."

"Have a good night," I called. "Stay safe."

The whispers at my back were strong enough to send me sailing. Outside the station, Wright stood, waiting, one foot propped against the bricks. "How'd it go?" he asked.

"Eh. Not bad. They bought it. You need me?" I asked. Certain he'd say no. If Wright were on fire, he wouldn't ask me for help.

"Yeah. Buy me a drink, after I check out. We'll meet at 5:30."

I stood agape, certain I'd heard him wrong.

"Meet you at Suds," he said.

$$\gtrsim \! \mid \! \diagup$$

Wright was seated at a table at the back of Suds, where he could survey the small crowd and drink his beer in relative quiet. Donna Daniels stood at the bar. She wore an orange tank top that was affecting the old timers' hearts. Her lip curled when she saw me, into a snarl.

"Hi, Donna. Can I get a Brooklyn?" I asked.

She held my gaze. "All out," she said.

"How about a Coors?"

"You want a lime with it?" She shouted the words.

"No."

"Just a minute."

I'd seen snails move with more hustle. Wright watched, amused. Lucky him. Six minutes later, I got my beer. "Donna seems upset with you," he said when I sat at his table.

"She resents me for being gay." His back stiffened. Wright hated it when I mentioned that I was gay. Maybe that's why I did it. "She wanted a chance at me."

"Whoa. How did you get your ego through that door?" he asked.

"It's true. Plus, she loves my boyfriend." He leaned back a foot. "And she saw me piss him off the other day." He cleared his throat and looked away. "You asked."

"Yeah, well, I've got to be at a baseball field in thirty-six minutes to pick up Joshua." His son, aged nine.

"Baseball? What's he play?"

"First base, third base. He's not exactly in the majors yet."

"Speaking of ball, who's team captain for our charity game?"

He rotated his glass. "Dix. Why?"

"Curious. Haven't heard much about it. I play shortstop and third."

He looked over my left shoulder. "Billy usually plays shortstop, and Hopkins plays third."

"Hopkins?" I asked, deadpan.

"Yeah."

"Why do I get the feeling no one wants me to play on the team?"

"Probably an oversight. You haven't played since you got here. Guys assumed you weren't interested." He never blinked. He was lying. "Back to the matter at hand," he said. "About Mike's sister, Susan. How'd you find out she was pregnant?"

"Her best friend from back in the day, Lucy, told me."

"But she didn't tell the family?"

"She was terrified. Scared for Susan and herself. And maybe it was easier, talking to somebody outside Boston, who never knew her as a child. Plus, she has a daughter in high school. I think me calling, it just happened at the right time. She looks at her daughter and sees what Mr. and Mrs. Finnegan saw when they looked at Susan. I think she wanted to tell someone, and telling me, a stranger, was easier than facing the Finnegans."

"Makes sense." He rapped out a soft beat on the table. "I want to help, with the case."

"You're not supposed to know about it, remember?"

He twisted his plain gold wedding band, not that he had much space to move it. He must've gained weight since he married, though it was tough to imagine him thinner. "Yeah, well, I do. Besides, we don't need to tell Mike I'm helping."

"Aren't you busy trying to identify the corpse in the woods?" I asked.

"Busy?" He traced a line through the condensation on his glass. "Not exactly. With the woods case, I need to keep Mike involved, and he's only part-time. If I hunkered down, I'd have her identified inside of a week."

"You're slowing down an active investigation to keep our part-time detective involved so that . . . what? His feelings don't get hurt?"

"We're going to find out who she is, and who put her in the ground. If it takes a few days longer, so be it."

I wasn't sure Finny would agree with this assessment. I thought he'd argue to identify the corpse stat and then notify her family, given where he stood with respect to that equation.

"You want to work a case, with me?" I emphasized the last word, hoping it would scare him off.

"Not at all, but I don't see you turning it over to me, so if that's what it takes . . ."

"You really don't like me, do you?" I asked.

"I could say the same." He pushed his drink away from him.

"I don't—"

"Save it. Let's just try to find Susan, yeah?"

It didn't look like I was getting rid of him. Now that I had a lead, some help would be useful. "You can help me find where she was going for her abortion."

"Great," he said. "We'll touch base in the morning, your office. Before Mike gets in."

A secret meeting in my office? What would the guys think? And then I laughed because thanks to Mrs. Dunsmore, they'd probably think Wright was trying to weasel his way out of the fitness requirements.

# SUNDAY, MAY 23, 1999
## 1400 HOURS

The house on Wood Street smelled of linen spray and potatoes. The alarm inside the entryway was disabled. "Ma?" I called. A radio upstairs played easy listening. I followed the sound to the bedroom I'd shared with David so many years ago. It was now the sewing room. My mother's machine and fabrics lived here, alongside tubes of giftwrap. In bygone Christmases, she'd made us save the bows and tags from our presents for future use. A recycler before anyone used the word. The radio sat to the right of the sewing machine. White fabric spilled from beneath the machine's needle. My mother made curtains, as wedding gifts or housewarming presents.

"Hello?" she called. "Bobby?" Why did it hurt that she expected my brother? He lived closest, kept tabs on her. She poked her head around the doorframe.

"You got new glasses," I said. The frames were blue and huge. Her pale eyes were tiny behind them.

"Marcy helped me pick them." She touched the sides, shyly. "Aren't they something?"

"They certainly are." I gave her a kiss on the cheek and a hug. She felt delicate in my arms, almost brittle. "Ma, the alarm was off when I came in."

"I didn't know you were coming! I'd have made cookies." Classic avoidance technique.

"I don't need any." I hadn't nursed a sweet tooth in years, but it was impossible to convince her. "The alarm won't work if you don't turn it on." The neighborhood was safer than it had been when I was growing up in it. But my dad was dead, and Ma was alone in the house.

"Come down to the kitchen." She walked ahead, her pace quick as ever. "Did you hear about Megan? She's engaged." Megan was my niece via my sister Carol. That explained the curtains.

"To anyone I know?" It was unlikely. I'd moved away twenty-one years ago. Only came back for holidays, weddings, and funerals. Most of the houses on our street had turned over to new owners. I recognized very few faces from the old days.

"His name is Pete Danforth. He's from New Hampshire. He sells computers."

Maybe one of Carol's kids would come out right. Her oldest son, Jimmy, was an addict, and her middle child, Allison, had been in five colleges and still had no degree. "Megan still teaching?"

Ma opened a cabinet. "Yes, third grade now."

Family photos hung on the walls, a procession of us kids through school, onto jobs and spouses, holding babies, our hair graying. Carol's hair didn't gray, because she colored it. Susan's hair didn't gray, because her last photo was from junior year of high school.

"Hey, Ma, why don't you sit? Take a load off?" I needed to tell her the news, and I wanted it done with, to be on the other side of this awful conversation. She ignored me and set the kettle to boil. Set two teacups on the table. She patted my shoulder as she wandered past, on her way to the silverware drawer.

"David was asking about you," she said.

"Was he?" I hadn't spoken to my older brother in ages. He'd been elsewhere last Christmas. That was the one time I usually saw him. "How are you feeling, Ma?" She'd complained of hip trouble when I'd seen her in February.

"Fine, fine." This from the same woman who'd sat through Carol's confirmation while her appendix ruptured. I didn't trust her self-assessments.

"Hip bothering you?" I prompted.

She gathered the kettle and poured hot water into the teapot she'd received as a wedding gift. The pot had nicks and chips that spoke of its long service. "It's worse when it's cold. Mrs. McDonald had her knee replaced last week. She's at a rehab facility now."

She finally sat down, and I took a breath. "Ma, there's a cop who's looking into Susan's disappearance." The words fell out of me.

She stared at the teapot's four-leaf-clover pattern. "Why? Has there been news?" Her voice rose. In it, I heard what I least wanted to hear: hope.

"He's learned something we didn't know back then."

"What?"

I took her hand, gently. "Susan was pregnant when she left."

"Pregnant? By whom?"

"I don't know. Lucy confirmed it."

"Lucy?" The shock in her voice. Oh, how I wished I could spare her it. Wished I could spare her all of what was coming. But I had to keep going.

"Lucy said Susan was going to have an abortion. Planned to come home after it."

"Susan . . . pregnant," she repeated. Her eyes flew to the picture of Susan on the wall. "She was moody around that time, but I thought it was teenage hormones, not . . ." She paused. "She was sick, twice. Told me she'd eaten bad Chinese. And I fell for it. I was worried about Carol, with her second child. You remember how sick she was back then. Oh, Lord. I was focused on Carol, and poor Susan was carrying a baby too. My poor girl." Her hands trembled.

"Oh, Ma."

"You have no idea who the father was?" she asked. "Not Andy Moretti, no matter what your father thought, God rest him."

"No, not yet."

"Well, maybe a new set of eyes will help." Jesus wept—she sounded like the chief. "It can't hurt. And, who knows?"

"Don't get your hopes up." I tried to temper her outlook.

"My hopes are my own, Michael Patrick Finnegan. Now, I know

you did everything you could to find your sister. But if I want to believe she can be found, that's my own business." She wiped at a tear that had escaped her eyes, and adjusted her crazy eyeglass frames.

"I just don't want you hurt, Ma."

She sniffed. "Susan vanished twenty-seven years ago. I don't expect that she'll come sailing through that door, smiling. Telling us what wild adventures she's gotten up to. I'm not foolish. The best I can hope for is a body I can lay to rest near your father and grandparents. That's all I want. To find her and lay her to rest."

Shame made my skin cold. All this time, I'd assumed she'd hoped we'd find her alive. She knew better. She'd been on this planet for seventy-four years, most of them in a neighborhood where bad things happened and where there was a code: you didn't talk to the police. It made my early days on the force interesting. But she'd seen it—organized crime, the busing crisis, the rise and fall of drug dealers—and she'd survived it, along with the loss of her youngest child and her husband.

"I'm sorry."

She reached for me. The back of her hand was a road map of ropy veins and age spots. Her fingers caressed my knuckles. "You're a good boy, Mikey. None of this was your fault."

I didn't believe it. I could've called in Susan's disappearance that first day. Ma had asked, had pleaded. But Dad had sided with me. What if it was a repeat of the last time? He knew what it would mean for me at the station. As if it mattered. As if my super would've cared all that much. Lord knows, I'd seen cops use their influence for things more trivial than a missing sibling.

"An abortion," she whispered. "Where would she have gone?"

I didn't tell her about the Combat Zone, the area of Boston known back then for pimps, drugs, and nudie flicks. No need to add that image to her mind.

She said, "Have some tea." I was a coffee guy. But I'd drink it down, if it would make her happy. "So, when will this policeman be showing up?" She took a sip of her tea.

"Not sure."

"What's he like?"

"He's my boss."

"The gay one?" She leaned forward. "I'll get to meet him?"

"Please don't call him 'the gay one.'" God, he'd hate that.

She put her hand to her chest. "As if I would. I'm so interested to meet him. He's from New York, isn't he?" Aging or not, her mind was a steel trap. "I wonder if he knows the Kilcunneys. They moved there back in '89 or was it '90? Yes, it was 1990. It was right after the roof got repaired."

My fears morphed. No longer worried about my mother's heart-break, I was concerned with how she would interact with the chief.

"Does he have a boyfriend? Oh, stop." She flapped her hands at me. "I'm not going to ask *him* that. I'm just curious."

"We don't discuss his love life."

"Probably doesn't ever talk about it. Poor dear." *Poor dear?* "Reminds me of Mr. Sheehan."

"Mr. Sheehan." Why did I know that name?

"Your history teacher. Susan's, too. Lovely man. Used to volunteer at the nursing home. Beautiful tenor voice."

"He was gay?"

"Of course. Got the stuffing kicked out of him one Thanksgiving. His attackers told him to get out. They said they didn't want a 'fairy' destroying the neighborhood. They sent him to the hospital with two broken ribs."

"Who did?"

"Adam McKee and his gang."

"I never knew that." Mr. Sheehan. Now I remembered. He wore horn-rimmed glasses, long after they fell out fashion. He liked to quote dead presidents. He'd been a good teacher. "Did he leave?"

She gave me a grim smile. "Wasn't safe for him to stay. Think he moved back west, where he was from." She set her teacup down. "You look tired."

"You always say that."

"Not always. Just the past ten years."

That cracked a smile. She always knew how. "Too many ex-wives," I said.

"I don't know why you married so often." She refilled her teacup. "You know what the definition of insanity is? Doing the same thing over and over and expecting a different result."

"Who said that?"

"Einstein." Ma was the only other person who read books like I did. Well, Susan had, too.

"Einstein, huh? Why you gonna listen to a dummy like him?"

She swatted my hand and laughed. Her crazy blue frames moved with each short *ha!*

"You should visit more often," she said.

True, but my heart couldn't bear it. Being in this house, with that picture of Susan from junior year, rebuking me from the wall. There were no pictures of her aging past sixteen, no photographs of her in a white gown or holding jolly bald babies. It was my fault.

No, my heart couldn't bear it. But I'd never tell her that.

# MONDAY, MAY 24, 1999
## 0750 HOURS

**M**att ate toast so dark it verged on charred. Its crunch set my teeth on edge. I sipped my coffee and asked, "You going into work?" It was nearly 8:00 a.m. He was usually out of the house by now, having run and done his weights set. This morning he'd lain in bed until I poked him awake.

"I'm going in a little late. Got to stop at my place first. You?" he asked.

"Headed to the station. Need to check in on a case."

"The body in the woods?"

"Yeah, that," I said, keeping my promise to Finny not to discuss his sister. I glanced out the window. Clouds turned the world gray and promised rain. The phone rang. Matt snorted. "You've got to get a phone that wasn't designed for the blind." The phone had oversized numbers, a legacy from my house's former elderly owner.

"Why?" I asked, before taking the call.

"Hi, Thomas." Damien Saunders greeted me. This was a surprise. I glanced behind me. Matt stood, finishing his toast.

"Hi," I said. "How are you?"

"Good, thanks. I hear your men found a body in the woods. Must be causing quite a stir."

"Now everyone thinks the ghost stories are true."

"A ghost? How wonderful. Idyll really does have everything."

"Seems like it." Matt left the room, humming.

"By the by, I wondered how your romantic gesture went," he asked.

"The flowers?"

Matt walked into the living room, his duffel on his shoulder. He swiped up his cards. He'd insisted on more poker lessons last night and had wanted to play with his own deck. I lowered my voice. "They were a hit." I wanted to tell him how I'd sent them to Matt's office, and how he'd endured some whistles and high-fives, along with some dirty looks. But I didn't feel right spilling all that with Matt seven feet away.

Matt grabbed his jacket and mouthed, "Almost done?" He tapped his watch.

"I've gotta go," I said. "I'll call you later."

"Oh, of course. Don't mean to keep you. Good-bye, Thomas."

"Bye." I hung up the phone and said, "Taking off?" to Matt.

"Who was that?" he asked.

"Dix," I said. "Giving an update on the clamshell case."

"Thought you told me that was all sorted."

"It is, but the neighbors are still upset. Complain the smell hasn't gone yet."

Matt glanced at the phone and frowned. "Buy 'em some air fresheners." He touched my cheek and said, "Be a good boy, huh?"

"Where's the fun in that? See you tonight?"

"Can't. I told my brother I'd help him install his new home-entertainment system. He's clueless when it comes to tech."

"Luis?" He had two brothers and a sister.

"He promised his wife would make me pastelón."

Outside, the skies had grown darker. Rain meant the last of the pollen would be washed away at last. Matt waved before he hopped into his SUV. A minute later, I got in my car and headed for the station to debrief with Wright.

When I got to work, the men were all aflutter about the exercise plan. One said, "Drop and give me twenty!" as I passed. I stopped and looked for the offender. The laughter dried up under my stare. Good.

Detective Wright came to my office later. He stopped and rubbed his shin. "Ow."

"Everything okay?" I asked.

He took his hand from his leg. "Banged my leg this morning. Stupid toy car was on the floor. I rolled onto it and pitched forward. My shin collided with the coffee table."

"And you want another kid," I said. Three kids meant more toys to trip over.

"Hey! Who told you?"

Oops. "No one. I overheard you talking. Congratulations."

He looked as if he was examining my kind words for flaws. "Thanks."

Maybe we should skip the small talk. "We need to figure out where Susan went for her abortion."

"Do we know anything?" he asked.

"Combat Zone."

"Rough area, back then."

"Her boyfriend might know where she went."

"Except no one knows who the boyfriend is," he pointed out.

"I have a few notes on guys who were suspected of being involved, and then rejected."

"Let me see the original notes," he said.

"They're in your car trunk. Two boxes."

"What? How?"

"You're kind of careless with your keys, Detective. Must be Idyll rubbing off on you." I'd swiped the keys from his desk when he went to the restroom ten minutes ago. It had taken only a few minutes to put the boxes in his trunk.

"I'll find out who she was seeing," he said, his voice all confidence.

I almost asked how he thought he could pull that off, where other, more senior detectives from the Boston Police Department had failed. Not to mention myself. And then I realized how Finny must've felt when I snatched his sister's case and discovered she was pregnant. How much it must've hurt to feel that he'd failed her. He'd never found her, and he never even knew why she left.

"Find the baby daddy," I said, "And I'll buy you a drink."

He shook his head and said, "Uh-uh. I find the baby daddy, and you buy me a bottle."

"Deal." I stuck out my hand. He eyed it. Good God. Did he think he'd catch something if he touched me? "Cooties cost extra," I told him. Then I dropped my hand to my side and said, "Keep me updated on the Colleen case, yeah? Mayor is already breathing down my neck."

He muttered about the mayor's priorities and exited my office.

Good. Let him chase down the phantom father of Susan's baby. I had other plans. An ace up my sleeve. Detective Lawrence Carmichael, from my old precinct. He'd worked Homicide, but before he suited up for the majors, he worked Vice. Some of his favorite stories were about abortionists he'd put out of business. Detective Carmichael was hardcore Catholic, and he believed he was saving souls by locking up men with scalpels. Kind of interesting since he also couldn't keep his dick in his pants and had likely benefitted from such doctors.

When I called my old precinct's number, I was surprised when they put me straight through to him. Carmichael had been on the verge of retirement when I'd left, in 1996. Some cops have to be carried out, feet first. Looks like he'd be one.

"Detective Carmichael, Homicide," he barked. The sound of that sharp New York bite brought him to my eyes. Too-wide tie, thinning hair, and eyes with pouches that spoke of poor sleep.

"Hey, Lawrence, it's Tommy. Tommy Lynch."

"Tommy," he said. "This is mighty unexpected."

"How you doin'? How ya been?" I asked, with each word my newly adopted Idyll speech patterns chipping off like a poorly applied coat of paint.

"Fantastic. Staring down the barrel of retirement, and my prostate is giving me hell."

"Sorry to hear that. Listen, you worked Vice back in the sixties and seventies. Busted a lot of backdoor clinics, yeah?"

"Sure did. Must've put twenty of them bastards into jail. Those were the days."

"I hear that. Look, I've got a stone-cold missing persons case out of Boston, and it looks like the girl went to see a doctor. I wondered—"

"They kick you off the force down there?" he asked.

"What? No. I—"

"I heard your big news. Made the station hum for a whole week. Jansen claimed he always knew about you, but Lee said he's full of shit." So, the news had made its way back home. Not surprising. Cops talked to other cops. Still, that old fear of exposure, it rose up in me, and it felt again like I was back inside, pretending that there was nothing better than Cindy Crawford in a pair of tight jeans.

"You think maybe you could look into this abortion angle for me? It's possible the operation went badly. She might've died on the table."

"I'm sorry to hear that," he said. "Terrible thing, but see the thing is, Tommy, I wouldn't piss on you if you were on fire. *Capisce*?" He slammed the phone down.

I sat, stunned, until the phone beeped repeatedly, and then I set it into its cradle and blinked. So much for my ace.

Did all the guys from back home feel this way? Jansen claimed he'd known I was gay. The hell he had. Not with the way he used to walk buck naked around me in the changing room. He'd known nothing. None of them had. Well, now they knew. And they hated me. For lying? For being who I was? For both?

A knock at my door. "Come in." My voice sounded scratchy, even to my ears. And I hated it, hated that I cared what a nutjob like Carmichael thought of me. Sanctimonious prick.

Billy came in, with his anxious face. "Hey, Chief. Did you sign those papers I need for my course?"

Damn it. "No, but I've got 'em here. Hold on." I found the sheets and flipped pages. Signed off on the last one. "Are these overdue?" He'd told me when they were due, and I'd set them aside for another day. Forgotten about them entirely.

"They told me if I got 'em in today it would be good."

"Glad to hear it."

"Thanks, Chief." Billy clutched the papers to his chest.

"No problem, Billy."

At least I could overcome some people's disappointment in me.

# MONDAY, MAY 24, 1999
## 0800 HOURS

The phone surprised me during my shave; I nicked my throat. Stuck a small patch of toilet paper on the wound. It was Linda, my first ex-wife, on the phone. I shouldn't have hurried to answer it.

"Did you forget your son's birthday, again? Or decide to cut him out of your life entirely?" Shit. It was the 24th. Four days ago, my oldest son, Brian, had turned twenty-three. The truth, that I'd forgotten, consumed by the news of Susan's pregnancy, would win me no sympathy.

My son, Brian, had come into this world crying, his face a raisin, all angry wrinkles and folds. His six pounds, ten ounces felt like feathers. I remembered it like it was yesterday, but his twenty-third birthday had come and gone, and I hadn't called or sent a card. "Is he still living at the place near the Laundromat?"

She sputtered. "You don't even *know* where your son lives. Can you hear yourself?"

"I'd like to send him a card. Is he at the same address?" My calm would only make her angrier, but I didn't see why we should both yell.

"If you ever visited him, you'd know where he lives!"

Sure. I'd show up, and he'd shuffle his feet, and we'd make awkward small talk in his cramped apartment, and eventually he'd take a verbal swing about how I'd mistreated his mother by not being around, about how I wasn't much of a father. And I'd have to take it, because pointing out that his mother had been a shrew wouldn't earn me love. Explaining her constant disdain of my job, which she'd admired when we first met, her nitpicking about why couldn't we afford to go on cruises, and why didn't I care more about my clothes wore me down so that I felt immobile, like a tool, not a person. Articulating that to my son would do what? Poison him against the woman who'd raised him most of his life? Prove to him that I was an uncaring monster? Best to stay away, and hope the memories he had weren't all bad, that he had some love for the man who taught him how to hit a baseball and tie a necktie and ask a girl to the school dance.

"You don't know where your son lives. He could've been abducted." She paused. "No. Then you'd care. You'd care *plenty*. It's only the missing ones that have your heart."

That, then, was that. My missing sister, subject of fascination and sympathy to all my exes during our courtships, always turned to an object of scorn and jealousy by the end. The famous wound they thought they could heal made them angry that it took attention from them, from our children. I should give up, forget about Susan, move on with my life. She was dead. Why couldn't I grieve and go on? This from women who'd wept over shampoo commercials and were still complaining about bad restaurant service they'd endured six years ago.

"Does he live at the same address or not, Linda? I'd like to send him some money."

"Yes, though he's getting a new place in July, so don't take too long sending it."

"I won't." I hung up and scrubbed my face, dislodging the toilet paper. My cut bled.

Forty minutes later, I walked into the station. Everyone noticed. Billy said a quiet, "Good morning." The others watched me take my jacket off. After Thursday's fireworks, were they expecting an encore? If so, they'd be disappointed. My fuse had burnt out. Dix sidled up to me and said, "Good job. Chief's exercise plan? It's absurd. And you were right to give him a piece of your mind about it. We're all with you." He nodded toward the others, who were watching us.

They thought I'd exploded because of the fitness regulations? I opened my mouth and then shut it. Contradicting that story wasn't a good idea. "Sometimes a man has to take a stand," I said.

"Here, here." Dix clapped me on my back. Guy couldn't run, but he nearly knocked me over with his palm.

"Thanks," I said. "Gonna go see the lion in his den."

In the chief's office, I found Lewis. He and Chief were bent over a document, the crowns of their heads nearly touching. Wow. This day was chock-full of surprises.

"Morning, Detective." Chief eyed me for mood and pushed the document aside.

"Hey," Lewis said, leaning back so he could take me in.

"Just came to apologize for my behavior the other day," I said to the chief.

"I understand you weren't expecting to be subject to the fitness rules," Chief said, nodding toward Lewis, "but as I was explaining to Wright here, modifications can be made."

So, the chief hadn't told Lewis why I was shouting the other day? He'd let him believe this was all about the silly fitness memo. Should've seen that coming. "Um, so we're good?" I asked.

"Apology accepted." Chief stood. Lewis took a paper from the desk and said, "Ready to find our girl today, Mike?"

My heart stopped. Then I realized he meant Colleen, not Susan, and I said, "Hell, yes."

We went to our desks. Lewis said, "I followed up on a few of our girls. Three are confirmed dead, and one is alive and living in Alaska."

"Good for her." The live ones made me happy. They got excluded from the search, and they were a welcome break from the unrelenting tragedy of the others.

He grunted. "Would've been nice if she'd sent a postcard home. Saved us some trouble."

"You're right. Very insensitive of her not to consider our needs."

He rubbed his nose and said, "That brings us down to . . . wait a second." He pulled a yellow lined sheet of paper nearer and started counting. "Thirty-eight possibilities. We might find our girl before the next millennium begins."

"I heard the new millennium doesn't begin until 2001," Jim Yankowitz said.

Lew gave him the look I'd labeled, "slow burn," but Jim held steady. Jim knew Lewis was afraid of his dog, and that he'd never say a word about it. Everyone else in the station loved Jinx. But then, they hadn't been attacked by a dog as a kid. Lewis had.

"What are you talking about?" Billy asked. "It's the year 2000 on January 1st." Another thing Lewis hated: Billy's frequent insertions into other people's conversations.

Jim said, "Yeah, but the Gregorian calendar counted from year AD one. There was no year zero, so technically the *current* millennium doesn't end until December 31, 2000."

"It's not gonna matter to the computers," Billy said. "The Y2K problem. All those double zeroes are going to be read as 1900."

Lewis vibrated in his chair. He wanted to work, and these two were debating math and talking computer glitches. On another day, I might've joined them, but we had a hard row ahead of us and I wanted to find out who Colleen was far more than I wanted to talk about Y2K.

"Fellas, you want to take your existential questions to the locker room?" I asked. "We got a case that needs solving, and the Gregorian calendar ain't gonna help us. Leave the big boys alone so we can do grown-up crime stuff, yeah?" Jim looked surprised; Billy looked shocked. It wasn't like me to pull rank.

"Fine," Billy said. He walked away. Jim followed. Jinx looked at me with his big liquid eyes, and then trotted off after Jim.

"Thanks," Lewis said, low.

"No problem. Why don't you gimme nineteen of those and let's see if we can't reduce them to a top ten by lunchtime?"

"Top ten? What is this, the Miss America pageant?" He handed me a stack of papers. "Can't wait for the bathing-suit competition."

"Me? I'm a talent guy, all the way."

He shook his head. "I had to watch it last year. Simone wanted to." Simone was his daughter. "The singing and the speeches?" He shuddered. "But she loved it. Loved the sparkly dresses."

My daughter, Carly, had been a tomboy. More interested in Wiffle ball than ball gowns. I'd been grateful. "You want another girl?" I asked, quietly.

He chewed his lower lip. "Yeah, but Janice says it's a boy. Says she can tell. I didn't point out she was wrong about our son."

"Wise man," I said.

Nineteen women were collected on my desk, missing from as far north as Millinocket, Maine, and as far south as Norwalk, Connecticut. Of course, our Colleen, as we still called her, might've come from outside New England, but we had to start with some limits. Six of the nineteen were from abusive families and in foster situations or juvenile homes. That didn't mean one of them couldn't be our girl, but, given the gold crown, it seemed unlikely.

Thirteen women. Two were married. Ten had pierced ears. I looked up. "Pierced ears?"

Wright pursed his lips. "Ummmmm." He looked for the medical examiner's report. Found it. Turned it, page by page. "They found earrings in the grave. The lobes were long gone."

"Great." I set aside the non-pierced women, knowing that perhaps the question had been answered incorrectly or never asked. We narrowed the field based on what we knew, but we'd found errors. A woman was excluded because she was too tall. Then we found there were varying heights reported, as different as four inches. Another set aside because she fell outside our date range later found to have been mixed into the "wrong year" by the police who'd sent the file. That one had made Lewis kick a cabinet and ask what we were supposed to do if we couldn't trust the paperwork.

"God, I wish there were a national database for adults," he said, leaning away from the papers and stretching his arms overhead.

"No kidding." Missing kids had a national clearinghouse set up in 1984. Adults? Nope. Many adults left home because they wanted to, and no foul play was involved. No crime, no need to track 'em. But if we had the database? Oh God, the time it would save! Consolidated reports nationally accessible? Be still my beating heart.

After several hours, I could recite the histories of the women whose pictures blurred before my eyes. Amy Holt: twenty-two years old, played clarinet, owned a parrot, lived with two roommates on Cape Cod. Went missing April 1980. Last seen leaving work at the Lighthouse Restaurant and Café. Roommates said she sometimes hitched rides home when she was tired. That day, she'd pulled a double. Had she gotten into the wrong car? Trusted the wrong person?

Lewis said, "I've got my pile down to twelve. You?"

"Nine, I think, if this one really was alive as of late June 1983." I tapped Nancy Quarterman's picture. "I think Colleen was buried earlier than that."

"Techs think so," Lewis said. "They think they narrowed the burial date by remnants of the jeans she was wearing?"

"Really?" I'd missed that report. "What brand?"

"Sasson."

I sang, "Ooh la la Sasson!" Lewis looked at me like I'd sprouted a hydra head. "Come on, you don't remember those ads? They had that one with the New York Rangers, where the players skated in the jeans."

"Must've been before my time," he said.

"Hardly."

He said, "Anyway, the jeans didn't exist before 1975, and that body couldn't have been in there after July 1983, because the bone you found belongs to the corpse."

"Our victim was put there between 1975 and 1983," I said.

"Correct."

That didn't eliminate anyone from my pile, but it might prove useful, later.

He looked down. "Huh. This one's birthday is today. She'd be forty years old today, or is forty. Who the fuck knows? No one can find her."

"Oof. Birthday. I've gotta run an errand before the post office closes. You mind?"

"Nah," he said. "I'll grab some grub."

Main Street was quiet. Kids were in school. Adults were working. I liked this time of day; I liked this town. The lilac bushes were abloom. I wandered the pharmacy rows until I found the birthday cards. There were so many. For Him. For Her. Age Five. Age Twenty-One. From Both of Us. Who had decided cards must be so specific? I picked one up marked For Son. Inside was a poem about how much the son meant to his parents, and how he was the pride of their shared life. The rhymes were clunky. I shoved it back into its slot. The other For Son cards were equally overwrought. I ended up buying a 99-cent card. It had a birthday cake on the front and read, "Happy Birthday!" on the inside. Short, sweet, and to the point. I slipped three twenty-dollar bills inside, signed it *Love, Dad*, addressed it, and dropped it into the outgoing mail slot. My parental duty for Brian completed, until Christmas.

My desk had a ham-and-cheese sandwich on it, a bag of chips, and a Diet Coke. "Trying to tell me something?" I asked Lewis, pointing to the soda.

"They were out of regular," he said. "Besides, I thought you could stand to lose some pounds before you start Chief Lynch's exercise protocol."

"Not us. We're the brains, not the brawn."

He pointed. "Not seeing a whole lot of brawn anywhere here."

I looked about the station. True. Most of us looked like the "before" in before-and-after weight-loss advertisements.

Billy, one of the only "afters" in the station, trotted up, papers in hand. "You got some stuff from the fax." He handed them to me, though he knew Lewis was lead detective. A bit of subversion, or perhaps my reward for going toe to toe with the chief over the fitness memo. Except I hadn't.

"These about the woods' bones?" he asked. What interesting phrasing. "The woods' bones," as if the body belonged to the forest.

"Yes," I said.

"I still can't believe that all this time there really was a dead girl in the woods." He scuffed the carpet with the toe of his shoes. "Even as a kid, I didn't think it was true."

"You ever take the dare and spend the night in the woods?" Lewis asked.

"No," Billy said, quickly.

Lewis grinned. "You believe in ghosts?"

I glanced at the top sheet. Elizabeth May Gardner, age nineteen, reported missing April 16, 1979, at 10:00 p.m., by very worried parents. I'd had only a badly photocopied photo to work from, so I'd requested a better one. Here it was. Billy looked over my shoulder. "Pretty," he said. She was, or had been. Big eyes and a winning smile. I squinted.

"Billy, does she have a gap between her teeth?"

He took the paper. It was black-and-white and fuzzy. The resolution wasn't great. "Yeah, I almost didn't see it, but yeah. Why?"

Where had she gone missing? Salisbury. In the northwest corner of the state, bordering New York and Massachusetts. Small town, smaller than Idyll. Didn't have a police station. Relied on the staties for help. Wealthy? Some sections were. Had Elizabeth May Gardner lived on the right side of the tracks?

"Is that her?" Lew asked, hand extended. Billy gave him the paper, and he looked it over like it was a treasure map.

"One way to tell. Talk to Dr. Finch." The forensic odontologist might tell us if the gaps matched.

"You go," Wright said, not looking up.

"This could be her," I said. Surely, he'd want in on this action.

"You check it out. I'm following up on a tech report. Might help us identify the murder weapon." Lewis loved the chase, and he was ceding ground to me. Why?

"Okay." If he didn't want it, I did, desperately.

At Dr. Finch's office, I had to wait. The receptionist didn't attempt to hide her curiosity. She watched me read and reread the details of Elizabeth May Gardner's missing person sheet. Born July 15, 1959. Dark-blond hair, blue eyes, height five feet four inches, weight 125 pounds, with pierced ears. She'd last been seeing walking with her camera on April 16, 1979, near a park.

A young man with a swollen face emerged from the hallway, touching his cheek. He mumbled to the receptionist. Then he left, and Dr. Finch came out. She wore a lab coat over a navy dress. "I've only got five minutes," she told me.

In her office, I showed her the photo. "See the gap?"

She nodded. "Possible. Anything in the file about a gold crown?"

"No. I'm going to track down her family dentist. Ask that he send you her x-rays."

"If he has them," she said. "It's been twenty years since she was his patient. He might've disposed of them by now."

"Even though she's missing?"

She shrugged. "If you can get me the scans, I'll be happy to compare them. Without them, I'm guessing." She handed me the sheet. "You really think this is her?"

"I've got a feeling."

"Policeman's hunch?" She brushed a strand of hair from her shoulder. "Like on TV?"

"Something like that."

She touched my arm, lightly. "Good luck."

The pressure on my arm made me wonder if she was single. No, I was not going down that path. Not because we were working together in a professional capacity, but because my track record for picking winners in this area was zero for three. And that was just the ones I'd married.

Back at the station, it took me four calls to track down a state policeman who remembered the missing persons case. An old-timer by the name of Dawson, due to retire in three weeks. He was surprised by my call. "Elizabeth Gardner?" he asked. Was I sure?

"No. That's why I need dental scans, or her family dentist's information."

He blew a long stream of air into the receiver. "I don't know. I'll have to dig through the archives."

"Can you rush it? I've got a body here, and it might be her. Her parents will want to know."

"They split. Mother left town ages ago," he said. "But, yeah, I'll look. The kids they hire these days don't know how to alphabetize. Probably waste half a week looking under the wrong letter." He went on for another few minutes about how standards had lapsed. Good thing he was due to retire. Malcontents on the force contributed very little. I gave him my number and told him to call anytime, though I suspected he'd knock off a few minutes before his shift ended.

There were other sheets to review, and reports to type up, but I kept sneaking glances at the telephone.

"You know staring at the phone isn't going to make it ring, right?" Lewis asked.

"How busy can Dawson be?" I asked.

"You said yourself he's half out the door. Look, if we haven't heard by tomorrow, I'll call and apply pressure." He was so calm. I was biting my nails and snapping at people. We'd switched roles, and it was disconcerting.

"I have to leave in twenty," he said. "I promised Joshua I'd go to his practice."

Wright was a model dad. He attended his kids' practices and games and helped them with their schoolwork. My children barely spoke to me. He left, telling me we'd have another crack at it tomorrow. Forty-five minutes passed, and I realized Dawson wouldn't be calling tonight. I looked into the grainy eyes of Elizabeth May Gardner.

I snatched up the phone and redialed Dawson. He was there. Maybe those prayers to St. Jude worked. "Hey, I know I just called earlier, but could you check if there's a note in Elizabeth's files about her teeth? I need to know if she had a gold crown?"

"Gold crown? I wish you'd asked that straight out. I remember because we all thought that was strange. Gold in your teeth."

"Okay." I pulled my notepad out. "Okay. Can you read me what she was wearing when she went missing?" He did. Jeans, blouse, boots. "I don't suppose you know what type of jeans?"

"Sasson. Her mother made a point of it. Guess they cost a fortune."
Tiny pinpricks along my forearms. This was what it felt like to be close,
so close to resolving a twenty-year-old mystery. "Hold on," he said. "I've
got her dentist's name here. Doctor Forrester. I'll put in a call to him,
but let me warn you, he's a bit of a grump."

"So?"

"So, he might not break an ankle running to help us."

"A woman's been missing two decades, and he's going to withhold
help?" My voice brought heads at the station up.

"I didn't say that. But don't expect a call at midnight saying we've
got the x-rays."

"Got it," I said.

I wouldn't sleep well. This close to an identification? No way. I'd lie
on my sagging double-bed mattress and stare at the ceiling and count
pretend sheep. Only I didn't see sheep. I just counted. Maybe I'd make
it to a thousand tonight. Maybe two thousand.

# MONDAY, MAY 24, 1999
## 2000 HOURS

**P**ost-shopping, I put away the bread and eggs and then the chips, pickles, and apples. I wiped my hands on a dishtowel and reached for the phone. Damien answered immediately. "Hello?" How was he single, given his telephone voice?

"Hi, Damien. It's Thomas. How are you?"

"Well, thanks. To what do I owe the pleasure?"

"I have a couple of questions. It's semi-work-related," I paused, "but not. An unofficial look into a missing persons case in which I'm sworn to secrecy."

"Intriguing. What can I help with?"

"The missing person, girl, in question, was going to have an abortion in 1972."

"1972," he said. "Go on."

"I need to find the doctor, but aside from knowing he was in Boston, maybe in the Combat Zone, I got nothing."

"And you're not partnering with the police there because . . ."

"Unofficial investigation," I reminded him.

"Right. How old was she, your missing girl?"

"Sixteen."

"Prostitute?"

"No. No. She was from a middle-class, Catholic family."

He didn't point out that a prostitute could be a middle-class Catholic. He said, "How do you suppose she found the doctor?"

"I have no idea."

"No, think about it. She's a sixteen-year-old Catholic girl in 1972. Not like those doctors advertised in the Yellow Pages."

"Let your fingers do the walking," I said, repeating the directory's old motto.

"Where would she have found that information? Maybe another girl at school?"

"Her best friend didn't know."

"Had her best friend had an abortion?"

"No."

"Well, then," he said, as if that settled things.

"So, I have to try to figure out who might've had an abortion at Susan's high school, back in 1972?"

"Susan?"

I swore. "Forget the name. Please."

"Well, unless you want the Boston Police Department's help, yes, I'd say start there."

It wasn't a bad avenue for exploration, and it might not be as hard to acquire the information as I thought. Finny had gone to the same school as his sister. He'd have known other girls her age. I'd ask him.

"Thanks. I'll try it. So, what's the state's most talented medical examiner doing tonight?"

"The state's most talented medical examiner is probably cooking dinner for her husband and kids," he said. "*I'm* having a drink and watching a baseball game."

"I didn't know you liked baseball."

"Love it," he said.

"Do I dare ask where your loyalties lie?"

"I'm in the Yankees part of the state," he said.

"There's a divider?" I imagined a ruler line within the state, something like the Mason–Dixon line for baseball fans. "I assumed people picked the team they preferred."

"It's generally held that Hartford and parts west are Yankees territory. East of that you enter into the hostile land of Red Sox fans."

"Who's your favorite player?" I asked.

"Bernie Williams. Did you know he's a classically trained guitarist?"

"Yes." Damien also played guitar. That's why he had calluses on his hands.

"Hey, while I have you on the phone, can I ask you another question?" I continued. "My brother's getting some award at NYU, and I'm going to the ceremony. Do you think it's okay to bring a date?" He went so long without speaking that I said, "Hello? You there?"

"Are you asking me if it's okay to invite the man you've been seeing to a family event?"

"No. I mean, yes? I mean, do you think it would be too much, for Matt?"

"I can't answer that for you, Thomas. Why don't you ask him?"

"He might say 'yes,' but then I'm afraid my mother will tell everyone she knows that her gay son is getting engaged."

He inhaled. "Are you?"

"We can't get married, and no! God, I just . . . don't want her to start thinking that way."

He sighed. "Do you want to go with Matthew?"

"I think so."

"Figure that out. If the answer is yes, then ask him."

"You make it all sound so easy."

"And you complicate every decision."

"I don't, not normally. You should've seen me in the grocery store earlier. I was a single-minded shopping god, unlike everybody else." What was it with people abandoning their half-full shopping carts mid-aisle?

"I'm sure you were. Any other questions I can answer?" His tone was light, but I sensed annoyance underneath.

"No. Sorry to bother you. But now that I know where your allegiances lie, maybe we can watch a game together?"

"Sure," he said. "Good night, Thomas." He hung up. Maybe I'd bothered him. Next time I had a romance question, I wouldn't call. I'd be an adult and handle it myself. Next time.

## DETECTIVE MICHAEL FINNEGAN
# FRIDAY, MAY 28, 1999
## 0900 HOURS

"Hello, Dawson?" I said. "Any word? But—. Hey, why don't you give me his address? I won't. No. Promise." I scribbled down the address, said thanks, and hung up.

"You got it?" Lewis asked, pointing to my notepad. "Let's pay him a visit." Lewis was as annoyed as I was by Dr. Forrester's stonewalling. He'd claimed to Dawson that such old dental files were in a storage unit and he couldn't get to them before next week. But I was sure that Elizabeth Gardner was our girl from the woods. Neither of us wanted to risk a positive identification without the dental x-rays, though. Telling her parents we'd found their daughter after all these years could only be made worse by one thing: if we were wrong.

Lewis drove. His car was cleaner and had a nearly full tank. He told me I couldn't smoke inside. His wife would lose her mind. "How is the missus these days?" I asked.

"Nauseous," he said. "And angry. It's been a great few weeks."

"You tell the kids yet?" I asked.

"We're planning to next week, after the quad marker test. I'm worried about Simone."

"Because she's the youngest?"

"Because she likes things a certain way, and a baby is going to throw that out the window."

"You think Joshua will be okay?"

"Joshua is so chill, we sometimes wonder if he's human."

"Sure doesn't get it from you," I said.

"Do we turn off here?" He squinted at the road sign.

"Next exit," I said. "So, what's our plan? Bribery? Good cop/bad cop? Handcuff him and toss the place?"

"You're ridiculous." He pushed play on his CD player, and a steady beat filled the car.

"Who are the Roots?" I asked, turning the CD case over.

He didn't answer. Shook his head and said, "Just listen."

"Are they saying 'the ha ha' over and over?"

He pulled into the right lane and said, "'The hot music.' That's what they're saying. Hearing going, huh?"

I held my hand to my ear and yelled, "Eh, sonny? A little louder into my ear, if you please."

Off the exit and around the bend, it was Ireland green. Dr. Forrester's house was on the outskirts of town. There were lots of trees and very few houses on the rough, pocked road where he lived. "Watch out," I told Wright. "Dawson tells me the good dentist is anti-authority."

"He sure has a lot of Private Property signs," Wright said.

"I also hear he buys a *lot* of soup."

"Soup?"

"He's one of those Y2K nutters. Thinks the world's going to go to hell come December 31st. He's stockpiling bottled water and canned goods." I'd heard of worries about computers flipping dates incorrectly, but I didn't see how that translated into an apocalypse.

He said, "Maybe we can bond over my fondness for Campbell's Chicken Noodle Soup."

Outside Dr. Forrester's shingled cabin were two No Trespassing signs posted on a waist-high fence. A security camera was installed near the front door. Beside the door was a No Soliciting sign. There was no doorbell, but there was a heavy, old brass knocker. I pumped it against the door and waited. When the door opened, a short, grizzled man with dirty eyeglasses sized us up and barked, "Can't read?" He pointed to the No Soliciting sign. He aimed the comment at Lewis. Oh, hell. Please tell me this bastard wasn't racist.

Lewis didn't blink. He said, "I read very well, thank you. I'm not soliciting. I'm a detective with the Idyll Police. My name's Lewis Wright. May I come in?"

Dr. Forrester said no like it was a reflex.

"Would you come outside and answer a few questions for me? It's about Elizabeth May Gardner."

"I told that state cop who called earlier that the x-rays are in storage." He adjusted his neck so as to keep both of us in sight. I walked to the side, to make the task impossible.

"I heard," I said. "The thing is, it seems very likely that a skeleton we've discovered is Elizabeth."

"What do you need her dental x-rays for?" He looked away from me to Lewis.

"Proof. I want proof before I go to her parents and raise their hopes for the umpteenth time. They've looked at other bodies that weren't their daughter, and I don't want to do that to them again."

"Do you have children?" Lewis asked him.

"No."

"Ever had your hopes dashed?" I asked.

He shuffled his socked feet and said, "Sure."

I said, "Okay. Well, imagine all of your hopes, all of your dreams, all of your energy is focused on one thing. It's not even a nice thing. It's this: you want your child's body back so you can bury it. So that you can say good-bye. So that you can sleep and not dream of the terrible ways in which she is being tortured as you sleep in your own bed in your own home, safe. So that you can have conversations that aren't interrupted with thoughts about where she might be, and who might be holding her, and what he's forcing her to do, again, and whether she thinks you've given up on her, for good."

"Enough!" He held up his hand, to ward me off. "Enough. God. I'll get the x-rays." He moved out of sight, but he didn't close the door. I wondered if the storage unit was far away, and how long it would take to get there. He reappeared, a manila folder in hand. The peeling label on its tab read "Gardner, Elizabeth M. (1959)." He opened the glass door and thrust it at me.

I blurted, "You had it here?"

"Take it." He waved the folder, like I was a fish and the folder was a worm.

I opened the folder and grabbed an x-ray. Held it up. The crown shone bright, just like it had in Dr. Finch's office, among the shadowy teeth. The same molar. "Gold crown."

"Yeah, she had a gold crown, when she was eighteen. Her parents understood the value of gold. Not many people did."

I raced to the car to grab the folder I'd brought with us. Back to the porch I held up the x-ray to the light. The dentist emerged from behind his door and stared at the two. "That's from the corpse?" he asked.

"Yes."

"It's her then. See that cavity, there?" He pointed to a molar. I didn't see what he did. It looked much the same to me as the one next to it. "Not filled yet. She was supposed to come in a week after . . . she disappeared. It never got filled."

Lewis said, "Thank you for your help."

Dr. Forrester stepped back and closed the doors. I heard him throw two bolts.

"Guess we go talk to the staties," Wright said. "You did good back there, with your speech. You got through to him."

"What a turd," I said.

"Well, look on the bright side. Come January 1st, he's gonna realize he bought a whole lot of soup for nothing."

Salisbury was served by Troop B of the state police, in North Canaan. The US flag hung limply on its pole in front of their station. The pole was surrounded by a bright circle of flowers. Everything neat and well presented, until you got inside. Inside, boxes were stacked to nearly the ceiling. Equipment was piled on a desk. We flashed our IDs and introduced ourselves. I asked for Dawson. Was told he was "packing up."

"You guys are moving?" Lewis asked, surveying a giant mound of tangled electric cords.

"Nope. We had a pipe burst. Had to box up stuff. Moving some of it offsite while they do repairs. Dawson's retiring soon. That's why he's packing. He's down that way, second office on your right."

"Office?" Lew said under his breath. "Ooh la la. Fancy."

When we got there, we saw "office" was an overstatement. Dawson had a cramped room with two shelves of pictures, books, baseballs, and work gear. On the floor were two empty banker's boxes. So much for packing.

"Help you?" a voice called.

"Dawson?" I recognized his voice from our calls.

"You must be Detective Finnegan." He came around his desk and I introduced Lewis. Then I handed him the envelope with the x-rays. His brows shot up when he saw what was inside. "You got the dentist to drive to the storage unit?"

"He had them at home."

He made a sound of disgust. "Ornery son of a bitch. He's still mad about some zoning law that affects his property. As if that's got anything to do with us. This proves it, does it? Your body is Elizabeth?" he asked.

"Yes."

"Was she murdered?"

"Looks that way," Lewis said.

"Raped?"

"Don't know."

"I remember when she went missing. Made the nightly news six days running, but we never heard a thing. Not really." He shook his head. "If there's anything we can do to help, let us know."

"I'd appreciate that," I said.

"We're going to have to tell the Gardners." He looked dismayed by the prospect.

"I'll go along," I said. "They might have questions I can answer."

Lewis said, "Three's a crowd. How about I find a place to grab a bite, and I'll pick you up back here when you're done?"

Three cops would be overkill. It should've been Lewis making the notification. Not that it's a job any cop wants. But it was his case. "You sure?" I asked.

"Yup. Later."

In the wake of their only child's disappearance, the Gardners had split town and had split up. Elizabeth's father had moved two towns away, and her mother had uprooted herself to San Antonio, Texas. It was to Mick Gardner's house we drove. He lived in a tidy community of two-story Colonials. Two cars were parked side by side in the driveway. Dawson parked along the sidewalk and said, "He remarried a few years after he and his wife divorced. The new wife's name is Kate."

The new wife answered the door, and I took a step back. Why hadn't Dawson mentioned that she looked so much like Elizabeth? A second later, her husband appeared, quizzical. He put a hand on her shoulder. Did he know? Had anyone ever told him that he'd married a vision of his missing child?

Both vibrated with curiosity. "Is this about—?" he began.

"Let's go inside and sit," Dawson made the command seem like a suggestion.

We gathered in a living room done in shades of white and beige. Some would find it tranquil. I found it unsettling. How could you relax in a room where every stain would show?

"Detective Finnegan is from the Idyll Police Station." Dawson hesitated, giving me room. Ready to plow on if I didn't pick up the slack.

"Our men recently recovered a body buried in the woods," I said. "We took dental scans. I've visited with your daughter's dentist and obtained a copy of her records. They match. The body we discovered is, I believe, the body of your daughter, Elizabeth."

He didn't cry out. He squeezed his hands together and said, "You found her? Was she recently buried, or . . .?"

"We believe she's been there are least sixteen years," I said.

A sound escaped him. A low keening. His wife put her forehead to his and whispered, "Now we know."

He reared back. "Where is she? Can I see her? Can I see my baby girl?"

He had no idea what she looked like, after spending years in a shallow grave. It wasn't just time that had abused her, but insects and scavengers and her killer. He didn't want to see the mummified remains of his daughter. He thought he did, but it wouldn't be a kindness to allow him to see her.

I ignored his question and said, "I know you've received a shock, but I want you to know we will be investigating the circumstances of Elizabeth's death."

Tears were on his face. But he wasn't sobbing. "She was killed." His tone contained no doubt.

"Yes."

His wife, Kate, cleared her throat. "Does Hannah know?" Ah, the former Mrs. Gardner.

"She still lives in San Antonio?" Dawson asked.

Mr. Gardner nodded. "Yes."

"Could you give us her current telephone number?"

Mick rose quickly. "She's going to be devastated. She always thought that Elizabeth would return."

"But you didn't?" I asked.

"No. After five years passed, I knew it was hopeless."

He led us to a home office. He had a computer with a large monitor. Books on patent law filled built-in bookshelves. He found an address book and pointed to his wife's address and phone number. "Hannah will want to come back, for the funeral. We can have a funeral?" He sounded like a child asking for candy.

"Of course," Dawson said.

"Where's Idyll?" Mr. Gardner asked. I told him, describing the route he'd drive to get there. "And the spot, where you found her? Was it—"

"It's beautiful," I said "Among trees, some of them birches. Lots of birds back there. Daffodils. It's peaceful." It was, I supposed. But she hadn't chosen it for her final resting place. Her killer had.

"That's good. She always liked nature. Loved taking pictures of birds and leaves and things. She wanted to be photographer. She was taking classes. This was hers." A print on the wall showed a bird in flight, but it was the skeletal tree behind it that grabbed the eye. The bird and tree both black against the grainy white background.

He led us to the living room. We said our good-byes. Kate thanked us for coming and delivering the news in person, playing hostess as best she could. Her husband leaned against her.

In Dawson's car, he said, "Guess we should call Hannah. What time is it in Texas?"

I checked my watch. "4:53 p.m."

"Quitting time. She works as a medical secretary, though she does transcription, so maybe she works from home."

We would call from his office. I asked about his retirement. "Sixteen more days," he said. "And then I'm off to a life of leisure."

"What'll you do?" I asked.

"Drive my wife crazy. Maybe travel. I'd like to see Yellowstone National Park, and the Northern Lights."

At the station, Dawson put his office phone on speaker and dialed the former Mrs. Gardner, who now went by her maiden name, Holliday. She picked up on the second ring, breathless. "Hello? Patsy?"

Dawson said no, he wasn't Patsy. He explained who he was, and she said, "I remember you." She didn't sound happy about hearing from him.

"We have news, Mrs. Gardner. A body was found in the woods of Idyll, Connecticut, recently. Dental scans show it to be a match for your daughter, Elizabeth."

One inhale followed by silence. "Ms. Holliday?" he asked, tentative. "You still there?"

"How far is Idyll? From Salisbury, from our old home."

I said, "A little less than two hours, ma'am." I introduced myself as the detective who'd found her daughter. True in 1983. Not true recently. But why complicate matters?

"She's been there this whole time?" she asked.

"We're not sure, yet. We're running tests."

"She was there that whole time," she said, ignoring what I'd told her. "That whole time, less than two hours away, and you never found her. Twenty years! It took you twenty years!"

Dawson's frown deepened. "We've spoken to your ex-husband."

"Mick? You told him *first*?" She exploded. "I was her mother! Mick barely spoke to her when she was a moody teenager. Told me to wake him when she stopped back-talking. And you talked to *him* first."

"We needed to get your number from him," Dawson said. "If you'd like to discuss funeral arrangements—"

"I want you to nail the bastard that killed her." We stared at the phone. What could we say? "I know who did it," she said.

"Who?" I asked.

"Donald Waverly."

"Her boyfriend," Dawson said. He didn't appear surprised by her accusation.

"Ex-boyfriend," she said. "That's why he killed her. He was jealous and abusive. Where is he now? Go arrest him."

Dawson shook his head. "We'll certainly look into it, ma'am. I'm going to give you my phone number, if you have questions." He recited the number.

"I'll be pursuing the investigation into your daughter's death," I said. "I'll need to talk to you about her habits, friends, enemies."

"She didn't have enemies except for a terrible ex-boyfriend who beat her up. She was a beautiful girl with a good heart." She cried. The hiccups between sobs made us examine our shoes. "But why did she—"

"Do you have someone who can come stay with you?" Dawson asked. "A friend?"

"Patsy should be over soon," she choked out, between sobs. "We're having dinner."

"I'm sorry for your loss," Dawson said. He waited, for more yelling. We would have welcomed more yelling. It was easier to bear than the gasping sobs. She hung up. We sat, in silence. Time ticked by. Each of us lost to thoughts of how it might've gone differently, but never different enough. We'd never get her girl back, alive.

"What's this about the ex-boyfriend?" I asked.

"Him," Dawson said. "She was on about him after Elizabeth disappeared, but he stuck around. Tried to help. Searched the areas with us."

I'd heard of many a murderer who "helped" with the case he'd created. "What about the abuse?"

"That's the trouble. Mr. Gardner says he never saw it. The mother claims Donald Waverly roughed Elizabeth up and threatened her after she'd broken up with him. No complaints were ever filed, and it was only after she was missing several months that Elizabeth's mother mentioned it."

Several months? Why the delay? My brain immediately pointed out that I'd waited a week to report Susan missing. *He that is without sin among you, let him first cast a stone at her.* I was in no position to judge, but I would ask Mrs. Gardner, later, about the delay.

"Where's Donald now?" I asked.

"He left town about nine months after Elizabeth went missing, when it was clear she wasn't coming back. He gave us his contact information in case we ever found her. He wanted to know she was safe. I'll send it to you as soon as I find it."

I thanked him and called Lewis, who said he'd pick me up in ten minutes. I waited outside the barracks, my eyes trained on the sky. A cloud shaped like a dragon passed by, and I found myself thinking of Elizabeth May Gardner's photograph of the bird and the skeletal tree. She'd had promise, artistic promise, but it was gone forever. Another cloud passed, a thick ribbon of gauzy white, and I blinked away the tears I felt burning on my eyelids. Susan hadn't had a talent. She liked a lot of things and was better at some—ice-skating, poetry, and braiding hair—than others. But she was young, and I'd had every confidence that she'd come out right. Find her path. Except she hadn't and never would.

# SATURDAY, MAY 29, 1999
## 0645 HOURS

"**Y**ou want me to what?" Matt asked. He paused, his hand on his refrigerator door. It was white, whereas my fridge was avocado green.

"Come to my brother's award ceremony," I said. "And then dinner, with my family."

His hand remained on the fridge handle. "And do what?"

"Nothing. Talk, eat."

He opened the door and pulled out a dozen eggs. "You're serious." He set the eggs on the counter and pulled out a block of cheese and scallions.

"Yes."

He shifted to the stove, then moved the skillet to the front burner. "Okay."

"Really?" I'd expected more resistance.

"Give up a chance to meet your family? Besides, I always enjoy a free meal." Back at the counter, he cracked four eggs into a bowl. Then he reached for the cheese grater. "But now you definitely owe me another poker lesson. Make that two." He chopped scallions.

"All right, all right. Hey, how big is that omelet? You invite an army?"

"I'm hungry. I hardly ate yesterday. We did surveillance, and the idiots in charge brought the worst snacks for the van. Seriously, who eats corn nuts?" He whisked the eggs and added shredded cheese and cut-up scallions and peppers and poured the mess into the heated skillet. At first contact, it sizzled and popped. "You want one?" he asked.

"I'm good, thanks." I'd had coffee and a piece of toast.

"How's your top-secret case coming?"

"Slow," I said, "though we've made some progress."

"We?"

"Detective Wright is helping me."

He turned to make sure I wasn't pulling his leg. "Don't you two get on like water and oil?"

"It's a process." His oven alarm beeped, prompting me to check the time. "I better get moving." I grabbed my coat and made for the door.

He jiggled the skillet. "Don't forget you owe me poker lessons!"

"I won't."

The second I walked past dispatch, it started. Dix strolled by me, humming the *Rocky* theme song. Hopkins stretched to one side, arms overhead. Wright was on the ground, doing push-ups. He had remarkably good form. "It's nice to see everybody taking my memo so seriously," I said. "Keep up the good work."

Wright stood up, dusted his hands, and said, "I'm good for six months."

"Me too," Hopkins said. "You don't want to *overdo* it."

I was a breath away from saying Hopkins *couldn't* overdo fitness when Yankowitz chimed in. "I think your memo might violate some laws."

"What laws?" I asked.

"Disability laws."

I set my hands above my belt and said, "Come on. None of you are disabled!"

"Not all disabilities are obvious, Chief," Wright said.

"You're telling me you have a mental disability?" I asked with a smile.

"Shots fired!" Billy called.

Wright shook his head. "A word?" he said.

"Come along," I said.

When we reached my office, he closed the door and said, "How's the hunt for our abortionist going?"

I dumped the dregs of my water cup onto my plant, and rotated it slightly so that its browning leaf wasn't facing the sun. "So far, nothing." No need to tell him about my conversations with Detective Carmichael or with Damien Saunders. "What about Susan's boyfriend? I owe you a bottle yet?"

"Not yet." He rolled his shoulders up and back. "All the boys we know about are dead ends. What if it was someone . . . older?"

"Older?" I asked.

"Maybe someone . . . inappropriate?"

"Teacher?" I asked. Such things happened.

"Yeah, or coach. She played field hockey."

"Any rumors that her coach was a lech?" I asked.

"No. I'm also looking through her yearbooks. The 1971 and 1970 ones. Checking out upperclassmen and club advisors."

Hmm. I might need those yearbooks later, to look for girls Susan was friends with, girls who might've had an abortion. But I'd let him have the books for now. I picked up a memo from Mrs. Dunsmore. Brought it closer to my face.

"You need glasses," he said.

I set the paper down and said, "Excuse me?"

"You've been squinting at your papers for a good six months now. Just grab a pair of reading glasses from the pharmacy."

I growled. Reading glasses. As if.

He said, "Maybe you can ask Finny about the coach thing."

Right. Because Finny couldn't know Wright was looking into his sister's disappearance. I was finding it difficult to navigate who knew what about whom.

"Good. Hey, nice work on getting an ID on the woods corpse so quickly," I said.

He was surprised by my praise. "Thanks. A lot of it was Finny. Guy's a bulldog when he thinks people are withholding information."

"Any ideas on who put her in the ground?"

"It's early days. Mother says it's the ex-boyfriend. We're trying to track him down. Last contact information we have for him is twenty years old." He left. I heard him call out, "Yankowitz, you call that a sit-up? You have to bring your torso up, man."

"This is a perfect sit-up!"

The peanut gallery weighed in with thoughts on form, the proper duration of a sit-up, and bets on how many Yankowitz could do in a minute.

Looked like the men were having more of a reaction to the fitness memo than I'd planned. On one hand, it had proved a great cover for Finnegan's outburst. On the other hand, it meant that Mrs. Dunsmore had been correct, again. And it wasn't likely she'd let me forget it.

# DETECTIVE MICHAEL FINNEGAN
# MONDAY, MAY 31, 1999
## 1015 HOURS

The contact information for Elizabeth Gardner's ex-boyfriend, Donald Waverly, was twenty years old and useless. The telephone number now belonged to a Thai restaurant, and his address, an apartment complex in New Haven, had turned up no record of him. My sigh ruffled the papers on the desk.

"Who died?" Dix asked, stopping at my desk.

"My sense of self-worth."

He slapped my back. I coughed. "Buck up, buddy. I'm sure it'll come back. Go get yourself another wife. That always cheers you up."

Funny fucker. As if a new wife would bring me anything but heartbreak and another siphon on my bank account. I went in search of the nearest typewriter. We'd lost one to an injury sustained during an in-station football pass gone wrong. I took a seat near the desk Dix liked best. The typewriter there had a ribbon and all its keys. Score. I rolled a sheet into it and began filling in details, such as they were.

"Oy, look who's got the only good machine," Hopkins complained, a bunch of papers clutched in his hammy hand.

"You snooze, you lose," I said, slowing my typing to one slow finger-jab every four seconds.

"Billy's using the other."

"You think watching me and complaining is going to advance your cause how, exactly?"

"I'm on call," he complained. "I might only have these five minutes to type this."

"And you might get called while typing. So, you'll have wasted my valuable time with this interruption and for what reason?"

"You detectives always think you come first in everything." He raised his voice and looked at the other guys, hoping for support. It didn't come.

Torturing him wasn't any fun. I finished typing and yanked the sheet through. "Your chariot awaits," I said, waving my hand with a flourish.

Back at my desk, I examined the reports Dawson had sent us. Elizabeth May Gardner was a well-liked girl who enjoyed photography and cooking. She had dated a young man named Donald Waverly. She broke up with him six weeks before she went missing. The cops looked into him, but he had no priors. He worked full-time at a landscaping company. He was interviewed, twice, and seemed very upset that she was missing.

A few men who'd asked Elizabeth out on dates (she'd refused) were checked out. None of them were pursued. She'd last been seen walking along Canaan Road. Her mother said she'd gone to take photographs. Her car was found near the Scoville Sanctuary's entrance. A few sightings of her had been reported as far as the Midwest in the weeks following her disappearance, but knowing that she ended up in Idyll, they were likely mistaken or crank calls.

Lewis's desk phone rang and rang. He was in the restroom. I checked my wristwatch. He'd been in there a while. He was too young to have gut problems. I thought back to my ulcers, acquired in my twenties. Okay. Maybe not too young then.

I tapped my fingers against my desk, one at a time. Horse trot noises. *Trot trot to Boston; trot trot to Lynn; trot trot to Cambridge, but don't fall in!* It was an old nursery rhyme. One my parents recited as they jogged us up and down on their knee. On "don't fall in," you got dipped into the gap formed between their knees, and you shrieked and clapped because it was a fun game. I'd played it with Susan when she was a baby. She'd start grinning at "Lynn" because she knew what was coming. After I'd done it, she'd gurgle and say, "'gain!" I played the same game years later with my own kids.

Lewis's desk phone rang again, and he appeared in time to snatch it up. "Yes?" He looked at me and mouthed "Medical Examiner." I listened in, but Lewis didn't say much. Lots of "huh"s and "okay"s and, at the end, "when?" He hung up. "More info on Elizabeth Gardner," he said.

"And?"

"They're faxing it now."

"We'll get it by Thanksgiving," I said.

"I'll go check the fax," he said. Paused. "Think that counts as exercise?"

I shook my head. It was the "new" office game. Doing something like stapling a report and then asking, "Hey, does this count as exercise?" Only a few men were bold enough to play it in front of Chief Lynch, but he knew about it, knew it was widespread. I'm sure Grace Dunsmore kept him apprised.

I looked again at the papers. There wasn't even a photo of Donald Waverly. Not surprising. You didn't photograph an interview subject. Still, I'd have liked something more than a name and a defunct address and phone number. I picked up the phone and tried again to reach the owner of the landscaping company Donald had worked for when he and Elizabeth dated.

Turns out late May is the busy season in the life of a landscaping company. Lawns to be seeded, mulch to be strewn, trees to be planted, and whatever else those guys did. Me? I'd maxed out at lawn mowing and hedge trimming. Not that I needed to do such things in my seedy little apartment complex. I'll say this for my ex-wives: They guaranteed I'd never have to operate a lawn mower again.

When I called Fern Landscaping, the phone was answered by a human, not an answering machine. That was where the good news ended. I got a temp who didn't know anything about nothing. No, she didn't know when Jim, the owner, would be in the office. No, she didn't know what his home phone number was or if she was allowed to give it out, and um, could I hold? I held. After seven minutes, I decided she was never coming back and I hung up.

Lewis returned, faxed report in hand. "I *hate* that machine."

"Did it eat the cover page?" I asked.

"No. It gave us every *other* page of the report. So, I've got pages 1, 3, and 5."

"You want me to call and ask them to resend it?" I offered.

"Would you?" he asked. "I wanna read this first."

"Sure." I dialed the ME's office and explained that our fax machine was cursed by a demon who hated even-numbered pages. The woman on the other end seemed less than amused by my flight of fancy, especially when I told her I needed her to fax the whole report, not just the even-numbered pages, because our fax-machine demon was anything but predictable.

Lewis said, "Why do I have a feeling they're going to put your picture up at the ME's office with a label that reads 'Crazy'?"

"No idea. So, what do the odd-numbered pages tell us?" I asked.

"In addition to her blunt-force trauma, Elizabeth May Gardner suffered multiple stab wounds. The jacket she wore was largely made of polyester. It was intact enough to reveal cuts and bloodstains. There was knife damage to some bones. There's a lot of cautious statements here, but it looks like a serrated blade, six inches or so."

"Defensive wounds?"

"Nature didn't leave them much to work with."

Smart killer. Dumping a body in a shallow grave in the woods wasn't super-genius-level stuff, but it wasn't stupid either. Much of our victim's body had succumbed to time and insects and scavengers and the earth. Without her gold crown, we might not have identified her for a long, long time.

"The report say anything about how long she was in the ground?" I asked.

"Based on decomposition and what they could recover of the clothing, it's likely she was buried before 1981."

"Between April 1979 and before 1981," I said.

"That's the best guess. Soil samples and leaf matter and nasty bug info says she likely went into the ground in spring."

"The guy snatches her in mid-April and doesn't keep her long," I said.

"Might have killed her the same day he grabbed her." He bit his lip. "Why'd he dump her there? It's not exactly well-known, yeah? For all he knew, he was going to wind up in someone's backyard. Kind of dicey."

"Maybe he knew the area?"

"Local boy?" he asked.

"God knows. I'm still digging into Donald. Can't make contact with the landscape owner."

"When is Ms. Holliday going to talk to us?" This wasn't the first time Lewis had posed the question. Elizabeth Gardner's mother was upset and angry. I didn't blame her. Discovering her daughter had been murdered and buried in the woods? That was devastating. But the unsympathetic detective in me wanted to ask her why, if she was so certain she knew who killed her daughter, why wasn't she calling us with information that could help us?

Lewis looked at the missing persons poster of Elizabeth. "Nice smile," he said absently. "When my kids smile, it's like they're practicing for Halloween. All teeth and gums." He gave me an example.

I said, "When my daughter, Carly, was young, she'd complain that people told her she didn't smile enough, and I'd tell her, 'You don't have to smile. Friendly is overrated. Friendly gets you killed.' And then I'd tell her how Ted Bundy lured many of his victims by faking an injury. 'A guy needs help,' I told her, 'you tell him to ask another man for help.' She'd shake her head and say that no one else's dad told them such stories, and I'd tell her that proved I loved her more than those other fathers."

When had I last spoken to Carly? February? Real father-of-the-year material there.

"You told your child not to smile," Lewis said. "Because friendly gets you killed?"

I nodded. It hadn't helped that, at the time, there had been a grisly murder splashed all over the news. A young woman only a few years older than Carly had been murdered by a stranger who'd given her a ride on a rainy day.

"What kind of a world we live in?" Lewis asked, his eyes looking at Elizabeth May Gardner's photo. "A world in which you tell your child not to smile."

# TUESDAY, JUNE 1, 1999
## 1100 HOURS

**M**rs. Dunsmore appeared, a folder cradled to her chest like a baby.

"Tell me that isn't the budget," I said.

She said, "It's not the budget."

"Oh?"

She set the folder down on my desk: *Idyll Police Budget, Fiscal Year 2000*.

"You told me it wasn't the budget."

"You told me to tell you that."

"What's the problem? We set the figures." By "we" I meant Mrs. Dunsmore, with some input from me.

"Don't you think we'll need to increase it?"

"Why?" I asked.

"I keep hearing rumors about Y2K."

"Such as?"

"Such as that the world's computers are going to fail, people will lose their money from banks, and there will be looting."

"If those computer geniuses can't figure this out and fix it before New Year's, then they're not so smart after all."

"Chief." She nudged the folder to me.

I sighed. "The mayor will blow his top if I amend this budget. You know that. You trying to get me fired?"

"If I'd wanted that, I'd have done it by now," she said. Probably true. And then who would she have to torture? "I think it would be smart to prepare for a worst-case scenario. Maybe we'll never need it. Besides, I hear the Fire Department has drawn up some scenarios." Ah, her trump card. Well played. She knew I didn't want to look less prepared than Captain Hirsch.

"Hey, can I ask you a question?"

"Questions are free. Answers will cost you," she said.

"Funny. Do you know why I wasn't invited to participate on the softball team? Do they usually exclude the chief?" This was a trap. I knew the answer. I'd dug back into the files and found that the chief of police always captained the team, except in 1978, when he'd been away, at some conference.

She asked, "Do you want to know the answer?"

*No.* "Yes."

"Some of the men are still . . . hesitant to embrace you as their chief. They worry too much about appearances."

"What? They think I'm going to make them wear rainbow-colored shirts?"

"I believe they voiced concern that the color pink would be involved."

"You're serious."

"Sadly."

"One more question. Can they keep me off the team? Is it allowed?"

She considered the question. "It's never come up before."

"Okay." I grabbed the folder she'd given me and opened it up. I muttered, "Where would people loot? The candy store? The garden-supply store?"

She didn't turn around. Just called out, "People will surprise you," as she left the office.

After I'd spent two hours trying to imagine worst-case scenarios—townspeople stealing gas from the Citgo station, all electricity going out (but that had happened in February during a blizzard), a computer blackout that meant we couldn't pull any driver's information while on patrol—Finny strolled into my office. He held a folder and looked worse for wear.

"Tell me that's not the budget." I distrusted all folders on sight now.

"What?" He glanced at the folder, as if it had perhaps changed its contents while he wasn't looking. "No. It's an update on the Gardner case. The plastic bag they recovered from the scene had nothing to do with the grave. Trash, mostly, and too modern to be related."

"Too bad," I said. "Would've been nice if it included a receipt with the killer's name."

"And home address and telephone number," he added.

"Sure. While he's at it, why not include a big old sample of DNA? What was inside?"

"Potato chips pack, crushed beer can, two broken pencils, a circular from the newspaper, a half-empty soda bottle, and three Tic Tacs, orange flavor."

"Orange? Yuck. What's the point of a breath mint if it's orange-flavored?"

"Beats me. We're due to meet Elizabeth Gardner's mother in three days. She's going to give us more information on the ex-boyfriend."

"Great. Hey, while I have you in here, I've got a question." I lowered my voice. "About the other case."

"Oh, yeah?" He closed the office door and said, "What is it?"

"Well, it occurs to me that your sister probably didn't associate with doctors, so how did she know who to visit about her situation?"

His brow furrowed. "I don't know."

"Maybe she asked someone at her school? Maybe someone she knew had an abortion?"

"Like who?"

"I was hoping you could help me there. High schools are usually gossip mills, yeah? You ever hear anything about a girl going away for a few days to take care of an issue?"

He bit the tip of his pinkie finger. "Maybe. There were some rumors about Melissa Kennedy. She was two years behind me and two above Susan. She got sick at school, and a few weeks later was gone for a whole week. Her parents took her out for a trip to California. That wasn't normal. Some of the girls said her boyfriend had knocked her up. Melissa was a grade-A student, headed for college, so I can see where a baby wouldn't have fit her plans or her parents' plans for her."

"Any idea where she lives now?" I asked.

"You want to call Melissa Kennedy and ask if she had an abortion nearly thirty years ago?" He didn't have to make it sound like a mission-impossible task, did he?

"You got any better ideas?" I asked.

"I could see if any of the guys back home I worked with arrested any doctors back then, but . . ."

"But?" That was exactly the resource I wanted, and couldn't get access to, what with my investigation being secret and not sanctioned.

"But I'd have to tell them why I'm asking."

He didn't want to tell the Boston Police that his teenage sister had slept around back in the day. Was it sweet that he wanted to protect her reputation? Or stupid? Maybe both.

"If you don't want to do that, I need Melissa Kennedy's phone number."

"I'll ask Carol. She and Melissa were friendly. Have sons the same age, I think."

"Melissa had kids later?"

"Sure, after she graduated college. Right after, I think. I'll see about getting you her number."

"Unless you'd rather have your sister ask her?" I suggested.

"Carol?" He considered this. "She'd probably worry it would end their friendship."

"Right." Leave it to the gay stranger to ask a woman private details about her high-school sex life. Fantastic.

"That all?" he asked.

"Yeah." He turned to go. "No. Um, do you play in the softball tourney?"

He winced, so fast I almost missed it. "Yup. Outfield." Outfield? Outfielders had to run. Our team was worse than I thought.

"Gonna play this year?" Maybe he hadn't known about my being excluded from the team. And maybe pigs were flying outside at this very moment.

"Sure, unless this case requires me to work that weekend."

"Who plays first base?" I asked.

"John Miller."

"Dispatch John Miller?"

"He played on his college team, back in the day. That all?" He edged nearer the door.

"Sure."

He left, without saying any more about the softball game. I was good enough to investigate his sister's disappearance, good enough to talk to her high-school friend about her abortion so he and his sister, Carol, weren't put in an awkward position. But good enough to play softball with? Apparently not.

## DETECTIVE MICHAEL FINNEGAN
# FRIDAY, JUNE 4, 1999
### 1400 HOURS

**M**s. Hannah Holliday, the former Mrs. Mick Gardner, had the spotted skin of a person who lived in the southwest and spent a lot of time outdoors, her bleached hair made whiter by the sun. She wore a large turquoise necklace and carried a bag embroidered with sunflowers. She was not what I expected. What had I expected? Black dress and gray hair and fingernails gnawed short? Perhaps. I stole a peek at her hands. Her nails weren't bitten. They were on the long side, and unpainted. She also subverted my expectation of animosity with her first words. "Thank you for bringing her to us, so we could lay her to rest."

Lewis pulled out a chair and urged her to sit. He'd asked Chief Lynch if we could borrow his office, and the chief had said yes without hesitation. "May I get you some water?" Lewis asked. She nodded, and he stepped outside. She looked around the office, her eyes settling on the plant in the windowsill. Lewis returned, water cup in hand. He gave it to her. She took a tiny sip and set the cup atop the desk.

I cleared my throat before I asked if she remembered anything odd about Elizabeth's behavior in the weeks prior to her disappearance.

"Odd how?" she asked.

"Did she seem nervous or scared or upset?" I asked.

She pulled her top lip down with her bottom teeth. "No. She was a little quiet. But then, when I went back and read her diary, I realized why." She reached into the sunflower bag and withdrew a cracked, red leather diary. She patted the cover. "I gave her this when she was seventeen. It's a three-year diary. She didn't write in it often." She wrinkled her nose. "I didn't like to read it. I waited, months, before I did. Well, not exactly. I read the last two pages two days after she went missing. I didn't read the others until later. If only I'd read those sooner."

"May I?" Lewis asked, extending his hand slowly, the way you would approach a shy animal you didn't wish to startle. Her fingers tightened on the diary. Then she extended it, with a soft sigh, as if releasing it from her grip cost her.

"January 28th," she said.

Lewis opened the diary and flipped pages. January 28, 1979, was two-thirds through the book. Those unfilled pages, awaiting news of boyfriends and squabbles with friends and concerts attended and hearts broken, those pages were a mirror to all the days she didn't live, and would never experience.

Lewis read, his brow furrowing. "Donald hit her," he said. "Because she contradicted him."

Ms. Holliday pulled her lip down again with her teeth. "If you read further, you see where she hid it, the bruise, with makeup. She didn't tell me or her father or anyone. She thought it would never happen again."

"But it did?" I prompted.

"Twice more, before she broke up with him. It's all in there. She broke up with him after the kicking incident. I remember I was surprised when she told me she was splitting up from him. When I asked why, she said they had other interests, and she didn't think he took her photography seriously. She loved taking pictures, so I believed her."

"When you read the diary, did you tell the police what you'd learned?"

"Yes. Of course! I called them and told them, and they promised to look into it."

Lewis cut a glance to me and then to the diary. They hadn't taken it as evidence. Why?

"They interviewed Donald," he said. "More than once." What he didn't say was that the interviews occurred in May and in June. Before she'd read the diary and reported the violence he'd committed against her daughter. We had no record of an interview after June. What had happened?

"They thought I was hysterical. Was making up accusations," she said. "I'd already accused the pharmacist of being too interested in her."

"Pharmacist?" I asked.

"Mr. Paxton."

"Ah, him," I said. There had been a mention in the files. He'd been looked into and dismissed, right quick.

"I didn't know then about the abuse. If I had . . ."

Lewis read the other pages.

"What did you know about Donald Waverly?" I asked. "Where he lived? Worked? Family? Friends?"

She gave us the information we already had about his job and where he lived. She thought he was from Vermont, originally, and that he had an older sister, Rose. "I think his parents were gone. An accident, maybe?"

"What about friends?"

She shrugged. "When they hung out in a group, it was mostly Lizzie's friends and their boyfriends. I don't recall anyone as being Donald's friend. Of course, he was a bit older than them."

"Twenty-four," Lewis said.

"Yes."

"What did he look like?"

"Dark hair, hazel eyes, and a slight cleft in his chin. He was vain about his hair. Wore it like Tom Wopat from *Dukes of Hazzard*. He had a large mark. Here." She tapped by her left eye. "Chicken pox mark. Don't you have a picture?"

"Would you have some more pictures of Donald?" I asked, the "more" implying we had a picture, which we did not. "Maybe some candids?"

She frowned. "In with Lizzie's things, yes. They're in San Antonio. I brought photos of Lizzie with me, for the service, but none that included *him*." The word "him" was full of venom.

"Maybe a friend could get them for you, send them on to us?" Lewis suggested. His voice was gentle but urgent, which made me think whatever he'd found in the diary had made him think Donald was our guy.

"I suppose I could ask Patsy, if it would help."

"It would," he said. "Very much."

"Did Donald mention where he planned to go when he left town, nine months after Elizabeth disappeared?" I asked.

She grimaced. "He didn't share his plans with me. And by that time, my marriage was breaking up. I wanted to hire a private investigator, and Mick wanted to start cleaning her room. Start boxing up Lizzie's things. She'd been gone less than a year!"

I could've told her it wasn't an uncommon reaction. Parents' decisions made after their child goes missing aren't always the same. Some parents can't stand to see the items that were touched daily by their missing child and want them gone from sight. Others preserve rooms like museum exhibits—nothing changed, not even after decades when the child would have outgrown the clothes and the toys and the pop-star posters. My parents had left Susan's room preserved for a decade, and then items began to creep inside: out-of-season clothes, toys for the grandkids they kept at the house, old furniture, until Susan's room was layered with items, hers buried at the bottom.

"Did you hire a PI?" I asked.

"No. Mick controlled the money. After we divorced, I wanted to leave the terrible memories behind, so I moved. San Antonio. It has a wonderful modern-art museum, and it's sunny two hundred and twenty days of the year." She recited the facts as if they were proof of happiness.

Her husband stayed, mere miles from where his little girl went missing, and she moved thousands of miles away.

"Did Lizzie say anything about Donald after they broke up?" Lewis asked.

"Only that she should've done it earlier. At the time, I was surprised, but after I read the diary, I saw why she said it. She thought he'd change, that the violence was the exception to the rule."

"You don't think so?" Lewis asked, casually.

"No. I don't." She looked at the diary in his hands and then at her sunflower bag. "I'll get you the photos."

"Thank you so much," he said.

"Is there anything else?" she asked, her eyes going from me to him.

"No," he said. "Thank you for coming in and talking to us. Again, we're very sorry for your loss."

She stood and teetered a fraction. I reached for her, but she stepped back and said, "I'm fine." She turned to go. "The funeral is on the 13th at 10:00 a.m. You're welcome to come, if you'd like."

"Thank you," I said. *If you like.* What a choice of words. The last thing I wanted to do was attend a funeral for a nineteen-year-old girl who'd been violently murdered. Whom I'd called Colleen for sixteen years. *If you like. Like* had nothing to do with it. "I'll be there."

# TUESDAY, JUNE 8, 1999
## 1730 HOURS

"It's such a pleasure to meet you," Mom said, taking Matt's hand into both of hers. She held on and gave him a thorough looking-over. Around us, faculty mingled, talking about their summer vacations and research plans.

"The pleasure is all mine." He let her hold his hand hostage.

"You a policeman, too?" Dad asked.

Matt said, "FBI agent."

"Oh my," Mom said. "Your parents must be so proud." And here I thought my mother had a low opinion of federal agents ever since the Waco mess.

"You came!" Marie cried. My sister-in-law was trailed by my nephews. Tyler wore a Yankees sweatshirt. Gabe wore a button-down shirt and had recently had his hair cut.

"Uncle Tom!" Gabe said. "I thought for sure you'd skip this!"

Marie shook her head and said, "And who's your friend?"

"Matthew Cisco." He smiled at her. "Tom didn't tell me there was a stone-cold fox in the family."

Marie blushed and put a hand to her chest.

"Ewww," Tyler said, uncomfortable with this description of his mother.

"Who is this guy?" Gabe asked. "I thought he was Uncle Tom's date."

"It's *lovely* to meet you," Marie said. "I hope you won't mind my children. They've recently become feral beasts. Onset of puberty." She said this last part at a slightly louder volume. Tyler put his face in his hands and Gabe cried, "Mom!"

The sound of a wineglass being tapped cut through the chatter. We looked toward the source of the sound. The dean of John's school stood near a lectern. "Good evening. We're going to start soon. If you could take your chairs, please?"

Marie rounded up the boys and we all sat in the second row of narrow folding chairs set up in the faculty library, where, John had assured me, the books were largely ornamental. "It's a space where we can escape students," he'd confessed. Matt was seated between me and Mom. The dean talked about the school's mission and its values. I zoned out. My face was pointed in the right direction, but I stared at a painting behind his right shoulder showing American Indians hunting buffalo. It seemed an odd choice for the room. My mind wandered back in time to Susan Finnegan, sixteen years old and pregnant. How was it no one knew of her boyfriend? From my experience, most teen boys ran their mouths about girls they'd scored with, so either our baby daddy was very respectful of her reputation, or he didn't want to be caught. Maybe Wright was onto something. Maybe Susan had slept with someone who was older, or married, or . . .

The first award recipient was a professor of chemistry. It was a career award. I hoped that meant he was retiring. It looked like a strong wind might blow him over.

If the boyfriend could land in hot water, that would explain the abortion. He'd probably pressured her. If we could find him, we might find the doctor who'd performed the surgery.

Next up was a professor of economics. She was a black woman, which made her a rarity in any department. John's department had one white woman, and she was on maternity leave. I once told him NYPD had better diversity stats, and he got all red in the face. We have fun.

John was the fourth awardee of the night. "How many are there?" Matt whispered as we clapped. My father leaned over my mother to answer. "Five. Home stretch now." He gave Matt a thumbs-up, and I realized you're never too old to be embarrassed by your parents.

After the ceremony, John made small talk with faculty and faculty spouses. Matt got trapped in a conversation with the school's dean, who'd heard there was a federal agent in the room. I kept the boys out of trouble while we impatiently waited to be released to dinner.

An older woman with a lipstick-stained wineglass wandered over to us. "Are you Sylvia's husband?" she asked me.

Tyler guffawed.

"He's gay," Gabe said.

The woman looked at me for confirmation. "True," I said.

"Might you be single? I have a son. He's a doctor."

"That's his boyfriend," Tyler said, pointing to Matt. He wore a suit though I'd told him it wasn't a formal event. He looked fantastic.

"My," she said. "Well done."

I looked to my nephews, and they shrugged and laughed. What was there to say?

We ate at an Italian restaurant that served dinner family-style, which meant we started off arguing. Gabe hated mussels. Tyler hated cheese. "What?" John said. "No, you don't. Stop it."

We ended up ordering too much, but I'd brought a secret weapon: Matt. After he'd eaten the veal, the ravioli, the octopus, and the chicken, Gabe asked, "How do you *do* that?"

Matt said, "I exercise a lot, and I have a high resting metabolism, so I require a lot of calories."

"Do you lift weights?" Gabe asked.

"Yup."

Tyler asked him how much he could lift, and Matt answered all the boys' questions, pausing only to fork more ravioli in his mouth.

"I like him," Mom mouthed at me. It was so obvious that Marie had to choke back laughter, and Dad nudged her with his elbow. "Well, I do," she said, loudly enough for the cooks to hear.

Marie asked what I was working on. Because of my oath to Finny I said only, "A cold case. Missing persons."

"Let's not dwell on crime," Dad said, silencing my job talk. "John, you've hardly touched your veal. What's wrong?"

He said, "The dean wants me to double up on classes next fall."

"What?" Dad half-shouted. "You're tenured. You don't have to do that."

John toyed with the broccoli on his plate and said, "They're short a professor with Henson leaving, and Phips is on sabbatical."

"Can't the new associate professor teach those classes?" Mom asked.

"She's on leave, remember? She doesn't get back until October."

Marie squeezed his hand and said, "Boys, do not play with your food."

"How many classes do you have to teach?" Matt asked.

"It should be one," John said.

"One." Matt gave me a quick look that asked, *really?*

"I'm writing a book this year," John said, defensive. "On rising sea levels."

"The classes being taught, do they have to be taught fall term?" Matt asked. "Could they move to spring term?"

John said they were core courses and must be taught in the fall, but then Mom interrupted to say that Intro to Ecology could be offered every other year, it had been done four years ago when . . . I stopped paying attention and watched the boys. They were busy arguing about someone named Jeremiah Higgs and whether he actually could do a 360 hardflip and had anyone seen him do it? Hardflip was skateboarding, right? Skateboards brought me back to Susan Finnegan. She'd been seen on a skateboard a week before her disappearance.

"That might work," John announced. He smiled and forked up a big bite of veal. I guess his work crisis was resolved.

When we'd finished dessert, we sat, stuffed and tired, talking about Columbine High School, where two teen boys had shot and killed twelve students and one teacher. "I remember when my biggest worry in school was whether my hair looked good," Marie said.

"I heard Jake Reever say the shooters were heroes," Tyler said.

"What?" John said. "Who is this kid? Does he go to your school? Does he own a gun?"

"Naw," Gabe said. "He just likes to say stupid things."

Marie shook her head and said, "It makes you seriously think about homeschooling."

"Did you see the latest *Star Wars*?" Matt asked the boys. He had two nephews, younger than Gabe and Tyler.

"Yeah, Dad took us," Gabe said.

"He *hated* it," Tyler said.

"They ruined it," John said. "Ruined it. There's this awful CGI character named Jar Jar Binks. Oh God, it was just awful."

"I liked it," Gabe said. "There were cool effects." John rolled his eyes.

"We need to hit the road," I said.

"Already?" Mom asked.

"It's almost 10:30," Dad said. "They've got a drive ahead of them." For my parents, who drove only on out-of-city trips, a multi-hour commute was a powerful and terrible thing.

I said my good-byes. Congratulated John again. My mother hugged Matt and said how *wonderful* it was to meet him. Tyler asked if he'd send him his weightlifting plan. Scrawny Tyler, who had never, to my knowledge, lifted anything heavier than a soup can.

In the car, Matt said, "They were really nice."

"I'm sorry my mom was all over you." I fastened my seat belt.

"It's nice to have fans," he said.

"It wasn't too much?" I pulled out into traffic. A cabbie honked at me. Ah, New York.

"Please. My family is too much. Yours is just right. Does your brother really only teach one class a term?"

"Mostly. But he also sits on faculty committees and advises and has that book to write."

"Whereas you just solve murders and catch kidnappers."

"Not daily. Not in Idyll." I took my hand from the wheel and squeezed his knee. "Thanks for coming."

"I had a good time." He reached over and touched my arm. "Plus, I'm not going to need another meal for six days."

"More like six hours."

He laughed. "Probably true."

# WEDNESDAY, JUNE 9, 1999
## 1500 HOURS

The drive to work was twenty-five minutes. In the passenger seat was a brown bag containing a sub sandwich, chips, and a can of Coke. Today I had a six-hour shift. The soda was prevention against boredom and naps. Working as a consultant at a security company supplemented my income and kept me afloat in an ocean of alimony payments. What it didn't do? Stimulate my brain. I reviewed security-camera footage and statements submitted by homeowners. The security company was always on the lookout for fraud. People who bought one of their systems, got robbed, and then submitted claims, usually within six months of the system's purchase. People who arranged their own burglaries are rarely patient. They buy the system, put on a balaclava, "break into" their house, and "steal" all the good stuff. As if most burglars know exactly where you keep your valuables. Sure, they'll hit your jewelry box, your portable electronics, and any closet with furs. But you think most of 'em know you keep antique coins in a cookie tin in the pantry? No. Dead giveaway.

My job could be done by a semi-intelligent teenager. But the security company liked my cop status. Thought it lent them credibility. And it seems that since I started, they've paid out significantly less money in claims. Michael Finnegan was worth something to someone.

ACE Security was in a long, low brick building off Route 84 in an industrial park near a towing company, an auto-body place, and a florist wholesaler. If you wanted food, you brought it in with you or called out for delivery. Given the location, your only option was Domino's, and I hated Domino's pizza. The puffy, undercooked dough tasted like disappointment. That's why I had a brown paper bag with a sub from Gepetto's.

Frank, at the front desk, said hello. I waved and swiped my card to get past the inner door, walked down a narrow hallway with dark-green carpeting, and entered the second room on the right. Milton was at his desk, listening to the Red Sox. One of the only guys left in America who preferred listening to baseball games to watching them.

"Hiya, Mike," he said, glancing up from a spreadsheet. "You believe this?" He jerked his thumb to the radio. "Pedro's slaughtering them today."

"Sounds good."

"You hear Donello quit Friday?" His finger traced a column on the sheet.

"No." I set my brown bag on my desk. "Why?"

"Said management was giving him a hard time about coaching his son's Little League team."

"Really? That's too bad." I didn't believe it for one second. Donello worked on the camera installations, but I'd breathed his fragrance enough to know he had a drinking problem. He missed work a lot for a guy his age. Plenty of excuses: sick kid, sick wife, car trouble, house trouble. I was surprised he hadn't called in with a plague of locusts yet. Looked like he wouldn't get the chance.

The Sox scored a run and the crowd went nuts. Milton lowered the volume and said, "One month until vacation." Milton was flying to Ireland, to go on vacation and find where his ancestors had lived in County Cork. He'd been planning the trip for years. He was a genealogy buff, our man Milton.

"I could look up the Finnegans for you," he offered for the umpteenth time.

I gave him my usual reply. "That's okay, Milton. I've got enough Finnegans to deal with on this side of the Atlantic. Why make life more difficult?"

"You're lucky. Having a big family. It's only me and Dad now. No siblings. No cousins. I have one aunt, but she's a lesbian, so not likely I'll be seeing any late-in-life cousins there."

I didn't disabuse Milton, tell him that family was hard, like marriage was hard, like living was hard. Four reports were stacked on my desk. I could have 'em done in two hours, but then I wouldn't get paid for six, would I? I shoved aside the baby ones and reached for the large one. Dessert before dinner. Ah, well. Delayed gratification is overrated.

"Whatcha got there?" Milton asked me.

I read the pages "Break-in. Thieves took some cash and a computer. Mostly they trashed the place, including some art." I read the report. "Somehow, the primary alarm failed, but a secondary one was tripped, and our guys arrived six minutes later. Take a look."

Milton took a photo from me and ogled the damage. Sofa cushions ripped open, lamps knocked to the floor, a glass coffee table smashed, and the very expensive paintings, split canvases drooping like tears, the strips hanging below the gilt frames. "Wowza," he said. "Looks like they wanted to find something, huh?"

No. It didn't. You didn't smash a lamp to look for something or cave in a glass-topped coffee table because you suspected it hid anything. What it looked like was rage. Someone had worked up a good old-fashioned case of anger and expressed it with primitive tools: a bat or a crowbar, and a razor or knife. I thought it likely the theft was secondary, perhaps a smokescreen. I didn't correct Milton's assumption. He was older than me, and I'd been raised to respect my elders. Besides, he didn't handle investigations. He handled the books.

"Might have to pay this one out." I checked the claim and whistled sharp through my teeth.

Milton raised his head, "What?"

"The paintings that got ruined were worth millions," I said.

"Holy moly."

"One was by Keith Haring."

Milton shook his head. "Management won't like it."

No, they would not. Of course, it was the insurance company that was on the hook for the paintings, but our security company could suffer a loss of face, or worse, in light of the alarm failing. They had better hope it was the fault of the owners, or an act of God. I was always suspicious of the first; not so, the second. Who was I to question God?

"Where was the house?" Milton asked.

"Williamstown, Mass," I said. ACE covered Connecticut, Massachusetts, and the western half of Rhode Island. Why they chose to cover only half of the country's smallest state never made sense to me.

"Lucky no one was home," Milton said. "Could've got nasty."

"Yeah." Only most of the time, it wasn't luck. Burglars preferred empty houses. A clean snatch and grab to a potential hostage situation. They'd seen enough movies to know those rarely ended well.

Milton said, "Gonna grab a snack. You want anything?"

"Trusting the vending machine again?" Milton had refused to use it for a month after it ate a dollar and refused to dispense his snack or return his money.

"Hunger knows no reason," he said, jingling coins in his palm.

"Good luck."

He left for the vending machine, democratically installed in the middle of the long building. I slid the burglary papers aside and took out the folder I'd smuggled inside my jacket. Opened it up. Inside were photocopied pages from Elizabeth May Gardner's diary.

Her handwriting was less bubbly than I'd expected. Her capital *G*s had horns and her capital *D*s were emaciated, as if they longed to be capital *I*s. Much of the diary was a record of small events: fights with her parents, trips with her friends, a leather jacket she wanted, and the hope that her photography might place in competitions. There were a few romances before Donald Waverly, but they seemed less intense.

*Donald drove me to the park today. I wanted to take pictures of the trees' budding leaves, the actual moment of budding. Donald said it was impossible. I said it wasn't. He asked if I was calling him stupid. Sometimes he gets upset over trivial things. None of the pictures came out as I wanted. On the way back, Donald stopped the car and told me I was the smartest girl he knew. Then he gave me a flower he picked in the woods, a lady's slipper. They're almost endangered, and you shouldn't pick them in the wild, but I didn't tell him. It would have made him feel bad. The flower is in a vase on my desk, tiger-striped and beautiful.*

Donald didn't know his wildflowers, or he didn't care about the vulnerability of lady's slippers. The passage established that he got angry over small stuff and would follow up with an apology. Classic abusive behavior.

*Went out with Donald and friends to the movies. It was hard to follow the film with everyone gabbing. After, we ate at Sandy's. Donald wanted to drive to the lake, but I told him I didn't feel well and that Aunt Flo was in town. He was annoyed and called me an ice queen. Later, he called to apologize. I've got a heating pad on my stomach. The cramps are awful.*

In January, he hit her.

*Went to see Gordon Lightfoot, with the birthday tickets Mom and Dad got me. Donald wore a tie, and he looked so handsome. The show was incredible. On the way home, I asked what his favorite part was, and he said, "'Reading my Mind.'" I said, "Oh, you mean 'If You Could Read My Mind,'" and he hit my face with the back of his hand while driving. Then he told me to stop correcting him. I cried.*

*He stopped at a gas station and bought me a stuffed bear and a Tab. He held the soda to my face and said he was sorry and he'd never do it again and he didn't know what came over him. Work has been making him take on crazy extra hours. He cried, saying I was the best thing in his life. He begged me not to leave him.*

*My cheekbone is blue-green, but I can cover it with makeup. If I pull my hair forward, you can hardly spot it.*

Lewis had followed up with the staties about Donald. About why, in light of his abuse, they hadn't pressed harder on his relationship to Elizabeth Gardner. They said they had, but the paperwork told a different story. They'd asked a few questions, sure, but given how he was the only guy in the picture, they hadn't grilled him. They'd checked that he was working the day she went missing. So? She wasn't reported missing until 10 p.m. He could've snatched her after work or between jobs.

We had his driver's license, a rental application for the apartment he'd had when he dated Elizabeth, and a copy of his auto-insurance policy. That was it. He hadn't committed any crimes. He hadn't married or divorced anyone. He hadn't bought a home. It was possible he was a squeaky-clean citizen. But I doubted it.

"It worked!" Milton said. He held up a bag of chips in his left hand. The game announcer reported that the score was now 7–1, Red Sox. He grinned. "This is turning out to be quite a day, isn't it?" Ah, Milton. Full to the brim with optimism.

"Yes," I said, closing my folder and returning to the claims work. "Quite a day."

Two and a half hours later, I ate my sandwich while checking the alarm logs on a recent break-in. The bread was very chewy. My molar wasn't happy about that. I needed a root canal but didn't want it and could hardly afford it.

"Tooth bothering you?" Milton asked, all sympathy.

Damn it. I hated being transparent. Loathed being the object of pity. "Fine," I said. "They used too much hot sauce today." There was no hot sauce on the sandwich.

"Hey, Milton," I said. He was eating spaghetti and meatballs he'd cooked from scratch. Milton was a bit of a gourmet. He looked up. His napkin tucked into the top of his shirt, prevention against stains. "When you're doing genealogy, you ever have trouble finding people?"

He stopped chewing and swallowed. "Sure. All the time. Especially when you're dealing with poorly kept records."

"Ever have trouble because someone changed names?" I asked. Donald Waverly. So little data made me think he'd adopted an alias, that he'd taken a new name. Lewis wasn't convinced, but he thought the idea had merit. The real problem was, if that wasn't his name, how did we find him?

"Well, women can be troublesome because they change their names when they marry. I once heard a historian tell a group of women that if children were named after their mothers, it would make his job a lot easier. You see, you always know who the mother is. But the father?" He shrugged. "Unless you run a paternity test."

"Sure." Not the direction I was going in. "What about false names? What if someone got in trouble and assumed a new identity?"

He exhaled through his nose, a high, whistling breath. "That's a toughie, Mike. If someone's new name is nothing like their family name, then what connects the two? Photographs would help, but only if you had both names, right? As a police detective, you probably know more than I do." He was forever deferring to my expertise, which felt particularly rich today, given that I felt I had none.

He twirled a long strand of pasta around his fork. He brought real silverware from home to eat his meals. No plastic utensils for Milton. "You'd be surprised at how many times people just use their mother's maiden name or their street name as assumed names. Maybe because it's easier for them to remember." He ate the mouthful of pasta.

How could I know what Donald Waverly's mother's maiden name was if all I knew was his assumed name?

"Look for a birth certificate with the mother listed as Mrs. Xavier if Xavier is the false name," Milton said, as if he'd heard my mental question. "Or look for addresses with a street name that matches the name."

"Milton," I said, "You're a genius."

His face matched the color of his red sauce, and he batted his hands around, deflecting my praise. Then he paused and looked up. "Are you interested in genealogy, Mike? Like I said, I can help you find your Finnegans."

My heart ached for one second as I considered that there was one Finnegan I'd pay for Milton to find. Only I didn't think his skill set would be of much help in locating Susan. I doubted he knew much about illegal abortionists in 1970s Boston. And just like that, my euphoria evaporated. I set the last quarter of my sandwich down.

"Tooth?" he asked quietly.

"Yeah," I said. "Aches like a son of a bitch."

# THURSDAY, JUNE 10, 1999
## 1530 HOURS

**W**right came into my office. Used to be, I could go months without the pleasure of his company in my space. Not anymore. Every day, it seemed, he had ideas and theories that translated into more work for me, like checking out whether a teacher at Susan's high school who'd been charged with indecent exposure had taught her. (He hadn't.) Between him treating me like I was his detective and him insinuating that I needed reading glasses, I had had my fill of Lewis Wright.

"Remember our bet?" His face was 100 percent smug. No way. He hadn't done it, had he?

"You found the father of Susan's baby!" We both started at the volume of my words and looked to the closed door. Nothing happened, so I repeated my question, at a normal volume.

"No. But what if I discovered that she didn't go through with the abortion?"

"What?" How did he know that? "What's in the folder you've got there?"

"If I show you, I think you'll agree that you owe me a bottle," he said.

"I'll be the judge of that."

He slapped the folder onto my desk. I turned the cover over. "A birth certificate?" I looked at the copied form.

Place of Birth: Suffolk County
Place of Birth: St. Ann's Hospital, Dorchester, MA
Mother's stay before delivery in hospital or institution: 16 ½ hours
Full name of child: James Michael Shaughnessy
If plural births, twins or triplets? If so, born 1st, 2nd or 3rd? N/A
Born alive or stillborn: Alive
Date of birth: April 6, 1973
Sex: M
Color: W
Father: Blank
Mother's maiden name: Susan Shaughnessy
Present name: Susan Shaughnessy
Residence: 15 Cedar St., Somerville, MA
Color or race: White
Age at the time of this birth: 16
Place of birth: Avon, MA
Occupation: student

I hereby certify that I attended the birth of this child who was born
at the time of 6:23 p.m. on the date above stated. The information
given was furnished by Susan Shaughnessy related to this child as
mother.

Signature of the attendant at birth: [illegible scrawl]
Physician, parent or other: Dr. Frederick Chambers
Received at the office of city or town clerk: April 9, 1973

A gold seal was affixed to the bottom of the form. It was raised. You
could see that, even on the photocopy.

"James Michael," I whispered. Finny's first name was the baby's
middle name, and their father's name was the baby's first name. Was
that who she'd named him for? Her father and brother? Or did the
baby's father share one of those names? The baby's father, unnamed
on this document. "She had the baby." I'd been so certain, we'd been
so certain, that it was the abortion that killed her. That she'd made a

poor choice and entrusted her life to some doctor more afraid of being caught performing illegal surgeries than he was for his patient's health.

"Didn't go through with it." He sounded pleased, as if he approved of her choice.

"She had the baby, and then what?" I asked.

"Don't know. My buddy in the BDP got this. He couldn't believe it. That it had been filed all this time and no one thought to look for it." He nodded at the form. "Shaughnessy is her mother's maiden name."

"This is great. Now we have leads to chase. Starting with . . ." I peered at the tiny type on the form, "St. Ann's Hospital. I don't know it."

"My buddy, Grant, says it's famous. There was a home for unwed mothers and for orphans attached to it, called Gracie's Place. Back in the day, girls got shipped there by parents who pretended their daughters had gone away to visit aunts or travel. The babies were given up for adoption, and when the girls came home, no one was the wiser."

"What about the babies?"

"Given to people who couldn't have them," he said.

"You know what this means?" I asked.

"Mike has a nephew he doesn't about."

"Bingo." How were we going to tell him? *Good news, your sister didn't die on an abortionist's table. Bad news: she had her baby and gave it up for adoption, and we have no idea where the baby is, or your sister.*

"They must have adoption records," I said.

"Might be sealed," Wright said. "Not sure if we'll be able to get them to give us a peek."

"We'll jump that hurdle when we get to it. At least we know where to search next." I laced my hands together and said, "Not looking forward to telling him."

He didn't ask "who." He knew.

"It's good news, in some way," he pointed out.

From outside, Finny called "Lewis? Where you at?"

"I've got to go." He hurried to the door.

"Hey!" I said, halting him at the door. "You did real good. You earned that bottle."

A rare smile lit his face, and then he ruined it by saying, "You're damn right I did."

\\\|//

It would've been cruel to withhold the information from Finny, but given the way he'd reacted to the last breaking news I'd shared about his sister, I decided telling him off-site would be best. I told him that I hadn't found Susan, but I had a promising lead. I asked him to meet me at a diner I'd heard him boast had a good Cuban sandwich. We took separate cars so as not to arouse suspicion at the station. "They'll think you're dating me," Finny joked.

"You wish," I said.

At the diner, Finny greeted the waitress by name, and I wondered if I'd done the wrong thing. If he ate here regularly, maybe I should've picked a different spot. One where he wouldn't have to relive this conversation over and over again. We put in our orders, and as soon as the waitress was six feet away, he said, "Tell me."

I told him about finding the birth certificate, though I glossed over how that happened. "She had a baby, a boy. Named him James Michael."

"James, after our father. Is the baby alive? Where is he?"

"I don't know. Not yet."

"I can't believe she was at St. Ann's. You know that's within spitting distance of our house? . . . She was maybe five miles away all that time?" His gaze got misty, and he sipped his beer. "Why didn't she call us? If she was going to have the baby anyway, she could've come home."

"Could she?" I asked. His jaw flexed. "I'm asking. It seems like your dad was strict. It was the old days. And maybe she thought if she did it this way, well, she could start new once the baby was adopted."

"Why didn't we check there?" he said, smacking his palm against the table. A couple across from us shot a look our way. I repaid them with a frosty glare. They went back to their meal.

Our dinners came, and neither he nor I ate much. He kept saying things like, "I have a nephew I've never met," and, "Mom is going to lose her mind when she finds out."

"Maybe keep this close until we know what happened to the boy, yeah?" I suggested.

"Why? Do you think something bad happened to him?" he demanded. He peeled the label from his beer bottle and put the tiny strips of paper on the table.

"I have no idea. I really don't. That's why I'm nervous about sharing the news."

He nodded. "You're right. Would be awful to tell them about him if something happened . . . Dave isn't going to believe this. When are you going up there? Are you going in person?"

The waitress stopped by, her eyes going to the pile of stripped paper. "Everything okay?" She aimed her comment at him.

"Yeah, great. Thanks, Cheryl."

Her eyes went to his plate and his uneaten sandwich. A frown crossed her face. "You sure you don't want anything else?"

"Some of your chocolate ice cream," he said. "It's amazing. You gotta try it," he told me. He was talking fast, too fast. He reminded me of my partner, Rick, when Rick was snorting lines, and his speech turned blurry with all the thoughts he couldn't control.

"Sure thing," she said, spinning on her heel and heading for the kitchen. I wished I could join her. It was painful to watch him this way. Fidgety, anxious, excited, scared. It was too much.

When the ice cream came, he made no move to eat it. Instead, he talked about his kids and how weird it would be for them to have a cousin they'd never known, and then he was off, speculating as to how his exes would take the news. I sat, listening, waiting for the adrenaline flame to burn out, to leave him worn and tired.

But it didn't. He was still chattering when we paid the bill. He thanked me for the hundredth time for finding where Susan went, for discovering the baby. He apologized for giving me grief earlier. He'd been so worn down by years of failure. He really didn't think she could be traced. But I'd done it! Here was where I wished I could give Wright credit, but even in Finny's excited state, I knew that would be a misstep.

"You're solid gold, Lynch, you really are. My mom's going to bake you a soda bread, you see if she doesn't."

I'd stopped trying to halt the rush of his words. I nodded, clapped him on the back, and told him to drive safe. He pulled out from the lot faster than I'd like. My eyes watched his red taillights until they winked out of sight.

My body felt as though I'd run a marathon. I was exhausted. I hadn't warned Matt I was coming. In fact, he'd told me he might need to work late, so I shouldn't come over. But I needed to see him. There were few cars on the road; the trip was fast. I parked outside his house at 12:45 a.m., glad to see his car was parked in the driveway. I knocked, not loudly, in case he was sleeping. I'd let myself in and find a spare bit of bed. He tended to starfish when asleep alone.

He didn't come to the door, so I used my key. The kitchen was dark, all shadowy shapes except for the glowing microwave and oven clocks. I stumbled over a pair of sneakers. Odd. Matt usually kept those by his gym stuff. He liked everything in its place. I sat in a chair and unlaced my boots. There was a set of keys on the table. Not Matt's. His set had seven keys and this had only three. There was a small, fuzzy dice attached to the key ring. Had Matt lost his set? Had to grab a spare?

I eased the boots off my feet, careful to keep them from thunking on the floor. Matt was a light sleeper. Hazard of the job, he claimed. Boots off, I stood and stretched. What was that smell? I sniffed. Cologne. But not Matt's. I knew that smell intimately. The room seemed in order, but something was off. I scanned the table and chairs, the counters and fridge and . . . back to the counter. A bottle of wine. I padded over and picked it up. An almost-empty bottle of red. I peered at it. Merlot. Matt didn't drink wine, not much.

A light flicked on. The brightness blinded me for a second. "Hello?" Matt, in boxers, one hand holding a gun.

"Whoa," I said. Hands up.

"Thomas? What are you doing here?" he whispered.

"I didn't mean to startle you." He lowered the gun but looked hyper alert. "I was in the neighborhood, and—"

"It's not a good time." His voice was curt.

"I was over in Vernon, and, what?" His words cut through my haze. "Not a good time?"

"Matt?" a male voice called from the back of the house.

I glanced at the bottle of wine. "You have company." The keys, the cologne. God, how dense could I be?

"I . . ." He rubbed his hair. It stood up in tufts. "I'm busy."

I stomped my feet into my empty boots. I'd tie them later. For now, I had to leave. Get out. Before this got worse.

"Matt?" He stood in the living room. He wore boxers and nothing else. It was hard to make out his features, but he was smaller than me, and younger, much younger.

"Sorry to disturb you," I said.

The guy's face was handsome and unlined by age. He looked utterly at ease standing nearly naked in the living room. He looked at me, tilted his head and asked, "Lynch?"

It felt like my blood had been replaced with acid. Everything inside boiled and burnt. I turned away and reached for the doorknob. How did he know me? Why? How long had this been going on? "Thomas," Matt said, his voice strained.

I left, my boots' laces flapping against the driveway as I ran to the car. It took three tries to get the key into the ignition. I drove too fast, wanting to be away from there. I hadn't assumed I was the only person he saw socially. But I'd wanted to see him tonight, and I hadn't thought he might be occupied. Clearly his date knew of me. But I hadn't known him.

I reached home after 1:20 a.m. I undressed in the dark and slid under my sheet and closed my eyes. Sleep didn't come. I turned, punched my pillow, and breathed, in and out. My heart was racing and I felt . . . angry. I got up and padded to the living room. Sat in my recliner and rocked, back and forth, waiting for dawn, when I could put on my uniform and go into work and forget what happened earlier.

And then I remembered that tomorrow was Friday and I had the day off. That's when I slammed my hand down, into my glass-topped Eileen Gray table, the same one Damien Saunders owned. The glass fractured in an unsteady crack along the table's length. But it stayed intact, not crashing to the floor as I expected, no shards to vacuum or to find with unsuspecting feet.

"Whatever doesn't kill you," I muttered.

# FRIDAY, JUNE 11, 1999
## 1045 HOURS

**W**hat a day. My old patrol partner from eons ago, Frank Murray, had called to tell me he'd scored me an interview with the director of St. Ann's Home for Unwed Mothers for next Thursday. Benefit of his new position as superintendent. "Watch out, Mikey," he said. "They're very touchy about privacy, especially around the adoptions."

"Because of that *Herald* article from 1994?" I asked.

Since the chief had told me about Susan's baby, I'd read up on Gracie's Place. I'd known of the place when I was young. We all had. There were rumors that Tracy Keppler had gone there senior year. Never confirmed, but still. "Gracie's Home for Whores." That's what the kids called it. It made me wince, knowing Susan had been inside those walls. Had we ever called it that in front of her? I hoped not.

Back in 1994, the *Boston Herald* ran an article about the home, painting it in an unflattering light. Several girls who'd gone there complained, decades later, about the food, the poor heat, and the scorn the nuns heaped upon them. Worse, one young woman claimed she hadn't wanted to give her baby up for adoption, and that she'd told the doctor and nurses, but that they'd given her a sedative and when she awoke, the baby was gone. Another woman said she'd had "second thoughts" days after her birth, but she was told her baby was gone and she had no parental rights.

"The *Herald* article fanned the flames, but even before that the home ran afoul of the neighborhood. The nuns were constantly lodging noise complaints, and the home created parking shortages," he said.

"Never get between somebody and their parking space in Boston," I said.

"No kidding. I guess plenty of people who adopted children from the home had nothing but glowing reviews for the place."

"Sure," I said. "They got a baby. What's not to love, from their viewpoint?" My mind imagined a chubby little boy with Susan's nose. *God, please let him have found loving parents who raised him well.*

"Hope your visit goes well. If there's anything else you want us to do, we're here, man."

"Thanks, Frank. I really appreciate your help. The whole family does." *Or will, once I tell them.* I felt terrible holding back, but until I knew more I didn't want to raise hopes. What if Susan had died after childbirth? What if her son had? I had no proof that anything had ended well, and I knew that if I called Dave or Bobby or Carol, I'd spend time saying, "I don't know" so often that they'd demand to know what I *did* know. And then old family arguments would become current. Naw. Better to wait.

"If you're in the neighborhood, stop by. Your godchild would love to see you." Gia, Frank's daughter, born when we were partners. I recalled her in pigtails, clutching a stuffed pig she called Harry.

"What is she, twenty-four now?"

"Twenty-five." God, he'd been a child himself when she was born. Who allowed us to have kids when we were hardly grown ourselves?

"Give Alice my love," I said. "And thanks again."

The station door opened, and I swiveled to check if Lewis was in yet. No. Damn it. He'd had to go to another pregnancy exam with his wife. I wanted him to distract me with Elizabeth Gardner case tasks. Didn't matter what. I craved distraction. Without it, my feet wanted to race out of the building and up to Dorchester to Gracie's Place, appointment be damned.

The door opened again. Lewis, at last.

"Hey!" I called.

He didn't hear me. He spoke to Hugh at dispatch and gestured toward the door. Then he turned around and walked back out. I waited a few minutes, but he didn't return. I walked to dispatch. Hugh was coordinating response for a fender bender by the library. When he finished, he said, "Hey, Detective? Help you?"

"Thought I saw Lewis come in."

"Oh, yeah. Right. He did. Stopped by to say he wasn't feeling well. Both him and the missus. He was going to drop her off at home. Said he'd be home, too."

"Sick?" He'd seemed fine yesterday. Not so much as a sniffle.

"Stomach thing," Hugh said.

Oh. Well, those could come on without warning. Could be food poisoning. My mind backtracked through what I'd seen Lew eat at the station. Hoped it wasn't the fries that came with his burger, because I'd eaten half of 'em.

"That's too bad." I meant it. Now I'd have to dig through the Vermont information we'd got Billy to pull for us all by myself. Such drudgework was made better by a partner, someone you could bitch to. Ah, well. I'd go it alone. I returned to my chair and lifted a phone directory. This one for Manchester. I turned the pages and found six Waverlys listed. Time to call them. And then I could move on to . . . I looked to the right, at the pile of old Vermont phone books tottering near the file cabinet. On top was Montpelier. I picked up the phone and cleared my throat. Time to get cracking.

"Hi, this is Detective Michael Finnegan of the Idyll Police in Connecticut. Who am I speaking to? Mrs. Floyd Waverly? How do you do? I'm calling because I'm looking for a man named Donald Waverly. He lived in Salisbury, Connecticut, back in the late 1970s. Might Donald be a relation? . . . Dennis? . . . Yes, I see. Any other men in the family around age forty? No, we want to speak to him about an investigation we hope he can help us with. . . . No, ma'am. . . . No. . . . Well, that's alright. I appreciate your time."

I did this six times in a row before taking a break. My ear was pink and hot, my shoulder cramped from tilting to hold the receiver there. Billy stopped by and asked how I was doing.

"I'm tired, my ear is hot, and I don't think I'll ever find this guy."

He stared at the pile of phone books. "Want me to help?" God bless, the kid had a good heart.

"Nah, pal. Save yourself. I'm going to the little boys' room to drown myself."

He watched me go, his face a mask of pity.

In the bathroom, I made the mistake of checking out my reflection. Dear God, when had this become my face? I looked like a bulldog. My cheeks hung like hams, and the whites of my eyes were pink from lack of sleep. Jesus. I looked sixty. I washed my hands and walked back to my desk, debating the merits of more caffeine.

Pro: It would keep me awake.

Con: It would keep me awake well past bedtime.

At Lewis's desk sat Billy, on the phone, the Burlington phone book at his elbow. My first thought: *Lew will lose his shit if he finds Billy there.* My second thought: *Billy didn't listen to me.*

"Yes, sir. Donald. But maybe he went by another name? Dark hair, yes. No, sir. I can't give details about the investigation. I'm sorry."

Third thought: *Bless him.* I told him I didn't want his help, and he waded into the cold waters of phoning strangers anyway.

When he hung up, he ticked off the name in the phone book and said, "They sure ask a lot of questions."

"They're curious," I said. "Not every day they get a call from the police looking for a family member."

"Can I make another?" he asked, pointing to the phone book.

"Be my guest."

A few hours back into it, and we'd cleared the phone book stack by a foot. My ear ached, and my jaw was sore from all that talking. Even Billy had wilted under the work, his hair mussed from rubbing it absently, his mouth turned down.

"Pack it in," I said.

"I got one more call for this book," he said. I glanced over. The Woodstock one.

"Just one more," I said, wondering again what was wrong with Lewis and hoping he was better by tomorrow.

"Good evening. This is Detective Michael Finnegan of the Idyll Police in Connecticut. Who am I speaking to? Mr. Marcus? Oh. This isn't the number for . . ." I peered at phone book entry, "Mr. Jeb Waverly? Ah, I see."

A snapping sound nearby made me look up. Billy was snapping his fingers and mouthing, "this one" at me.

"Thank you and have a good night." I hung up the phone and listened to Billy say, "Rose? You say you had a younger brother? His name? Daniel."

Rose. Mrs. Gardner said Donald had an older sister named Rose. Daniel. Donald. Not very different.

"Do you know if he lived in Salisbury back then?" he asked. "What about afterward? . . . No. When was the last time you saw him? . . . I see. . . . Yes. . . . What did he look like? . . . Yes. Ummm." He scribbled on a paper. "Right. Yes. . . . He did? Okay. Okay. Thanks very much. We may call back with more questions. Thank you for your time. Yes, good night."

He hung up, his face stunned. "What happened?" I asked.

"Her name was Rose. She had a younger brother named Daniel. Born 1955, which is the right age. She said he moved to Connecticut in the late 1970s. Not sure where exactly. They didn't keep in touch much. Both of their parents are dead."

"Were they dead when he moved?" I asked.

He nodded. "Car accident when she was twenty-two and Daniel was almost eighteen."

"She say what he looked like?"

"Dark hair and hazel eyes. Thin. Mark near his left eye, from when he had chicken pox."

"Cleft chin?"

"She didn't mention it."

"No matter." The pox mark. Had to be him.

Billy looked around. "You need me for anything? Help you follow up?" He glanced at the clock behind me. Shoot. He should've been gone an hour ago.

"Gimme her phone number. You did real good, Hoops. Real good."

He gave me an *aw, shucks* smile I'd seen make girls' hearts go pitter-patter.

Lewis would be so happy that we'd finally found a lead. Billy grinned, and I laughed at the image of Lew's face when I told him who had chased down our best suspect. He'd have to concede that Billy was more than a pretty face, just this once.

# SATURDAY, JUNE 12, 1999
## 1300 HOURS

It took me three and a half hours to find where the Finnegan clan had lived. Boston's lack of signage and my own confusion added delays. The city was still working on the Big Dig, a project so over budget and time it was beyond absurd. When I finally reached Wood Street, I noticed how close the houses were. In some, you could touch your neighbor's house if you leaned out your window. Most were paneled in siding. The narrow street was a riot of colors: red, blue, yellow, sea green. Each house had many windows. No wonder so many people had seen Susan the day she went missing.

I stood in the middle of the street, looking at the house Detective Michael Finnegan had grown up in. It was tan. A potted plant stood on the top of the front steps.

"Can I help you?" someone called from across the street.

"Just visiting," I called. With the neighbor's eyes on my back, I rang the doorbell.

The door swung open. A small woman with white curls and a pair of blue-framed glasses stood inside. "Hello?" Her face looked prepared to be pleased, seconds from a smile.

"Good afternoon, Mrs. Finnegan. I'm Thomas Lynch, from Idyll, Connecticut. I work with your son, Michael."

She smiled and clapped as if I'd arrived with a million-dollar check made out to her. "Oh, come in!" She spotted the neighbor and called, "Hi, Joan!" Then she shut the door firmly behind me and said, "Mikey said you'd be coming."

We walked up to a landing where family photos were displayed. I saw Finny with one of his wives and a small, ginger-haired boy. I'd never seen a picture of his children. He didn't display pictures at work. "Come to the parlor," she said. The parlor was for company. There were china knickknacks and a mantel clock keeping time. The sofa was spotless and stiff. She said, "Let me put the kettle on. I'll be right back." Kitchen sounds came: the rush of the tap, the clank of metal. I surveyed the room. On the coffee table, a cut-glass candy dish held mints fused to their crinkly-edged wrappers by time.

She returned with two photo albums. "I thought you might like to see these." She laid the albums carefully on the table. "Susan is in quite a few of the pictures. Mostly from elementary and middle school. She got shy about having her picture taken when she was older."

"Thank you." I picked up the first album, bound in faux white leather. Snapshots were tucked behind plastic onto adhesive sheets that held them in place. "Is that Michael?" I asked, pointing to a picture. His face was thin and young; his grin, wide and joyful.

"Yes, with his brother David. Let me check on that tea."

I flipped the pages, finding photos of Susan throughout. She had short hair when she was very young, but over the years it grew and grew until she looked like Rapunzel. Her smile was gap-toothed. She had freckles. She wore wildly mixed prints and fabrics. A photo of her wearing a plaid skirt with a gingham top made me wonder if she was colorblind.

When I asked Mrs. Finnegan, she laughed. "No. Susan had perfect vision. She liked bright patterns. Carol used to tease her. Said she looked like she'd dressed in the dark." Maybe the tendency for outrageous patterns was genetic. Finny had terrible taste in ties and sports coats.

"Sugar? Cream?" she asked.

"No, thank you."

She handed me a teacup. I worried I'd crush it, but saw no safe place to put it. No coasters on the coffee table. I cradled it in my right hand and flipped album pages with my left. "Who's this?" I pointed at a young girl beside Susan. They held their lunches in brown paper bags at their sides and smiled at the camera. First day of school, fourth grade.

She sat beside me, her weight not denting the unyielding sofa. "Oh, that's Lucy, Susan's best friend. You can't tell from that picture, but she had bright-orange hair. The kids called her Raggedy Ann, but really, her hair was beautiful." She sighed. "She lives in Maine now, Portland, with her husband. She has two kids, a son in the army, and a daughter in high school. Oh, but you know that, don't you?"

"I spoke to her."

"And she told you, about Susan being pregnant?"

"Yes." No need to tell her that I'd tricked the information out of Lucy.

"Pregnant." She stared at the window, but her gaze was unfocused. "I still can't believe we missed it, that *I* missed it. She was sick, a couple of times. And you know, there was one thing."

"One thing," I said.

"Church."

I waited a few moments before asking, "What about church?"

"Susan went a few times, without us, to arrange flowers and help with the fall fair."

"And that was unusual?"

"Well, she used to like church when she was little, but as a teenager she was less involved. Started asking questions about whether God was real, and if He was, why he permitted wars and other atrocities."

"Reasonable question," I said.

She snorted. "Not to her father, it wasn't. Anyway, it was a bit of a surprise, that's all, when she said she'd offered to help out."

"Is it possible she didn't?" I asked. "That it was an excuse?"

She set her teacup into its saucer. "To meet her secret boyfriend, you mean? No. She really had been at church. After she disappeared, Father Corcoran stopped by, and he told us how kind it had been of Susan to help out at the church and how he'd pray for her."

So much for using her church duties as a smokescreen, then.

"Maybe she went to pray for God to take care of her problem," she said. "She wouldn't be the first girl."

"When did she start going to church?" I asked.

"June or July of 1972. Why?"

"Creating a timeline." I was counting backward. If she was two and a half months pregnant in late September, she wouldn't have gone to church to pray it away in June. Even July seemed a stretch.

I flipped the photo-album pages. Birthdays, with young Mikey, Susan, Bobby, David, and Carol. Mrs. Finnegan must've been the photographer because she was rarely captured on film. Mr. Finnegan also appeared infrequently. When he did, it was with a goofy expression. Mugging for the camera. That explained where Finny got it. There were pictures taken on the street or outside the house, with smoking neighbors smiling. A close-knit place, rather like Idyll, only more crime-ridden if history had it right.

Susan evolved, from little girl to teenager. Her mother was right about her camera shyness. There were fewer photos as she got older, most of them candids. No more smiling head-on. Instead, she was at the edge of the group, watching the action or looking pensive.

"Do you think I could talk to Father Corcoran?" I asked. There'd been no statement from him in the boxes of material.

"Oh, I'm afraid he passed on, three years ago," she said. "Lung cancer."

"I'm sorry."

She frowned. "You know, Abigail Waters might remember that time. She was awfully active in the church. I suspected she had a crush on the organist, Mr. Williams. Anyway, Abigail was in church all the time, volunteering at Sunday School and on all of the committees. She and Susan saw each other during the summer."

"Is Abigail still around?"

"She lives up on Bartlett Street. Would you like me to contact her?"

"That would be wonderful. I don't suppose . . ."

"You want me to try her now? Let me see if she's home." She rose from the sofa and rubbed at her hip.

"Are you okay?"

"Yes, yes. Don't tell my son, if you please. He's convinced I'm falling into disrepair."

"Your secret is safe with me."

She left to make the call, and I paged through the album. Susan was the one I'd come for, but the images of Finny, freckled and young, distracted me. His wide, goofy smile. His thin frame, hidden now under pounds of fast food and beer. Finny had always been quick with a joke and a smile at work, but these pictures showed me a young man with no shadows on his face, a happy guy with no dark secrets.

"You're in luck!" Mrs. Finnegan called. She appeared, a plate of cookies in her hands. "Abigail can see you as soon as she's finished with her knitting group. They knit blankets for refugees. I suppose the refugees don't mind the color schemes." She set the plate down and smacked her wrist. "Naughty of me. But they are *garish*."

"Mike sure was slim back in the day," I said, pointing to a photo.

"Oh, him and Bobby. That's from when they went fishing with my brother, Bernie. Mikey said fish were gross. He didn't like the way they felt, all slimy." She smiled. "He used to be a fishing pole himself, all elbows and knees. Took after his father." She leaned in and looked at the photos. "Of all of my kids, I think Susan's absence hit him hardest. Carol was starting her own family, and Dave was never close to Susan. Too many years between them. Bobby was close, and I know it was hard for him, at first. But he made peace with it. Mikey . . ." she shook her head, "Mikey won't know peace until we find and bury her, and even then . . ." She looked up from the page, her eyes small behind her giant eyeglass frames. "He thinks it's his fault. Because he made us wait to report it. But he didn't make her go. Susan chose to leave. That breaks my heart." She held her hand to her chest. "It does. But that isn't his cross to bear." She sighed. "He thinks I don't see how it eats at him. It made him a crazy parent, always worried for his own kids."

Really? My first months on the job, I didn't even know he'd had kids. There were no pictures. No stories. Nothing. Then, one day, Wright mentioned Finny's son, and I said to him, "You have a kid?" and everyone laughed.

"Have a cookie." She thrust the plate at me. "And can I ask you a question?"

"Sure." I took a cookie, to be polite.

"Do you have a boyfriend?"

The half-chewed crumbs got stuck in my windpipe. I coughed, spraying cookie bits all over the pristine room. "Oh, sorry." I gulped air. "Sorry. Let me clean up the mess."

"Not at all. I caught you by surprise." She picked up a crumb from the sofa and then said, "Well, do you?"

⚝

I saw what Mrs. Finnegan meant about the refugee blankets. The colors had to have come from the discount yarn bin. No one liked acid green and burnt orange. And together? Perhaps the blankets doubled as visual aids? Anyone wrapped in one could be seen from half a mile, easy.

"What a lovely blanket," I said. "Did you make this yourself?"

Abigail Waters nodded. "My knitting circle makes blankets for refugees." She checked me out. "Patricia says you're looking into Susan's disappearance. Has there been new information? A sighting?" She was all but drooling over the idea of a gossip scoop.

"Sorry, no." I wasn't going to tell her about Susan's pregnancy. "I'm told Susan helped out at church the summer before she went missing."

"Yes, she helped out with the kids at Sunday School and other tasks. She had a good eye for the flower arrangements. Many don't."

"Did she seem upset?"

"Upset?" She bit her lip. "No. She was a bit quiet, but she never was a rambunctious girl, not like some, and she was in church. She certainly didn't seem like she was planning to run away."

"Was there anyone at the church she hung out with, a friend?"

"Like I said, she helped with the children, and the flower arrangements and some of the mending. I know priests are men of God, but they are *tough* on linens. Susan could sew well. Not many her age did. Her mother taught her."

"Were there any boys who volunteered at the church?" I asked.

"The altar boys," she said. "Luke and Peter."

"Luke and Peter." Was there a Luke mentioned in the files? The name seemed familiar.

"Susan's age?" I guessed.

"Luke was. Peter was a bit younger. Fourteen, I believe." Would Susan have dated someone two years her junior? "I think Luke had a crush on her at the time. He seemed very upset when she went missing."

I'd look into Luke. Maybe he was our missing baby daddy.

"What were Luke and Peter's last names?" I asked. "I might want to speak with them."

"Luke Kelly and Peter Walsh. Luke's still local, but Peter moved to Alaska, of all places. Works on a fishing boat up there. I can't imagine."

"Did Susan go to confession?"

"Confession?" She recoiled as if I'd said a filthy word. "It's a sacrament, and it's between a person and God."

"And the priest," I said.

She harrumphed. "I didn't pay attention to when she went to confession, *if* she went."

I gave it up. It was a moot point. Confession was protected. I couldn't demand a priest tell me what someone told him, and the priest I wanted was dead. It had been a question prompted mostly by curiosity and a dark thought. What if the priest had been the one Susan had slept with? I blamed Wright. He'd planted the thought of an authority figure, someone older, into my brain.

My question had annoyed and upset Abigail Waters, so I thanked her for her time and made my escape.

Driving out of the city, with its frequent one-way roads and construction detours, my mind tried to get a grip on Susan Finnegan. A smart girl who helped at church, but who'd run away two years before, and who, as far as I'd found, told only one person besides the baby's father that she was pregnant. Susan was excellent at keeping secrets. Far better than most criminals I'd encountered. No wonder Finny had managed to keep his sister and her missing status hush-hush for so long. Keeping secrets was a family talent.

# SUNDAY, JUNE 13, 1999
## 1000 HOURS

Funeral services for Elizabeth May Gardner were held at the Congregational Church in Salisbury, the same church the Gardners had attended when Elizabeth had been alive, the church they'd attended less frequently in the wake of her disappearance, the church they left when they divorced. Now Mick and his former wife, Hannah, sat beside each other, only their upper backs and heads visible from the tall pew they sat in, up front near the giant photo of Elizabeth that was propped on an easel. There was no coffin inside the church.

Lewis wriggled on the cushion-covered pew and cleared his throat. He looked a little off. Must've had a stomach bug after all. Hope it wasn't catching. My toilet wasn't clean enough for me to hug it.

The church was three-quarters full. The light coming through the large windows was oyster-colored, gray with a rainbow inside it. The minister rose and began talking about Elizabeth and how she'd made it home, to the bosom of Christ, years ago. Only now were we able to share in that good news.

Lew turned to me and whispered, "Good news?"

I said, "He's going positive."

A woman behind us in a large purple hat shushed us.

Sure enough, the minister, rather than go Old Testament and discuss justice and retribution, went very New Testament and spoke of Elizabeth's eternal grace, of how she was delighting in paradise and having the eternal spring break everyone wanted but not all were invited to take part in.

I stared at the photo of Elizabeth. Her gap-toothed smile was hidden behind closed pink lips. Her hair was feathered and long, and she wore a blue sweater.

The minister introduced Regina, a cousin who was "like a sister to Lizzie." He invited her up, to read a poem in honor of Elizabeth. Regina's voice trembled as she read the poem's title, "Away," and its author, James Whitcomb Riley. She unfolded a piece of paper and read:

> I cannot say and I will not say
> That she is dead.—she is just away!
> With a cheery smile, and a wave of hand,
> She has wandered into an unknown land,
> And left us dreaming how very fair
> Its needs must be, since she lingers there.
> And you—O you, who the wildest yearn
> From the old-time step and the glad return,—
> Think of her faring on, as dear
> In the love of There, as the love of Here;
> . . .
> Think of her still as the same, I say:
> She is not dead—she is just away!

I'd heard that poem before, but with male pronouns. Regina sniffled into a tissue and made her way, unsteady, down the stairs to the second pew. Then it was time for more happy thoughts from the minister on why death wasn't bad, not really, not for the good people among us.

Lew's face was grim as he watched the family stand and proceed up the aisle, toward the doors. He said, "Let's get to the car." We'd driven in his ride. He'd complained that mine was filthy and smelled like the inside of a Marlboro pack. A funeral home employee gave us a flag to attach to our window, so traffic would recognize us as part of the funeral caravan.

"What'd you think?" he asked, cracking the windows. The air smelled of freshly mown grass.

"The poem was awful."

"I meant about the attendees," he scolded.

"I think they were sad, except for the minister. He seemed pleased as punch. Never knew anyone could be so delighted in the face of a murder."

"I meant, did you see anyone behaving oddly?"

"You're kidding, right?" I watched as mourners poured out of the church, toward cars, anxious not to be left behind. "You expected the killer to show up to watch the havoc he wrought? Maybe he'll be standing graveside, clutching a red rose." I snorted.

"Glad you think this is entertaining." He started the car, pushing too hard on the gas. He was gonna flood the engine.

"Oh, come on! You're not serious? You think we're going to find her killer here?" I waved my hand toward the people carefully picking their way to the cars in too-tight loafers and heels they rarely wore.

"Whatever. Just drop it."

We pulled out, to join the caravan as it wound through towns until we reached the cemetery. Fewer people made the trip to the grave. Large floral bouquets dominated a dark wood coffin. The parents made a strange tableau. Mr. Gardner stood alone. His new wife had her arm around his ex-wife, who was sobbing into a handkerchief. Mr. Gardner's face looked as if it was hewn from the same rock as his daughter's headstone.

Elizabeth May Gardner
July 15, 1959–April 16, 1979
Beloved daughter
And flights of angels sing thee to thy rest!

Interesting. They'd picked the date she'd gone missing as her date of death, though we were not sure the two were the same. And the quote was unexpected. Horatio's words to Hamlet as he lies dying, post-poisoning. How was Elizabeth like Hamlet? I was overthinking it, no doubt. They probably thought the phrase pretty. That's it. No more. It was a fault of mine to look for meaning everywhere. Used to drive wives #1 and #2 crazy. Wife #3 had been more forgiving of that fault, but less tolerant of others. Leaving the toilet seat up was, it turns out, grounds for divorce.

The minister kept the service very brief. People picked their way back to their cars, careful not to step on the grass under which the dead lay.

"Well?" I asked, when nearly everyone had gone.

"Well what?" Lewis said.

"See the killer lurking behind those gravestones?" I pointed toward two massive stone angels guarding headstones several rows away.

"Fuck off," he said.

"Jesus, take a joke."

"No, you show some respect." He walked forward, his right shoulder driving into me as he passed by.

"Whoa! What the hell, Lewis? What is up with you?"

He started to walk for the car, and then he stopped. Shook. He came back to me, his eyes all anger. "The baby has Down's."

"What?" What baby? What was he talking about?

"Our baby," he said. "The amniocentesis."

It hit me. His baby. Their baby. "Are they sure?" I regretted the words. Not helpful.

He made a face like he was chewing rocks. "Not 100 percent. They can't be. But it looks that way."

What would they do? Keep the baby? Terminate the pregnancy? Unbidden, my mind went to Susan, my baby sister, pregnant all those years ago. Willing to terminate her pregnancy so she could have a life. And then deciding against it. I'd never know why. Never know what drove her to make her choices.

We stood, a few yards from Elizabeth's grave. Workers came to lower the coffin. To cover it with dirt. To make it look like all the other graves in this place, its newness distinguishable only by the lack of moss on the headstone.

"What will you do?" I asked. The men worked quickly, ignoring us, talking sports. Just another grave, another corpse, another day.

"I don't know. Janice, she's so upset. I asked her if she wanted—" He shook his head. "She doesn't know. She's trying to digest it. We're both trying."

"I'm sorry if I was being an ass earlier."

He rubbed his face. "No. I'm snappy. The past day's been really tough. I hardly slept. It's not your fault."

"Sometimes I don't know when to shut my mouth."

His smile was tired and brief, but I saw it flash. "That's true," he said. "About a hundred percent of the time."

We walked to the car, the sound of dirt falling on Elizabeth May Gardner's coffin keeping time with our footsteps.

# MONDAY, JUNE 14, 1999
## 1600 HOURS

**M**y Y2K worst-case scenarios were on Mrs. Dunsmore's desk. She'd done no more than glance at them and said, "Better not be any sci-fi nonsense in here." Good thing I took out the zombies. "I'll look it over after I sort through this equipment mess," she said. Yesterday, somebody had taken delivery for twelve boxes from an electronics company. Turned out they were full of equipment we hadn't ordered. She was determined to figure out how the mix-up occurred and who'd signed the delivery sheet without checking with her first. I put my money on the new dispatch guy.

Finny and Wright were hunched over their desks, trying to track down their victim's ex-boyfriend. Apparently, there wasn't much to go on. They suspected he'd not used his real name. Or he'd disappeared into thin air after he left Salisbury. Either way, they were feeling it. I'd assigned Billy, Dix, and Halloway to help them. Wright had bitched about their capability, telling me that Dix was a "nice guy," but he couldn't make decisions. Not true. What Wright hated was that Dix asked him too many questions. Dix only did that because he was afraid Wright would chew his head off if he made an error. If I tried to point this out, Wright would deny it and we'd have wasted more time, so I kept my mouth shut on the subject.

Finny lifted his head and scratched his armpit. Then he wadded up a ball of paper and tossed it at Wright. It missed, but Wright looked up, his lower lip in a pout. Finny asked him a question, and Wright chuckled. Then Wright took a ruler from his drawer and smacked it into Finny's open palm. Finny took the ruler and held it to the front of his pants. Thank God his back was to the door. I didn't need some citizen with a parking ticket wandering in to see my detective measuring his dick, joke or no joke. Wright reached down and withdrew a tape measure. Pulled it out so it was a yard or more and held it below his desk. Finny howled.

The other men watched, shaking their heads and laughing. I walked to my office. The detectives were sleep-deprived and annoyed by their lack of progress. I'd let them make jokes, for now.

My phone rang. I snatched it up. "Chief Lynch."

"Mayor Mitchell, please hold."

Goddamn it. Mayor Mitchell had figured out that I didn't answer his calls, ever. Not when they came from his direct line. He made his secretary call me and then she patched him through to me. I hated being outwitted by that country-club-loving moron.

"Chief Lynch," he said.

"Mayor."

"What's this I hear about alterations to the police annual budget? As you know, we already approved next year's spending plan. Hope you're not looking to hire."

He loved to give me hell for hiring police, when the only times I'd done so was to fill vacancies.

"We're just running numbers in case this Y2K virus ends up affecting the community," I said.

"Y2K. Can't those computer nerds figure out how to solve that problem?" he asked.

"I assume they're working on it. Doesn't the fire captain have a plan in place for Y2K?"

"Perhaps," he said. Perhaps? Mrs. Dunsmore said he did, and if she said he did, he damn well did. Why was the mayor being coy?

"Would be terrible if a fire broke out and their software didn't work," I said. Not elaborating on what software I was referencing.

"It would," he said, concerned.

Excellent. Now he could call Captain Hirsch and demand details. This day wasn't a total wash.

"About that body recovered from the woods," he said. So much for him leaving me alone. "Are we certain it's a homicide?"

"Yes." Why ask him how he thought the body managed to get into a shallow grave?

"People keep talking about the ghost," he complained. "Now they're saying she's real."

"And what do you tell them?"

"That there is no ghost!"

"Sounds good to me," I said.

"No, what would be good is no more bodies, no more homicides." He referred to the murder of Cecilia North in summer 1997, and now this. Two murders in three decades? He had no idea how good Idyll had it.

"The body had been there for many years," I said. "It's not as though we've got gangs doing drive-bys on Main."

He went silent. Uh-oh. Silence meant he was formulating a response.

"Chief, the day we have gangs in Idyll, doing 'drive-bys' as you call them, is the day you'll be looking for employment elsewhere."

"It's nice to have job security. Have a great day, Mayor Mitchell." Click. If he thought I was going to let him make threats about my employment, he was dumber than I thought.

I stalked outside the office. Stood at the bulletin board, looking for something to distract me. Front and center was a green sheet advertising

Police vs. Firefighters! Annual Softball Tournament*
July 10th at NOON
*All proceeds benefit St. Jude's Hospital

For one second I fantasized about ripping it from the board and tossing it in the trash. But I didn't. I walked back to my desk and read a report about drug abuse and related crimes, or tried to. The report was drier than sand.

A soft rap on the door.

"Come in."

Wright came in, looking over his shoulder. Did he have an update on Susan? I wondered if anyone had noticed how much time he'd spent in my office lately. Hopefully they assumed he was updating me on the Elizabeth Gardner case.

"Hey," he said.

"Hey. Any news?"

"We're trying to get Donald, or Daniel, Waverly's sister to meet with us. She insists we come to her."

"Why?"

"She's running a business and can't step away from it."

"What's the business?"

"Antiques."

"If you have to go to her, do it. Just let Mrs. Dunsmore know, in advance."

He said, "Oh, I know. She's a damn grizzly about driving reimbursements."

"Any news on the other case?" He met my question with a blank look. "Susan Finnegan."

"No. I haven't had time. What with the other case and Joshua's baseball team. Now, Simone wants to take dance lessons. Speaking of family, I need to take time off Wednesday." He'd finished telling me how busy his caseload was, and he wanted time off?

"What for? You're my lead detective on this homicide. And according to you, none of the other men are capable of sifting through evidence, case notes, or finding their asses with their elbows." He'd said that of Halloway yesterday.

His face grew rigid. "Janice has another pregnancy test scheduled. I need to be there."

"Thought they only needed to test the pregnant person."

He crossed his arms. "I have more than enough time accrued."

"I'm sure you do, but you're in charge of a big case that's stalled. How often will you need to attend these tests?"

"It's none of your business what I do with my free time. I came in and asked, as a courtesy. I'm sure my union rep would back me. Should I give him a call?" Great. Pull in the union rep, and soon we'd be talking through lawyers about scheduling time for Wright to attend his daughter's dance recital.

"No," I said. "Whatever. Go to the test. Make sure Finny's in when you're gone, though, huh? I want someone who knows the case on call should something come to light."

He didn't acknowledge my request. He left, slamming the door behind him. Great. We were back to square one of our working relationship: mutually hostile.

# TUESDAY, JUNE 15, 1999
## 1130 HOURS

Rose Waverly's home, like London Bridge, was falling down. It had once been grand. An imposing two-story house with slate roofing and good, strong bones. Two columns in front should've lent majesty, but the columns looked as if they had rashes, gray spots appearing from below the flaked-off white paint. Knee-high weeds wrestled anemic yellow grass on the lawn. Two long tables, covered with oilskin cloth, stood on the lawn. The tables were covered with junk sporting colored stickers. A rusty egg beater was next to a bent spoon with a Disneyland logo. A roll of purple ribbon was propped atop an old white princess phone missing its cord. Water-damaged paperbacks were cluttered at one end of the table, beside a two-foot-tall doll with blue glass eyes and blond ringlets. The doll wore a blue flower-patterned dress and patent leather shoes. It didn't have a sticker.

"That costs twelve dollars," a voice yelled.

I looked up toward the house but saw no one.

"Twelve dollars is a bargain."

She appeared around the corner of the house, coiling a garden hose. She dropped it, half coiled, onto the ground. She patted her hands against her slacks and walked to me. Her face was big and round. Her orange lipstick matched her hair, which was askew on her head. She pushed it up and said, "Make a mighty fine gift for a little girl." When she got closer, I smelled something, strong, floral but piercing.

"I don't have a little girl." My daughter had left dolls behind years ago. Lewis looked at the doll with suspicion.

"Ah, well then." She lowered herself into the saggy-bottomed lawn chair by the table's end. "Just browsing?"

Two men dressed in suits, whose very bearing screams cop, and she asks if we're browsing? Either Rose Waverly had a very dry sense of humor, or she'd been born without a clue.

Wright took the lead. "I'm Detective Lewis Wright and this is Detective Michael Finnegan. We called earlier."

She groaned and moved side to side, trying to get comfortable. "That's right. So much for supposing you've got one of them big checks from Publishers Clearing House."

"Afraid not," Lewis said.

She wiggled in her chair and extended her legs. "What do you want to ask me about?"

Lewis cleared his throat. "As we mentioned, we want to talk to you about your brother, Daniel."

"Daniel? What's he done now?"

"Done now?" I asked.

"He was always getting into scrapes." She rolled her eyes.

"You grew up here together?" Lewis eyed the columns. One of them was crooked.

"Not here. Halfway across town. This house belonged to me and my husband." She stressed the last word. "He passed two years ago, Lord bless him." She looked at me from under lowered lashes. Hoo-boy, no. I was not looking for my next wife. Not here.

"I'm sorry to hear that. What was Daniel like as a boy? Did he play sports? Or keep to himself mostly?"

Her laugh was a short, sharp cough. "Daniel? He was always rambling. Liked to explore in the woods. Pretend he was some famous adventurer. He was goofy." She scratched her ear. "Me? I prefer air-conditioning."

"What about girlfriends? Daniel have many of those?"

That harsh laugh came again. "Daniel liked the ladies. Even from a young age. Used to flirt with the Avon lady when his voice hadn't so much as cracked."

"So, he had girlfriends."

"Sure. He was no Casanova, but he always had a date to the dances." Her tone made me think she hadn't had it quite so easy. "Of course, after it got out about Bridget, he found himself not so popular."

"Bridget?" Lewis asked.

"Bridget Cutterson. Nice girl. Rode horses. She and Daniel dated. Her sophomore year, his junior year. She got a busted ankle and claimed Daniel did it. He said she had a riding accident. Mr. Cutterson came by with his rifle and made threats. Our parents got involved." She waved her hands. "It was a kerfuffle."

"What happened?" Lewis asked.

"They broke up. Mr. Cutterson threatened to make it a police matter, but he didn't."

"Why?"

She rubbed her nose. "Dunno."

"What do you think happened?" I asked.

She flicked her gaze my way. Her eyes were bright green. "He probably did it. Like I said, he was a troublemaker."

"He hurt anyone else?"

"One of the other girls he dated, what was her name? Shauna. Shauna had a couple of bruises. Might've been Daniel, but it might've been her old man. He was a drunk. Everyone knew it. Sad, really."

"Did Daniel ever hurt you?" Lewis asked, his tone gentle.

"Ha! Me? Not likely. I used to beat the snot out of him when he was little. He was forever going through my things. He opened my diary, and I kept him in the closet until our parents got home. One time, he stole my bra. I found it in his room. I tied his hands together with the straps and locked him in the cellar. Nosy brat."

"You locked him in the cellar?"

"Just for a few hours, though I think he lost control of his bladder. I made him do *that* load of laundry. What a baby he was."

"And now? Where is he?"

She moved her wig again. "No idea. After our parents died and he left home, we didn't keep in touch."

"Does he ever visit?"

"Here? Hardly. He can't stand me. Says I made his life a 'misery.' Boy never could take a joke. I haven't seen him since 1978. What did he do, to make you come here and ask so many questions?"

"He might know something about a case we're working. Girl went missing in Connecticut. Turns out she was murdered."

"Murdered? How?"

"Sorry. Can't discuss details."

"Hmmm. You think Daniel had something to do with it?"

"We'd like to ask him some questions about it."

"He used to collect knives," she volunteered. "Set up a target board out back in our yard and would toss knives at it, hour after hour. One of the neighbor ladies complained it was dangerous. Her car got egged the next day."

"Daniel?" I asked.

"Probably. She called the cops, and they gave him a talking-to. Thought he was gonna wet himself all over again. He was such a scaredy-cat."

"Did he ever work in Connecticut?" I asked.

"I think so. Only because I got some paperwork once with his name on it. IRS looking for their tax money. Said something about land-scaping." Lewis flashed me a smile. Landscaping sounded like our boy.

"You ever get anything else for him?" Lewis asked. "From the IRS or anyone else?"

"No." She shuffled her sneakers in the grass. "Wait. There was one thing. From the Red Cross of all places."

A car stopped in the drive, and her head swung toward it like a vulture spotting prey from above. "Might be some buyers." She set her small hands on the lawn chair arms and heaved herself upward.

An elderly couple emerged from the car. The man squinted against the sun. The woman looped her arm through his, and they walked up the incline toward the tables.

"You better scat," she said. "I don't want any murder talk scaring 'em away."

"We need that Red Cross paper," Lewis said, crossing his arms. Making it clear he wouldn't leave without it.

"I'll fetch it for you. Promise." She made a cross over her heart, like a child would.

"One more thing. Do you think Daniel is capable of hurting someone, badly?"

She laughed. "That chickenshit? Barely. Only thing he ever truly destroyed was my Barbie collection."

The elderly couple skirted around the weeds, making a slow approach.

"Yeah. Little shit came into my room one day when I was at choir practice and ripped all the arms out of my dolls. You ever try to reattach a Barbie doll's arms?"

As a matter of fact, I had. My daughter, Carly, had once removed her Barbie's arm and then cried when she couldn't get it back in.

"Damn thing is impossible," she said. Experience told me she was right. You could never get the arm back in the socket. It just wouldn't fit.

## CHIEF THOMAS LYNCH
# TUESDAY, JUNE 15, 1999
## 0920 HOURS

The birds and sunshine woke me, both too high and bright. I'd fallen asleep in my recliner. My legs ached. I stood and rubbed my lower back, eyes bleary. That stupid dream. Matt kissing Ed Harris and me watching it all from the parking lot of a diner. The same diner I'd gone to with Finny and told him about his sister's baby. The place where painful secrets were revealed. Jesus. My brain was as subtle as a brick through a window. I stumbled into the kitchen and squinted at my answering machine. No messages. Over four days and Matt still hadn't called.

The oven clock read 9:20 a.m. Hell. I'd never been this late to work. Never. My fingers felt the stubble on my chin. I'd also never taken a sick day. Today was a day of firsts. Dix, who took the call, said he hoped I felt better soon. What to do next? I couldn't be seen rambling about town. People would talk, and it would get back that I had been 'active' on my sick day. I spent a long time in the shower's spray, my thoughts veering toward Matt. So what if he'd had a midnight visitor? I'd made too much of it. He could spend his time as he wished. I wasn't always available to spend time with him. And we'd never said other people were out of bounds.

Showered and dressed, I opened the door to a world that looked like it was dreamed up by an advertising executive. Sunshine, fluffy clouds, grass so green it looked fake, and people driving freshly washed cars at a reasonable speed. Lord. Some days it felt like I'd up and moved to a pretend TV community.

I drove to the gas station, filled up the car, and headed west. Getting home to New York took anywhere from two to three hours, depending on traffic. Stamford was always a tangle of brake lights. I turned the radio on and listened to a story about Boris Yeltsin surviving impeachment. NATO had stopped airstrikes on Belgrade, and Slobodan Milošević was indicted for crimes against humanity and war crimes. Cheerful stuff.

I drove to my parents' house, not sure that either would be home. It was a school day. Then I recalled that Mom had taken a sabbatical to write a book about Anne Brontë's heroes, so she wasn't teaching, only advising. Sure enough, she was home, a pen stuck in her semi-wild hair. "Tom!" She pulled me forward and down and hugged me like I'd returned from war. "What brings you here?" She pushed me back and peered at my face. "Is everything okay? Is anything the matter?"

"I'm fine, Mom." I patted her arm and looked past her. "Dad around?"

"He's teaching, and then he's got a faculty committee meeting, poor sod." Mom's speech included Briticisms when she wrote about them.

"I thought he'd sworn off faculty committees."

She laughed. "He tried, bless him. But it was rejoin the committee or let Old Klepper have a seat at the table." Old Klepper was a fellow philosophy professor my father loathed. He'd taken on an almost-mythic presence in our household. When things were broken or malfunctioning, we'd shake our heads and say, "Old Klepper's at it again."

"How old is Old Klepper?" I asked. "He must be ninety."

"He's seventy-six, only six years older than your father."

"Huh." Maybe it was the name. He'd been "old" to me for so long that I assumed Klepper was ancient.

"What brings you here?"

"Can't a son surprise his mother?" I countered. "Nice flowers," I said, noting the bouquet on the dining table. "Dad do something wrong?"

"It was a thank you from a colleague. I caught a typo before his book went to print."

"He sent flowers?" Seemed excessive for a typo.

"The typo was on the cover. Have you had lunch yet? I've got some leftover pastrami from Loeser's."

"Ooh." Idyll might have its charms, but a good pastrami sandwich wasn't one of them. I grabbed the mustard and pastrami from the refrigerator. "Where's the bread?"

"Here." My mother handed me half a rye loaf.

She poured me a glass of ginger ale and set out a plate. It felt like I'd come home after school, and she was fixing me a snack. "Thanks," I said. Seated, with my mouth full of delicious pastrami, I hummed contentment. "Idyll's ideas of deli meats are piss-poor, and don't get me started on the bagel situation."

She patted her hair. Felt the pen and pulled it from her updo. "One of these days I'm going to impale myself."

"Please don't. We'd have to keep explaining to Dad that you're dead, and that would be awkward." My father was absentminded. He'd once famously returned from the park without my younger brother. Nowadays, he'd be in serious trouble for that. Back then, a neighbor just brought John home.

"How's things?" she asked as I chewed. "How's the house coming?" She found it amusing that I'd become handy in my middle age. It certainly wasn't anything she or my dad had passed on to me. As New Yorkers, they believed any and all problems were the building super's area of expertise.

"I should tackle the bathroom next, but it's gonna take forever. And I don't have a second one, so I'd be without one while it's renovated. You know, if you ever came and visited, you could see for yourself."

"I'd love to," she said.

I stopped chewing. "Really?"

"Don't talk while you're eating."

I finished my bite and said, "Sorry. You're really going to come see my house?"

"Of course! We've been waiting for an invite for two and a half years."

"Waiting?" Since when did my family wait to be invited?

"Sweetie, I respect your privacy. We thought maybe you wanted to get settled, or maybe you were ashamed of your big-city family." She pouted.

"Right." I didn't buy that act for a minute. "Hey, did you and Dad ever have . . . a misunderstanding?"

"Ha!" The laughter erupted from her. "Oh, you're serious. Sorry. Honey, why? Did you and Matthew have a disagreement?"

I'd leaned backward, in my chair. "Uh-huh."

She patted my hand. "All couples fight and have misunderstandings. It's the human condition. Plus, your father's an idiot at times." She gazed at me with so much love I had to duck my head and look at the bread crumbs on my plate. "Did you mess up or was it him? Because he seems *perfect*," she said.

"Hey!"

"I was kidding, sort of. What you have to do—and you're going to hate this, but listen to me: You have to talk."

"Talk."

"About your feelings."

"Sounds like therapy."

"Communication is the bedrock of a good relationship. That and sex."

"Mom!"

She laughed. "You're too easily embarrassed. When we visit, we should bring you a housewarming gift. What would you like?"

"More pastrami from Loeser's."

"Done."

"Bagels, too."

"Of course."

I turned my head and sneezed. "You getting a cold?" Mom stood up. She hated germs.

"No. Allergies. Idyll is filled with things that are trying to kill me, slowly."

"Your grandfather had hay fever something awful."

"Really?"

She smiled. "He used to say Nature was out to get us all."

I glanced at my watch.

"You got to be somewhere?"

"Habit," I said. "I should be at work. I played hooky."

"You played hooky?" She looked scandalized. "I don't think you've ever missed a day of work in your life. You're too much like your father and me." Huh. I always thought John was their mini-me, the child formed in their image, what with his academic career and heterosexuality. She did the creepy mother mind-reading thing, and said, "You always worked hard, even at things you didn't like. John would give up on things he wasn't good at. You'd plug away at them."

"Feels like I'm plugging at the moment."

"On what?" She got up and brought the cookie jar from the counter to the table. I opened the lid and peered in.

"Are those rugelach? From Zabar's?" I ought to play hooky more often.

She smiled. "I'll send you home with some if you don't eat them all now."

I didn't have a big sweet tooth, but I made an exception for Zabar's rugelach. "You know what's wrong with Idyll? No Jews. There's no good smoked meats or rugelach." I hadn't quite put my finger on it before. But it was clear to me that Idyll's lack of diversity crippled its food production.

"You were telling me about what you're plugging on."

"Was I?" Ah, hell. What could it hurt to tell her, and for once, my work didn't involve murder. "Missing person case."

"Another?" She meant like last year, with Cody Forrand.

"This is recreational."

"Recreational Missing Persons." She enunciated each word carefully. "Why not take up golf?"

"Because I'd run into Mayor Mike every other day."

"You know, you talk about Mayor Mike the way Dad talks about Old Klepper."

She wasn't wrong. "I guess we all have our Old Kleppers." I finished my cookie. "If you really want to hear what I'm working on, here goes." I told her about Finny's missing sister, about her pregnancy, about our mistaken assumption she'd died during surgery, and then the revelation that she'd given birth to a baby boy.

She asked, "Is it possible she died after giving birth? It happens."

"It's possible, though the Boston cop who found the birth certificate was smart enough to look for a death certificate with the same name she'd listed, and he found nothing. Finny's going to see someone in charge of the home soon. If she died while there, he'll find out."

"But you don't think she died there?" she asked, measuring my expression.

I shrugged. "It's possible. It would explain why she was never in touch. But why was there no death certificate? Plus, we have no idea who the father of her baby is, and it's making Finny crazy."

"No ideas?"

"There were a few boys questioned." I summarized those interviews.

She scratched between her eyebrows, her thinking face on. "It was 1972, and her parents would've been shocked, but do you think she didn't tell them about the pregnancy for a reason?"

"What kind of reason?"

"Maybe she felt ashamed, or knew that revealing who the father was would get him in trouble?" She frowned. "Or her family in trouble?"

"How would her family get in trouble?" I stopped. "What if . . .?"

"What?"

"Well, the neighborhood. According to Finny, it had a lot of Mob activity back in the day. Supposing she slept with one of those boys, it's possible she'd worry about her family. Her brothers find out and go after the guy, and then maybe their 'associates' go after Susan's brothers."

"Would she have hung around those types?" Mom seemed doubtful.

"If the neighborhood was full of 'em . . . I'm sure she wasn't allowed to fall in love with one of them, but that doesn't mean it didn't happen."

"Fall in love, huh?" She smiled. "You always were the romantic."

"Me?" I snorted.

She pushed another cookie toward me, "*You*." I bit the cookie in half. "Now what about the guy at Bunker Hill?" she asked.

"What about him?"

"You mentioned she backtracked to go to the monument."

"Yeah."

"Why?" My mother had never shown interest in my work. Certainly, she'd never wanted to puzzle through a case with me before.

"Maybe she was saying good-bye to the neighborhood historical landmarks before she left?" Out loud, it sounded nuts.

"Or maybe she went to see him."

"The ranger?"

"Anyone else there?"

"No, but we know she didn't leave with him. She made it to a corner store later."

"Where it looked like she was waiting to meet someone, right?"

How did it play out? Susan stops by the monument to tell him she needs a place to stay overnight before she has the abortion? He closes up the monument and meets her later? It seemed like quite a stretch.

"It could've been one of the altar boys," I said.

"Maybe Susan was inspired to lust by the sight of those surplices the altar boys wear."

"If Nana could hear you," I said, "she'd be shocked."

"Oh, she hears me."

"She's dead."

"Mothers never stop listening." She grabbed a rugelach from my plate. "Remember that."

# THURSDAY, JUNE 17, 1999
## 1400 HOURS

Gracie's Place for Unwed Mothers used to be in Dorchester and was affiliated with St. Ann's Hospital, where they sent their "girls" to the maternity ward. Six years ago, it moved to Brighton, incorporated into St. Ann's Medical Center's Women's Health Pavilion. The word *pavilion* made me imagine a world's fair, but nothing about the place looked like that. It looked like an administrative unit of a hospital. There was that Lysol smell and the floors shined. Inside, there were lots of women. Many in chairs, waiting, but some behind desks, answering phones and handling folders and scheduling appointments. I waited only five minutes in the company of all these women before I was escorted down the hall by a tall young lady named Beth. She brought me to the director's office.

I merited the director of the home? Well, well. My heart was all pitter-patter. Would she tell me Susan was dead? Surely that could be the only reason a director would be required to speak with me.

"Detective Finnegan," she said, standing behind a large desk covered with papers. On the neat scale, it fell between mine and Lew's desks, skewing closer to Lew's since there were no food crumbs on it.

"Ms. Hoskins."

We shook hands and she said, "Please, sit."

I sat. Waited. She sat and drew in a breath. "I must say I was surprised to hear of all this. I became the director eight years ago, so of course I wasn't around when your younger sister, Susan, came to the campus."

"No, I didn't think you were." Ms. Hoskins was my age. When Susan was there, Ms. Hoskins was probably in college.

"I've had a time finding the records. Sadly, organization of files isn't our number one priority, and it shows. But I was able to get my hands on her admission form." She set her hands atop a folder. It had a label on it, typed on a typewriter and attached with tape. The tape was nearly orange with age. *Susan Shaughnessy*, the label read.

"She used our mother's maiden name."

"Yes. I'm still surprised they didn't get the truth out of her." She met my steady stare. "Lots of girls came into the home with false names and grand stories. The staff tried to help them by getting them to face the truth of their circumstances so they could best decide how to move on. Your sister must have been an accomplished . . . story-teller. She came here in October of 1972 and gave birth at St. Ann's Hospital in April of 1973. She stayed five and a half days in the hospital, and then left."

"Left? You're sure?" I leaned so far forward I nearly tumbled off the chair.

"Yes." She examined my face. "Oh, did you think—" She put her hand to her collarbone.

"Yes."

She leaned forward. "I'm so sorry. No, your sister was fine when she left us. Her pregnancy went well. She had a bit of a crisis afterward. Her blood pressure dipped very low, but they gave her oxygen and she bounced back. She was healthy when she was released."

"It's just, we never heard from her, after. I have no idea what happened to her."

"I'm sorry." She nudged a box of tissues my way. "I truly am. We discharged her from the hospital on April 11th."

"Wait. Did someone have to accompany her? To bring her home?"

"Yes. We don't let the girls leave on their own. In extreme circumstances, where the family relations were irrevocably broken, we might allow a friend to pick her up. Or the father of the child."

"Who picked her up?" It wasn't me, or my brothers. Not Carol or our parents. So help me God, if it was Lucy, I'd bawl her out. But no. Lucy hadn't known.

"I don't know." She opened the folder and turned pages. "Here it is." Her eyes roved the page. She blinked. Scanned it again. Shook her head. "It says she was released to her brother, but the signature is illegible."

"Her brother?" No way. "May I see?"

She hesitated. It was a medical record. There were rules. She turned the sheet so I could read it. Sure enough, the form said Susan had left the hospital in the company of her "older brother." The scrawl was unreadable. A series of peaks and valleys that looked more like one name than two. But it wasn't David's signature. That much I knew.

"Could I get a copy?" My mind was at work. Older brother. Likely the father of her child had been older than her. I'd taken it for granted, but now that fact seemed confirmed.

"I really can't—"

"Ms. Hoskins, I've been looking for my sister for twenty-seven years. Until recently, I assumed she was kidnapped and murdered." She winced. "Then I discovered she was pregnant and thought she'd bled to death on an abortionist's table." She bit her lip. "It's very unlikely that my sister's story has a happy ending. And the person who acted as her 'brother' may be the person who knows what happened to her, who made it happen."

"If she's still alive . . ." she said. Still trying to do her job and protect the privacy of my sister's medical files.

"My sister was many things, Ms. Hoskins, including, as you noted, a gifted storyteller. But she wasn't cruel. There is no way that she ignored my parents for over twenty years, that she missed my father's funeral, that she chose to cut us out of her life completely."

She looked at the file. "And yet she told none of you about the baby. She could've stayed at Gracie's Place and been in touch." Her words stung like lemon in a fresh cut. Yes, Susan could've told us she was safe and sound and pregnant and living mere miles from us, and she hadn't. It made us look like monsters, like we wouldn't have cared for her in her condition. And it hurt, oh God, it hurt.

"I'd like to talk to the girls who were there at the same time as Susan."

"I'm afraid that's impossible. Patient confidentiality. Plus, many of those girls elected to give their babies up for adoption. Several of them hid the pregnancies from family and friends. We can't share their details." Her tone was certain.

"What became of Susan's baby?" I asked, switching topics.

"It was adopted," she said.

"By whom?"

"Detective, I'm sorry, but I can't reveal those details. I know you must have a lot of questions, and I want to help, but the system—"

"Give me the discharge sheet, and I'll go." I stood, a half-promise.

"What?" My sudden shift, my quick bargain threw her, as I'd intended.

"Give me a copy of the discharge sheet, and I'll leave. No questions about the adoption asked."

"Well, I . . . one moment." She had a copier in her office, a large machine that made a mechanical hum when it started. It took a minute to get the copy. I folded the sheet in half and carried it out with me.

The women in the waiting room looked to be exactly where they were when I'd left them. I spared them a brief glance before striding outside. In the parking lot, my brother Bobby sat at the wheel of his minivan, drumming his fingers against the steering wheel. He always did that when he was nervous.

"Well?" he asked.

I closed the door and settled myself into the seat. "She didn't die in the hospital." I handed him the discharge paper. "Some guy picked her up from the hospital. Claimed to be her older brother."

"Her brother?" His outrage was tangible. He read the sheet, slowly. "What the hell does that say?" he asked.

"The signature? Hell if I know. Dickhead probably scribbled on purpose so he couldn't be found."

"But we'll find him," Bobby said, the words less a statement than a question.

I looked at him, my baby brother. His face getting fat, his middle expanding in the same way Dave's and mine had before him. We all started skinny and wound up pudgy. Look on the bright side: We all had our hair, mostly.

"We'll find him," I said, because I was the older brother and had to say such things, and because, for the first time in a long time, I hoped it was true. Maybe we could find Susan, after all these years.

# FRIDAY, JUNE 18, 1999
## 1945 HOURS

**M**y cell phone rang from inside the house. Where had I put it? The mechanical ring stopped. I found the phone in my bedroom. One missed call. I checked the log. Matthew Cisco. My eyes scanned the digital letters, searching for meaning. He'd called once since I'd last seen him, at his house, with a young guy in boxers looking on. Once. But no voicemail.

I carried the phone with me to the kitchen, where I was assembling dinner. A ham sandwich that made me long for New York delis. I layered the ham slices on the bread and grabbed some spicy mustard from the fridge. One thing you could say about the people of Idyll: they loved their condiments. You could walk into a store and find a whole shelf devoted to chutneys, and don't even get me started on jams.

My sandwich made, I sat at the kitchen table and sorted my mail. Always a fun activity. Bills, fliers, a catalog from L.L. Bean (how had I gotten on that list?), and a notice about the annual Police vs. Firefighters Softball Tournament. Damn. That was in three weeks. Had they even practiced? Tried hitting a ball or two? Probably they avoided talking about it in front of me. Jerks. I could see some of the guys voting to exclude me. Some of them assumed I'd see their bodies in motion on the field and be unable to control my insatiable man lust. But some of them knew better. Had those guys even tried to convince the others? I mean, Hopkins on third? Maybe they wanted to lose.

I ate the sandwich and wished I'd bought chips when I was last at the grocery. I'd been eating healthier. Or trying to. And why? Because when I looked at Matt's body and I looked at mine, I got worried. Never mind I was almost ten years older. I washed my dishes and limited myself to one beer, which had 154 calories. Then I sat in my recliner and mentally reviewed what Wright and Finny had told me of their case. Looked like Elizabeth Gardner's ex-boyfriend, Donald aka Daniel Waverly, was abusive. He'd threatened her. She broke up with him. Wright had shown me her diary. The relevant passage:

> *Donald said he'd rather see me dead than dating another guy. He said I'd regret leaving him. I told him that it's over, and that he should never contact me again. Tonight, the phone rang three times and every time Dad answered, the caller hung up. I think it was Donald.*

Unfortunately, Wright and Finnegan's number one suspect had disappeared. Their last known information on him came from 1982, when the IRS sent forms to his sister's house about back taxes owed. The forms showed he'd worked a landscaping job in New London. Finny said his sister, Rose, was supposed to fetch more mail that might provide a better address, but neither he nor Wright seemed optimistic about her doing so.

They'd spoken to neighbors, who'd lived in Woodstock, and the picture of Daniel Waverly they painted was disturbing. One neighbor caught young Daniel harming a stray cat. Another saw him setting fire to a doll that belonged to his sister. And several complained he'd bullied girls. But he had no criminal record. Just the never-lodged complaint that he'd broken a prior girlfriend's ankle. "Not that abuse victims always notify the police," Wright said. He should know. His issues with abusers told me his mother had been hit, often. No other way to explain his hatred for domestics.

On top of my cracked side table were notes on the park ranger from Bunker Hill who'd spoken to Finny the first day he canvassed the neighborhood for Susan. Gus Saunders. Gus had been twenty-two years old when Susan went missing, and he'd worked at the monument for a year. Enough time to get to know her and impregnate her. Gus now lived in Kansas City. Inconvenient for interviews. Gus had a criminal record. Assault with a deadly weapon. It landed him in prison for six months. The guy he'd assaulted was a known thug with a temper. They'd fought outside a bar, late at night, over remarks made about a Boston Bruins game.

Had Susan fallen in love with that idiot? Gotten pregnant by him? Gus didn't get into his fight until 1974, so he would've been around to check her out of the hospital, pretending to be her brother. Finny had told me about that, certain whoever had checked her out of the hospital had to have been the father of her baby. He was also convinced the same guy killed her. Why else would she disappear?

He didn't consider she'd rather go away, live another life, than return to the family home in Charlestown. Then again, no contact in twenty-seven years was extreme unless her family life included abuse or trauma, and Finny was adamant it had not. "Unless you count attending Mass weekly a trauma." As someone who had done that for sixteen years of my life, I was willing to consider it.

We had two cases of missing women. Elizabeth Gardner and Susan Finnegan. One found murdered and buried in a shallow grave. One never found. One with an abusive boyfriend. One with a boyfriend we knew nothing about. One who'd had her arm removed. One who . . . we had no idea. Simply no idea of where Susan's remains were, if she was even dead.

Unable to make headway, I decided to work out. I changed clothes and headed for the ships room. It was a guest room that had once had sailing-ship wallpaper. Mentally I called it the ships room even though I'd removed the wallpaper and painted the walls a flat white. I was as bad as the locals. Referring to places by their former owners' names. Like the Old Graham place. Was I turning into one? Getting picky about blueberry pie and expecting to see chutney on the shelf next to the jams? As I lay against the bench and lifted, I realized I'd never be a local. Not even if I lived here fifty years. Locals were born, not made.

The house was quiet, the only sounds my huffed exhalations and the clank of metal as I lowered the bar down. When I stood, my heart beat against my chest, hard and steady. I lowered into squats and counted. A hard burst of sound brought me up from a squat, fast. Someone was knocking on the door.

Matt stood on the side porch, his shoulders sagged inward. His face was aimed toward my backyard. I wondered if the robins were out there. I opened the door. The suction sound it created made him turn toward me.

"Hi."

"Hey." He stepped to the side and back. "Can I come in?"

"Of course."

He came in, knocking his boots against the riser. He knew how much effort I'd put into rehabbing my kitchen floor. "Working out?" He'd clocked my outfit, and my sweat.

"Finishing up." I poured myself a glass of water. "Can I get you a drink? Beer?"

"Nah." He sat at the kitchen table. Perched his elbows on the surface, and said, "About the other night."

I remained standing. "I shouldn't have assumed—"

He held up a hand. "No, look, we never talked about it, and you have a key, so I can see where maybe you thought . . ."

"Yeah." I rubbed the back of my neck. "I get it. You're right. We never had a conversation, and, truth be told, I'm not surprised."

"By what?" He was alert.

"That you'd want to play the field, so to speak. You're young and incredibly hot. I don't expect to be your one and only. I mean, I didn't even give you my letterman jacket."

He grinned. "Do you have one? Have you been holding out on me?"

"I did, once upon a time. Haven't seen it since I graduated. I'm guessing it's long gone or one of my nephews has taken it because it's retro cool."

"You're not upset?"

I had been. I hadn't wanted to, but I had been. "I'm not. You want me to give your key back? Maybe prevent future incidents?"

He said, "Nah, just call next time."

"I can do that."

He stood.

"You leaving?"

"Well, I thought maybe you wanted to finish your workout. I kind of barged in on you." Not as bad as I had the other night. I could see his thoughts had gone there, too. "Not that I'm—"

"It's fine. You had dinner? You want to grab a bite to eat?"

"I had a late lunch." He patted his abs.

"Hey, there is something you can do for me."

"What's that?"

"You played baseball in college, right?"

"You're looking at the pride of Puerto Rico, baby, right after Roberto Clemente, and Ivan Rodríguez."

"And Roberto Alomar and Edgar Martínez," I said.

"Don't forget Jorge Posada."

"I never forget Jorge." I was a die-hard Yankees fan. Posada was an outstanding catcher *and* a switch hitter.

"Okay, so maybe I'm not the pride of Puerto Rico, but I can outhit the idiots on my league team," he said.

"That's what I'm counting on. I need batting lessons."

"Batting lessons?"

"It's been forever since I played."

"When are you playing? Oh, is it that town matchup against the firemen? The one where they routinely decimate your department?"

"Maybe."

"Well, you've been giving me poker lessons, so I think I can repay the favor with some hitting tips."

"Great."

He looked at the papers spread on my floral loveseat and atop the cracked table. "Case?"

"Looking into a cold one for a friend."

"When's the softball game?" he asked.

"Three weeks." I held up the postcard from the mail.

"We better get to work," he said. "Three weeks isn't much time."

"What, now?"

"Sure. I know of some batting cages that stay open until 10:00 p.m. Let's go." He stood, certain in his decision, eager to start.

I hesitated. Why? "Sure thing," I said. Unsettled by my gut. This was what I wanted, right?

# MONDAY, JUNE 21, 1999
## 1030 HOURS

"God, why are these so blurry?" Lewis complained. I didn't answer. He was looking at the photographs of Daniel (Donald) Waverly that Elizabeth's mother had mailed to us from San Antonio. Six snapshots in all. Three of Elizabeth and Daniel. One of Daniel alone. The other two were of a group of friends that included Daniel. The quality of the photographs wasn't great. Eyes were red, faces blurred, and none of them gave us what we wanted: a close-up, perfect image around which to build a murder investigation. To be fair, no one who took those photos in 1978 and 1979 realized these pictures would be used this way. I held my breath. Lew had been grousing since he set foot indoors. I wouldn't be the one to ignite his short fuse.

"We should use the one of him and her on the porch," I said.

"Only decent one in the bunch," he muttered. He snapped his head up and asked, "His sister give us anything?"

"Says she's still looking. Says there's a lot of paperwork in the house."

"I'm surprised she hasn't tried to sell them," he said. "Did you see she was selling old copies of *TV Guide*? Who would buy old copies of *TV Guide*?"

"You guys want old copies of *TV Guide*?" Billy asked. I locked eyes with him and shook my head, silently telling him to get out of harm's way. Across from me, Lew rifled through his desk. "Who took my stapler?" he roared.

Billy mouthed "thanks," and walked to the other side of the station.

"It's by the phone," I said.

"Oh." Lew glanced at the stapler like it had betrayed him by appearing where I'd said it would be. "Guys are always stealing it."

I went back to completing a report of a burglary from a car parked on Oak Street. I'd been out there at 8:00 a.m., interviewing Mr. Stottler about the roll of quarters and music CDs he'd lost as a result. He seemed more upset about the quarters than the CDs. Maybe because the CDs belonged to his wife and, according to my notes, were "terrible pop music that makes you want to jam a screwdriver in your ears." While Lewis was getting his coffee, I'd been in the trenches, listening to Mr. Stottler's opinions on music, the neighborhood, and, inexplicably, khaki pants. Mr. Stottler hated them.

After completing the report, I decided to reward myself with lukewarm coffee. At the coffee table stood Billy and Jim. "Where's Jinx?" I asked Jim.

"Day off. Injured ankle. Was doing a sniff test near the dump and got stuck in a hole. Wrenched his paw out. It's a bit swollen, but nothing permanently damaged."

"Poor dog. Should we send flowers?"

"Try treats, or tennis balls."

"What's up with Wright?" Billy whispered. "Thought he was going to decapitate someone over that stapler."

"He's got some home issues, so go easy, yeah?" It was as much as I could say without betraying his secret.

"We all have home issues," Jim replied. "You don't see us yelling like lunatics over office supplies."

I took my coffee to my desk to find Lewis gnashing his teeth over a Department of Motor Vehicles report. It must have come up empty.

"How was this guy driving a truck for a landscaping company without a valid license?" he asked. I didn't ask who he was talking about. It was Daniel Waverly. Everything was these days.

"He might've gotten a fake one. He wasn't using his real name in Salisbury." As aliases go, the jump from Daniel to Donald wasn't much, but he may have grown more creative. "No Waverlys?" I asked.

"None that fit his age range, except one. Timothy Waverly. He had a license issued in Old Saybrook in 1985, but he's dead now."

"Could still be our guy."

"He was black."

"Or not."

"How's it going, detectives?" Chief Lynch asked. He seemed sunnier than usual. Had he learned something about my sister? No. This was a different face.

"We just discovered Daniel Waverly didn't get another license with his last name in the state of Connecticut," Lewis said, his voice tight.

"That's too bad. What name was he using when he worked in New London?"

"His own," I said. "That's how the IRS caught up to him."

"You've been in touch with the landscape company?"

"Went out of business twelve years ago," Wright said, rubbing his brow, aggrieved. "They've got nothing for us."

"Did he have any hobbies?" Chief asked.

"Photography," I answered. "That's how he met Elizabeth. At some photo club near the college she attended."

"Maybe he kept at it."

"And?" Lewis said.

"And so maybe there's a photo club in or around New London that he belonged to. Also, you have to drop off film to develop photographs. And the equipment is expensive, or was, back then. Maybe a developer or camera store recalls him."

"Great," Lewis said. "I'll get right on calling every camera parts store in the tristate area." Wow. His insolence was going to land him in hot water.

"Make one of your lackeys do it," Chief said. "That's why I gave you additional support." Smiling, he walked off, hands in his pockets. Disaster averted, for now.

"It's not a terrible idea," I said.

"I know that." He seemed pissed off, all the same. "Billy!" he shouted. "We need you!"

Billy approached with caution, ready to be snapped at. "What's up, detectives?"

Lewis said, "I hear you're excellent on the phone."

Billy looked from Lewis to me. "Um, yeah? Who do you need me to call?"

"Every photography club and camera store in Connecticut, starting in New London. We're looking for anyone who might've encountered Daniel Waverly."

"Okay. Is there a list?" Billy's face didn't change. He looked as hopeful and expectant as ever. God love him.

"No list," Lewis said.

"Check local colleges," I suggested. "They might have photography clubs."

"With co-eds," Lew said, snapping his fingers. "Good thought."

"I'll be over there," Billy said, pointing to a desk near dispatch.

"Okay, thanks," Lewis said. Billy left. "He never bitches," he said his voice full of wonder.

"Billy is the best of us," I said.

"No, he's the *nicest*," Lew said. "Doesn't make him best."

※

"Maybe we should check the military," I said.

"Come again?" Lew asked, rubbing crust from the corner of his eyes.

"Our guy just ups and disappears for years. Could be possible it's because he joined up, went overseas."

"Kind of a stretch. Though he is violent. Military likes violent, in certain conditions. Hey, Hopkins! We need you to contact military personnel records."

Hopkins's groan was audible across the station. "Why?"

"Because we need to find a murdering son of a bitch," Lew called.

Hopkins came over, and I explained what we wanted, and how many names we needed checked. He made a point of writing it down in his notebook. Smart ass. He walked away, to make the request. We heard him say, "Guys there are gonna think I'm the local retard, can't get the guy's name right."

"What did you say?" Lewis asked, his voice cutting through the station chatter. Conversations halted mid-speech. People turned and looked. A UPS guy by the front door froze.

"What?" Hopkins said. "That you're going to make me look like a retard in front of the military folks? It's true."

Lewis stood. Oh no. I could see it. All his pain and anger over his baby's diagnosis was wrapped into what Hopkins said. And the lummox had no idea. How could he? Shit. Lewis was going to hit him. He'd get to him faster than I could and . . . shit, the chief was out of his office now. Lewis would get suspended for sure. Lewis hurried for Hopkins. Fuck. I jumped up from my chair, and Billy charged into the fray like a bull who'd spotted a red flag.

"What did you say?" Billy poked Hopkins in his chest with his pointer finger. I swear he left an impression in Hopkins's torso.

"What's your beef?" Hopkins asked, eyes wide. Billy never confronted anyone. Well, except when he enraged the chief into declaring he was gay.

"My beef? My beef is with you using that word," Billy said.

"What word?" Hopkins was leading with his jaw. Not a good move. Lewis was still looking to punch him, and Billy hadn't given an inch.

"You *know* what word. My cousin, Jake, is slow. I hear someone call him that word, there's going to be problems." Billy wasn't shouting, but he wasn't quiet either.

The UPS guy looked all around for someone to sign his form, but everyone was watching Billy and Hopkins.

"I didn't call your cousin a retard!" Hopkins wailed. "I was just—"

"Don't use the word again," Lewis said. He'd come up behind Hopkins. Hopkins turned, his face red. Lewis raised one finger. "Don't," he said, so quietly I strained to hear.

"Okay, guys, enough," the chief said. He clapped his hands and said, "Back at it. Someone sign for that damn package." He pointed to the UPS guy. "And don't use the term that was bandied about a moment earlier. It's insensitive and rude. We don't only uphold the law. We uphold standards, including standards of civility and respect."

Hopkins said, "Okay, okay. You fellas wanna back off?" A bead of sweat rolled from his brow to his neck. Lewis took a step back and Billy stepped aside, waving Hopkins before him.

Lewis looked at Billy and said, "Mike was right. You're the best of us, Billy."

Billy looked like he'd seen Santa Claus in person. He nodded, unsure what to do. Lewis clapped a hand to his shoulder and patted it twice. "The best," he said. Billy blushed and ducked his head.

The UPS deliveryman asked, "Can someone sign for this package?"

# TUESDAY, JUNE 22, 1999
## 1900 HOURS

The baseball pitching machine spat a ball at me. Right over the plate. Matt had said he'd give me more coaching, but he'd cancelled an hour earlier. When I'd pressed, he said, "I'm busy. Sorry. I can't see you, and, um, don't drop by later." He had company. No, he had company he'd dumped me for. I swung hard and whiffed it. Jesus. Damn machine handed me a home run on a platter, and I couldn't nail it.

"You swung early," Wright said.

"Thanks, Sherlock."

We'd agreed to meet at the batting cages. I'd invited him to my place first, but he'd demurred.

The next pitch came in low. I struck it with the tip of my bat, and it swept short and low.

"Too slow on that one."

Five minutes of Wright's eagle-eyed observations were driving me to thoughts of violence. "I have a bat in my hands."

"And?"

"Maybe you should keep your comments work-focused, yeah?"

He sighed. "I looked into the altar boys at the church, Luke Kelly and Peter Walsh. Luke had a girlfriend when Susan was volunteering at the church. Doesn't rule him out."

"Nope." I swung hard and whiffed the next two pitches. Matt would despair of his coaching if he could see me now. Not that he could. It was one thing to arrange another date, but then tell me

about it, in his roundabout *I'm busy, don't stop by later* way? That was
bullshit.

"What rules out Luke Kelly is that he's infertile," he said.

"Infertile." I smacked the next ball, high and away. It had been a
meatball, but still. "How do you know that?"

"He told me. Turns out his two kids are adopted."

"You sure?"

"He sent me copies of their paperwork."

"Why?" That seemed excessive. And excessive volunteered information always made me suspect that there was a secret the person was
trying to hide by misdirecting attention elsewhere, like a magician.

"He seemed troubled I'd try to lay that baby at his doorstep. Said
Susan was a nice girl, but she never seemed interested in him. He got
the impression she had eyes for someone else."

"Peter Walsh?"

"Peter, or Petey, as they called him, was two years younger than
Susan. He says she treated him like a little brother. Taught him how to
dance."

"Sounds like romance."

"Sounded like she was doing him a favor," he said.

The next pitch went high, and I swung for it even though I knew
better.

"Give me the bat." Wright removed his jacket. While I stood, away
from the plate, he rolled up his shirt cuffs and removed his tie. He held out
his hand as a ball whumped past. I slapped the bat into it, none too gently.

"Get closer to the plate." He demonstrated, by stepping to it.
"You're treating it like it's a woman," he said. "Try not to be afraid of it."

*Oh, funny. I hoped he choked on this pitch. I hope he did a damn pir-
ouette chasing its tail.*

Wright squared himself at the plate, tapped it twice with the bat,
and said, "Come to Daddy." The machine spat a low pitch, and Wright
laid into it, knocking it clear and far. An outfielder would be hard-
pressed to get it. The next one came in perfect, and his bat cracked
against it, sending it into home-run territory. *Fuck. He's good.*

"Of course, we play softball, so the ball is bigger, and the pitches are slower," he said, "So maybe that's more your speed."

"The softball-pitching machine is broken," I said between clenched teeth.

"Turns out our Petey is also unlikely to have been romancing Susan, as he was too busy. He had two summer jobs, altar boy duty, and he helped his elderly grandparents with their shopping."

"Good boys don't always stay good," I said.

"Petey did provide an insight, though. He said Susan was dropped off twice from a Ford Mustang. He recognized the car. Belonged to a neighborhood bad boy."

Wright kept hitting them out of the park, one after the other. It would've been beautiful if it had been anybody else. He set the bat down.

"This bad boy have a name?"

"Jack McGee."

"Bullshit," I whispered.

"No, that's his name."

"No, I mean that's what Mike wrote, Finny wrote, on his interview statement. He wrote 'bullshit.' Jack claimed he was working on his car the day she went missing, and I don't think Mike believed him."

Bullshit. Like Matt leaving me alone at the batting cages while he kept company with some younger guy. I'd told him it was okay, but I was wrong. It wasn't.

"Maybe his instincts were good. We should follow up," he said.

I grabbed the bat. Got closer to the plate. Bided my time. I let one pitch go past. Then swung hard at the next one and connected. Line drive to first. No home run, but no strike either.

"Better," Wright said. A phone rang. He glanced around. Realized his jacket was a yard away and hurried to retrieve his mobile. I kept swinging. "Yeah, I'm on my way. . . . I am. . . . I know. I said I would. . . . No, honey, I'm—. I am. I know. . . . I understand you're under a strain. I do. I'll be there," he glanced at his watch, "in twenty minutes. . . . No. I had to stop off at the dry cleaner's. I forgot. Yes. . . . Okay. See you soon. Love you." He snapped his phone shut. "I've got to go."

I didn't look his way. "If juggling this case with the other is too much, you can drop it. I want you focused on the Gardner case."

"I can do both."

"Sounds like you might be stretched." I swung and missed. *Damn it.*

"I can do both," he said, his voice tight. "I'll look up Jack McGee. See if he has a criminal record."

"Okay." My next hit went high and far. I turned to smirk at Wright, but he was walking away, my batting average gone from his mind. He had other things to think about, like the people waiting at home for him.

Me?

I had nothing but time on my hands.

## CHIEF THOMAS LYNCH
# THURSDAY, JUNE 24, 1999
## 1230 HOURS

Finny burst into my office, his face pink. Had he run here? What had happened? Had he found Susan? Or had he and Wright managed to find their chief suspect, Daniel Waverly?

"You dick!" he shouted. "You let the entire neighborhood know Susan got knocked up. That she had a baby."

"Wait. What?" I hadn't done that. I hadn't. When I'd spoken to Abigail Waters I hadn't breathed a word about Susan's pregnancy. And I hadn't told . . . Damn it. Wright. When he'd asked the altar boys about their relationships with Susan, he'd revealed that she'd had a baby. He'd told me as much.

"Now my brothers and sister are fielding questions about my sister from classmates they haven't spoken to in twenty years, and how she was easier than everyone thought, and how come we don't know who the father of her kid was."

I couldn't tell him it wasn't me. I'd have to absorb the blowback and ask for forgiveness.

Wright stormed into the office. "What's going on?"

Finny turned to Wright. "This jackass just told everyone in my old neighborhood that my baby sister was a slut."

I stood up. "Hold on, now."

"You're denying it?" Finny said. "Jesus, Chief, you can't even admit to your own mistakes? No wonder they wanted to be rid of you in New York."

That hurt, so I said, "Watch your tone, Detective! You're two seconds from suspension."

"Where have I heard that line before? Oh right, when you were handing me ultimatums earlier. I bet the mayor would love to know about that exchange."

"It was me!" Wright yelled. "I told your neighbors."

Finny, full of steam, didn't register what he said. "And another thing, if you think I'm gonna keep quiet about the North case—"

"Mike, stop! He didn't tell them," Wright said. He pointed to himself. "I did."

Finny reared back, his flustered face uncertain. "What are you talking about?"

Wright sighed and rubbed his face. "I revealed that Susan was pregnant when I spoke to some boys she knew from back then. Luke Kelly and Peter Walsh."

"Luke? Peter? Wait. What? Why are you looking into Susan's disappearance? Did he tell you?" He waved his arm at me.

Wright clucked his tongue. "You really give me no credit, Mike. You think I didn't know about Susan? That I haven't seen those pictures in your wallet? I'm not stupid. No matter what you think."

"You knew?" Finny asked.

"Of course, I knew! You're not exactly a pro at keeping secrets, and you left a scene behind you in Boston. I have a buddy in the police department there. You're known. Okay?"

"Instead of asking me about it, you go behind my back with him?" Again, the pointed finger my way, the reference to me as "him," as if I was below naming. "You didn't think to ask me before you went poking in my life, before you revealed to everyone that Susan was knocked up at sixteen?"

"She's dead!" Wright shouted. "She doesn't care about her reputation. Why are you so concerned with it?"

Finny lunged at Wright. Wright sidestepped, too late. Finny punched him. The blow glanced off Wright's jaw. "How dare you!" he screamed. "I didn't tell everyone your secrets!"

I ran around my desk. Finny was swinging at Wright. Wright cupped his jaw, stunned. I stepped between them, and Finny's next punch landed on my ribs. "Oof." I pushed him back and held my arms out. "Stay back!"

He stood still. His face was red, and he panted, shallow breaths. "I didn't tell people about your baby," he yelled at Wright. "How would you like that, huh? If I told everyone your baby has Down's?"

Wright lunged, and he caught my side as I tried to intercept him. His weight threw me off balance. I stumbled and fell, knocking into my desk. Thump. I hit the carpet. My vision went gray. Ouch. I touched my head. Ow! Everything went white. A low buzzing sound started up. I couldn't see. Ow. I tried to sit up, but kept leaning too far over.

"Oh, shit," one of them said, low and quiet.

"Back off." That was Wright. "Chief, you okay?"

I moved my neck. My head hurt. My vision was clearing, like a windshield clearing snow with wipers. I stood up, holding the desk as I elevated myself. A wave of nausea passed through me, and I gagged. Hot liquid at the back of my throat. I choked for a second and swallowed it back down. Gah. That was nasty. My throat burned from the acid I'd ingested. Wright's arm was under me, supporting me.

"I'm fine." I stepped away from him. My vision blurred again, and my knees buckled.

Finny said, "Chief, your head is bleeding. You knocked it on the way down. I think you need a doctor."

I waved my arm, or tried to. It felt wrong, like the movement was slower than it should be. "I don't need a doctor." Was my tongue thick? That was odd.

"You do," Wright said. "You're bleeding, and you're not steady on your feet."

Way to rub it in. "It's your fault." When he opened his mouth to protest, I said, "The two of you. If you hadn't come in here screaming and scrapping, my head wouldn't have connected with the desk. Just bless all the saints you can name that Mrs. Dunsmore isn't here." *Thank God. She'd hold me responsible.* A burst of pain made me groan.

"Chief?"

"I'm fine," I said, but that wasn't true, because I could feel more vomit damming near my esophagus, and then it was out of me, splashing on the floor and my shoes.

"Call an ambulance," Wright ordered. "Now!"

I didn't argue.

In a surprise move, it was Wright who insisted on accompanying me to the hospital. He was the one to override my objections that I didn't need an ambo or a doctor. He was the one who threatened to call Grace Dunsmore right this minute if I didn't shut up and do as the nurse asked once we were inside the ER.

They flashed lights in my eyes and asked me all sorts of questions like who the president was. "Clinton," I said. What day was it? Where was I? Did I know how I got to the ER? Could I count backward from ten? Yes, yes, I could do all of those things, but did the lights have to be so bright, and could they please *stop* touching my head. The cut I'd endured required cleaning and a butterfly bandage, but not stitches. "Am I gonna have a scar?"

"You must be feeling better," Wright quipped.

"Why?"

"Your vanity is intact and on display."

"This is your boyfriend?" the nurse asked, nodding at Wright. I don't know why the question surprised me. She knew my name and had probably read one of many articles announcing my "First Gay Police Chief" status.

He looked ready to jump out the window. "No," I said. "I have taste."

She laughed and then touched my head again. I swallowed a yell. "How's the nausea?" she asked.

"Better." Mostly true. I hadn't thrown up again, and my stomach felt steadier, if not steady.

"When you're released," she said, "You'll need to go home and rest." This last was delivered in a firm tone. "I mean it. No going back to work. Your brain got a wallop, and it needs to relax. You have a slight concussion, so you'll need someone to check on you each hour, to make sure you're conscious and well." She glanced at Wright.

"Not it," he said, quickly.

I closed my eyes. I wanted a nice dark room. "As if I'd pick you."

"Do you have someone who can stay with you? If not, I can see if we can scare up a bed." She sounded doubtful.

"I can find someone." I didn't want to call my family. They didn't own cars, and my parents would make a fuss. John would have to come to my place, and it would be a whole thing. I could hear the stories he'd tell about the time he had to mind me because I'd bumped my head. Nope.

It was another hour and a half before I was allowed to leave. We had to wait for someone to read my scans and make sure my brain wasn't going to . . . what? Explode? Whatever it was, it seemed I was safe.

Billy chauffeured me home, with Wright in the backseat, handling the questions.

"What happened?" Billy asked. "We all heard shouting, and then it sounded like fighting, and the next thing we know an ambulance shows up and you two get in it."

"We were discussing the Gardner case," Wright said. "Working out how the crime might've taken place. Chief was playing the victim, and we had a slight mishap. He tripped and hit his head on his desk. Concussed himself."

Oh, that was rich. I played the victim and was klutzy? Not Finny and Wright were fighting like children, and Wright assaulted me and I got injured?

"That's not what Finny said," Billy said.

Uh-oh. We hadn't thought about Finny, about the fact that we hadn't coordinated stories. Too late now. "What did Detective Finnegan say?" Wright used his best "detective" voice.

"Not much. Said you tripped Chief as a joke and he hit his head. He left right after you guys. Haven't seen him since."

"He was joking," Wright said, his tone making it clear this was the official version and no further questions were allowed.

I wondered where Finny had gone to but gave up because thinking hurt.

They tried to assist me into my house, and I barked at them that I was fully capable of walking into my own home. Then I dropped my keys trying to open the door, and after Billy got the door open, I tripped on the riser into the kitchen. My language turned blue.

I headed for my recliner. Collapsed into it. "You can leave now!"

Billy looked around, eyes stopping on every ancient artifact that had come with my place: floral loveseat, misshapen homemade key holder, avocado-colored fridge. "It's true," he said, under his breath.

"Who should I call?" Wright asked.

I met his stare. He wasn't leaving without a guarantee that someone would come and watch me, as if I was a damn child.

"Matt's number's on the fridge," I said, each word costing me.

"Great." He stalked to the fridge, grabbed the card, and picked up my phone.

"You have trouble seeing, Chief?" Billy asked, eyes on the giant phone numbers.

"Previous occupant," I said. He flipped a light switch. "Lights off!" He flipped it again. "The light hurts my head."

"Oh, sorry. You got quite a bruise," he said. While Wright murmured into the phone, Billy asked, "Did it really happen that way? You were practicing the crime, and you tripped?"

"Yes." I closed my eyes. The nausea had passed, but I felt shaky. Like I was on a boat. I wasn't great on boats.

"You can't?" I heard Wright ask. "Are you sure? Okay. . . . Okay. No. I'll figure it out." He lowered his voice.

"You need me to stay?" Billy asked.

Oh, God. Matt couldn't or wouldn't come. Billy wanted to play nurse. I opened my eyes. He was gazing at me with pity. It made me itch. I hated pity.

Wright picked up the phone and pulled a card from his wallet.

"Who are you calling?" I called. My hoarse voice broke.

"Let me get you some water." Billy leapt up and headed for the
kitchen cupboards. Wright kept his back to me. I couldn't hear what he
said. God help him if he was calling Mrs. Dunsmore. I'd go back to the
hospital before I'd let her play nursemaid.

Billy gave me a glass brimming with water and asked, "What's with
all the boxes?"

I lifted my head. Did I have any evidence lying about? Interviews?
"Just sorting through old stuff," I said. "Spring cleaning. A little late."

"I hold onto stuff, too," he said. "Mom calls me a pack rat, but what
if I want some of that stuff someday to show to my kids, or it becomes
valuable?" I pictured Billy surrounded by baseball cards and G.I. Joe
figures. I closed my eyes.

A hand shook my shoulder. "Hey, wake up." It was Wright. He
looked tired. His jaw was shadowed with a faint bruise. That's right.
Finny had hit him, earlier, in the office. I'd forgotten.

"Where's Billy?"

"Sent him back to the station. I'll hang here for a bit until my relief
comes."

"Who?"

He didn't answer. "Those the other boxes?" he asked, pointing.
I hadn't given him all of Finny's stuff on Susan. Only the pieces that
seemed most relevant. I nodded. My head felt thick.

"How many fingers am I holding up?"

"Four."

"Fuck you," he said.

I smiled. It had been two, and I knew it was two, and he'd said
"fuck you" like we were buddies, like I wasn't his gay boss, whom he
loathed.

"Hey, was that true? What he said about your baby?" I asked.

Wright's face had a way of closing. It reminded me of watching
bodega owners pull down the roller shutters over their stores at night,
the distinctive sound that accompanied the motion. I heard that sound
now, seeing his face change.

"Yes."

"What are you going to do?" I asked. Raising a child with special needs was no joke. He already had two kids.

His Adam's apple bobbed when he swallowed. "Janice has decided to continue the pregnancy."

"And you?"

He said, "I—"

The sound of the door opening stopped him. We both looked to the kitchen, to see Damien Saunders enter, a leather duffel bag in hand. Was he going somewhere?

"Damien?"

"Looks like the patient is awake and alert," he said.

The patient. Me. He was coming to watch me. Wright walked to Damien. "Thanks," he said. He'd called Damien? How'd he known? How had he guessed that Damien would come to watch over me?

"I'll let everyone know you're okay," Wright called. "Stay at home. Two days. I'll tell Mrs. D. you're not to be in the office before then." He left.

"Traitor," I muttered.

Damien dropped his duffel on the kitchen floor. "I like what you've done with the place." He'd visited over a year ago. Had seen the house in its mostly original form.

"It hasn't changed much," I protested.

"Oh, I'd say it has." He glanced at my recently refinished hardwood floor, but I had the sense he was discussing another topic altogether.

"How are you feeling?" He leaned in to take a look at my eyes and to touch the wound on my head with his long fingers. He looked good and smelled like . . . mint.

"Confused."

His face got alert and worried. "How?"

I leaned forward, tugged at his jacket, and said, "like this," before kissing him.

# THURSDAY, JUNE 24, 1999
## 1730 HOURS

**D**amien tasted of mint. He sighed low, in the back of his throat, as we kissed. Then he pulled away. "Wait."

"Why?"

He stood up and stepped backward. Shook his head. He looked a little fuzzy, like I felt. "You're in a relationship."

"An open relationship."

"Since when?" He grabbed my water glass and went to the kitchen. Refilled it and brought it back.

"Since I found Matt with another guy."

"Oh." He cleared off papers from the table, exposing the crack in the glass. "What happened?" He sounded pained. He owned the same table. It was a collector's piece.

"I might've smashed it."

"After you found Matt with another guy." His words were wooden.

"Yes."

He sighed and grabbed a kitchen chair. Brought it into the living room and sat opposite me. "I thought so. Look. Thomas, I like you, but I'm not going to be your weapon in this war."

"What war?"

"The one you're waging against Matthew Cisco."

"I'm not; we're fine."

"Uh-huh."

"I'm sorry, then."

"Sorry for what?"

"Kissing you," I said.

"I'm not," he said. His eyes were so blue. "But I'm sorry you did it because you're angry at Matthew. If you ever kiss me again, I'd want you to do it because you want to kiss me." He held up his hand to keep me from rebutting. "Let's let it go, for now. How are you feeling?"

"My stomach has stopped heaving. My head aches."

"They give you something for it?"

I waved a prescription form that Wright had left beside me. "Need to get this filled."

"I'll do it," he said. "Pharmacy in the center of town?"

I nodded. "Can you get it filled without me?"

He stood. "I don't want to leave you long, but do you need anything else? Food, drink?" He walked to the fridge and peered inside. "The answer is yes. Any requests?"

"Morphine."

"Not one of the major food groups." He grabbed his car keys and said, "I will be back in a half hour. If you get sick or feel ill, call 911. Do not be a hero and die of a head injury." He left.

My head ached. The throbbing made it hard to do anything. I tried TV, but it was too bright and loud. Eventually, I closed my eyes and then the throbbing stopped.

"Tom. Tom." I felt a tickle on my cheek, like a feather. Why was there a feather? "Wake up, Prince Charming. Or do you need a kiss?"

"You said we couldn't," I murmured. I turned my head and opened my eyes and saw Matt. He knelt before me, his dark brows slashed downward.

"I told you what?"

"Nothing," I said, pushing myself upright. "I was dreaming."

He peered at me. "How'd you get injured? Your colleague, Wright, was short on details."

"Bit of a scuffle in my office led to an accident. I tripped and hit my head on my desk."

"That massive thing?" he asked. "No wonder you had to get your skull checked out."

"I feel better."

"Right. Explains why you're wincing. Sorry I couldn't come right away. I was on duty, and then—"

"It's okay. I understand."

"I was worried when I got that call," he said.

My head's throb was back, and I felt like part of it was triggered by Matt. I had thought he wasn't coming. I had kissed Damien. I had punched my glass table. I thought we were headed down a path that forked, and now? He was here, worried.

The kitchen door opened. We both turned to see who was visiting. Damien untangled plastic bags in his hands "Hey, I didn't know what you wanted to eat, so I got—" He looked up and stopped. "Oh. Sorry. I didn't realize you had company."

"Hey," Matt said.

"I got your meds," Damien said, handing me the small waxed paper bag from the pharmacy. "Do you need water?"

"Got some," I said, gesturing to the glass Billy had given me.

An awkward silence fell, broken only by me ripping open the bag and rattling the pills in the bottle. After wrestling the childproof cap without success, Damien said, "Let me," but Matt was faster. He grabbed the bottle from my hand and opened it. "How many?" he asked.

"The instructions are on the label," Damien said.

"One," Matt read. He handed me a single white capsule and rotated the pill bottle. "Don't drink alcohol while taking this. Don't operate heavy machinery." He read in a robotic voice.

I swallowed the pill with a mouthful of water. The capsule was large. It felt as if it was lodged behind my breastbone.

"You okay?" Damien asked. He must've noticed my slight gag. I nodded.

"Thanks for your help," Matt said. "Think I can take it from here."

My eyes went to Damien. He'd gone rigid. His bright eyes sought mine. Whatever he saw there made him say, "Okay. Don't let him sleep for more than an hour without waking him to check that's he's responsive. Ask him the date, the president, and what he last ate. Check his pupils."

"Got it." Matt had his arms crossed.

"Okay, then. Thomas, I hope you're feeling better soon."

"Thanks for coming," I said. He grabbed his duffel and was out the door. I heard the low rumble of his car start.

"What the fuck!" Matt yelled. His shout made me recoil. My head still throbbed.

"*Shhhhh*," I said.

"You invited *him* over?"

"No, Lewis did."

"Lewis?"

"Detective Wright. He was with me when I hit my head. He called you, but you couldn't come so I guess he called Damien next."

"Why's that?"

"Because we're friends."

"Friends?"

"Are you jealous?" I still felt wobbly, but I stood. I didn't like him looming over me. "You've got some nerve. I thought we weren't exclusive."

"We're not exclusive because you're still two-thirds in the closet. Touching you in public is forbidden. Heaven forbid anyone know that their gay chief of police is actually, you know, *gay*."

"I sent you flowers at *work*. I introduced you to my *family*. I was, I am, trying to get over my public-affection thing, but I've never been that way. And how dare you criticize me after you fuck whoever you want and blow off dates?"

"What dates?"

"The batting cages."

"The batting cages? That's helping you with homework, not a date."

My head throbbed. "Like teaching you poker isn't a date, but I notice you didn't seem to mind that."

"You think I'm stupid, that I didn't know you've been talking on the phone to him? The other day? Claiming you were talking to Dix? You weren't."

Fuck. He knew. "I should've told you the truth, but I was embarrassed. He's been helping me, with relationship advice. He told me to order the flowers." The second the words left my mouth, I knew they were wrong. "I wanted to do right, but I'm not good at this stuff."

"You talked about me to him."

"He's my friend. I'm not exactly up to ears in them around here. You have family, you have tons of guys at work and the neighborhood."

"He isn't your friend, Thomas. He wants to sleep with you. He's been angling to do so ever since he met you."

"That's not true."

"You're even dumber than you look."

"Get out." My whole life I'd been the dumb one of the family. He knew that. If he'd spent months analyzing hurtful things to say, he couldn't have done better. "Now."

Matt assessed me. "Who's gonna watch over you?" He hesitated, as if the question mattered.

"Out. Now."

He slammed the door behind him. My skull juddered as if it, too, had been handled roughly. I collapsed back into the recliner, the chair rocking under my sudden weight shift. I cradled my brow on the heel of my palm and inhaled and exhaled.

I had no one to check me for brain injury. Maybe it was knowing about Lewis's baby, with its diagnosis, but I didn't assume any longer that I *would* be okay, that something might not be wrong. I needed help, so I stumbled to the phone and dialed.

"Suds." The background noise made Nate difficult to hear.

"Nate, it's Thomas, Thomas Lynch. I need help."

# FRIDAY, JUNE 25, 1999
## 0945 HOURS

Lewis gave me a twenty-yard stare, though he sat three feet from me. What had I done now? I popped another salted peanut in my mouth and considered not asking. Let him stew in his broth. But that wasn't my way. "What's up?" I asked.

He didn't shift his eyes my way. "Nothing," he said in the exact tone each and every one of my three ex-wives used when I'd ask them that question. "Nothing" meant I was supposed to know the answer; that I wasn't supposed to need to ask.

"Cool." Another peanut went into my mouth.

His gaze drifted to me. "Why'd you have to go off, big guns blazing?"

"Look, I apologized for throwing that punch." Lew's jawline was blue-purple with bruising. He hadn't shaved today. He always shaved. He was hiding the bruise, from the others, forestalling their questions.

"You should apologize to the chief," he said.

I set my plastic tube of peanuts down and said, "I'm not the one that sent his head into the desk." Lewis's stare could set the paperwork afire. "Fine, I might've provoked you, and I'll apologize as soon as he's back in the office."

"You could stop by his house."

"You want me to bring him flowers? When did you become his biggest fan? Wasn't two days ago you were bitching about him and his memos."

"He's a thousand times better than Stoughton ever was, and you know it. He didn't give you grief when you showed up at our girl's crime scene. And he isn't going to tattle and suspend you or me for fighting in the office when you know he has every right."

I did know that. I'd thrown a punch back in Boston and gotten automatic suspension and a review. They made me talk to a shrink. There were forms in triplicate and whispers. Guys talking, speculating about what set me off. I could've told 'em. One of the cops tasked with finding my sister had referred to her as "a lost cause," so I'd punched him. Didn't think about it. My fist formed and met his face before I had a chance to evaluate the decision. I'm not proud, but I'm not ashamed either. It was a move that made me leave Boston, and I needed to leave because I was tired of seeing Susan in places where she wasn't.

"Detectives," Billy said. He had three sheets of paper in his hand. Lewis perked up. Ever since Billy had nearly punched Hopkins over saying "retard," the kid could do no wrong. Not this month, anyway. "I think I might've found some leads."

"Leads?" Lewis repeated. "As in multiple?"

"Maybe. I called around to camera stores and photo-developer places. There was one in New London that seemed possible. It was two blocks from where Waverly lived."

"Still in business?" I asked.

"Still run by the same guy. He remembered that there was a man who came in pretty regular. He'd check out camera lenses. Didn't often buy anything but he liked to talk shop. He sounded like he was the same age and build as Waverly."

"He give the owner a name?" Lewis asked.

"Donald."

"Not his real name," I said, "but the name he used in Salisbury."

Billy looked at his papers. "Yeah, so the place sold camera parts, but it also transferred film tapes to VHS."

Lewis and I exchanged a look. Film? What was this about film?

"Owner says Donald was really interested in this service. Said he had old footage he'd shot on a Super 8 camera, and he'd like to have it transferred. But he didn't want to hand over the reels."

"Why not?"

Billy looked like we'd asked him the meaning of life, and he'd come up short. "I don't know. I asked him, and he said Donald asked if he could learn how to do it himself. That he offered to help out at the store in exchange for training."

"Owner take him up on it?"

"He did. Gave him a few lessons in exchange for moving some inventory and unloading supplies. Seems he'd thrown out his back that season and needed help. But then one day he comes in late on a weekend, after he'd closed the store, and he finds Donald in the dark-room, making prints. He was upset and asked how Donald had got in. Seems Donald had a spare key made off the original. Guy yelled at Donald. Donald apologized. Said he'd come in to transfer some film to VHS, and he was working on making prints as an anniversary present for his parents."

"His dead parents," I said.

"If it's our Donald," Lewis observed.

"Right. Owner kicks him out and never sees Donald again," Billy said.

Damn. That abrupt ending took the wind out of my sails. "What, never?"

"Nope. But he said Donald left a film behind."

"What's it of?" Lewis asked.

"Owner said it's mostly footage of a girl."

"That it?" I asked.

"Yup. He didn't finish watching it, said it was pretty boring and not well shot."

"And he threw it out," I said. Because of course he had. It would be too much to hope Donald aka Daniel Waverly had shot video of Eliza-beth Gardner and this store owner still had it in his possession years later.

"No, he still has it," Billy said.

"Really?" Lewis was as surprised as I was.

"Yeah, and he said he'd transfer it for us onto VHS."

"When can we get it?" Lewis asked, standing. He reached for his jacket.

"I was going to ask if I could fetch it now," Billy asked. "Do you think that's okay? Or do you guys want to go?"

"We'll go," Lewis answered. He glanced at me. "Hurry up." Like I wasn't on my feet, coat in hand, waiting on him.

The inside of Stan's Cameras reminded me of a jewelry store. Only instead of diamond rings behind the glass, there were lenses and cameras and flashes and battery packs. I'd never been much of one for photography. Did I still own a camera? Nope. Pretty sure ex-wife #3 took all the electronics, including the coffeepot. And she didn't drink coffee.

Lewis spoke to Stan, the owner, a small man with a comb-over that brought tears to your eyes. Why bother grabbing those six strands of hair and pulling them over his freckled scalp? Who did he hope to fool? He wore an outfit that reminded me of Mr. Rogers from TV, a cardigan over a button-up shirt and tie, and sneakers. He'd told us he was finishing the transfer of the 8 mm film now. He'd looked at the pictures we brought and confirmed that *yes, that man was Donald.* Lewis asked more questions about Donald. Where did he work? *Landscaping company.* But we knew that. Where he lived? *Around the corner.* Close enough; it was two blocks over. If he had a girlfriend? *Yes, he talked about a Stacy once. He had to leave to pick her up for dinner.* Stacy have a last name? *Sorry, no. It was so long ago. I only remember Stacy because that's my sister's name.*

"Let me just pop to the back and have a look," Stan said.

While he was in back, the door opened, and the bell over it jangled. A harried woman entered, hair a tangle, tentative. She saw us, and shied away. "Stan here?"

"He's in the back," Lewis said.

She stepped around us and looked at the lenses farthest from us.

Stan came through, a VHS tape in hand, and cried, "Ah, Sherry. I have your lens. Came in yesterday. Just one sec."

He got the package and produced the lens. Much shop talk ensued about apertures and f-stops and shutters. My eyes stayed on the tape. Maybe we could just grab it and go? Lewis cleared his throat, quietly. Sherry and Stan stopped talking, swung their eyes his way.

"I should be going," Sherry said.

"Nice seeing you," Stan said.

Damn. I couldn't do that. Make people hop to it with a cleared throat or cocked brow. Lewis could. The chief could. Me? I needed a club or a gun to make people do that, and I didn't enjoy using either.

"You have a video player." Stan made it a statement as he handed me the tape.

"Actually," I said, "It's busted."

"It is?" Lewis wrinkled his nose. "When?"

"Since a kid on a station tour stuck a pencil inside it."

"We arrest him?"

"Nope. Turns out we can't incarcerate eleven-year-olds."

"You have a video player we might use?" Lewis asked.

"Of course. In back."

"In back is perfect." Lewis started walking before the owner could disagree.

In back was full of inventory in various states of packed and unpacked, plus machines for transferring film. A tiny space to the right was marked "Darkroom."

There was only one chair. "I'll stand," Lewis said. Stan slipped the tape into the video player. The bell out front jangled. "I need—" Stan said.

"Sure thing," I said, eyes on the screen. "Go take care of it."

Stan hurried away, ready to sell cameras.

The screen showed snow at first, just black-and-white streaks. Then it was outside, a bright day. And then a girl was in frame. If we hadn't known the footage was old, her outfit would've been a dead giveaway. Peasant blouse and bell bottoms and clogs. She smiled and waved at the camera. "Closer," a voice said, from the video, a male's voice, the person shooting the film.

"Daniel," Lewis said.

Elizabeth smiled and walked closer. We'd seen photos, of course, and her rotted corpse and skeleton arm, but nothing had shown how she was in life. Here she smiled, revealing that gap between her teeth. Her laugh was low-pitched. She twirled and cried, "Wonder Woman!" Her blouse billowed as she spun.

The screen went to snow, and then Elizabeth was all dressed up in a green dress, her hair pinned up, lips bright pink, dangling earrings nearly kissing her collarbone. "Yeah, just there. Stop. Smile!"

Elizabeth did as commanded, but then she fidgeted. "Are you done?" Her voice both plaintive and annoyed. "We'll be late."

The camera suddenly filled with a cowboy boot and gravel. He must've lowered it. Furious whispers. The words "why" and "nag" the only ones I was sure of before there was footage of Daniel and Elizabeth, she still in the green dress. People milled around them, drinking and laughing. He wore a bolo tie and sports jacket. There was the cleft chin, the dark curly hair. "Give it back," he said, hand outstretched. "That's enough."

"Let him take our picture," Elizabeth implored, kissing Daniel's cheek.

"It's a film, not a picture," he corrected.

"Pedant," I muttered.

Another few seconds and then we were outside again, and Elizabeth was taking pictures, aiming her camera at the sky, then at trees. "Let's go," he said, voice terse.

"Just a couple more minutes." Elizabeth didn't turn around. It was winter. She wore a long gray coat and pink hat. They'd broken up in late February.

"Camera got shaky," Lewis complained. True. The next footage we watched was less stable. Elizabeth was so far away I wasn't sure the speck was her. But then I saw she stood outside the house the Gardners had lived in before the parents split and moved. We'd seen pictures. Elizabeth was fuzzy.

Then it was closer but a different day. She walked along, never looking back.

"He's taping her without her knowledge," Lew whispered.

"You think?"

She turned, a quarter-turn, and the footage went to pavement, as if the camera had been lowered abruptly.

She was in a car with a girlfriend, next, laughing and singing, "I Will Survive." The camera shook. And then went black. We waited for more. Nothing, not even snow.

"Is it over?" I asked.

Lewis looked at the video player for information.

Snow appeared again.

"Looks like it," he said. He leaned forward to press eject.

The screen filled with Elizabeth, wearing jeans and a jacket, carrying her camera. "That's Scoville Sanctuary!" I shouted. We'd visited the site. We knew what it looked like. "That's her car!" Her car, parked near the entrance, found hours later, when they began searching for her. The camera followed her as she walked up an incline. Her camera was down, at her side. She didn't know he was behind her. She was utterly relaxed, walking, humming. You could hear it. Very softly, she was humming.

And then the camera got close enough to show her jacket had a small tear in the back, and those were Sasson jeans. A loud snap made her turn. Her face, scared, eyes wide. "Don—"

And then it was a blur as it sped toward her, the screen all hair, and a crash, and "Ah!"

"He hit her with the camera," Lewis said.

She was on the ground, touching her head, scrambling backward. He'd hit her with the camera. Why hadn't they found her blood there? It was spring, it was muddy but . . .

"Don't," she said. "Don, don't." She had got to a half-crouch, her camera abandoned on the forest floor. Her hand was at her skull.

"You stupid bitch." His voice was hard and cold and disgusted. "You'll pay."

And then all we saw was mud and rocks and a bit of cowboy boot as he grunted and she screamed and then it was silent, so fast it felt like another blow. Nothing. Nothing. And then the camera was being lifted, and there was a little bit of her shoes, her ankles crossed and lying still, and then, "That'll teach you." Blackness.

We watched until the tape stopped, in case there was more. But there wasn't.

"He killed her," I said.

Lewis was vibrating. I could feel it from where I sat. His body was trembling. "We need to find that fucker," he said.

## CHIEF THOMAS LYNCH
# SATURDAY, JUNE 26, 1999
## 1400 HOURS

**D**onna Daniels missed her calling. She shouldn't have been a bartender. She should've been a prison guard. I told her that after she woke me for the sixth time to check that I was lucid and that my concussion wouldn't kill me. "Not that I'm sure it would be such a loss," she said, her cool fingers pressing my wound. I'd yelled. She'd told me to quit being such a baby.

She slept on the floral loveseat, left crumbs from her meals all over the place, and sang off-key, loudly, a lot. After a day of this, I kicked her out of my home. "You think I don't have better things to do than babysit you?" she asked, hoisting her giant purse onto her shoulder.

"I think you have *other* things to do."

Before she left, she made me promise that I would stay home today. "No work," she said. I'd made the same promise to the hospital nurse, the doctor who'd checked my head, Lewis, Damien, and Nate. No going to work for two days. But this, *this*, I told myself, was a hobby. It wasn't an active investigation. And besides, being in my house wasn't restful. I kept reliving yesterday's scenes, kissing Damien and then the blowout with Matt. And my head felt great, well, good. Almost as good as usual. Going on a drive would be beneficial. Fresh air, etcetera, etcetera. Though there wasn't a lot of fresh air on the highway.

Jack McGee's house was across the street from the Finnegans' home. His place was painted blue and had a wide driveway, unlike every other house that necessitated its owners park their cars two wheels up on the curb.

I rang the bell. Waited. Rang again. Nothing. Hell. I'd driven two hours for nothing. My head started up again. I walked toward my car. So much for making progress. Lewis had given me a summary of Jack McGee's criminal exploits: reselling stolen goods, assault, breaking and entering, arson (that charge was dropped), and running numbers. But this same petty scum was seen dropping Susan Finnegan at church more than once. That was a disparity that I needed to investigate.

I reached into my car and grabbed my pills and a bottle of water. Recalled I wasn't supposed to drive on the meds. Damn. I'd have to wait until I got home to take my pills. I set them down and leaned against the car. Closed my eyes and felt the hot sun baking me. Behind my lids, everything was red.

A cool hand on my forearm startled me. "Chief Lynch? Thomas?" Mrs. Finnegan stood beside me, worry all over her face. "Are you okay?"

I straightened up and said, "Yeah, I'm fine. Trying to pay a visit to your neighbor."

She looked at the houses. "Jack?" Her voice leapt. "You want to talk to him?"

"I do."

"He won't talk to you. You're a stranger and a cop." I glanced down at my polo and khakis. She laughed. "You look like a cop, and there's your car on the street, announcing you."

Fair point. "But if I go with you . . ." she trailed off.

"Why would he let you in?"

"He owes me. Are you sure you're all right? Looks like you bumped your head."

"Looks worse than it is," I said.

"Liar," she said, cheerfully. "Let's go get come cookies."

"I don't need cookies."

"Not for you," she said. "For him."

She went home and returned with a round cookie tin featuring the Bunker Hill monument. I could see the great stone structure from where I stood. It was imposing, a big granite obelisk that dominated the view and made me feel as if it was watching the neighborhood. Silly. My head must be worse than I'd thought.

She rang his doorbell and yelled, "Open up, Jack! I brought cookies." Under her breath she said, "He just got back from the hospital. Heart operation."

The door swung open to reveal an old man in a bathrobe. He had a three-day beard, all gray. His face matched. Had the surgery been successful? Didn't look like it. He was Finny's age, but he looked twenty years older.

"Patricia, you didn't say you'd brought a friend." He had the voice of a longtime smoker. "And a cop to boot! The doctors said I shouldn't have any excitement, you know." He took the cookie tin from her and pried open the lid. He smiled at the contents. "Shortbread. My favorite. From Mrs. Keeley's recipe?"

"As if the old bat would share that!" She laughed alongside him. He closed the front door and seated himself in a battered recliner. Reminded me of my own, though mine didn't smell like a pack of cigarettes or have burn marks all over it. He'd fallen asleep more than once with a ciggie in hand. Miracle he hadn't burned this place down.

"To what do I owe the pleasure?" He wheezed.

Mrs. Finnegan said, "I'll leave you to chat." She opened the door and was on the steps before the surprise registered. I'd assumed she'd stay. But she'd gotten me inside, and that's all she intended.

"That's a favor repaid," he said under his breath.

"I'm looking into her daughter Susan's disappearance," I took a seat. The springs in the sofa were worn. I felt one trying to poke its way into the back of my thigh.

"Susan." He rubbed his mouth. "She thinks you're gonna find her after twenty-some-odd years? Poor thing."

"You claimed you didn't see her the day she disappeared."

"I lied." He leaned back.

"Why?"

"I'd been up to no good that day, and I didn't think sharing that info would win me any points with the boys in blue. Besides, Susan was on her way down the road the day she went. I heard it from the neighbors. My story just backed up everyone else's."

"You could've told the truth later, no?"

He stared at me. "Right. Cuz me and the local cops were so close. They kept busting up every little operation until they ran us out of business. And for what? So the neighborhood could get overrun by blacks and spics? So the murder rate could *increase*?"

"What else didn't you tell them, back then?"

He snickered under his breath and smiled. Oh, this guy. I knew this guy. I'd met a hundred like him back in New York. They thought so highly of themselves, maintaining a corner or two and thinking they controlled the city. They were aggressive bullies who liked nice things and who hated having their superiority questioned. They were easy in interviews because they could never keep their damn mouths shut.

"You knew more about her, didn't you? Things you never told them."

"Yeah, well, it wasn't hard to outsmart those stupid pigs. They couldn't find their asses with their elbows. I mean, did they ever find where she went the first time?"

"When she ran away."

"Yup." He rubbed his hands together.

"She was picked up in New Hampshire."

"Yeah, but where was she headed?" His voice took on that tone. The "I know something you don't" tone. I loved it. He'd spill soon, for sure.

"North, obviously."

He made a buzzing sound, like I'd guessed wrong on a quiz show. "Wrong. She told me she was heading where it never snowed. Besides, she didn't know anyone up there. She tried to go south, but it didn't work. Poor kid. Maybe if she'd made it the first time she'd have been okay."

"Why do you think she's not okay?"

He looked up at the ceiling, like he couldn't bear to stare at my dumb mug. "No way she leaves her mother to hang like this for decades, worrying. Nah. Something happened to her."

"Any ideas?"

"I didn't have anything to do with it." Shit. Now he was pouting.

"I didn't say you did, but since you know more about where she went, or tried to go, the first time, I'm thinking maybe you have insight into her disappearance."

He coughed. His hand went to his chest. "Goddamn that hurts." There were no medicine bottles in the room. No hospital paperwork. I glanced at his wrist. No plastic bracelet.

"You talk to her best friend?" he asked. "Lucy?"

"Yeah. She confirmed that Susan was pregnant."

He massaged his chest, rubbing a slow circle, around and around. No sign of an IV mark on his hand. How long had he been home?

"About time you figured that out," he said.

"You knew."

He looked like the cat that ate the canary. All that was missing was a bright feather poking from his mouth.

"You knew all this time."

"The real questions is, How didn't *they* know? She was wearing loose clothes, but you could see she was changing." Was that true? I'd let it slide.

"Bet you know who the father is, too."

He smiled. His teeth were yellowed. "They all thought she was pure as driven snow."

"You dropped her at church, so she could help out there."

"Did I?"

"Stop playing coy. Didn't take you for the church-type."

"Everyone was the church-type back then. Stone-cold killers sat next to their grandmas back in the day. It was a better time then, more," he spun his hand, searching for the word, "congenial."

"Right. Which one of those congenial gents got Susan pregnant and then abandoned her?"

"You make it sound sinister. You ever knock up the wrong girl?"

He looked me over. Wasn't gonna find a "yes" anytime soon. "Maybe the congenial gent couldn't take care of her, right? Some of us were already working, supporting families."

I made a show of looking around the room for evidence of his family.

"Fuck you," he said.

"This gent. He was a friend of yours?"

His eyes flicked to the TV in the room, an older model. Everything in the place was slightly out of date and worn past its prime. He didn't answer. My head was starting up again, thumping. The cigarette smell, and this guy, and his attitude. But he might have answers. He knew more. I needed to stick it out.

"Maybe you and she spent time together," I said, trying a different tack.

He grunted. "She might not have been pure, but she was damn close. I liked my women more experienced. Not like some Boy Scouts who weren't as great as they seemed."

Boy Scout? Who was the Boy Scout?

"She had the baby," I said.

He didn't startle. He gave a slow, reptilian blink and said, "Thought she had it taken care of."

"Who told you that?"

"She did. She crashed here the night before the procedure."

"She stayed here, across the street, the night before she was supposed to have her abortion?" I asked. If that were true, why had she gone on that winding walk for all the neighbors to see? Why stop at Bunker Hill? Why stand on a corner near the convenience store? Unless it was all misdirection. But why? She'd been planning an abortion. She had a cover story with her best friend. "I don't believe you," I said.

"Nobody ever does." His voice was singsongy. "She should've come straight over, but I wasn't home. Running late. So, she took a walk."

"And you drove her to the clinic."

He wasn't quick enough with his, "Yeah." His nod lacked conviction.

"No, you didn't." Why was he lying about this? Where had she stayed?

"Just like the fuzz never to believe the truth staring you in the face."

"You don't have an altar boy's record," I said.

He slapped the chair's arms. It squeaked madly as he rocked forward. "Everybody thinks I'm some sort of devil, like they didn't all buy from me back in the day, as if they thought those stereos actually fell off a truck. Like I didn't help fix their problems when they needed me. Nope. Now, it's 'Don't go near Mr. McGee's house. He says and does bad things.'"

"Look, I only want—"

"You want what they all want. Information. But when it comes time to pay, you never do. Same as it was, back in the day. Think I trust police?" He coughed, a hard cough that shook his body and wouldn't stop. His face got red. I stood. He waved me back even as his body shook from the force. He'd rather die than ask for my help. After two minutes, he stopped. Sighed and leaned back into his chair, his face worn.

"You never got that heart operation." I looked down at him, at his deep-set eyes. He had long lashes. They made his eyes look more sunken in his ashen face.

He tapped his chest and said, "They found a lump in my lung." He hacked up a loogie. Spit it into a tissue. "Said they couldn't do the surgery until the 'mass' was taken care of."

"Surgery? Chemo?" I asked.

He laughed, low. "Probably both. I ain't going bald and losing pieces of myself, bit by bit. I won't be dragging one of them IV poles behind me while I puke every five minutes. I've seen what cancer looks like. That ain't for me." He looked scared as he said it. I wondered if the decision had been solely his. The Mob didn't offer health insurance, last I knew.

"Thanks for your time." I opened the front door. A guy walked his dog past the house.

Behind me Jack said, "Fucking queers. There's three of them just in these two blocks." He pointed ahead. "It's not like it was."

"I bet it isn't."

I left him to his memories of happier days and wondered how many he had left.

# MONDAY, JUNE 28, 1999

"**W**hat if he never committed another crime?" Billy asked. He'd overheard us grumbling that Daniel Waverly didn't appear in the NCIC database, nor did Donald Waverly.

"He's an abuser," Lewis said. He tossed a tennis ball overhead and caught it. "They don't stop."

"Does that count as exercise?" Dix asked as he walked past. Lewis had been tossing the ball for a full half hour.

"Sure does," Lewis called. "I'm getting ready for the game."

"You know we play softball, right?" Dix replied.

"What if he died?" Billy asked. He was allowed to ask these questions after he led us to the videotape. He'd won the detective's version of a golden ticket, and he was getting full use of it today.

"If he's dead, that would explain why we can't find him," I said. "God, I hope he isn't."

"Why?" Billy asked.

"Because we want him to suffer behind bars," Lewis said, using his dad voice. "We want him to know we caught him, after all these years, and that what he did to Elizabeth Gardner will not go unpunished."

"I think death is a pretty good punishment," Billy opined. "I mean, if he died young."

"He didn't die as young as she did," Lewis said.

"True. . . . I'm surprised he left the film behind," Billy said.

"That's been bothering me too," I said.

Lewis set the tennis ball on his desk. "Why? Stan came into his store, surprised Daniel, yelled at him, and told him to leave. Daniel probably didn't have time to gather everything."

"Yeah, but it's damn incriminating footage," I said. "I mean, all he had to do was take the film. What else did he need to grab?"

"Shit," Lew and I said, in sync.

"What?" Billy asked.

Lew groaned. "We assumed this film was what Daniel was working on that day, but we didn't ask, not specifically. Maybe this wasn't the film he was transferring. Maybe that's why it got left behind."

It took him a moment, but Billy got there. "You think he was working on something else. Something *worse*?"

Lewis said, "We need to call Stan."

"On it," I said, snatching up the phone.

Ten minutes later, I reported that Stan wasn't at all certain about exactly where things were years ago in his back room, but that he thought Daniel had taken the film he was transferring that day, along with the VHS tape. But he wasn't sure.

"If he's remembering right, Daniel wasn't transferring the video of Elizabeth," Billy said.

"What was more important than that video?" Lewis asked. "You don't think . . ."

I shook my head. Daniel had killed another girl and was working on that tape the day Stan interrupted him? Maybe the second tape was more incriminating?

"It happens," Lewis said. "Only the caught ones are famous."

"We have no evidence," I said. "And even if it's true, how does it help us find him?"

"You assume a pattern," Lew said. "Patterns repeat."

"Young woman. Photographer. Trusting, maybe a little naive. I don't know."

Billy watched us go, back and forth, as if we had picked up rackets and were batting Lew's ball back and forth. "Are you guys saying he's a serial killer?"

"Lower your voice," Lewis hissed. "Only thing worse than the boy who cried wolf is the cop who cried serial killer. Got it?"

Billy, cowed, nodded. "Don't they have profiles for those sorts of killers?"

Lewis and I made noises. Cops like to argue about the value of psychology, of killer profiles. We're suspicious about all the psycho-pop babble about childhood traumas and wounded psyches. Because we see people beat down by life every day who don't murder people. Those people have suffered the same but have chosen to abide by what's right. And, besides, the profiles always look the same: loner white male who was abused as a child and may have tortured animals as a kid in a lead-up to his becoming the chief monster of his neighborhood. Some of these facts are as accurate as bull's-eye darts, and others? No evidence of them. And when you ask the psychologist why they were wrong, they say it's a growing field, an inexact science. And that's when the cops hear, "I'm making all this up, fellas," and they swear off relying on these doctors ever again.

What evidence of the common profile did we have? Daniel Waverly was a white man whose parents died young and who lived on his own. Was he abused as a kid? His sister seemed like she might've worked him over, but was it a sustained pattern of abuse? Was he responsible for maiming or killing animals? One neighbor said he was. Did he fantasize about harming others? We had no idea what went on in his head.

"If he was a serial killer," Billy whispered, "How does that help?"

"We could start looking for dead women," I said.

Lewis massaged his brow. Imagining the work that would entail. "Maybe he took arm bones?"

"But he didn't keep the arm bone," Billy pointed out. "Looked like some animal did."

"Yes, but he separated it. The animal didn't remove the arm with a weapon," I said. "Okay, let's look. Billy, you want to help?"

He straightened, his spine a perfect column, his face bright. "Absolutely!"

Lew smiled, in spite of himself. He shook his head. "At least one of us is excited."

# MONDAY, JUNE 28, 1999
## 1300 HOURS

We found eight corpses missing body parts within the past twenty years. Four were men, and one's missing appendage was something that made us all inhale and cross our legs. Four women. One was missing a foot, but that was an antemortem injury. She'd lost the foot in a childhood accident. Three women. One missing hand. Two missing skulls.

We reread the reports, which were short. The woman missing a hand, Lisa Fairway, was found in Lake Zoar in 1987. Her co-worker was accused and convicted of the crime in 1988. Apparently, the cutthroat world of real estate was more violent than I suspected.

"So, you don't think he's a serial killer?" Billy said. "Maybe his other victims haven't been found."

"Lower your voice," Lewis said. We were trying to keep the term "serial killer" on the down low, especially now that it looked as though Daniel Waverly wasn't one after all.

"Sorry. What do we do now?"

"Keep looking for him," I said. "He didn't vanish into thin air. People leave traces." And yet, look at my baby sister. She had disappeared for twenty-seven years. Although now, we knew where she had been for some of that time. We needed to know the rest. I poked my sore tooth with my tongue. "He'll have done something stupid. We just have to find it."

"Billy, why don't you call Stan back and see if he can recall what Daniel was doing the day he found him in the back of the shop? Maybe we got it wrong. Maybe he wasn't doing something worse than transfer-ring film that showed him to be a killer," Lewis said.

"I'll revisit the database," I told Lew. "I'll focus on domestics." He had another pregnancy appointment today with his wife. He hadn't told me more than that, and I hadn't asked. It was hard to know what to say.

After an hour, I found a possible match. A man abused his live-in girlfriend. Name? Daniel Waves. Not the same, but awful close. The man listed was three years younger, but that could be faked.

Lewis grabbed his coat and left, and I pled my case over the phone to a detective in Hartford. He said he'd try to track down the files on that offense, though he sounded less than enthused.

"Look, my chief is a bear and he's on a rampage right now," I said, willing to spin a story to get what I needed.

"Is that the gay one?" he asked.

This was not the first time I'd been asked this question. Not since the news broke. "Yup."

"That must be weird."

"What?" I asked, playing clueless.

"You know."

"No. What?"

"Having a gay man as your chief. Does he wear makeup?"

"Not much. Mascara and blush. Very tasteful. Accents his eyes nicely."

He hesitated, uncertain. "You're pulling my leg."

"I might be. But I mean it about my chief. He's big, and he's mean."

"Okay, okay. I'll see what I can do."

That would have to do, for now.

In the station, men started buzzing. Guys ran out the doors. What gave? Hopkins rushed over and said, "Bank robbery!"

"What?" No way.

"Federal Bank on Main just got hit. Call came through twenty seconds ago."

Sure enough, more guys were running for the door, shouting. "Robbers inside?" I asked.

"Don't know. Wanna ride with me?"

"Sure."

It wasn't every day the Federal Bank on Main Street got robbed. Last time the alarm sounded was in 1994, and it turned out some rookie teller hit it by accident and didn't tell anyone, so four squad cars rolled up and officers emerged, armed, for nothing. Scared the crap out of the customers inside the bank.

Today, the squad cars were staggered on the street, and I saw two dudes in cuffs, sitting on the sidewalk, Dix keeping watch over them.

"Aw, shit!" Hopkins yelled, hitting the steering wheel. "We missed it!"

We got out and talked to the guys, who informed us that all the cops had missed it. Turned out our robbers were carrying semi-realistic water pistols that didn't fool one of the tellers or the security guard. The guard yelled, "Water pistols!" and a high-school football player took down one of the robbers. The second guy fell victim to the security guard, a mustachioed seventy-year-old who looked like he was having the best day of his life.

Billy clapped a well-built young man on the back. Must be the football player. "Hiya," I said.

"Hey, Detective. This here is Dylan Jax. He brought down one of the robbers."

"Congratulations," I said. "Wait. Aren't you the QB for the Marauders?"

"Sure am." His young face was tanned, and he stood like a rooster in a coop full of hens.

"You're the guy who caused the clamshell mess," I said.

His face fell. "That wasn't my fault. Shanice did that."

"Because you told everyone your ex-girlfriend had an STD."

"Um, hi, I just tackled a bank robber. I'm a *hero*."

I looked at the guys on the sidewalk, hands cuffed behind them. They were in their late twenties and looked like drugs had driven them to this place and time. Too skinny and pale and shaking.

"Those guys? They're sad addicts with water guns. Congratulations." I made the last word an insult.

Billy's face was a mask of surprise. Fuck it. Guys like Dylan Jax thought they ruled the world, and, for now, in this small town, perhaps they did. But that didn't make it right for them to smear the name of a girl.

I was hot under the collar. Rumors of Susan's behavior, innuendos and gossip about her messing around, were swirling around the old 'hood, according to my brother Bobby. As if anyone knew anything back then.

"I'm going back to the station," I said. "You don't need me for this nonsense."

Miracle of miracles, when I returned to the station, a hot pile of pages awaited me on the fax machine. The report on the domestic I'd requested. And all the pages, including the cover sheet, came through. The victim had been punched and stabbed with a serrated blade by her live-in boyfriend, Daniel Waves. That's where the good news ended. The report included a picture of Daniel Waves's arrest picture. He was short and had light hair. He didn't have a pox mark near his eye or a cleft chin. He had a tattoo that read "Gangsta" over his left brow. Daniel Waves was not Daniel Waverly.

"Goddamnit," I whispered.

Around me the station was loud, the men buzzy from the bank robbery. Their chatter was white noise to me, nothing more.

"I leave for an hour and a half, and a bank robbery happens?" Lew said, dropping into his chair.

"They had water pistols," I said.

"I heard." He watched the guys laughing and cheering. "Chief's gonna be sorry he missed the excitement."

"Will he?" Seemed to me the chief, who'd come from NYPD Homicide, would hardly rate this bank robbery "exciting."

"What you got there?" Lewis asked.

"Daniel Wave's file."

"That was fast."

"It's not great." I passed the sheets to him.

He scanned the pages. "That tattoo," he said.

"Right?"

"Why would any woman with half a brain date that guy?"

"Women are optimists."

"You think?"

"I convinced three of 'em to marry me."

"Solidly argued," Lewis said.

"Hey, detectives," Billy said. "I heard from Stan. He said he recalls Waverly was inside the darkroom when he caught him in there, after hours."

"The darkroom?" I asked. "Doing what?"

"Processing photos. He said that they were black-and-white, and he thinks they were nature shots."

"Huh." It hardly seemed worth the bother of duplicating a key to get into a camera store to develop artsy nature photos, but what did I know?

"Oh, and I got a match on the name."

"Nah," I said. "It's a dead end. The domestic? Doesn't match." Lewis showed him the photo.

"Does that tattoo say 'Gangsta'? Geez. No, wait. That's Daniel Waves." He read the name on the mug shot.

"Right," I said.

"I meant the other name."

Lewis strained not to yell. I could see the struggle. "What other name?" he asked, managing to sound only mildly annoyed.

"Waverly Daniels. You said reverse the names, and I did, but Daniel came up empty, so then I tried Daniels, like Jeff Daniels. Have you guys seen *Dumb and Dumber*? That's like my favorite movie. So funny—"

"You got a match?" I asked, cutting short Billy's monologue on comedy.

"Yeah. Waverly Daniels got locked up for hitting his girlfriend. She claimed he threatened to kill her. And guess where they met? A photography club run out of the town's Continuing Ed program."

"When?" Lewis said.

"1984."

"Where's the file?"

"I've only got the highlights, but I can get the full one—"

"Yes, please," I said.

"You think it's him?"

"I think we need to look into it," Lewis said.

Billy went off to do our bidding.

I said, "I don't know." We'd had theories knocked down and one false trail to our names. I wasn't ready to invest a lot of hope in Waverly Daniels. Not yet.

"We'll find him," Lewis said. "Whether it's this guy or the next or the next."

I admired his bravado and shared his hope, but there's nothing like having a sibling go missing for nearly three decades to make you doubt that you'll find the person you're looking for, no matter how strong the need.

"Let's hope so," I said, which was as much as I could commit to in this moment.

# TUESDAY, JUNE 29, 1999
## 0910 HOURS

Everybody wanted to talk to me at the station, ask me about my injury and how I was feeling. It was to be expected, given that the last time they'd seen me, I was being escorted into an ambulance. I said I was fine, no lingering effects. Dix suggested I pad my desk with rubber bumpers. "Why not pad the whole office?" I asked.

Once we'd established that I hadn't broken my skull, everybody and their sister wanted to tell me, again, about the bank robbery. Though, in point of fact, nothing had been stolen, and the robbers were armed with nothing more than plastic water pistols and bad breath. This from Billy, who said one of the robbers had "teeth rotting out of his head you could smell from two blocks away." I thanked him for that sensory detail and escaped to my office, where I collapsed into my chair. Overhead lights weren't doing me any favors, but my vision was clear today, and I'd had no ill effects after eating breakfast.

Three raps on the door were followed by Mrs. Dunsmore entering, her serious frown in place. "You got hurt."

"I'm fine now."

"And I'm to believe you tripped and hit your head on your desk?"

"Yes."

She stared, unspeaking. Two could play this game. She pursed her lips. I cleared my throat. She shifted her weight. I glanced to the window. She came to the desk and said, "Funny. I'd expect to see a dent here." She pointed to the desk's corners. "Given that your head is so hard."

"What's that?" I asked. She had a folder in her hand. Folders meant work. Maybe I should pretend to be feeling not quite well.

"Citizen complaints," she said, setting the folder atop my desk.

"You sure know how to make a guy feel better."

She harrumphed. In her hand was a plastic shopping bag. Odd. She usually used tote bags she'd gotten from the library fundraiser or public radio station.

"We've got two units out on fireworks calls," she said.

"Already?" Fireworks, except sparklers and fountains, were illegal in our state. That didn't prevent people from buying them and lighting them off at odd hours. Hell, it wasn't even 10:00 a.m. and yahoos were already out exploding stuff.

"It's the twenty-ninth," she said. "Seems to me, they waited longer than usual."

I rubbed my head. It hurt, so I stopped. "Just as long as no one loses fingers." Last year, one of our town's residents had taken Idyll's Blast Off! motto to heart and had done just that to two of his fingers. Idiot.

She saw me looking at the bag she held. Her lips curled, ever so slightly. "Station softball tournament is approaching."

As if I'd forgotten the one I'd been excluded from. "And?"

"I got you something for it." From the bag, she withdrew a t-shirt.

"For me?" I took it from her and held it up. The color could double as a visual-alert system. "But I'm not playing."

She crossed her arms and said, "Says who? You're the chief of police, Thomas. You think Dix is going to tell you that you can't compete? Only person who can tell you that is you." And with that, she left.

The t-shirt hung from my hands, the brightest thing in the room. I looked at it, trying to decide what surprised me more: her calling me by my first name or her agitating for me to play in the game.

I folded the t-shirt and put it inside my bottom desk drawer, to take out later. Maybe.

# TUESDAY, JUNE 29, 1999
## 2020 HOURS

Lewis and I were working overtime, poring through the assault report on Cassidy Peterson. It was our boy all right. Daniel Waverly reborn as Waverly Daniels. He'd picked the wrong girlfriend to beat this time. Cassidy's uncle was a retired policeman. She was his god-daughter. He did not take kindly to her boyfriend breaking her collarbone. Daniel sported a nice shiner in his mug shot.

"He gets arrested and does time for two months," Lewis said. "And then?"

"And then he becomes a magician and 'Presto! Change-o!' He disappears from the face of the earth," I said. My sore tooth was worse today. My tongue kept probing it, which only made it hurt more.

Lewis sipped from his coffee mug and grimaced. Probably cold or bitter or both. He glanced at his watch. "Janice is gonna kill me." He stated this as indisputable fact.

"Head home. I can read myself blind and curse at these files same as you can."

He rubbed his face and shook his head. "Billy make any headway on those searches?"

"He's working on it. You want me to grab it from him?" Billy was no longer a rookie, but he wasn't a seasoned detective either.

"If he hasn't got it by tomorrow," Lew said. "Not like we're going to nail him tonight."

I admired his optimism.

"You think he's dead?" he asked. This wasn't the first time he'd posed that question.

"We haven't found any likely obituaries or death certificates with that name."

"Maybe he's sunning himself on a beach in Hawaii."

"Also possible, though I hope not." Scumbags like Daniel Waverly shouldn't have an easy life when their legacy is pain and destruction. But then the world doesn't operate on the "life is fair" principle.

"Why was he reproducing black-and-white photos? You think they were pics of Elizabeth, after he killed her?"

"Stan said they were nature photos, remember?"

"Yeah, well, maybe that's what he saw. Maybe only a piece of her was visible and he didn't catch it."

Lewis would talk all night if I let him.

"Maybe. I'm just glad we have that video." Elizabeth's diary, detailing his abuse, was great, but the videotape was gold. A jury would devour it.

Billy came over, his uniform creased to hell. "I thought you went home," Lew said, checking his watch. "You're off."

"I wanted to finish looking through the reports. None of the men match his birthdate. There's only one who looks possible."

"He was using fake names, so faking his date of birth would be par for the course," I said.

Billy said, "This guy was arrested on a domestic and on an assault, and he did time for both."

Lew sat up in his chair and leaned forward. He made a 'gimme' gesture, and Billy handed him the sheet. Lew scanned it. "Can't be him," he said. "He was in jail for Cassidy Peterson at the time of the assault."

"You sure?" Billy asked.

"We've been reading this report since yesterday, Billy," I said. "We're sure."

"No others?" Lewis asked, his disappointment audible.

"There's this guy, but he's in a nursing home."

"Nursing home?" Daniel Waverly would be forty-four years old today. There's no way he'd be in a nursing home.

Lew made the "gimme" gesture again.

"He's only forty-four," I reminded him, sighing.

"What's this guy's date of birth?" Lew asked.

"1956," Billy said.

"And he's in a nursing home?" Lewis asked. "Why was he in the system?"

"DWI," Billy said. "In April 1990."

"Did he drink himself into a home?" I asked.

Billy shrugged. Lew and I shared a look that our young patrolman noticed. "What? Did I screw up? What is it?"

"Nah," I said. "Only we'd really like to know what landed him in the nursing home."

"And what he looks like," Lewis asked. He read the sheet. "He's at Meadowvale in Mansfield."

Mansfield was a twenty-five-minute drive from here. "It's after eight o'clock," I said.

Lew swore under his breath. Because he'd be reamed out by his wife when he finally dragged himself home, or because he knew there was no way we were getting into Meadowvale today. "Can't do anything tonight," I said, as much as to myself as to him.

He nodded. If, by some miracle, this man was Daniel Waverly, we had to do everything proper. Contact the Mansfield Police and share our suspicions. Get clearance to work on their patch. Plus, not piss off the folks running the nursing home. We'd be wrestling red tape. If this was our guy.

"Guess we'd better call it a night," Lew said. He sounded sorry about it, and I wondered how things were at home. He hadn't said another word about his baby since I'd spilled the beans to the chief. That bothered me. I shouldn't have done it.

"See you in the morning, fellas," I said, with plenty of false cheer. Billy lost a little of the anxiety pinching his face. I wasn't sure if I was acting for him or for me. Being the station jokester for so long had taken its toll. You do a thing for so long and you forget you're doing it.

## CHIEF THOMAS LYNCH
# TUESDAY, JUNE 29, 1999
## 2100 HOURS

"Lewis, you got a sec?" I asked. He stopped, jacket over his arm. He'd been headed home. The Elizabeth Gardner case was running him into overtime. I was preparing justifications to the selectmen about why we'd gone over budget on overtime, again. He came to my office, worry lines etched in his brow that I suspected had nothing to do with the case.

"Any progress on Susan's baby daddy?" I'd given him my update from Jack McGee earlier.

"No. The Gardner case is taking all my time. That and . . ."

"Your baby."

His hand tightened into a fist. But then his rigid body went soft and he said, "Yeah. Between the two, I haven't had any time to look into it. I'm sorry."

"It's fine. Understood. You're working your priorities. I can manage on my own."

"Thanks. I've got to go. Janice will have my head."

He left, and I wondered whether the Gardner case was good for him or bad for him. Some detectives, in the midst of a personal crisis, pour their hearts into a case. Distraction. Others miss things, important things, when preoccupied by problems at home. I was the first type, and I suspected Lewis was, too. Finny once told me we were two peas in a pod. I hadn't believed him. Still not sure I did.

Thoughts of Finny brought me back to his sister, Susan. She'd been alive as of April 11, 1973. Her "brother" had checked her out of the hospital. What were the chances anyone who worked at the hospital back then would recall this brother? Employees would be long gone, and "the brother" would be just one of a sea of men coming to collect a recent mother to bring her home. No, it would be impossible. There had to be something from the investigation, some clue I'd overlooked, some connection I wasn't making.

I bid the men good night and told them to be safe. Then I drove to Pino's Pizza, where I failed to order a salad with my pizza. Screw it. Not like I needed to keep trim. No one was looking at my body these days.

At home, I ate slice after slice and rummaged through the remaining boxes of interviews. I pushed it aside and flipped through other mementos and objects. The rabbit's foot and a worn postcard depicting Bunker Hill that said "Wish You Were Here!" penned on its back in faded blue ink. Silly, given that she'd lived a few blocks from the place. I glanced at where the postage stamp should be, but there wasn't one. She'd bought it and wrote on it. A joke? Because she had wished herself elsewhere for years? She'd run away, after all.

She'd been a Girl Scout. In the box were badges in childcare, folk dancing, ceramics and pottery, animal kingdom (bird), and good grooming. The badges were circles with embroidered images inside. Good grooming had a pumpkin with a high heel in front of it. Cinderella? Girls got badges with a Cinderella symbol, for what? Bathing regularly and styling their hair? Or makeup application? I doubted today's Girl Scouts had such a badge.

There was no diary. Too bad. Diaries were insights into a person's life no longer available once the person died. People thought they knew everything about their daughter or sister or lover, but a look into her diary might reveal secrets never shared. That's why I'd never been tempted to write in one. To me, diaries were evidence to be used against you.

How many times had I read these interviews? I returned to Jack McGee's. He'd said he was working on his car in the driveway the day Susan went missing. Hadn't seen her. He had seen her the day prior. I bit my lip. Who cared? No one was asking about that day. Maybe he'd said that because they asked when he'd last seen her? No, he'd volunteered it. Then again, other neighbors had done the same. But I knew Jack had lied. What if he'd lied about seeing her Thursday? But why lie about that date?

I grabbed the other neighbors' interviews. Seen Thursday? No. Set it aside. Seen Thursday? Okay. At the end, I had two piles. Seven neighbors saw Susan on Thursday, including Jack McGee. Where and when? Coming home from school, around 2:30 p.m. Walking with her book bag, around 2:25 p.m. Outside the monument, around 4:30 p.m. Walking on Wood Street, around 6:00 p.m. Leaving her house at 4:10 p.m. Outside the Bunker Hill lodge at 5:30 p.m.

Finny said she liked the monument, that the giant stone structure had fascinated her as a child. But she was sixteen years old. Did she still care so much? My mother had thought it fishy, but I'd dismissed her insight, because she was a mother, not a detective. I returned to the interview with the park ranger, Gus Saunders. He hadn't seen her the day she went missing. Busy with visits from schoolkids. Okay. There was a mention of a Kevin McGee too. Finny had known him, from the old days. They'd played as kids, and Kevin had worked at the monument for a year.

Finny had talked to him two days after he knew his sister was gone. Kevin said he hadn't seen Susan in "ages." He was sorry he couldn't be of more help. But, according to the reports, she'd been at the Bunker Hill lodge the day *before* she went missing, *and* the day she went missing. Kevin's co-worker, Gus Saunders, said Kevin was on shift Thursday. If Susan went to Bunker Hill, Kevin should've seen her. Unless he was working inside the monument. Or he lied. I looked at the postcard. "Wish You Were Here!"

No. There was something wrong. I called the number listed on the report. Gus Saunders no longer lived there. But his second cousin, Kathy, did. God bless large families. She gave me his number in Kansas City. It was only at the end of the call that she thought to ask, "Why do you need his number?"

I told her I was on his high-school reunion committee and hung up.

What time was it in Kansas City? 9:45 p.m. Late to call a stranger on the phone. He might be asleep. Then again, my old super used to say, "Nothing ventured, nothing solved, you thick shit-for-brains."

Five rings and no answer. Ah well. I'd try tomorrow. "Hello?" The voice was creaky.

"Gus Saunders?" I asked.

"Who's this?"

"My name is Thomas Lynch. I'm the Chief of Police in Idyll, Connecticut."

"Connecticut?" He made it sound like Mars, like a place he'd heard of but hardly believed was real.

"Yes, sir. I wanted to ask you a question."

"You calling me at ten o'clock at night to ask me a question? About what?"

"Back in 1972 you worked at the Bunker Hill Monument."

"Yeah," he said. His "yeah" matched Finny's for sound.

"A girl went missing in the neighborhood."

"Susan Finnegan. I remember."

"You do?"

"Sure. Not a lot of girls went missing back then, not girls like her. Plus, my buddy at work was acting up."

"Acting up?"

"Kevin asked me to lie about his shifts for him."

"Kevin?"

"McGee. He was a piece of work. Young guy. Married with a kid on the way. He must've been chasing some skirt again, cuz he asked me to say he wasn't there."

"What date did he ask you to lie about?"

"The weekend."

"Friday?"

"Must've been. Back then, the old timers worked the Saturday and Sunday shifts. Kev and I were the low men on the totem pole."

The day Susan went missing, Kevin was at the monument she'd visited, and he'd asked his co-worker to lie about his whereabouts. My palms tingled. "Why do you think he wanted you to lie?"

"There was a room in the lodge for employees. Kevin used to take some of his girls there. Used to put an Out of Order sign on the door when he was, um, occupied. Anyway, he got freaked when he heard the police were poking around. Was afraid word would get back to his wife. Asked me to tell the cops he'd been off on Friday, if they asked."

"And that didn't concern you?"

"No. Why? He told me he'd been shut up with some Bunker Hill co-ed when he should've been at his post. He said he was gone ten minutes, max." He laughed. "Wasn't even embarrassed by it."

"You still in touch with Kevin?"

"Nah. I moved out here and don't really keep in touch with the old crowd. My parents left Charlestown for Florida. Don't have much family back there now. A few cousins."

"Why was Kevin so worried about his wife finding out?" I asked.

He laughed. "You kidding? Kev's wife was Diana Killeen. Her uncle was Mack Killeen, a player in the Mob. You didn't cross those guys' family members, yeah?"

"And Kevin was related to Jack McGee?"

"Jack? Yeah. He and Kev were cousins. Practically grew up in each other's pockets."

"I see." And I was, at last, beginning to see how it might have been.

Jack McGee and Kevin McGee, cousins, and best friends.

"Thanks for your time."

"Wait. Why are you calling? Have they found her? Susan Finnegan?"

"No," I said, and then I hung up the phone.

I hadn't found Susan Finnegan, not yet, but, for the first time since I started investigating, I thought I knew who might have landed her in the predicament that started it all.

# WEDNESDAY, JUNE 30, 1999
## 0910 HOURS

**M**y footfalls sounded absurdly loud in the Idyll Public Library. At 9:10 a.m., the place was populated by one elderly man reading the newspapers, two librarians, and me. The librarians stood behind a waist-high counter. One sorted books. The other, Mrs. Lindhurst, tapped at a computer keyboard, her lips pursed.

"Good morning," I said.

Mrs. Lindhurst looked up from the screen. "Hello, Mr. Finnegan." Though I lived in Ellington, I used Idyll's library for my reading. It had a better selection, and because it was near the station, I could drop in and pick up items. If I waited until my shift was over to collect from Ellington, the library would be closed. "We've got your copy of *The Girl with a Pearl Earring*," she said. "Caroline, could you get that please?"

The younger librarian bent and rummaged below the desk. Popped up with two books in hand, "And you've got another." She turned the book so I could see its cover.

"Ah, the Lahiri," I said. "I've heard great things."

"It's marvelous," Caroline said.

"And set in your old stomping grounds," Mrs. Lindhurst said.

"Charlestown?"

"Boston."

As if they were exactly the same. I didn't bother correcting her.

"I came today because I need help with a research question."

Mrs. Lindhurst checked out the books, stamping the due dates onto the label affixed to the back. I had two weeks to read both books. Not a problem. I read two books a week on average. A lack of wives gave me a lot of free time. She handed me the books and asked, "What's the question?"

"I'm trying to discover why a young man might be living in a nursing home."

"How young?" Mrs. Lindhurst asked.

"Mental disability," Caroline suggested.

"Forty-four years old," I said.

"Accident," Mrs. Lindhurst said. "With a mental impairment, he'd likely live in a group environment, but not a nursing home, not usually."

"Accident," I said. I'd had the same thought. "Could we check the newspapers?"

"For when?" she asked.

"Sometime in April 1990 or later." He'd had a DWI in April 1990, so it had to be after that. The DWI report indicated that he'd been swerving between lanes. He'd paid a fine and spent a night in jail. His insurance must've gone up. But he wasn't harmed. The report listed no injuries. Whatever landed him in a nursing home happened after that event.

"Don't suppose you could narrow the time frame?" Her tone implied I was being difficult.

I couldn't. I'd called Meadowvale this morning but was told that the person who could help me was out sick today. No one else had access to intake records. I doubted it, but I'd decided not to push too hard. We'd need the facility on our side later if this was the same guy.

"Between 1990 and 1996." Billy had found the listing for Waverly in a 1996 census listing, so he'd been at Meadowvale that year.

"You have the man's name?" Mrs. Lindhurst said.

"Yes."

"Caroline, you have the desk." Mrs. Lindhurst sounded as though she was handing over control of a flagship to a petty officer. Caroline nodded and straightened her cardigan. "We'll be with the microfiche."

I followed Mrs. Lindhurst down the hall toward the stairs, which led to the basement where the children's library, reading rooms, and microfiche lived. She paused near the stairs. "Wait. Let's try the web first."

"The World Wide Web?" I asked.

"Searching on the computer might save us time."

"You're web savvy?" I didn't own a computer.

"Libraries are living institutions and must keep up with the times." She led me upstairs, where the large-format books and most of the non-fiction books were shelved. We went through a door marked STAFF. A few desks, a coat rack, a coffeepot, and a tiny galley sink plus a very worn orange sofa and scarred coffee table.

"So, this is what the inner sanctum looks like," I said.

She walked to the largest desk, atop which squatted a heavy computer screen. "I'm going to use a new search engine called Google. My colleagues tell me it's better than Lycos."

"Sure thing."

She sat and tippy-tapped on the keyboard. I looked at the magazines and books on the coffee table. Several dog-eared *New Yorker*s lay along mystery paperbacks.

"What's the man's name?" she asked.

"Waverly Daniels. Or that's what I think will show up."

"Alias?"

"Mmm-hmm."

She asked me to spell the name, and then she typed. I waited. "Got it," she said.

"What?" Was she kidding? It had been less than a minute.

"December 1990. A man named Waverly Daniels was injured in a car accident outside Manchester. We can pull the original article from the *Hartford Courant*."

I peered at the screen. "All you did was enter his name?"

She turned and gave me a stern librarian look. "I did a little more than that, but," she tilted her head, "not much. Soon you'll be able to find out almost anything here."

I sniffed. "I'm not sure about that."

She shook her head. "I am. Come on, to the microfiche."

A half hour later, I had a copy of the article describing Waverly Daniels's two-car accident. I handed it to Lewis, who sat at his desk, sipping coffee and muttering under his breath about police cooperation.

"Here you go," I said.

"Where have you been, and what's this?" He read the article. "Oh, God. It's him. It's him!" A few of the guys turned his way, but most ignored him. We'd done a lot of yelling the past few days as we thought we got closer and then realized we hadn't.

"His picture!"

"It's him." They'd printed a photo of Waverly Daniels. A smiling photo as a counterpoint to the horrific details of the accident. His car had been sideswiped at an intersection. The driver's side was crushed. He'd been pinned inside while emergency responders wrestled the Jaws of Life to extract him from the car. His injuries included fractured ribs and a spinal cord injury.

"Couldn't happen to a nicer guy," Lew said. "December 1990."

"You think this is why he stopped?" I asked, knowing Lewis was running the same track with me. Abusers rarely stopped abusing. But his confinement to a wheelchair might have ended his career.

"Would explain it," he said.

"Now we just have to get inside and talk to him."

"Just," he repeated, his deadpan delivery forecasting all the work it would require.

"You want me to work on the nursing home or the police?"

"Nursing home," he said. "Charm the hell out of them, okay? I know a cop who worked in Mansfield. He's not there anymore, but he may know who's the best person to approach."

"Okay," I said. "Wonder Twin powers activate." We touched fists together, like the cartoon twins. "Form of a charming bureaucrat," I said.

"Form of persuasive detective," Lewis said.

Then we picked up our phones and got to work.

# THURSDAY, JULY 1, 1999
## 0950 HOURS

I'd reached that point where I couldn't do more, not without doing harm. I had a solid lead: Kevin McGee. I had his co-worker who attested he'd been asked to lie about Kevin's work schedule. Kevin had a wife whose family was heavily involved in organized crime. Kevin's cousin was Jack McGee. Susan visited the Bunker Hill Monument more often than any sixteen-year-old girl would. And she'd headed that way the day she disappeared, when it was out of the way of her path, or seemed to be. And yet, it was circumstantial. Thin as air. Nothing but guesswork. No forensics. No confession.

Mrs. Dunsmore looked surprised when I came to her office. She said nothing when I closed the door and sat opposite her. "I need to run something past you," I said. Her phone rang. She glanced at it. "It's about Susan Finnegan." She hit a button, silencing the ringer.

"What is it?"

I told her, about Kevin McGee and his lying cousin, Jack. How I thought Jack and Finny had some history, maybe. "If it's Kevin, I can't touch him. It's well outside my patch."

She nodded. "And you can't tell Michael."

It was my turn to nod. Telling Michael Finnegan my suspicions would be the last thing I would do. He'd go after Kevin McGee, and he might take his brothers with him for company. No. I didn't know for sure whether Kevin was guilty, and I wouldn't let Finny endanger his career for my hunch.

"What will you do?" Her hands were gathered on her lap.

"Contact the Boston Police. Hope someone there still cares about this case and has time to investigate."

"Sounds like the right move." I was glad. I'd wanted confirmation. And I couldn't bother Wright, not now with everything else he had on his plate. "I know someone at the BPD who might be able to help." She had a Rolodex, and she spun through it, searching for the name. "Here he is. Detective Fred Williams. When you call, tell him Grace Dunsmore sent you his way, and ask how his sister is doing."

"Okay." I looked at her fat Rolodex. "You got a detective in every city in there?"

"No."

I rose to exit, and she added, "But I've got a sailor in every port."

"Mrs. Dunsmore!" I put my hand to chest, faking outrage. "I never!"

Her laughter boomed outside the office, causing heads to turn. When they saw me, their looks grew even more confused. Good. Always keep 'em guessing.

$$\gtrless \! \lessgtr$$

Had Mrs. Dunsmore given Detective Fred Williams a kidney? How else to explain the raptures he went into when I mentioned her name? I was to tell her "how happy he was to hear she was well" and how "delighted" his sister would be to hear from her.

It certainly greased the wheels of my request. Fred Williams wasn't familiar with the Susan Finnegan missing persons case, but he paid attention because of Mrs. Dunsmore, and he perked up when I mentioned the missing person was a policeman's sister.

"He still working?" he asked.

"Yes, for me, actually."

"Ah, so that's how you got involved."

"Yeah." Better to say that than that I blackmailed my detective into letting me look into his sister's disappearance because I was bored at work.

"You know anything else about this Kevin McGee?" he asked.

"Only what I've told you. Once I found out about him, I thought it best to pass it off to your department."

"I'll see what I can scare up. Might take some time."

"I understand." I wanted more, but I had no right to ask it, no authority. After the call ended, I felt like a shaken soda can about to erupt. I took a walk around the station. A couple of guys started to do crunches, but they soon tired of the activity. This was why I'd wanted a fitness plan. They couldn't keep up exercise, even for the sake of a joke.

Lewis and Finny reviewed papers. They gestured with their hands and finished each other's sentences. They were deep into it. "But this one—" Finny said.

"You think he'll respond?"

"How's it going?" I asked. They pulled apart and regarded me with bleary eyes. Men woken from the dream of nailing a killer. I knew that look. Hell, I'd once had that look.

"Getting there," Lewis said. "The nursing home says we can visit tomorrow. We're just finalizing details with the police. They're concerned about his impairment."

I said, "Really? Thought they'd be more concerned that they have a murderer living in their backyard under an assumed name."

"Right?" Finny asked. "We're getting confirmation from the nursing-home staff that he's physically, not mentally, disabled."

"What is his status?"

"Paralyzed from the chest down. He can still use his arms and hands. But he's wheelchair-bound," Lewis said. "Requires assistance to eat and other activities."

"How you feeling?" I asked.

"Nervous," Finny said.

"Why?"

"His situation. I worry it'll play for sympathy. Juries don't love convicting people in wheelchairs."

"You don't worry about a jury. Worry about the arrest. What's the plan? Gonna hit him with good cop, bad cop?" I asked.

"Nah. Too predictable. I was thinking bad cop, worse cop," Lewis said.

# FRIDAY, JULY 2, 1999

Lewis glanced at me, did a double take, and asked, "What is *that*?"

"My lucky necktie." It was yellow and printed with shamrocks. I'd gotten it as a gift in 1989 from my son, Max. Back then, my kids got me one of two presents for Christmas and my birthday: a tie or a bottle of Old Spice. I still had four bottles of the cologne, unopened, in my bathroom.

"Never seen it before," he said. "I'd remember."

"Never needed it before."

He harrumphed and got out of the car. I followed. We stood, surveying Meadowvale Nursing Home and Rehabilitation. The grounds were pleasant. A wide lawn dotted with walking paths. The building was a hodgepodge. Originally a large family home, it had, over the years, had wings added to create the giant building before us. The original home was still visible in the middle of the newer additions.

We checked in at the reception desk. The director was on hand to lead us to Mr. Daniels's room. He had a short stride, but it was fast-paced. He talked as he led us through the lobby, down a hall toward the living quarters. The hallway smelled of cinnamon candle and burnt oatmeal. "He's on the first floor, of course." I assumed he meant because of the wheelchair. Difficult to evacuate in case of a fire if the elevators weren't to be used.

"He's awake at 6:30 a.m., every day. He often naps around 2:00

p.m., but he should be quite alert for you. He usually keeps to his room after breakfast. He likes his privacy. I think it's because he's so much younger than the other residents."

He stopped before a door. To the left of the frame was the name Waverly Daniels, written in marker. Nothing adorned the door, unlike the one next door or across the hall. Both of those doors were marked with stickers and fake flowers. Attached were photos of smiling grandchildren and pets and vacations taken years ago. Before us, a blank wooden door. Waverly Daniels wasn't one for displaying his memories.

The director knocked a quick, light series of raps, and then he called, "Mr. Daniels? You have visitors!"

"What?" a voice called.

"Visitors, Mr. Daniels. We told you yesterday, remember?"

Lewis reached forward to stop the director from turning the knob. "You told him we were coming? We specifically requested he not know."

The director dropped his hand and frowned. "Well, yes, but that's not our policy. Mr. Daniels never has visitors, and we thought it might be jarring if the police showed up, unannounced, to ask him questions."

We had *planned* on it being jarring. It's what we wanted. I looked at Lewis and shook my head. Nothing we could do now. Daniel Waverly had the advantage of knowing we were coming.

Lewis opened the door, an expression of his annoyance. The room was eastward-facing. Sun streamed inside. Dust motes danced by the window and near the center of the room. And with a book on his lap sat Daniel Waverly. His hair was grayer than brown, and his face and body looked bloated, but he still had the pox mark and the cleft chin, and it was him all right. His eyes hardly blinked as he examined us.

"Good morning," he said.

We returned his greeting. Looked around for seating. There was none. I guess he didn't have much need for chairs. A twin bed made up with a pale-blue blanket afforded the only place to sit. The director noticed too. "Let me go fetch some chairs," he said.

"It's fine," Lewis said. "We won't be long." What he didn't say was that we didn't want him interrupting our interview.

"It will only take a moment," he insisted.

"We're good," I said. "Really." I stepped forward, edging him to the door.

The director looked about the room, as if he'd find a spare chair hiding in the corners. "Well, if you're sure."

"We are." He left, and I closed the door.

Daniel looked from me to Lewis. "I was surprised to hear I'd be hosting two policemen this morning. What can I do for you?"

"He didn't tell you?" Lewis asked. He, meaning the director.

"He said you had questions, about a case you're working?" He adjusted the book on his lap. I read the cover. *The Talented Mr. Ripley* by Patricia Highsmith. Was he kidding with that shit? Ripley was a sociopath who was always one step ahead of everyone, including the police. I fought back a smile. Cocky. We could work with cocky.

"Elizabeth Gardner." Lewis produced a photograph, the one used for her missing persons posters.

"Elizabeth Gardner," he repeated, as if hearing the name for the first time. This might be easier than we'd expected.

"You dated," Lewis said.

*Let him deny it. Let him deny it.* Then we'd have caught him in a lie.

"We did," he said. "Briefly."

"Nine months." Lewis laid a photo of Daniel with Elizabeth atop his book.

Daniel picked it up by the corner and stared. "That was a long time ago. She went missing, back in '78?"

"1979," I said. "Surely you remember that?"

"Right, 1979. You'll have to forgive me. I get confused about when things happened, since the accident." Bullshit. But we'd let it stand for now.

"We discovered Elizabeth's body," Lewis said.

"Really? Where?" he asked.

"In Idyll, on our patch," I said. "That's why we're here."

"She was . . . killed?" Lord, hand the man an Oscar award for that delivery. The hesitation before "killed," the wide eyes.

"Yes," I said. "Murdered. Know anything about it?"

"Me? How would I? I've been living here since 1991."

"She's been dead since 1979," Lewis said.

"All that time? How awful. Her parents must be devastated." He put his hands on his chair and wheeled himself to a desk with an open space for a chair. He set the book atop the desk, next to an alarm clock.

"When was the last time you spoke to Elizabeth?" I asked.

He wasn't facing us but was looking at her photo again. "I told the police, back then. It must've been a few weeks before she went missing."

"You never saw her after she broke up with you?"

He stiffened. Hadn't liked that dig. Good. "No. Never."

"What's this?" Lewis asked. He'd crossed the room to examine a framed photograph on the wall. It was black-and-white and focused on a skeletal tree. The focus was on fallen leaves before the tree, so that the tree was a bit fuzzy, its sharp, bare limbs made softer by the contrast. It looked a lot like the photo Mr. Gardner had hanging on his wall. Elizabeth's photo.

Daniel had to spin his chair around to see what Lewis was examining. "That's a picture I took," he said. "It placed second in a national competition a few years back."

"You take photographs?" Lewis asked. "Must be difficult." He eyed the wheelchair.

"Not at all. Camera equipment has come a long way. And I can manage fine with my arms."

"Second place," I said. "Who got first?"

"I don't know. It was a *national* contest."

"You win anything?" Lewis asked.

"My picture was printed in a magazine, and I got two hundred dollars."

"Not bad. What did the winner get?" I asked. I'd wandered to the window and was adjusting the shade.

"Would you mind not fiddling with that?" he asked. "If it's too high, I can't reach it."

"Oh, of course. How thoughtless of me. Why did you change your name?"

"What?" he asked.

"Your name," I said. "It's Daniel Waverly, only you went by Donald when you dated Elizabeth, and now you're here under Waverly Daniels."

"Made you hard to find, I don't mind telling you," Lewis said.

"I . . . I was young, and I'd never liked the name Daniel. There were too many of them in the town where I grew up."

"Woodstock," Lewis said.

His eyes flicked to Lewis. He didn't like this. Didn't like us knowing much about him. "Yeah, so I went by Donald."

"Like Donald Duck," I said. "Th-th-th-that's all folks!"

"Porky Pig says that, not Donald Duck, and no, not like Donald Duck." He was irate.

"Why'd you pick it, then? Easy to remember? Donald, Daniel."

"I liked it." He spat the words out.

"So why go by Waverly?" Lewis asked.

"I got tired of it again. I was opening my own business, and Waverly was a more distinct name."

"Your own business?" I asked. "Doing what? Lawn care?"

"Photo processing."

"Where was that?"

"Hartford."

"When?"

"1990. But then I had my accident."

"So, you had a business under a false name?" I asked.

"It's not a false name if it's a business name. You think the guy who runs Papa Gino's has the first name Papa?"

I pretended to mull it over. "Why not?"

"That's not how it works."

Lewis said, "Don't mind him. His momma dropped him on his head when he was a baby." He pointed to me. "*Several* times."

"Look, what does any of this have to do with Elizabeth?" he asked.

"Were you upset when she broke up with you?" Lewis asked.

"More or less upset than when Cassidy Peterson pressed charges against you?" I asked.

"Who?"

"You know. The woman who had you locked up because you didn't know your own strength. Snapped her collarbone. Too bad about her uncle, the cop. They don't let things like that go, am I right?"

"You got kind of a bad track record when it comes to ex-girlfriends," Lew said. "I mean, one dead. One assaulted. How many girls you dated total. Three, four?"

He sputtered. "I don't know how many girls I've dated. Twenty?"

"Twenty," Lew said. "Well."

"You marry any of 'em?" I asked.

"No."

"Why not?" Lew asked. "Not the marrying type?"

"Guess not."

"When did you last see Cassidy Peterson?" I asked.

"I don't remember. That was years and years ago."

"But more recent than Elizabeth Gardner," I said. "Did you maybe not like Cassidy as much as Elizabeth? How long did you and Cassidy date?"

"Three months."

"Only three months? No wonder he's had twenty girlfriends." I winked at Lewis. "Can't keep 'em for long."

"I can keep—" he began.

"Don't mind him," Lewis interrupted. "He's just jealous. Not much of one with the ladies. I mean, look at him."

"That tie," Daniel said, smirking.

"Right? I told him, dressing like that, you might as well hang a sign around your neck that says 'Single and Desperate.'"

Daniel laughed, a small hic-hic sound.

"Hey now," I said. "I like this tie."

"You're proving my point," Lew said. Turning back to Daniel, he said, "We spoke to your sister. She's a character."

Daniel said, "Rose? When?" For the first time, he sounded scared.

"She hasn't seen you in a while. Glad to know where you are now. I mean, I guess you don't get many visitors, and now that she's divorced, she'll have more time to spend with you."

"I don't want her here." He looked at the door, as if afraid she might appear behind it.

"No? I must admit, she's a bit colorful. But, hey, family is family, right?"

"She locked me in our cellar for a day because I touched her headbands."

"Sisters, am I right?" I asked. "But that was a long time ago, yeah?"

"People don't change," he said.

"Hey, you can't know that," Lew said. "I'm sure when she sees the situation you're in, she'll behave very differently than when you were kids, and you took all the arms off her dolls, which, I gotta say, sounds like a crappy thing to do."

"She loved those stupid dolls. I changed the outfit on one, and she made me eat a dog biscuit."

"She what?" I asked. "A dog biscuit?" I laughed. "Kids."

"It's not funny." He slammed his right fist on his chair's arm. "She cut my hair once, as punishment. For what? For not helping her clean up after dinner. It wasn't even my turn. So, I hit her. Gave her a black eye. And my parents, you know what they said? 'Don't hit girls. It doesn't matter what they do to you. You must never, ever hit girls.'" His voice shook. "How is that fair?"

"Well, you showed them," Lew said.

"Sure did," I agreed. "And yet, he didn't win that national contest with his own work. Kind of sad." I strolled to the picture.

"What are you talking about?" Daniel was breathing hard.

"This." I tapped the glass of the tree photo. "It's Elizabeth's. I wonder if he got the film out of her camera that day."

"Oh, *that* day," Lew said. "Makes sense. Or it could've been in her car."

"True. Keys would've been on her, so he could've used them to open it up. Search it. I mean, she didn't need 'em anymore."

"Why the arm?" Lew asked. "You think it's the Barbies, all over again?"

"You two are crazy," Daniel said. "Talking gibberish." Were we? His hands trembled, and he was sweating.

"We've heard that before," I said. "I think maybe he didn't want her to be able to use the arm. After all, she used it to take better photos than he could."

"She didn't take better photos!" Spittle formed at the corner of his mouth.

"Oh dear, we've upset him," I said. "I think it's all back to Rose. He just wanted to hurt her."

"He's dumber than we thought," Lew said, pointing to me. "He never even hurt Rose. Hell, those girls looked nothing like her."

"Cassidy did. That old photo we have of Rose and our boy here, remember? Cassidy looked like Rose did, back in the day."

"Oh, that's right."

"Cassidy looked nothing like Rose!" he yelled.

Lew locked eyes with me for a nanosecond.

"I don't know," I said. "Her hair, her eyes. I see a distinct resemblance."

"She had brown eyes!" he said. "Cassidy's eyes were brown. Rose's eyes are green. How stupid are you?"

"Not as dumb as some folks. I mean, leaving your DNA all over the crime scenes. That's just stupid," I said.

"My DNA is not on any crime scene!"

"Back in the late 1970s we didn't have DNA testing," Lew said. "Gosh, we've come a long way. But what's truly extraordinary is that we can go back and test crime-scene evidence for DNA from old scenes. It's just incredible."

"Not that we needed it," I said. Daniel had gone silent. His hands gripped each other. "I mean, that film you left at Stan's, well, who the hell needs your blood when we've got film of you murdering her?"

"I guess he really didn't like her being a better photographer," Lew said. "I wonder if that affected his, ah, performance in other areas?"

"Explains why she dumped him."

"She wasn't a better photographer! She was just lucky and pretty, and people liked her little pictures because she was a girl! That's it!"

"Seems like she could've given you pointers," I said.

"No!" he wailed. "I didn't need her damn advice! I didn't need any of her advice. Thinking she knew better than me. Thinking she was smarter because she'd taken some college classes. Well, she wasn't so smart after all, was she? And she's got nothing now. Nothing."

"She has our sympathy," Lewis said. "Which is more than you'll ever have. Daniel Waverly, I am arresting you on suspicion of the murder of Elizabeth Gardner."

"You'll never prove it! Never. It took you twenty years to find me." Twenty years. The time between Elizabeth's death and now. How nice for him to mention.

"Actually, it took us a few weeks," I said. "And only cuz we're kind of busy right now."

"Bank robbers," Lewis said. "And that domestic terrorist."

"Yeah. Those."

Daniel would never know the robbers had water pistols or that the terrorist was a teen girl chucking clamshells. Lew looked over his head at me and smiled, a wide, sunny smile like he'd won the lottery. I felt it too.

"Maybe we should give Rose a call," I said. "See if she wants to visit her brother in jail."

"No!" Daniel shouted.

Lewis said. "Nothing like a family reunion to warm the heart." He looked my way and winced. Thinking about Susan no doubt.

To make him feel better, I said, "There sure isn't. Come on, Daniel. Time to get your photo taken. Maybe you can give the guy doing it some tips."

# SATURDAY, JULY 3, 1999

"I'm sorry," Detective Williams said. "If anything changes, I'll let you know."

"I'm sorry too." I hung up the phone before I said something more, something about loyalty and doing your job and how fucked up was it that the department had "other" priorities.

They weren't going to interview Kevin McGee. They didn't see any connection between him and Susan Finnegan. The lie about not being on duty? Probably was to cover an affair, but we had no proof that the affair was with Susan. Damn it. I'd been sure I'd finally found the guy, and BPD didn't want to look into it. What could I do? He still lived in Boston, and the crime, if there was one, happened in Boston.

The phone rang. Outside call. Maybe Detective Williams had changed his mind? Maybe his super had come through?

"Hello?" I didn't bother with my rank and name.

"Tom." Oh, Matthew. This was unexpected.

"Matt. Hey."

"How are you?"

"Fine. You?" This was excruciating.

"Good. Fleeced Vic at poker last night. He couldn't cover his bets, so now I have access to his boat."

"His boat?"

"I don't even care about the boat. He thought he had me beat with three of a kind. I had a full house. Ladies and tens. You should've seen his face."

"That's great."

"Anyway, I called because I left my sweatshirt at your place, and I wanted it back."

Oh. The navy-blue sweatshirt in my bureau's bottom drawer. The one he'd brought over six months ago. That one.

"Sure. Stop by anytime." Or never. Never sounded good.

"How's tonight at 6:30?"

"Fine. Good."

"Great. Thanks." Click.

That was that. He wanted his stuff back. I guess that's how things ended. This was new to me. My prior relationships had never involved stowing clothes at other people's apartments or homes. If anything got left behind, well, finders keepers, losers weepers.

Finny walked into my office while I was considering what I had left at Matthew's place. Sweatpants, boxers, a t-shirt, a toothbrush, and a comb. Anything else?

"You okay?" he asked. "You look like you swallowed a June bug."

"Aren't those the big black bugs you find on your screen doors?" I asked.

"Yup."

"Gross."

"Your appreciation for the natural world is a wonder to behold. Looks like the prosecutor's going to try for Elizabeth Gardner," he said.

"That's great. I mean you have video, so he'd be a Grade-A idiot not to, but . . ."

"But Grade-A idiots always go on to be lawyers, right?"

"Right. Where's Lewis?"

"Off today. He and his wife are going shopping for the baby."

We both sat with that news for a bit.

"Any news?" he asked. "On the other thing?"

The other thing meaning his sister's case. Fuck it. "I think I found a lead."

He perked up. "Yeah? That's great. What is it?"

I shouldn't tell him. There was no predicting what he'd do with the information. On the other hand, the Boston police refused to pursue it. Nothing would happen if I stayed silent. Nothing would ever happen unless God intervened with a miracle. God seemed mighty busy these days.

"There was a park ranger who worked at Bunker Hill. I think maybe he dated Susan, but I have no real evidence he did. It's a glorified hunch."

"Who?"

"Not sure I can tell you that."

"You think I'm going to go rogue?" He laughed, but it was too hollow for my liking. "Have you notified the BPD?"

"I did."

"And?" He didn't wait for me to answer. "And they declined. That's why you're telling me. Because they decided it wasn't strong enough, or they have other, more important cases than solving some old missing persons case, no matter that the girl was the sister of one of their cops. Nah." He paced the length of my office, window to wall. "How hard could it be to look him up? Check his record. Stop by for a talk?" He stopped pacing.

"Finny, I'm not sure I should tell you. If I do and you go chasing after him . . . I don't want to see you fired."

"They can't fire me. You can."

"I don't want to see you arrested by *them* and then fired by *me* because you lost your temper with this guy."

"Chief, I understand, completely. I don't want to beat this guy up. I just want answers. If he's the one, I'd much rather he rots in jail. Let him spend the next twenty-seven years of his life suffering."

"Even if he dated her, that doesn't mean he hurt her."

"Sure. I know that. I'm a detective, right?" He was too agreeable. Too sunny. He was turning on a dime. "What's his name?"

I shouldn't tell him. But this was day one. He'd ask me every day. He was a bloodhound. I'd seen him working the Gardner case, placing call after call, coming up empty and pressing on. And then I thought of his mother. How much more time should she wait, wondering what had happened to her youngest child?

"You promise you won't hurt him? You won't endanger yourself or your job? They'll know I told you if this goes sideways." Not that I thought he'd care much about protecting me.

"I promise."

"Kevin McGee."

"Kevin?" Finny narrowed his eyes. "The Kevin who used to play Red Rover with us when we were kids?"

"Yeah."

"Didn't he marry into the Killeen family?"

"Yes."

He mulled that over. "Most of 'em are behind bars now. Thanks for telling me, Chief."

"Don't make me regret it," I said.

"Me?" He held a thumb to his chest. "Never."

I so wanted to believe him. But I didn't. Even from here I could feel the heat coming off him.

*God, watch over this one, yeah?*

I didn't trust God to listen to me either.

# MONDAY, JULY 5, 1999
## 1610 HOURS

C hief was worried about me, but he should've worried about Dave. Not that he knew my brother Dave would accompany me to visit Kevin McGee. Since Chief had told me about Kevin, and since I'd promised I wouldn't beat the stuffing out of him, I hadn't spoken a word on the subject to him.

I'd told Dave and Bobby, but not Carol and not Mom. In case things went south or in case it turned out Kevin had never so much as looked at Susan. The only news I wanted to give Mom and Carol was good news, and we didn't have good news. Not yet.

Dave thrummed his fingers against the steering wheel. "I thought he got off shift at four." His car's clock showed it was 4:14 p.m.

"He's probably dicking around. He'll be out soon. That's his car." I pointed to the red Ford we'd parked near. "He isn't going anywhere without it."

We watched tourists explore the USS *Constitution*.

"You go there on a field trip?" Dave asked.

"Only about ten times. 'Old Ironsides,' the oldest commissioned naval vessel still afloat."

"You paid attention," Dave said.

"Speaking of." I nudged him with my elbow. "Ten o'clock. That's him, that's Kevin." I wouldn't have recognized him from memory. He was unremarkable. Brown hair going gray and slightly stooped shoulders. But I'd looked him up. Seen a semi-recent picture. He waved to a guard as he walked to his car.

"Let's go," I said. "Remember. Calm and friendly."

We stepped out of the car. The heat punched us in the solar plexus. Kevin was reaching for his keys when I cried, "Kevin? Is that you?" He looked up. Frowned. Not able to place me. "It's me, Michael Finnegan, from Wood Street."

He dropped the keys, and Dave scooped them up before he could. "Hiya, Kevin. I'm Dave, Mikey's older brother. You remember me? We played ball back in the day."

Kevin shifted back a step, looking around. "Sorry, fellas. My mind ain't what it used to be." He laughed, a weak laugh. "Wood Street, Yeah. I used to play over there, with my cousin."

"Your cousin Jack," I said. "Jack McGee."

"That's right. What brings you guys to the yard?"

"Doing a little sightseeing," Dave said. "Visiting old haunts. Hey, we were just gonna grab a drink over at the Tavern. You should come with."

"Aw, I don't know. I got to get home. My kid's got a game tonight."

"Baseball?" I asked. He said "yeah," and I said, "Terrific. Just one drink. Won't take long."

Dave had his keys. He made no move to give them back to Kevin. "Drive with us," he said. "Then we can take you back to the car." Dave opened his driver's door and hopped in.

"I really think I ought to go home."

"Come on, Kevin," I called. "Tick tock!" I got inside and closed my door. It was a good ten degrees cooler inside.

He stood outside, weighing his choices. Go back in and ask his work buddies for help? And tell them what? Some guys from the old neighborhood wanted to meet him for a drink? No. He reached that conclusion and opened the door behind me. "Just one drink, yeah?"

"Of course. We don't party like we used to, do we, Dave?"

"Can't. Once you hit thirty, your liver takes notice of you, yeah?" Dave drove, one hand on the wheel. The radio blasted "Mambo No. 5." I sang along for a bit. "You like this song?" I asked Kevin.

"Not really."

"Aw, come on," I said, turning up the volume. "Ladies love it! It's got all their names in it."

"Hey, you missed the turn," Kevin said. He tapped on the window.

"What's that?" I called over the loud music.

"The Tavern's back that way. Now you're going to have to double back."

"Nah," Dave said. "I know a shortcut."

Kevin looked out the window, trying to determine our route. When he decided we weren't going to the Tavern, he yanked on the door handle. It didn't open. "Childproof locks," Dave said. "When you've got kids, you'll do anything to keep 'em safe, am I right?"

We parked under Route 93, not far from the Sand and Gravel Lot. We turned in our seats to regard our guest. "What do you want?" Kevin asked. He was sweaty. Odd, given that we were running the air-conditioning full blast.

"We want to talk about the old days," Dave said. He looked ahead, at the gravel and dirt. A broken bottle glinted on the ground.

"And ask why you knocked up our baby sister," I added.

"I didn't," he said. "I never."

"Kevin, lies aren't going to save you. They're going to piss us off. You don't want that."

"Look, I don't know nothing about your sister Susan."

"You used a double negative. And we didn't say which sister we were talking about."

That threw him. Dummy. "Come on, Carol was married with a young kid. I guessed that you meant Susan."

"Right. The two guys you couldn't place earlier. You recall both their sisters' names easily. Interesting. Did you tell her to have an abortion cuz you were afraid of your in-laws?" I cracked my knuckles. Gah. They didn't crack easily, not anymore.

"You know who my wife's uncle is?" he said. "He ran the family. He had guys whacked for cutting him off in traffic after church."

"So, you figure if he finds out you're cheating on his niece with a teenager, he might get upset?" Dave asked.

"I didn't say I—"

"She gave the baby up for adoption," I said. "But you knew that. Did you know they can run DNA tests? I don't even need your DNA. I can get some from your mom."

Kevin leaned forward. Put his hand on Dave's headrest. "Hey, don't you bring my mother into this. She's suffered enough."

"Don't you talk to us about suffering!" Dave screamed, whipping his head around. "Twenty-seven years we've waited. Twenty-seven years we searched, and all this time you knew, you son of a bitch." His fist shot out and grabbed Kevin's shirt by the collar. Kevin pulled back, trying to escape.

"Tell us where she is," I said.

"I don't know!" He struggled while Dave pulled him forward. I opened the glove box. Inside lay my gun. Kevin saw it.

"No, no, no."

"Tell us where she is," I said. My right hand reached for the gun.

"I don't know."

"We should get him out of the car," I said. "I don't want to stain your seats."

Dave said, "Good idea. Bloodstains are a bitch to get out."

I opened my door, gun in hand, and Kevin yelled, "Miller's River!"

I paused. "Miller's River?" It wasn't a river, not exactly.

"That's what he told me. I didn't do it. I didn't put her there."

"Who did?"

"Jack."

Dave pulled Kevin forward, and I said, "No," and put my hand over Dave's. "Jack cleaned up your mess, huh?" I asked Kevin. Dave released him, and he fell back against the seat, as if he were boneless.

His voice was low and shaky. "I didn't mean to kill her. I really, really didn't. I picked her up from the hospital, after she had the baby. She was going to go home. Everything was fine. It would've been fine, but she was angry. Said she hadn't wanted to give up the baby once she held him. She was going to tell her parents, about us, about where she'd been. She wanted to look into getting the baby back, getting custody. If my wife's uncle found out, my life wasn't worth a nickel, and neither was hers."

"And then?" I asked.

"I hit her."

I shot a glance at Dave. He looked like he was going to lose it. "Breathe," I told him.

"You hit her," Dave said. A vein in his neck pulsed red.

"We were outside. We'd driven to the park. I'd brought her food, and she was eating it. When I hit her, I think a piece of the sandwich lodged in her throat. Her face turned red."

"She choked to death?" I asked.

"I hit her on the back, but nothing happened. And then she stopped. Her eyes were open, and she didn't blink. I called her name. But she didn't respond."

Of all the terrible scenarios I had imagined, of all the awful ways I imagined her lost to us, I had never pictured it so ordinary, so pointless. Choking to death on a sandwich.

"You told Jack?" I asked.

"I put her in the car. I couldn't have someone find her. I drove the car to Jack's and told him what happened. He was pissed. Said I'd get us all killed with my blubbering. Told me he'd take care of her and to keep my mouth shut."

"He buried her by Miller's River," Dave said. It was a ten-minute walk from our home, maybe five minutes from where we were parked right now. We sat with this knowledge until Kevin asked, "What are you going to do to me?"

"Why Susan?" I asked.

"She used to visit the monument all the time. She was nice. She asked questions, and she cared about my answers. She thought I was handsome."

"She was a child," I said. "You're going to walk into the police station and confess."

"What? No! My kids, my wife."

"You'd rather wind up in the police morgue with a bullet hole between your eyes?" I asked. "You have one chance. You confess now to dating our sister, to getting her pregnant, to killing her."

"I didn't mean to!"

"Shut up," Dave said. Kevin stopped talking.

I closed my eyes and said, "You do this, and I won't recommend that you be incarcerated at Norfolk."

"That's where Mack is! You can't! He'd have me killed within a minute. I'm better off outside."

"Are you?" Dave asked. "I understand your wife's brother, Paul, he's out now, yeah? How's he feel about his younger sister?"

"For that matter, how do we feel about ours?" I asked. I picked up the gun.

"This is blackmail," Kevin said. "You're entrapping me."

"You want to get out of the car? I'll warn you. My gun skills aren't what they used to be. I'll probably wing you before I get a kill shot. You'll probably suffer more than you'd like."

His teeth chattered. "If I confess, they won't put me in Norfolk?"

"That will be my recommendation," I said.

"How you gonna recommend anything? You're not BPD anymore, right?"

"You haven't been paying attention, Kevin. I came back a year ago. I been trailing you for ages, dum-dum. I know how you like your coffee. Iced, one sugar. We know your kids' names and where they go to school. Your son's no math whiz. Maybe you ought to get him a tutor."

"Enough! I'll go."

The car smelled of flop sweat. My own torso was wet, and the adrenaline was making my hands shake. I put the gun back in the glove box.

Dave started the car. "We'll be watching you. Don't think about running or going out a back exit of the station. You won't be free for two minutes before the lights go out, permanently."

At the station, we dropped him off. I followed him inside and waited until a policeman fetched him. "See you later," I called to the cop. Kevin didn't see the cop's look of confusion, didn't understand that we didn't know each other. He'd fallen for my act.

Back in the car with Dave, I waited.

"You believe him?" he asked. "That she choked?"

"It's so stupid, it's hard to believe he'd make it up."

"I can't believe it," he said. "She wanted the baby."

"Yeah. Susan always was stubborn about keeping her stuff."

"Remember that time Bobby took Mr. Growls and hid him, and Susan crumbled Ex-Lax atop his ice cream and he ate it?"

I laughed. "He shat everywhere."

"Including your bed."

I groaned. "He did."

"Oh God, that was classic."

I don't know when the laughter turned to tears. But it took some time before it stopped, and even then we knew it was only the eye of the storm.

# THURSDAY, JULY 8, 1999
## 1900 HOURS

Lewis and I sat at a table in Suds, beers before us. We hadn't taken a sip. "They've got permission to excavate tomorrow," he said.

"Do you think they'll find her?" I asked. Susan Finnegan had been underground for twenty-seven years. According to Finny, the ground where she was buried was a filled-in marshland. They had no precise area to search, just a rough idea based on Jack McGee's description.

"I'm surprised Jack McGee talked," Lew said.

"Mrs. Finnegan paid him a visit," I said. "Think she played the Catholic guilt card. And he's dying. I don't think he has a year left in him. If they prosecute, he'll never see prison. He hasn't got enough time left."

"Catholic guilt that powerful?"

"You've no idea. Any idea when Finny will be back?"

"He didn't say. He's hoping they'll recover the body and have a service, but even if they don't, they'll have a memorial. Now that they know for sure what happened."

We both drank. "Part of me wishes I'd never stuck my nose in," I said.

Lewis made a face. "But you helped find her . . . or who killed her."

"I don't know. They'd resigned themselves to not knowing. Me poking around? It made it clear she led a double life and lied to them. Before, they had their image of her. We've torn it to shreds."

"And you found them a family member they didn't know they had."

The baby, given up for adoption. Finny was making moves to discover his identity and to reach out to the boy, if he was willing, to let him know he had family interested in him, in knowing him.

"And now some guy who's twenty-six is going to find out he has another family, that he was given up for adoption?" I shook my head.

"You assume he doesn't know. Plenty of parents tell their kids they're adopted. It's not so taboo nowadays."

"Yeah, but he was adopted in 1973, when people didn't discuss it."

"You're determined to feel bad about this, aren't you?" he asked.

His question threw me. Was I set on a course for guilt? After all, I hadn't altered what had happened. I'd helped bring it to light, and I wasn't the person responsible.

"I don't know." I drank my beer and watched a group of young men at two tables near the bar. They were loud with their laughter and drink.

"They're fine," Lewis said. "Just having a good time."

"You were watching them too," I pointed out.

"Habit."

"Ditto."

Donna came by and said, "How's the head?"

"Great, thanks."

"Is Matty gone?" she asked.

"I don't think you'll be seeing much of him."

She pouted and stomped away.

Lewis stared at his beer intently. "She was asking about Matthew Cisco?"

"Yeah."

"You broke up?"

"You're kidding, right? Everyone knows. I'm surprised they didn't run updates in the paper."

"I don't pay attention to your love life."

I drank a healthy swallow, and said, "That makes you the only one, then. Everyone is super interested in what their gay chief will do next."

"Like how?"

"Let's see. The other day a woman I don't know approached me in the grocery and asked if I thought her outfit was too color-coordinated. Apparently, as a gay man, I'm an authority on the subject."

"Please tell me you didn't tell her she looked less than perfect. No, wait," he leaned forward. "No signs of bruising. You didn't. Smart guy."

"I told her she looked great. Now I'm terrified she'll lie in wait for me by the deli counter, looking for fashion advice."

"Go to a different grocery," he said.

"Are you kidding me? I've finally taught the deli guys how to slice my cold cuts. I'm invested."

Donna came over and served my beer, if slamming a glass atop a table could be described as "serving." She put a hand to her hip and said, "The annual baseball tournament is this weekend. I can't wait."

"Yeah?" Lewis asked. "Gonna come cheer us on?"

Donna gave him a look filled with pity. "You guys are gonna get slaughtered. Have you seen Dave Jacobson, their new guy? He played in the minor leagues for a year."

Lewis sighed. "Well then, I guess we know how Saturday will go."

Donna said, "We sure do."

# FRIDAY, JULY 9, 1999
## 1340 HOURS

We were gathered at the kitchen table, the same table we'd sat at so many years ago to discuss how to find Susan. Now we had gathered to discuss what to do about her death. "There's no body," Carol said, for the seventieth time.

"They're looking," I said. "But that's not an easy area to search, and they may not find her."

"You said that already," Bobby said. I wanted to smack him. It felt like we'd all regressed, back in time. Bobby was annoying me and Carol was playing big, bossy sister.

"Any update on Kevin?" Dave asked.

"They're holding him. That's all I know."

"They won't try him if they don't find her body," Bobby said. As if he knew a damn thing about policing and prosecuting. "Where does that leave us?"

"Waiting," Carol said. "Like before."

"*Not* like before," Ma cut in. "Before, we didn't know what had happened to her. Now, we know." She clutched a handkerchief, but her eyes were dry. Possibly because she'd cried every bit of water out of herself over the past few days. "We'll have a service."

Chastised, we murmured that it was a good idea.

"But should we wait, to hear if they find her?" Bobby asked. We all turned on him, united in finding a target. "What?" he said. "I'm just asking! I mean, it would stink to have a memorial and then find her body."

"We'd have another service, Bobby. Geez, stop being an asshole," Dave said.

"Language!" Ma said. "Honestly, the way you're all behaving makes me want to send you to church, for a week."

"Sorry, Ma," we said, in unison.

Carol smiled. Dave caught her eye and grinned. We were down and up, like carousel horses. We couldn't seem to stick to an emotion longer than the time it took to express it.

"Should we tell everybody?" Carol asked.

"Who's everybody?" I asked.

"Old classmates, neighbors, the people who helped search for her."

"We'll invite them to the service," Ma said.

"What about the baby?" Dave asked.

We went silent at that. I'd had more time than the rest of them to absorb the news, and even I had a hard time accepting that there was a Finnegan running around the world, not knowing us, his family.

"He's no baby," Ma said. "He's twenty-six years old."

Twenty-six. When I was twenty-six, I was on my way to marriage #2, with one ex-wife and son in my rearview. When I was twenty-six, I'd left Boston for Connecticut, trying my best not to look back.

"Can we find him?" Carol asked. "Would they let us try to contact him? Gracie's Place was strict about no contact from the biological parents."

"How do you know that?" Dave asked.

"I knew a girl who had a baby there, in '77. A friend of a friend, younger than us. She tried to find out who adopted her baby girl years later and didn't get anywhere."

"When was that?" Ma demanded.

Carol bit her lower lip. "The late eighties, I think."

"Well, times have changed," Ma said. "People are more open to knowing about adoptive parents." My siblings' faces showed that they didn't agree, but they weren't going to be the one to speak up, to pop this last remaining balloon of hope belonging to Ma. I didn't mention I'd begun asking questions on the topic.

"We should play 'Amazing Grace,'" Carol said. "At the service."

"Why?" Dave asked.

"Because it was Susan's favorite hymn."

"God, she couldn't carry a tune if it had a handle on it," Dave said.

"David Matthew Finnegan!" Ma scolded.

"It's true," I said. "You know it's true. Remember that talent show from second grade?"

"Third grade," Carol filled in. She groaned. "It was tragic."

Bobby, always eager to be included said, "She was so excited to wear her new dress."

"Didn't you let her wear lipstick?" Carol asked Mom.

"I may have let her apply a smidge," Mom said. "What did she sing?"

"'Ring of Fire,'" Bobby said.

Dave dropped his head into his hands. "It was my fault. I was into Johnny Cash."

"Oh, God," Carol said. "The teacher didn't know what to do with her. Her little voice trying so hard to go lower and lower."

"Could have been worse," I said.

"How?" Bobby asked. "Did you go? Did you see it?"

I hadn't. I'd been home, sick. They'd gone without me. At the time, I was delighted. It meant I could watch TV all by myself. But even though I hadn't been there, I knew all the details. It was a family legend of sorts. Our baby sister singing Johnny Cash at her third-grade talent show.

"It could've been worse. She could've dressed like Johnny Cash," I said.

Carol erupted into squeals of laughter, which set off Dave. Soon we were hiccupping and wiping our eyes. The phone rang. I didn't hear it for a moment, because we were making so much noise. I saw Ma stand and wondered where she was going. Then I heard the ring. She walked to the wall and lifted the receiver. "Hello. . . . Yes, he's here. Just a moment."

The laughter stopped, sudden, like a tap being turned. Ma held the receiver out to me. "Hello?" I said into the phone.

"Mike? It's Fred Williams. I wanted to let you know, they found a corpse at the site. Now, we don't know yet who it is. It's . . . badly decomposed."

I'd seen a body buried in the woods for twenty years. My mind had a good reference for what "badly decomposed" looked like. "I understand."

"Did your sister have a stuffed animal with her?"

"Mr. Growls," I said. "A teddy bear. It was missing from her room."

Now everyone in the room was watching me. My mother clutched a teacup. I feared she'd snap the handle. Carol repeated, "Mr. Growls," softly.

"I see. We'll likely need to do dental comparisons. I don't want to raise your hopes, but I didn't want to leave you wondering if we'd found anything either."

"I appreciate it."

"I hope it's her," he said. "I mean . . ."

"I know. Thank you." I hung up the phone.

"Did they find her?" Dave asked.

"They found a body. They'll have to run tests," I said.

"Oh, my baby," Mom said. The tears came again.

We gathered to hug her, and I offered a silent prayer, the first in many, many years, for Susan, for bringing us together again.

## CHIEF THOMAS LYNCH
# SATURDAY, JULY 10, 1999
### 1200 HOURS

The baseball stands were filled with townspeople eating hot dogs and popcorn. This being Idyll, there was no alcohol. Soda, water, or lemonade only. All sales proceeds went to benefit St. Jude's Hospital. The mayor stood on the pitcher's mound. His khakis were white, which seemed a bold choice. He talked about how this was an annual tradition and although historically the "firefighters won *every* year, well, you never know what may happen. So, let's get out there and play ball!"

"That seemed unnecessary," I said.

"But not unexpected," Mrs. Dunsmore said. Her sunhat attacked my face, and I shifted in my seat. We sat behind the police dugout and watched as our team took the field. The firefighters would bat first, the result of a coin toss Dix had chosen "tails" on. Who the hell chose tails? Our team captain, that's who.

"That's the new guy," Mrs. Dunsmore said, pointing to the very fit man practicing his swing. "The one who played for the Sea Dogs."

"The Sea Dogs?"

"Double-A team out of Portland."

"Ah," I said. "I thought he came from the PawSox." Not that a Double-A team was anything to sneeze at, but to hear our guys tell it, this guy was the second coming of Sammy Sosa.

"Did you know the new dispatcher could pitch when you hired him?" she asked.

Hugh was on the mound, rotating at the waist, clockwise,

295

counterclockwise. Turns out, he'd coached his daughter's softball team for years.

"How would I know that, or care? I wasn't included in the softball recruiting, if there was such a thing."

Hugh was an adequate pitcher. He managed to strike out the first batter. Wasn't so lucky with the second. Guy hit a line drive that Hopkins hopped over.

"Does he realize he's supposed to stop the ball?" I asked.

The person seated behind me nudged me. "Isn't he supposed to try to stop it, Chief?"

I turned. My nudger was my next-door neighbor, Mr. Sands. "Hi," I said.

"Hey, how come you aren't out there?" he asked. "Is it because of your head injury?"

"What head injury?"

"The one that sent you to the hospital the other day." How did he know about that? "My sister-in-law works in the ER." Of course she did. Whatever happened to patient confidentiality?

"I'm fine. Thanks for asking." I turned around in my seat. Mrs. Dunsmore said, "Popcorn?" and shoved a red-and-white striped box in my face.

"No, thanks." The butter-salt smell was too much in this heat.

"Suit yourself. Ooh, he's up." *He* being the minor league player turned firefighter. Chanting erupted from behind the firemen's dugout.

"Are they spelling his name?" I asked.

"The ladies think he's a catch," she said.

"I remember when I was a catch."

She snorted. "That was before they knew you."

Dave Jacobson smacked the ball out of the park. Hugh looked chastised as Dave ran the bases. The score was two to zero. Not good. I adjusted my sunglasses and crossed my arms.

An hour later, the score was twelve to two.

"This looks familiar," someone said.

"Yup."

"Hopkins looks like he's going to expire," said someone in the dugout.

"Yeah, well, we don't have anyone to take his place what with Finny out and Hallihan on vacation."

"Still can't believe he took vacation during the game."

The sixth inning ended, and the high-school marching band came out to play while the guys took a breather. "It's so damn hot!" I heard Hopkins complain.

"Just three more innings," Dix said.

"Maybe we should've adopted the chief's fitness plan," Billy said.

"Shut it, traitor," Dix said. "Come on. Not too much water, guys. You'll be sloshing as you run the bases."

"Run the bases!" Hopkins said. "Ha!"

"Come on, guys. Just three more innings. We got this!"

They jogged back onto the field. As luck had it, it was Hopkins at bat. He leaned over home base, his arms out too far. The first pitch whizzed past him. He didn't react at all. And then, on the windup for the second, he fell. Collapsed to the ground. I stood up and vaulted over the low railing to reach the field. Men hovered over him.

"He okay?" I yelled as I ran.

Billy touched his forehead. Hopkins's eyes fluttered. He moaned. "He fainted," Billy said.

"I saw."

Hopkins rolled his head to the side and asked, "What happened?"

Dix stood over him, casting a shadow on his face. "You passed out. Shit. Get him back to the dugout, would you?"

Billy and Lewis helped him up and half carried him from the field. The crowd erupted in cheers. Great. This was our highlight moment. Limping off the field.

"I'm sorry, fellas, but we're gonna have to call it," Dix said.

Captain Hirsch ran over from his dugout. "You ladies ready to call it? Without your guy, you can't field a team."

"Yes, we can," I said.

"Chief, didn't see you there," he said. Funny guy. I was hard to miss.

"I can take Hopkins's place."

"You?" He sounded delighted.

"Me."

"But your concussion," Lewis said.

"Was weeks ago. I'm fine to play." I had called the doctor about this, a week ago, but I'd die before I admitted it.

"We don't have another shirt," Dix said. He looked embarrassed.

"I have my own. Is this my at-bat?" I asked.

"Sure thing," Captain Hirsch said, bowing. "Remember, you have one strike." How kind of him to remind me.

"One moment." I strode to the dugout and stepped down and in. Then I pulled my t-shirt over my head. Revealing the t-shirt I wore underneath.

Billy said, "Whoa!" and Lewis said, "That is *pink*!"

"Mrs. Dunsmore made it for me."

They stared. Some of 'em had to know why it was pink and that their office gossip had contributed to its creation. But none of them said anything except Hopkins, who held an ice pack to his neck. "What does the front say?" he asked.

I walked closer so he could sound it out. "Hail to the Chief."

"That's right," I said, snatching the bat and walking to the plate. A breeze of whispers ran around the stadium as people eyed my shirt.

The firemen's pitcher didn't seem to care much. He tossed the ball and I froze. Was it coming in too low? Or should I swing? I swung, late, and missed it. It had been perfect and I'd missed it.

"Strike!" the ump called.

I backed off from the plate and took a breath. Remembered what Matt had taught me. What Lewis had said about the plate. I got close and glared at the pitcher. *Come on. Show me what you got, knucklehead.*

The ball came and I swung and the contact of it sent tremors down the bat to my hands. It went high and far, and the outfielder leapt to catch it, but it went over him. I ran, sprinting to first and looking briefly to the field where they were still after the ball. I ran to second. The fielder had the ball, and he switched to throw it and dropped it! The ball was on the ground! I took off, headed so hard for third I couldn't stop, so I rounded it and ran for home. I could feel the ball coming for me, but it whizzed past as I slid into the base and into the catcher. The ump screamed "Safe!"

The guys started screaming. Hirsch yelled "butterfingers" at his outfielder, and I walked back to the dugout, wondering if I'd just wrecked my ankle with that slide. My foot had caught on the edge of the base.

Before I went down into the cool depths of the dugout, to join my team, I gave Mrs. Dunsmore a smile. Above her, almost at the back of the stands, was a familiar face. Damien Saunders. And he was doing the classic New York taxi whistle with his fingers in his mouth. I waved and he stopped and grinned.

Then I got into the dugout and the guys clapped me on my shoulder and wondered aloud if they should've worn pink shirts since they seemed to be lucky. And we laughed and I batted twice more, hitting a single and a double.

We lost, thirteen to six.

According to Mrs. Dunsmore, it was the "best loss" in the history of our matches against the firefighters.

We toasted to the "best loss" over drinks at Suds and refused to let the firefighters in when they showed up, because we'd booked the whole space "for a private event."

"Come on," Hirsch said, when he saw we meant business. He stood outside the front door. "You can't take over the only bar in town." The entire fire crew stood behind him, sweaty and smiling. Confident that we'd let them inside for some good-natured ribbing.

"We can and we did," Lewis said. "See, while you were busy practicing, we were busy scheduling."

"Better luck next time," Billy called.

"Come on, Chief," he said. "You can't let them do this."

"I'm not team captain," I said, "And they can do what they like, especially if they booked the space . . . how long ago?"

"Three hundred and sixty-four days," Dix said.

"Well, enjoy your private party. We'll enjoy our trophy," he said, holding it aloft.

"Can't drink a trophy," I said as I closed the door.

The men roared with laughter, and for weeks, "can't drink a trophy" was used at the office as a catchphrase. It lasted longer than "Hail to the Chief," which lasted only two days and four hours.

# ACKNOWLEDGMENTS

Thanks to everyone at Seventh Street Books: Dan Mayer, Jill Maxick, Jade Zora Scibilia, Jackie Nasso Cooke, and Lisa Michalski. You make my books so much better with all that you do.

Thanks to my agent, Ann Collette, who is always a champion for Thomas Lynch.

To my beta reader, Belle Brett, thank you for wading through the murky waters of my draft.

To Amanda Stoll for wading into editing waters, again, on my behalf. Thank you!

To my sisters in crime, Emily Ross and Kelly J. Ford, thank you for your friendship, stalwart advice, and understanding that all meetings should include food.

To anyone and everyone who ever wrote to say they liked my book or who wrote positive reviews online or in print, thank you. You'll never know how much those words cheer me.

And to Bao, who is a bunny, and so cannot read this, thank you for every bink and every nuzzle, you sweet, furry love.

# ABOUT THE AUTHOR

Stephanie Gayle is the author of *Idyll Threats* and *Idyll Fears*. She works at the MIT Media Lab, doing finance because accounting runs in her blood. She lives in Massachusetts along with her partner, Todd, and bunny, Bao.